HOLLY WATT is an award-winning  worked at the *Sunday Times*, the *Daily Telegraph* and the *Guardian*. Her first novel, *To The Lions*, won the CWA Ian Fleming Steel Dagger, and was followed in the Casey Benedict series by *The Dead Line*. *The Hunt and the Kill* is her third novel.

Holly Watt

THE HUNT AND THE KILL

R A V E N BOOKS

LONDON · OXFORD · NEW YORK · NEW DELHI · SYDNEY

RAVEN BOOKS
Bloomsbury Publishing Plc
50 Bedford Square, London, WC1B 3DP, UK
29 Earlsfort Terrace, Dublin 2, Ireland

BLOOMSBURY, RAVEN BOOKS and the Raven Books logo are trademarks of
Bloomsbury Publishing Plc

First published in Great Britain 2021
This edition published 2022

A catalogue record for this book is available from the British Library

ISBN: HB: 978-1-5266-2558-8; TPB: 978-1-5266-2556-4; PB: 978-1-5266-2554-0;
EBOOK: 978-1-5266-2555-7; EPDF: 978-1-5266-4538-8

2 4 6 8 10 9 7 5 3 1

Typeset by Integra Software Services Pvt. Ltd.
Printed and bound in Great Britain by CPI Group (UK) Ltd, Croydon CR0 4YY

To find out more about our authors and books visit www.bloomsbury.com
and sign up for our newsletters

To Isadora

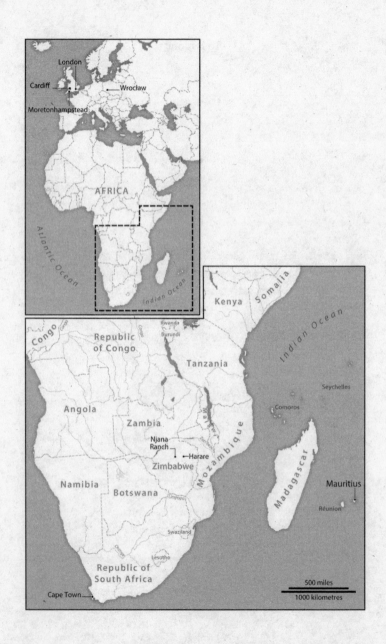

'You have,' Miranda said patiently, 'to stop hacking my emails.'

'I'm just keeping my hand in.' Casey leaned back in her chair. 'You wouldn't want me getting rusty.'

Miranda was standing beside Casey's desk as the *Post*'s newsroom rumbled around them. To Casey's left, the home affairs editor was picking a fight with the Met Police. On her right, a junior reporter was going through a particularly turgid report about housing, muttering random lines aloud.

'I might,' Miranda sighed.

'Besides,' Casey went on, 'if you make your password a combination of your ex-husband's name and a particularly rude word, you're asking for it.'

'Can't you concentrate, just for a minute, on,' Miranda read over Casey's shoulder, 'heart transplants?'

'Heart transplants haven't been interesting since 1967,' Casey said moodily.

They fell silent as Sophie, one of the opinion writers, walked past Casey's desk, heading for the coffee machine. The junior reporter, Eric, made a muffled excuse and bolted after her.

'How's that sweepstake going?' asked Miranda.

'I've got next Tuesday,' Casey flexed her fingers. 'And I am quietly confident.'

'I had last Friday,' the home affairs editor said crossly, as he slammed the phone down on the Met. 'And it was an absolutely sure thing, but Aaron

– who has a week on Monday, by the sodding way – packed Eric off to Great Yarmouth, of all places. Cheating git.'

Aaron, the current night editor, was in charge of dispatching journalists in the direction of breaking stories.

'What was happening in Great Yarmouth?' asked Miranda.

'Nothing ever happens in Great Yarmouth,' spat the home affairs editor. 'It was blatant fraud.'

'Shameless,' nodded a passing sub.

'We were all down the Plumbers,' moaned the home affairs editor. 'There was magic in the air, I tell you. And I'd bought loads of sodding rounds.'

'In itself, a miracle,' the sub grinned. 'Although I bet you'll expense them anyway.'

'And the next sodding thing, Eric's halfway to Liverpool Street.'

'How do you know,' Miranda asked, 'that Eric and Sophie haven't hooked up already, when no one else was around?'

'The newsroom's divided into shifts.' The home affairs editor pursed his lips. 'Twenty-four-hour cover. We reckon we've got all the bases covered, although Carlos lost them on the Tube last week. Useless prat. Comes of letting the property section do anything important. Amateurs.'

He stamped off towards the newsdesk.

'So what's happening next Tuesday?' Miranda dropped her voice.

Casey smiled. 'Eric and Sophie are going on a romantic date,' she murmured.

'How?' asked Miranda.

Casey's smile became beatific. 'There will be an exchange of emails. I'll just have to make sure I bump into them in the same bar, so they can't cross-ref too early on.'

'How …' began Miranda, then stopped as Casey's eyes flicked towards her computer screen. '*Casey.*'

'Casey!' Ross, the news editor, bawled across the room. 'If I don't get that heart transplant copy soon, you'll be a buggering donor yourself.'

Casey cast Miranda a despairing look.

'It's not my fault,' Casey grumbled. 'I'm so bloody bored.'

It had all started when the health editor went on maternity leave.

'I need you to cover Heather,' Dash, the *Post*'s head of news, informed Casey. 'Just for a few months.'

'Health?' Casey had rolled her eyes. 'You're joking. I don't know anything about health.'

But Dash was firm. 'You need time off from investigations,' he said. 'It's an order, I'm afraid.'

'I'm fine.'

'You're not.'

'Miranda?' Casey had appealed, in outrage.

But Miranda had shrugged. 'Dash is in charge, Casey. Nothing I can do.'

They had been a team ever since Miranda had joined the *Post*. Casey, a junior reporter back then, quivering with nerves and determination. Miranda, blonde and confident, with a smile like a bow on a present.

Miranda hadn't been sure about Casey when she first arrived as investigations editor. Miranda had been poached from the *Argus*, the *Post*'s great rival, arriving with fanfare and gloating and Buck's Fizz with the editor. 'You can choose your own team,' Dash had promised. 'Is there anyone else at the *Argus* we should nick, by the way?'

Casey had pleaded and schemed, and Miranda had given her a chance. *We'll see how you go, all right?*

'Go doorstep the Wynford CEO,' Miranda told Casey, one Friday evening. Doorstep: a verb in journalism. 'He lives in Holland Park, I'll message you the address. Ask him about that Coventry deal. Go in hard.'

It was their second day of working together. Casey had disappeared out of the office, a whirl of dark hair.

On Monday morning, Casey had been late. By 11 a.m., Miranda was impatient.

'Where the hell are you?' she'd snapped down the phone. 'I've been here since seven.'

'Outside the Wynford CEO's house.' Casey sounded apologetic. 'He's not been home yet.'

3

Miranda had looked out the window at January. She briefly remembered an old friend at the *Argus*, whose father farmed a hundred scrappy acres in the Lakes. Up the mountain in a blizzard, the father told the dog to *stay* by the sheep while he checked a gate. Three hours later, the father had wondered – idly – where the dog was. Thought back. Sprinted up the hill in heavy work boots to find the dog lying stock-still. Covered in a thick layer of snow, eyes gleaming hopefully, can I come home yet? *Stay*.

'I didn't mean "spend the whole weekend outside his house",' Miranda protested.

'It was no problem.' Casey was breezy. 'A friend's gym is just around the corner, so I've been able to ... Anyway, I can be back in the office in twenty minutes if you need me.'

'See you in a bit then,' said Miranda, and thought: *remember this*.

Since then, they'd raced around the world together. Triads in Macau, mafia in Moscow. Drug traffickers in Kosovo, people traffickers in Turkey. Once, sitting in a small van in Poland – chasing a money launderer turned out to involve endless waiting about – Miranda had passed Casey a cupcake, with a tiny candle on top. *Happy birthday*. They'd smiled at each other, for a second. Then the money launderer came out of his house, and without another word they'd followed him. Poznań to Katowice, hundreds of tedious grey miles.

Bolivia, Tanzania, Japan, Romania.

Countless planes. Waking up in hotel rooms, sleek and silver.

Where am I? Oh, yes. Who am I? Better check.

And undercover of course. A different costume, another life.

Tiny cameras, smaller microphones.

Oman, Switzerland, Mexico, Sierra Leone.

Happy birthday.

Kenya, Australia, Libya, Bangladesh.

Happy Christmas.

'But I can't do health,' Casey cried. 'I just can't.'

Libya. Bangladesh.

'Just for a while,' said Dash. 'A few months. After last time.'

2

'Casey,' Ross yelled across the newsroom. 'Get over here.'

Casey stamped over to the newsdesk. 'What?'

'Don't give me that fucking attitude.' Ross barely glanced up. 'There's a girl stuck in the Royal Brompton down in South Ken. Got cystic fibrosis. Flora Ashcroft or something. Friend of a friend.'

'You have friends?'

'Go and have a chat with her, yeah? The hospital's going to announce some breakthrough with its treatment of lung damage next week, and that can be the hook for a nice little feature.'

'But I don't know anything about cystic fibrosis,' Casey protested. 'And a *feature*?'

'There's this thing called research.' Ross's sarcasm could strip paint. 'You might give it a try.'

Out of the corner of her eye, Casey could see Hessa and Tillie – the two young investigative reporters working for Miranda now – rushing for the *Post*'s exit. They had the hurried stride, the excited smiles that Casey knew so well. She felt her throat burn.

Ross was watching her, eyes narrowed. 'Get on with it, Casey.'

For a second, Casey wavered mutinously.

'He's not exactly known,' the newsdesk secretary looked up, his eyes a warning, 'for his prisoner count.'

'Fine.' Casey whirled away. 'Bloody fine.'

Casey read her notes as the bus trundled down the street.

Cystic fibrosis is an inherited condition that causes sticky mucus to build up in the lungs and digestive system.

Casey's eyes drifted away. Sitting on the top deck, she watched people swirl along the pavements. The streets were clogged with traffic. It was the end of summer: heat rising from the tarmac and a taste of metal in the air. The London plane trees – brushing against the upper windows of the bus, odd to have them at eye level for once – were beginning to crackle to brown.

This causes lung infections and problems with digesting food.

The bus stopped at roadworks, damming the crossing so that pedestrians swirled in front and behind the big red shape. A drill thudded like a headache. Bored, Casey gazed up at the sky. Far above, a plane was tracking across the blue, west to east. Where was it going? The Hague, Berlin, Minsk? I wish …

Symptoms usually start in early childhood and vary from child to child, but the condition gets slowly worse over time, with the lungs and digestive system becoming increasingly damaged.

Casey's phone bleeped: Ed. Her face eased into a smile. *What do you want for dinner?* For a second, she saw herself as if from a distance: hair in a neat ponytail, sensible work clothes, pondering dinner with her boyfriend. Boyfriend, it was such a *practical* word. Pasta? Risotto? A jacket potato?

The build-up of sticky mucus in the lungs can cause breathing problems and increases the risk of lung infections. Over time, the lungs may stop working properly.

The bus wheezed forward, and then stopped again. Casey kicked the seat ahead in frustration. The pedestrians found their way round the bus, streaming away down the pavement, as bicycles wavered in the flood.

Treatments are available to help reduce the problems caused by the condition and make it easier to live with, but sadly life expectancy is shortened.

Poor Flora Ashcroft.

The bus creaked to a final halt, and Casey ricocheted down the steep, narrow steps.

The hospital loomed above her, all ugly red bricks, yellow stone and Victorian disapproval. Inside, it was a rabbit warren, modern medicine squeezing into cramped rooms and awkward corridors. Doctors and nurses hurried past, always overstretched. The tang of bleach stung, and the decor defaulted to beige.

Really, Casey should have told the press office she was planning a visit, and then been escorted by a twittering comms woman, pointing out silver linings everywhere. But: 'This Ashcroft girl's happy to talk,' Ross had said. 'Just say you're a friend, popping by.'

The secrecy was instinctive, always. Not least because the competition might overhear, start digging.

It was always easier to get permission afterwards, they knew. And, anyway, Casey hated interviewing with an audience. Nothing worse than some extraneous person filling the quiet: *I think you'll be interested to know* … When silence was the best tool of all.

Casey checked Ross's directions again. Up three flights of stairs, along a corridor, through double doors, down a half-flight of stairs and the ward is right there, on your left. She set off.

Flora Ashcroft was a surprise. Casey had expected frailty, fragility, an Elizabeth Barrett Browning pallor. Flora was pale – unquestionably – and thin, with narrow wrists, and a dry tautness around the eyes. Her fawn hair was plaited back tightly, and there were shadows under the deep brown eyes. But there was a vigour about her, and an urgent energy that made her vivid in the grey of the hospital room. Twenty years old, Casey knew. A patient at the Royal Brompton for almost her whole life.

'Hello,' Casey said. 'Thanks so much for agreeing to talk to me.'

They contemplated each other thoughtfully, and then Flora smiled.

'Welcome to the Royal Brompton,' said Flora. 'What would you like to know?'

Casey glanced around the room, reaching for her notepad. 'This room is nice. Do you all have your own rooms?'

Flora spoke with a deliberate air hostess chant. 'Room 25 is my favourite. Room 23A is the worst. It's the A that gives it away, because they've cut one room in half, so you only get half a window. 23A's also got a horrific apricot feature wall, which is supposed to make you feel jolly. It really doesn't work.'

Casey laughed, and started to like her.

'Half a window does seem a bit unfair.'

'I think it's meant to be symbolic.' A quick grin. 'And, yes, we all get our own room.' Flora paused, sobered. 'You don't know much about CF, do you?'

Life expectancy is shortened …

'Not really,' Casey admitted. 'I was only asked to do this article this morning.'

'With cystic fibrosis,' Flora recited, 'patients are vulnerable to different infections in our lungs – bugs that wouldn't affect you at all. We all sign contracts when we arrive, promising we won't have any contact with other CF patients. So, yes,' a firm nod, 'we all get our own room.'

Flora was sitting on her bed, trying to smooth out the wrinkles in the sheet. Back and forth went her slim fingers. Back and forth, back and forth.

'I'm sorry.' In the face of the calm acceptance, Casey felt inadequate. Abruptly, Flora's loneliness seemed to fill the room, a tide lapping higher. 'Could you possibly explain a bit more?'

'No two patients are exactly the same,' said Flora. 'And they haven't had exactly the same antibiotic treatment. That means their bugs are slightly different too.'

Outside the room, Casey could hear a man's voice echoing down the corridor. He was talking to one of the nurses, Somerset in his vowels.

Flora read her mind. 'I've never met him, for example.'

'How long have you been here?'

'I've been in for ten days this time,' said Flora flatly. 'Over my whole life? I don't know. Months? Years? I had to shield for ages during Covid.'

Casey thought about it. That Flora had spent weeks of her life next door to someone that she had never even met. Someone fighting an almost identical, but subtly different battle. Outside, a trolley rattled, and a door slammed.

'You get used to the noise,' said Flora. 'Sort of.'

'Why are you in hospital right now?' asked Casey.

'I have Mycobacterium abscessus,' Flora enunciated carefully. 'It's a bacteria, which is a sort of third cousin to both tuberculosis and leprosy, which is nice.' She glanced at her watch. 'The nurse will be along any minute, you'll see.'

'Do you know how you caught it?

'No one knows,' said Flora. 'It could be anywhere. You can catch it in old buildings, and I live in an old building.' She shrugged. 'No one knows,' she said again.

Flora smoothed the sheet again, pushing the wrinkle out of sight under the blanket.

'How are they treating it?'

'Treating it?' Flora's brown eyes glittered with laughter. 'They're aiming to get it under control for now. Lots of antibiotics, basically. At the moment, it's three different kinds. Some of them are intravenous – not ones you can swallow – which is why I have to come into hospital.'

'It must be very tedious. I am sorry. What does it do?'

'Abscessus? Lung infections, mainly. And the problem is … ' Flora was fighting to sound matter of fact, 'you can't have a lung transplant if you're infected with abscessus. It makes it all too risky.'

Over time, the lungs may stop working properly …

'Do you need one?'

'No.' Flora lifted a brave chin. 'Not yet.' Outside, the trolley rattled again. 'Hello, Ali,' Flora said brightly.

After the nurse was gone, the trolley clattering away, Flora moved across to the window. She stared down at the snarl of traffic.

'When they built this hospital,' she remarked, 'Brompton was a village, with market gardens. London swallowed it up.'

There was another knock at the door. This time a doctor, neat in his scrubs.

'Good afternoon, Flora,' he smiled. 'How are you feeling today?'

He took Flora's temperature and blood pressure with quick precision. His eyes – both concerned and calm – met Casey's over Flora's shoulder.

'I'm Casey,' she spoke quietly, making herself forgettable out of habit.

'A friend,' Flora added hastily, unnecessarily. 'This is Dr Noah Hart, Casey.'

'Hello.' Noah barely registered Casey, tapping notes into a handheld tablet. His mouth tensed slightly as he read one line. 'The old abscessus isn't responding exactly as we'd like, is it?'

'No.' Flora sounded almost apologetic.

'Have you coughed up any more blood?'

Flora's eyes went to Casey. 'A bit.'

'I'll go,' Casey said quickly.

'No.' Flora shook her head. 'Don't.'

As he pondered his notes, Noah sat down in the uncomfortable chair next to Flora's bed, the grey plastic creaking cheaply.

'Noah specialises in antibiotic resistance,' Flora told Casey. 'Antibiotic resistance is a constant problem for CF patients. And everyone else, really.'

Noah looked at Flora's visitor, and explained simply. 'When you give a patient antibiotics, you knock out most of the bacteria, but sometimes not all of them. Some of the original bacteria may have been resistant to that specific antibiotic, and the moment you stop the antibiotic, they start growing again. Only this time, the new bacteria population are all resistant to that antibiotic. It's why it's – ah – problematic when people don't finish a course of antibiotics. Effectively, they're just giving the bacteria a bit of a workout, and then they bounce back stronger than ever, having learned some fun new tricks.'

Casey was nodding, uncertainly.

'So for me,' Flora said briskly, 'who takes antibiotics all the time, it can get quite complicated.'

An understatement, Casey saw. Noah turned back to Flora, his pale face lit up by the utilitarian bedside lamp.

'As you know, we're treating you with amikacin and imipenem.' Noah spoke the drug names with the fluency of familiarity. 'But the Adsero antibiotic, zentetra, isn't working quite as we'd like it to.'

Casey pictured the nurse's trolley. The white packets with the prosaic writing on the side. There was no need for a hard sell with this audience.

'Adsero are bringing out a new antibiotic soon,' Flora said, in an aside to Casey. 'Hopefully. They're doing a last round of tests. But it might be a breakthrough.'

'It's provisionally called saepio,' Noah said to Casey. 'And it'll be at least a year.' And they all knew: *there might not be a year.*

'And it only *might* be a breakthrough,' Flora filled the short pause. 'Drug companies are always talking up miracle drugs that never actually appear.'

Noah stared at a crack in the wall. 'We can start you on a different drug regime, Flora,' he said. 'I think … '

The doctor fell into silence, his eyes hazing with calculations.

Casey watched him. Noah looked as if he rarely went outside: black under the eyes and a hospital-grey face. His pale blond hair was thinning, fading to cream at the temples already, although he was only in his early thirties. Casey sensed a blaze of intelligence beneath the despondent face, a mind whipping through a thousand possibilities. There was a sadness about him, too, as if the ward's melancholy had seeped into him over the years.

'Casey's a journalist,' Flora spoke into the stillness. 'Sorry,' she added to Casey, 'I didn't want him not to know.'

Noah flinched, his eyes went sharply to Casey's face.

'Casey Benedict from the *Post*,' she said smoothly, equably. 'I may write a short feature next week. Just about life with CF, what it's actually like for patients. I should have talked to the comms team first, but … '

Casey shrugged. Noah hesitated, eyes flickering to the window, and then he shrugged too, deliberately mimicking her, and forcing himself to relax.

Noah didn't care about the comms team, Casey saw. Like many doctors, he'd seen too much to care about a middle manager's tantrum over a few words to the press. On her first day as health correspondent, at a rickety A&E in Bassetlaw, Casey had watched the staff turn away – ostentatiously – from the professional smile of a junior minister. And heard the rude, half-muffled comments as they'd proceeded on a ward round. The politician had beamed widely for the cameras throughout, just the same.

But Noah's concern ran deeper, and was covered up more carefully.

'Why did you first get interested in antibiotic resistance?' Casey asked, making conversation, changing the tone.

He looked straight at her. 'Because it's going to kill you.'

3

He tried to lighten the mood afterwards, joking with Flora, and forcing a wide smile.

'Bacteria are a truly worthy enemy.' He turned the grin on Casey. 'We can talk off the record, if you want. Then you can check in with the press officers for proper quotes later.'

That was normal; interviewees often spoke openly – rambling freely, umming and ahhing – and then agreed the actual words for print with the journalist later.

'All off the record,' Casey promised.

'It's a numbers game with bacteria, then.' Noah's enthusiasm was abruptly real. 'It's Darwinian selection at a million miles an hour. Evolution on a scale that you would never normally think about. You've got 7 billion people on the planet and you can have 7 billion bacteria in a few millilitres of liquid, and they're all multiplying as fast as they possibly can. You can start using any antibiotic, and they will immediately try and find a way to overcome it.'

'You make it sound great.' Casey matched his smile.

'It's not,' he said brightly. 'But it is fascinating.'

'So how do you win?'

'You don't,' he said. 'Whatever we invent, whatever we find, the bacteria will defeat it in the end. AMR – that's antimicrobial resistance – is expected to kill an extra 10 million people a year by 2050 if we don't work something out. That's more than cancer. It'll be Covid, but all the time.' There was a zeal in his eyes, a glitter of fervour, and then his face changed, sharply. He turned to Flora. 'Don't worry, Flora, we'll work something out.'

He moved quickly, making for the door.

'See you tomorrow, Noah,' Flora called after him.

'See you tomorrow,' he echoed, closing the door.

'That's odd,' Flora said, when the sound of footsteps had receded down the corridor. 'He seemed quite stressed out.'

'Sorry,' said Casey. 'I should have got permission to come here. It just all takes time.'

'No, he wasn't worried about that. It was something else.' Flora coughed, reached for a box of tissues. 'You get to know the doctors here pretty well over the years. Well, never mind.'

Casey smiled at her. 'So tell me, how did CF affect your time at university?'

'I'm studying journalism.' Flora smiled shyly. 'And it's tricky anyway, of course, breaking into that world ... '

'You'll love it,' Casey grinned. 'And journalism is the best fun in the world. Some of the time, anyway.'

'How did you get into the *Post*?'

'Oh,' Casey stared at her notepad. 'One day, I just realised I was meant to be working at the *Post*. That I *had* to be there. They didn't see it quite like that though, unfortunately.'

'So how did you get started?'

'Um.' Casey felt the laugh bubble up. 'I got a job at a call centre.'

'A call centre?'

'It was during an election.'

A call centre set up during a general election, where dozens of students on zero-hour contracts read from scripts hour after hour. *Can I ask you how you are planning to vote, madam? And then ...*

Push polling dressed up as market research: illegal.

Casey – a student then, barely undercover – got a job at the call centre, photographed the scripts and called the *Post*. A minor scandal, a slapped wrist.

'Oh, yes,' Flora nodded. 'I remember.'

'And after that, the *Post* offered me work experience.'

'And?'

'Basically, I never left.'

'How did you manage that?' Flora's eyes were keen.

'After the work experience was over,' Casey started to laugh, 'I just kept coming in. They told me I couldn't because it was someone else's turn, but I managed to get to my desk every single morning.'

'How?'

'Oh, you know. There was a service entrance out the back, and that guard liked croissants. And the lavatory windows weren't guarded twenty-four hours a day. All the usual stuff.'

They were both laughing now, at the ludicrousness of it all.

Once, Casey had slept under one of the boardroom tables, because it was easier to stay overnight than find her way back past the guard the next morning. And when an Italian bridge collapsed in the middle of the night, Ross was delighted to see her trot towards the newsdesk at 3 a.m.

'Get me a fucking coffee' – a warm greeting by his standards.

At 4 a.m., taking a breather, Ross had given her some career advice.

'How would you feel about knocking on someone's door twenty minutes after they've been told their eight-year-old's been killed by a drunk driver?'

'Not great, but I'd do it.'

'In journalism, you can be told to fuck off twenty times in one day. That bother you?'

'No.'

'Good, then.'

When the managing editor finally barred her from the *Post*, Casey doorstepped Ross outside his Balham home at 5.30 a.m.

'Fuck off.' He hurried through the grey morning, carrying his stack of newspapers.

'No.'

'Fuck off.'

'I need a job, Ross.'

'Fine, I'll talk to the fucking editor.'

'I can do that,' Flora's eyes were gleaming. 'That's what I'll do.'

'No,' said Casey hastily. 'I'll organise some work experience for you.'

'Oh, thank you,' Flora glowed.

They talked for another hour, Casey making careful notes until her phone shrilled. Ross: *Siamese twins about to be born in Cardiff. Get on it. We're behind already FFS.*

Looking up, Casey realised it had got dark. Saying goodbye to Flora, she stepped out into the empty corridor. No one loitered here, gossiping away the hours. As she pulled her phone out of her pocket, Casey's attention was caught by a painting hanging opposite Flora's room. It was a gaudy burst of colour in the relentless magnolia. Someone had sketched an old-fashioned map with the ward as a fantastic archipelago. In this illustration, Debbie and Tony and Lauren and Marcella were grass-green islands, separated by oceans of disease. The careful script named the Gulf of N.T.M., the P. Aeruginosa Strait, the B. Cepacia Sea, and a galleon bobbed so bravely. Blue sea monsters, evil eyes glowing, skulked between the islands.

Casey glanced around for the way out of the ward. The exit signs were bright, simple, designed for people in distress. She typed out a message to Ed as she headed towards the ward exit. *Sorry, darling, have to go to Cardiff for the night. Won't be back for dinner.*

She looked up as someone came through the swing doors. It was Noah, brisk in his scrubs.

'I'm just off,' Casey explained.

'There is a quicker way out, just down that corridor,' he pointed. 'They've mothballed a ward, but you can nip through and then it's straight down the stairs to reception.'

'Thanks,' said Casey. 'Goodbye, Noah.'

'Goodbye.'

He disappeared through another set of double doors. Casey sent her message, and with a last glance at the jaunty sea monsters, she headed off.

The corridor floor was filthy, builders' footprints traipsing to and fro. They must be in the middle of a refurbishment. Casey hurried down the narrow passageway, thinking about the intro for her cystic fibrosis story. She had been a good interviewee, Flora. Articulate and thoughtful and sympathetic. They weren't all like that.

As the words flitted around her mind, Casey pushed open the ward door. It was a long, dark room, a few beds shrouded in plastic dust sheets. Almost everything had been stripped out, apart from the curtains around the beds. They drooped, pale as ghosts. Electric wires hung from deep-gouged walls, and the side rooms were taped off.

The muddy footprints led across the floor. Casey felt along the wall for a switch, but no light flickered into life.

You can nip through and then it's straight down the stairs to reception …

Casey followed the footprints. There were double doors at the end of the ward, and she pushed them open into another long room, an orange glow oozing in through the windows. The curtains dangled, gallows-heavy. Casey hurried along.

This ward ended in a dusty reception area. Left or right or straight on? Casey muttered aloud, trying to remember Noah's words. She checked her watch. *Come on.* She chose right randomly, scurrying through another ward, around an abandoned nurse's station.

There were double doors at the end of this ward. Nearly there, this *must* be it. She pushed at the doors.

They were locked.

Casey tugged at the doors irritably. *I'll miss my train.*

But the doors were impervious.

She scuffed the grimy floor with her toe, and spun around crossly. Now she would have to go all the way back to Flora's ward, and follow the maze back out again.

Just then, Casey felt the air shift very slightly. It was almost unnoticeable except for a plastic dust sheet shivering, the curtains whispering quietly to themselves.

Somewhere far in the distance, someone had opened a door.

The ward now seemed very dark. There were more light switches by this set of double doors and she pressed them hard. Nothing happened.

She shoved at the double doors again, but she was trapped, no way out.

For a second, Casey stood, her back flat against the hospital doors, a ripple of fear in her spine.

'Who's there?' She felt the words catch in her throat.

Silence.

In the distance, a door closed hiss-quiet. The curtains beside her shuddered, and stilled.

Someone had come into the ward. A silence settled over the room, a waiting, watchful stillness.

Casey's eyes flickered around the room, searching for another way out. But there was nothing. Moving quickly, instinctively, she slid behind one of the curtains, a strange echo of the child's game.

Her breath was shortening, her hands clenching. But then she squared her shoulders and shook her head. *You're being pathetic. Come on.*

She took a deep breath and stepped out from behind the curtain, walked down the ward and peered into the next room.

It was even darker in here. The bed curtains reached to the floor, and there were a dozen places a person might hide. The clutter and rattle of the rest of the hospital must be only a few dozen yards away, but it might have been a hundred miles. This ward felt abandoned to strange Victorian spirits, to dusty, fateful ghosts and watchful, dangerous eyes.

'Who's there?' Casey could hear a shake in her voice. 'Stop playing games.'

Silence.

She tried to peer around the drifting curtains, tried to see into the shadowy corners.

Nothing.

And then she lifted her chin and marched down the long room.

She passed the first bed, with its spectral curtains, then the next and the next.

And she was nearly at the doors, nearly back in the bright chaos of the hospital, nearly *safe*, when a curtain jerked aside, and a shape surged towards her.

4

Casey opened her mouth to scream.

'Shut *up*.' She realised it was Noah, still in his scrubs, his pale face smudged with grime.

'What the hell are you *doing*?' Casey spat. 'Are you insane?'

In the gloom of the ward, Noah was staring at her, eyes wide, hands shaking.

'You have to … ' Noah spun away, jaw gritted. 'You need to … '

The doctor's frustration took him across the room in a couple of strides, ending up by one of the windows, his hands gripping the sill.

'What?' Casey let herself sound angry. 'You *scared* me.'

'You need to … '

'What do I need to do, Noah? This is ridiculous.'

'I looked you up.' The words were staccato. 'You don't write features. You're an investigative reporter. Casey Benedict. You did that story in Libya.'

'I'm not on investigations.' Even now, Casey resented saying the words. 'I've stopped doing that. I'm covering Heather Webber, our health editor, while she's on mat leave. You can check with the *Post*. Or just look up the last few bloody stories I've written.'

'But you were … '

'Yes, I *was*,' said Casey. 'But now I'm just writing a piece on cystic fibrosis. Look me up properly, Noah. Yesterday, I wrote 900 unbelievably dreary words about tax breaks for pharmaceutical companies. I couldn't be bothered to go through all the hoops with the wretched press team here, that's all.'

'That doesn't matter.'

'Well,' she said. 'What do you want then, Noah?'

'It's … ' Casey waited. Noah pushed himself away from the windowsill, turned back towards the room. 'Flora is very ill,' he said.

'I know,' she said. 'I can see that.'

'No,' he said. 'It's worse than you realise. It's worse than she realises, even. Flora is going to die. And she's going to die very soon, unless we can get the abscessus under control. She can't fight it much longer.'

'The Adsero antibiotic isn't enough?'

'No. Nowhere near. Even the new one, saepio, probably won't help much. Flora will need a lung transplant, much sooner than she knows. And if you operate on someone with abscessus in their lungs, it gets into their bloodstream too, and then it really is the end. It makes it far too dangerous to do the operation. And because of that, they won't give donor lungs to a patient with abscessus. It's a waste of precious lungs.'

'So,' Casey calculated, 'She needs a different drug? A better one?'

'Yes. You could … ' He stalled.

'You must see very ill patients all the time,' said Casey slowly. 'What's different about Flora?'

'There is a different antibiotic. A much better one. But they've stopped it … '

'They've stopped what? Who's they? I don't understand, Noah. Why don't you just—'

'It could save people, and they've buried it instead. They're suppressing it.'

'How—'

There were sounds from the corridor. Noah turned, the fear juddering up.

'I have to go.' His eyes were wide. 'I'm sorry, Casey … I can't … ' He dived for the door, jerking it open. He stopped in the doorway just for a second, tugging his scrubs straight. 'I'm really sorry, Casey' – and he was gone.

'No,' said Miranda. 'You can't.'

'But … ' Casey's arms flailed with frustration. 'I have to.'

'You don't have to,' said Miranda. 'In fact, you have to go to Wales. You're meant to be halfway to Cardiff by now. All the other papers will be there, already. Ross will go absolutely ballistic if you're not there first thing tomorrow.'

Casey gestured away the conjoined twins. 'You didn't hear this doctor, Miranda. Noah was desperate … '

'What,' Miranda tried for patience, 'did he say exactly?'

Casey read aloud from her notepad. There was no recording, she thought with exasperation. She, who recorded everything. As soon as Noah had gone, she had sat down on an empty bed in the quiet ward, and scribbled down everything she could remember into her notepad. But even as she read Noah's words aloud, Casey could tell: there was not enough here to convince. It had been the fear in the voice, not the words.

'Stop,' Miranda interrupted. 'What does any of that mean?'

'I don't know.' Casey let out a sigh that was almost a groan. 'Not exactly.'

They were in the *Post*'s investigations room. Miranda sat at her desk, while Casey stood before her like a disgraced private. The room was small, shabby, three desks crowded together. There was a scruffy sofa, a faded print on the wall and a shelf of cheap gold trophies for various journalism awards. Secluded though, for plotting.

Casey stared at her old desk, now holding Tillie's notepad, a couple of files, a framed photograph of a small brown dog. Casey forced herself to look away. Hessa and Tillie were out somewhere, and Casey felt a burn of envy as she wondered where they were.

'It's important, Miranda.'

But Miranda met her eye. 'What's important is that you're on the next train to Cardiff, Casey. I can't protect if you don't even try to do your bloody job. You know what Ross is like.'

'Miranda … '

'I said no.'

Casey threw herself on the old sofa, defeated.

'Bloody Cardiff.'

'Besides,' Miranda looked at her watch and stood up, 'I'm meeting a friend for dinner.'

'Who?' Casey was still sulking.

'Delphine's back from South Africa.' Miranda's smile gleamed briefly. 'My old boss at the *Argus* before she packed in journalism. Taught me everything I know.'

'I'm quite sure Delphine Black,' Casey glowered, 'wouldn't pack me off to Cardiff.'

Casey brooded all the way to Cardiff, tapping at her laptop. She booked into an uninspiring hotel, and the next morning, she sat outside the grim concrete of the University Hospital with the rest of the press pack as they were fed dollops of news, bland as baby food, by pink-cheeked press officers.

Isn't it exciting?

Oh, fascinating.

All the reporters filed the same thing, at the same time, in different styles. From *Conjoined twins born in Cardiff* to *Welsh Mum in Siamese Shocker!* Casey stared into space.

The next day, Casey called Flora to check a few facts, casually also establishing that Noah was on duty. Jumping on the train back to London, she headed straight for the Royal Brompton. She loitered in a corridor until Noah's shift ended – long hours later – and then followed him cautiously down the street. In the sunlight, Noah looked even more exhausted, a sharp contrast to the manicured Chelsea women jogging along the wide pavements.

Casey waited until he was on a quiet street – tall white houses with scarlet geraniums spilling out of window boxes – and then sprinted forward.

'Noah.'

The doctor looked horrified, eyes roaming up and down the empty road. 'Casey, I can't speak to you.'

'I want to understand what you were trying to tell me about, Noah. I think it's important.'

'Go away.'

'Noah, you know about something serious. Something important.'

'It's nothing. I was just having a bloody tough day.' The swear word was awkward on Noah's tongue. 'There's nothing to talk about, Casey.'

'Please.'

'No.'

For a second, they stared at each other. She couldn't read his face. It was always harder reading unhappy people, people used to hiding their feelings.

'Please, Noah.'

'No. Just talk to the press office about a quote for your article, and leave me alone.'

Casey put a hand on his arm, but he twisted away and was gone, leaving her alone on the beautiful tall white street.

Her phone bleeped. *One of the twins is dying, and the other is looking dicey. Get back to Wales.*

In the middle of the grey Cardiff rain, Casey typed messages to the Royal Brompton.

Would it be OK if … Obsequious.

After a dozen tedious exchanges, they agreed, unwillingly. *You can have half an hour. And you have to anonymise any patient.*

Sure. So obedient.

Later, the press office agreed quotes from a Dr Noah Hart. Sentences clipped into words in an order no human would ever speak aloud.

Sitting in her hire car, Casey transferred the quotes to the article and sighed. She stared out through a rain-spattered windscreen and her mobile phone rang. A split second of hope, maybe *this* would be a story.

'Hello?' Casey's shoulders sank. It was the honeyed tones of a PR. 'I just wondered if you had a moment to talk about our new drug—'

'Has it killed anyone yet?' Casey snapped.

'Of course not.' The sugary tones stumbled, then whipped back to the script, 'It's a brilliant—'

'Well, let me know when someone dies. Then I'll be interested.'

Casey hung up and immediately felt bad. The woman was only doing her job. Dozens of calls a day to extol a contraceptive, a vaccine, the next miracle cream.

Industrial distortion, maybe.

But.

Casey sighed and climbed out of her car, heading off to get a sandwich. Chicken salad, raspberry smoothie, crisps, bored.

As the twins clung precariously to life, Casey stared out over the heave of the Bristol Channel, and tapped out messages to Ed.

What shall we do on Saturday night?

Because she worked Monday to Friday now, mostly, and could make plans for the weekend for the first time in years. Book tables, buy theatre tickets, wander down the South Bank hand in hand, maybe.

We could drive over to Wiltshire for Sunday lunch?

His parents – it startled her still – lived in a beautiful old rectory, long lost to the church. His mother smiled and bustled, made strawberry jam and chocolate cakes. He was a kind son. Always took flowers, tied with a pretty ribbon. Whereas her parents … No.

Or Pinks and Squash are in London for the weekend … We could –

Ed's old Royal Marine friends, the loyalties irrevocable. Ed had been chasing pirates across the Indian Ocean when he and Casey had first met: an odd sort of first date. The *Post* had dispatched Casey to Oman at the height of the piracy crisis, and she had skipped on board the huge Navy ship at Salalah with a fleeting hello to the quiet young Marine captain. During the slow days off the coast of Somalia, they had started to talk. One afternoon, they had raced across the waves in a fast boat with eight of his men. 'The boys needed some extra training,' he had laughed, as the boat skimmed from crest to crest and the sun sparkled over the ocean. He'd glanced back over his shoulder at her, just once. Kind eyes, turning down at the corners. By the time the ship turned towards the nearest port – the Seychelles, all silver gold beaches and wind-blown orange flowers – she had known.

Or we could sort out the spare bedroom.

They had moved in together. Tufnell Park, more prosaically. In a row of grey houses with that headmistress austerity. Ed had picked out paint colours, slapping uneven squares on the wall. Cat's Cradle or Kissing Gate? Feather Pillow or Wood Smoke? Come on, Casey. You do have to choose.

I land back early Saturday morning, but free after that.

Ed worked in security now, a bodyguard for a secretive billionaire who commuted from Belgrade to London, from Shanghai to Cape Town. Never the US, Casey noted cynically. And his plane would land at Northolt a minute after midnight, a minute into Saturday morning, so the taxman couldn't count a day.

See you soon. Can't wait.

The sun broke through the clouds over the Bristol Channel, and a seagull shrieked overhead, tempted by a dropped chip and some fried chicken. Maybe this job was enough.

Routine. Sensible. Day after day.

Mundane, Casey's mind filled in. Boring. Impossible.

A siren howled far in the distance, and she saw the fear in Noah's eyes again. *What?* The question flared up. *Who?* An almost physical urge. *Why?*

Later she messaged Miranda, a peace offering. *How was dinner with Delphine?*

Casey had only met Delphine a few times. Half French, she had a ballerina's poise, and was always immaculately turned out. Her crisp white shirts made Casey feel scruffy. Delphine wore her hair in a dark pixie crop and her dancer's slight figure made her look fragile, although Miranda laughed and said that Delphine was one of the toughest people she had ever met. It was Delphine who had introduced Miranda to undercover work, years ago.

Delphine's well, Miranda messaged back. *It was so nice seeing her. She sends her love. Told me some very funny stories about working at the Western Evening News back in the day. With Ross, can you imagine? Before they both moved on to the nationals, of course. She said he was a nightmare, but could be really good fun.*

Sounds unlikely.

Delphine had quit journalism around three years earlier, after her husband died unexpectedly.

'I have two young sons.' Delphine's eyes had been steady on Casey, over a glass of white wine in the bar next door to the *Post*. 'It was those hours, such a killer. So I had to choose, and it was the only thing I could do.'

Delphine had lived in South Africa since resigning from the *Argus*. 'My brother lives down there,' she said. 'And it is very beautiful. And it's a long way away.'

It was where her husband had died, too. Finlay – an architect, a rising star – had been dispatched to Cape Town for six months by his company. The *Argus* had agreed to send Delphine down to South Africa too, covering stories all over the continent.

I'm glad Delphine's well, messaged Casey now. *Cardiff, in notable contrast, is very dull.*

You won't be down there for long, surely?

God, I hope not.

Casey's cystic fibrosis article was published on Friday. It was listed for Thursday, but 'it'll hold, right?' Ross had asked. 'It's not exactly time sensitive.'

'Sure,' said Casey, thinking of all the times she had sprinted across Departures at Heathrow to be first on the plane, the first to the story. *First.* 'There's no rush on that one.'

When the article came out, she flipped through the paper idly. Poor Flora. Poor Flora Ashcroft.

5

On Monday morning, Casey marched into the office.

'Ross,' she said. 'I want to do a big read on antibiotic resistance.'

Ross was dealing with a ministerial resignation by shouting down his landline and his mobile simultaneously. He looked up at Casey vaguely.

'Did you know there's a form of gonorrhoea going around that makes you infertile within two years?' Casey asked cheerfully. 'It was first discovered in Leeds, oddly. Antibiotics bounce off it, basically. That's just one of the things that happens with antibiotic resistance, you know? Weapons-grade STDs.'

Ross lowered one phone for a second. 'I think I was happier not knowing that, to be honest, Case.'

'Don't worry, Ross,' the home affairs editor shouted across. 'It's hardly likely to affect you, is it?'

'The article will be riveting.' Casey looked pious.

'What's happened to the Cardiff twins?'

The political editor appeared in the newsroom, out of breath, his arms waving.

'Stable,' Casey said quickly. 'All right?'

'Sure.' Ross's attention had vaporised. 'Whatever, Casey.'

From the outside, the public laboratories looked like a sprawling office block, set back from rows of dingy Edwardian semis. Old brick walls covered in ivy sagged gently.

Behind the walls, however, the security was impressive.

'They kept cows up here, years ago,' a burly guard explained, as he walked Casey to the main entrance. 'For smallpox vaccination research, back when it was countryside all around.'

Casey imagined London spreading north, engulfing Colindale like a pandemic.

'Quite a difference,' she said.

Inside, Professor Brennan welcomed her with an absent-minded benevolence. He was tall and avuncular, with a grey beard and horn-rimmed glasses. His shirt – broad cream and vermilion stripes – clashed horribly with a green and yellow tie. The jacket of his well-worn brown suit had been abandoned somewhere, his shirtsleeves were rolled up to his elbows.

'Good afternoon, Miss – ah – Benedict.' Brennan peered at her over his glasses. 'Welcome to the Colindale National Institute for Health Protection, as I think we're called at the moment. How can I help you?'

The professor showed her around one of the laboratories, generous with his time.

'As you know,' he said as they walked down a long corridor, 'We analyse both viruses and bacteria here at Colindale. Viruses are – well – tiny. The simplest form of life, they have been called. They're just a strand of genetic material surrounded by a protein coat and they need a host to survive more than a few hours. That's your – ah – flu virus, your herpes, your Ebola. And your coronavirus, of course.'

'Yes.'

'Bacteria, however, are infinitely more – well – sophisticated, you might say. They're much bigger, and they can live independently of a host. And whereas almost all viruses cause disease, not all bacteria are a bad thing. You need them in your gut, for example. But, of course, they can be – err – a disaster.'

Brennan had an odd way of speaking, his words damming up, and then gushing out in a flood.

'I see,' said Casey.

'In here,' Brennan opened a door with a flourish and pointed to a long row of Petri dishes, 'we do the tests for what you journalists call – um – superbugs.' Through his thick glasses, his eyes twinkled. 'Hospitals all over the country send us a sample of a bacteria by courier, and then we grow it on agar. Agar is a solid – ah – growth medium, if you will. We give the bacteria twenty-four hours to colonise, and then we start testing a range of different antibiotics on them. If – ah – one of the antibiotics works, we tell the hospital, and they give it to the patient.'

'Twenty-four hours, just to grow the bacteria?' Casey thought of a world where information ricocheted like a pinball. 'But what if the patient is really ill?'

'Well. Yes. Sometimes, we – ah – tell the hospital what should cure the patient, but it turns out it's a bit late for the patient.'

'But isn't there a better way?'

'Not really.' He blinked at her over a row of test tubes. 'Not yet. The system's not changed for years. Fleming,' he gestured at the agar plates, 'would recognise this lot. Instant diagnostics would be – um – our holy grail. I think Great Ormond Street are working on something, but it's still rather theoretical.'

Casey thought about Alexander Fleming accidentally discovering penicillin in 1928. The world's first antibiotic: a billion miracles in one.

'Are the new antibiotics any better?'

'New antibiotics?' A hairy eyebrow rose an inch. 'It depends what you mean by *new* antibiotics, of course.'

'Why?'

'There are only about fourteen different antibiotics,' Brennan explained mildly. 'Or groups of them, I should say. And about ten of those were found in the two decades after penicillin was discovered. There have been very few substantial discoveries of new antibiotics for the last forty years. Most of our so-called new antibiotics are what you could call slight tweaks on old ones.'

'I didn't realise,' said Casey.

'Yes,' he said. 'And yet still people walk into their GP's surgery and demand antibiotics on tap. When they are the … ' he pushed his glasses back up his nose to emphasise the point, 'most precious thing.'

'But I was talking to someone recently about a possible new antibiotic, produced by Adsero?' said Casey. 'They said that it might be effective on Mycobacterium abscessus for CF patients?'

'Ah, yes,' said Brennan. 'I've heard good things about Adsero's new antibiotic. But of course it would only be an enhancement of their current one.'

'Their current one is zentetra?' Casey checked her notes. 'And the new one is due to be called saepio. So saepio would only really be a tweak of zentetra?'

'Precisely.' An approving nod. 'But, you never know, the new one may be much more effective. It can work like that. We live in hope.'

'But surely a really new antibiotic would be worth a fortune to any pharmaceutical company?' said Casey.

Brennan smiled. 'There isn't much of a pipeline for new antibiotics,' he said. 'They cost a vast amount to develop, and then if you did actually find one, you would want to use it as little as possible. Because as soon as you started using it widely, drug resistance would start building up. It's an endless cycle, you see?'

Brennan drew circles in the air with his fountain pen.

'The companies don't invest in antibiotics because they wouldn't make them much money?' asked Casey.

'It could take ten years and cost – ah – a billion dollars to develop a new antibiotic.' Brennan pushed his glasses up his nose again. 'And then you'd see resistance within two years.'

'But the big pharmaceutical companies make billions every year,' said Casey.

'It's much more fun to invest in something that the public will keep buying.' Brennan gave her a surprisingly wicked grin. 'If you were ill, you might use an antibiotic once or twice, and then be cured. But a cancer drug? Or – ah – a heart drug? Well, with a bit of luck, you might be on that for the rest of your nicely lengthened life. There are eight hundred ongoing trials with cancer monoclonal antibodies. Eight *hundred* trials. In antibiotics, there are maybe fifty drugs in the whole pipeline.'

'But a good antibiotic could save millions of lives,' said Casey.

Poor Flora Ashcroft.

'Yes,' said Brennan gently. 'Indeed.'

Brennan shuffled back towards an untidy office, waving Casey into a chair.

'I'll make you a cup of tea,' he said. 'How do you take it? I think I've got some milk somewhere. At least, I do hope it's milk.'

'How would you go about trying to find a new antibiotic?' she asked.

'Well, at the moment,' Brennan was prodding around in a small fridge, 'some scientists are going back through abandoned antibiotics. That is to say, antibiotics that were developed in the sixties and seventies, but not taken forward commercially because there was no market for them back then. But now, because everything else has stopped working, they're worth a shot.'

'Right.'

'And then there are antibiotics like colistin, which scientists never expected to be used by humans in the first place because the side effects are pretty dire. And since they never expected to give colistin to humans, they've been giving truckloads of it to animals for decades because it makes them fatten up nice and fast. And now it turns out we actually *do* need to use it on humans, because we haven't got anything else, but that means we are starting to see colistin resistance.'

The kettle was boiling. Brennan waved a carton at Casey, eyebrows raised.

'Yes, please,' said Casey.

'And then, of course, there are unintended consequences,' Brennan went on, lobbing a teabag in the general direction of a mug but missing. 'In the eighties and nineties, there was a big push to bring through cephalosporins, for example. A lot of companies developed them, and now we know that not only was that driving cephalosporin resistance, but – worse – it was enabling bacteria to produce a little enzyme called ESBL. And it turns out that ESBL doesn't just block cephalosporin, it causes resistance to a whole raft of antibiotics.'

Brennan retrieved the teabag from the floor and dusted it off.

'So by using one antibiotic, you actually created resistance to a whole range of antibiotics?'

'Exactly. In hindsight, it wasn't – er – ideal.'

As he was about to pour the boiling water, Brennan's phone rang. He smiled apologetically at Casey as he answered.

She half-listened to Brennan's conversation. 'Oh, how good to hear from you … I've got a young journalist here! Casey – ah – Benedict from the *Post*. Someone interested in AMR for once, can you believe it?' As Brennan spoke, Casey checked her own phone. A message from Ed. *I could meet you in Naples the weekend after next? Best pizza in the world. Fancy it?*

'We've been having excellent chats about everything from agar to zentetra.' Brennan laughed heartily at his own joke.

Young journalist? wondered Casey, and went back to her phone.

She was startled by Brennan dropping the phone back into its cradle. The avuncular smile had disappeared.

'I'm afraid,' Brennan stood up sharply, 'that I'm going to have to ask you to leave, Miss Benedict.'

'What?' Casey was bewildered. 'Why?'

He was bustling round his desk, hunting for her bag.

'I'm very sorry, but … '

Casey refused to be bustled. 'I don't understand. Why on earth do I have to leave?'

'I'm afraid … '

'What's changed, Professor Brennan?'

He stared at his jumbled shelves for a moment. 'There's – ah – some urgent work coming in. I'm sorry, but I'm going to be horribly busy for the next few hours.'

Brennan was a terrible liar, Casey thought. His eyes wouldn't meet hers, flickering right to left.

'I don't believe you,' she said.

But Brennan was refusing to let go of his excuse.

'It's absolutely imperative that I get this work done straight away, I'm afraid. I really must ask you to leave.'

'All right, but I really don't understand … '

And a few minutes later, she was out on the dingy street, slouching crossly towards the Northern line.

As her Tube rattled along the tracks, Casey looked at her watch. Late afternoon, sunny day, no point in going back to the office. Nobody would miss her anyway, she thought bitterly. Might as well get out at Hampstead, and wander round the shops, meander to the Heath.

Later, dawdling along the high street, she messaged Ed. *Popping to Hampstead Heath on my way back from Colindale. I need a walk.*

Did you have a good day? What did you find out?

Casey thought of herself being chucked out of Brennan's office, and suspected she might cry if she typed it out. *Really interesting. Very glad I went.*

What did you find out?

It's complicated. I'll tell you later.

A short pause. *Why don't I come and meet you on Hampstead Heath? I can finish up early.*

Despite herself, she smiled. *That would be lovely.*

I'll see you at the top of Parliament Hill. Be as quick as I can.

Casey drifted slowly along the paths, gazing up at the copper rust green of the trees as the sun sloped through the leaves. Someone was mowing a lawn in the distance, the smell drifting on a warm breeze. People in the mixed bathing pond were laughing, splashing about in the khaki-green water.

Where are you?

I'll be there in a minute.

It didn't take long to reach the top of Parliament Hill, looking out over the whole sweep of London. The Shard, the Walkie Talkie, the Gherkin, all jigsawing into a steel blue sky. And there was St Paul's, so perfect, alone in the crowd.

Casey's eyes softened as she thought about meeting Ed on another hill once. Twice, really. Crimson tulips, silver dark clouds and a city lit up by a storm. Thunder and lightning, and *you don't have to choose*.

That first kiss.

She sat down on the grass and hugged her knees.

A discarded *Standard* lay in the grass. Casey scanned the headlines idly, out of habit.

Tourists flown home after Anglo Air collapse.

Norovirus crisis: Hospital bosses warn 'Stay away from A&E.'

Teenagers were idling by the viewpoint at the very top of the hill. Flirtation and the indisputable smell of weed. Casey grinned to herself.

The teens drifted off, down towards Highgate Cemetery, and for a moment there was silence except for the breeze whispering over tussocky grass. Casey enjoyed the strange tranquillity of the huge park in the middle of the chaos of London.

Her eyes drifted across the grass. Far away, at the bottom of the hill, a small child was flying a kite. The kite was a flutter of neon in the sky, his family watching on proudly. Casey heard footsteps behind her, and looked around lazily, wondering if it was Ed. A tall man in a sweatshirt, navy blue, the hood pulled over his hair, something in his hand.

Not Ed: she turned back to the view.

In his hand.

A knife.

A knife.

6

Casey was scrambling away before the thought was complete, fear like a bomb blast. The man surged forward, all ruthless athleticism. In a frenzy of motion, Casey scrabbled to her feet. *Where?* Even in her fright, the thought: *not towards the child*, and she spun round and bolted towards the trees, terror transformed into speed.

It was darker in the woods. Casey could hear the man catching up with her, barely out of breath. His pace was terrifying. She darted between the trees, but already he was drawing closer, bounding effortlessly over the roots and brambles.

In the twilight of the woods, the park seemed endless, empty, desolate. Casey ran, diving under low branches, dodging past saplings. As she ducked round one vast oak, her shoulder smashed into the trunk, and she cried out in pain.

No time to stop. Who is he? Mugger? Rapist? Wallet, here, throw.

Her lungs were burning and her legs were agony. The man was closer now, almost able to grab her. A fleeting glance back. A glimpse of hollow eyes, short dark hair, and she sprinted as fast as she could, the world a blur.

A slash of his knife and she screamed as he tried to trip her, snatching at her jacket. She wriggled out of it and leaped from his grasp, running, racing, everything terror.

Out of breath now, couldn't go much further, legs tiring.

Ahead was a thicket of trees, lower to the ground. She dived towards it – last chance – scrabbling under the low-slung branches as the bushes tangled over her head. Casey forced her way through, caring only about survival. The bushes ripped at her face, her hands.

Those teenagers.

Casey spun towards Highgate. *They must be here somewhere.* She broke out from the thicket and darted with a dying surge of energy. And at last there they were, the same small group, all baggy clothes and studied nonchalance. She ran to them faster than she ever had, and almost skittled them over.

They were surprised, polite, sweet-natured. Nice kids, it turned out.

You all right, miss? What's happened to you? It's OK. It's OK.

'A man.' Casey fought for breath, her body juddering with exhaustion. 'Back there … A man … '

But they all looked, and there was no one.

'Don't be scared.' A tall boy, their natural leader, it appeared. He was amiable, slightly stoned. 'We've got you, don't worry.'

'But he was chasing me. I ran … '

The teenagers were excited by the drama, almost enjoying it. Loud voices and wide eyes. But the woods were empty, the quiet only broken by shouts from a rounders game starting in the far distance.

'Shall we call the police?' one girl said, uncertainly, the whiff of weed in her clothes.

She saw them all hesitate.

'No, it's OK,' said Casey. 'I can report it later.'

They relaxed at once.

'Thank you,' said Casey, meaning it. 'Thank you so much.'

Exuberant now, they escorted her to the road and waited while she called a taxi.

'You take care now, miss. Look after her, yeah? She's had a shock,' they said through the window to the taxi driver, and he grinned at their adolescent importance, and promised he'd look after her all right.

In the back of the car, Casey dug her phone out of her pocket.

Something horrible happened. Someone chased me in the park.

A pause. No answer.

Can you meet me back at the flat? I'm in a cab. Hurry. Please.
Silence.
Are you there?
Ed?

A flood of fear, visceral. To the taxi driver, calmly, urgently: 'Can you be as quick as you can, please?'

She knew. Before she even entered the flat, she knew. A pain like she'd never felt before.

Through the hallway, up the stairs, running her fingers along the wall as if to touch something real. The front door to their flat, the scrape of her key. Into the bedroom.

A shape on the floor.

A wail started from somewhere, and swallowed her up. She stumbled forward, a puppet, strings slashed.

There was no point in rushing, she could see. No point in screaming down the phone. *You have to hurry. You have to save him.*

His eyes, his beautiful eyes, flecked with grey and green, blue and gold.

They were fixed, staring at nothing.

She dropped to her knees, touching his cheek, his forehead, his hair. He was warm still. She stroked his chest, his arm, his hand, so gently. Held his fingers for a moment, as if she might lead him back.

Then she pulled away, and looked at him again. That grey jumper, so familiar. The tatty old jeans, all ready for a walk on the Heath.

No blood, he looked perfect.

My love.

She pushed herself backwards, leaning against the cool of the wall as the world whirled. Bile in her throat, and she shoved her fists to her mouth, hard. Blood was metal against her teeth.

No. No. It was impossible.

Beloved.

Impossible.

Behind her, she heard a commotion. Felt no fear though. Nothing worse could happen now. Nothing.

It was only a neighbour, a voice timorous but brave, calling through the front door left ajar. 'I thought I heard a scream, dear. Oh, no. Oh, no. Oh, dear.'

And then there was nothing, as the world folded her into a clamour of sirens and ambulances and uniforms, and finally a merciful silence.

7

'No,' said Casey. 'That's not right.'

The policewoman looked at her sympathetically. 'It's what they said it looked like. I know it's very difficult when you've had a shock like this. I'm so sorry.'

'But it isn't true.'

'It's a terrible tragedy,' said the doctor. 'Especially when he was so young. It does happen though.'

'No,' said Casey firmly. 'He didn't have a heart attack. They have to check again.'

The doctor gave her a smooth, professional smile, her eyes on the cut on Casey's forehead from when she'd fainted. They had brought her to hospital to get it checked out.

'There'll be an autopsy, of course.' The doctor was making conversation as she smoothed a large plaster into place. 'And they'll run a tox screen anyway, to make sure there wasn't anything in his bloodstream.'

'Did he take drugs?' The policewoman was leaning against the wall of the hospital's small waiting room.

'No,' Casey muttered. 'Ed was a Marine.' The policewoman's eyes were world-weary. 'He would never do drugs.'

There was a rising babble in the hall outside, and Casey felt the doctor's eyes go past her, the attention switching to people who might survive.

'I'm very sorry for your loss.' A last flick of sympathy as she hurried away.

Casey stared at the policewoman.

'You have to understand.' She could hear the hysteria in her voice, 'Ed didn't just die. Someone killed him.'

'Would you like a cup of tea?' asked the policewoman. 'It will help.'

A memory surfaced, as if it had happened a thousand years earlier and not a few hours ago.

'There was a man on Hampstead Heath earlier. He chased me. He had a knife.'

The policewoman regarded her.

'When did this happen?'

'A few hours ago?'

'Why didn't you report it?'

'I was going to.' Casey felt the frustration boil up, 'I was going to call the police as soon as I got back to the flat.'

'What did this man look like?'

'Tall. Wearing a dark blue hoodie, I couldn't see his face very well. I only caught a glimpse of him ... '

'And did anyone else see him?'

'There was a group of teenagers.' Casey's despair rose. 'But they didn't see him. I ran towards them, and when we looked back he had gone.'

Her voice wobbled. She could feel the policewoman's scepticism.

'Is there anyone,' the policewoman's eyes were kind, 'who I can call?'

Miranda raced into the small waiting room in a flurry of distress. 'Casey, I am so sorry. I can't believe it.'

'I couldn't think,' Casey was crying again, 'of who else to call.'

'Don't be daft,' and Miranda enfolded her in a sweet-smelling hug. 'Now, let's get you home. You need a hot bath and bed.'

'No.' Casey jerked away. 'I want to go to the office.'

'The office?' Miranda's eyes widened. 'You need to go home, Casey. You're in shock.'

'I'm not.' Casey scrubbed away tears. 'And I have to go. I have to go to the office.'

'Casey. No.'

They argued for several minutes, until Casey stood. 'Fine. I'll make my own way.'

And Miranda gave up.

They were all very sympathetic, oddly soft voices in the quiet of the investigations room.

'Did you get the teenagers' names?' asked Ross.

'No.' Casey struggled to stay calm. 'They were up there smoking weed. They wouldn't have wanted to speak to the police.'

'Right.' Ross looked down, made another note.

'I'm not delusional,' Casey protested. 'It happened.'

'Of course it did,' Dash said evenly.

They were sitting in the investigations room. Casey was on the sofa, Miranda at her desk. Dash was leaning against the door, with Ross perching on the radiator. Tillie and Hessa had made some excuse and faded out of the room.

The news had already spread around the office. They all knew Ed, knew what he meant to Casey, and she had felt dozens of eyes on her as she walked through the newsroom to the little office.

In the office, Miranda handed Casey a cup of tea and a slice of dry chocolate cake from the canteen. *You need to eat.*

Casey took it awkwardly, shoving away the thought of a mother in a beautiful vicarage on a hill, turning to an unexpected knock at the front door.

'Take us through it again,' said Dash.

'I was messaging Ed as I walked up the hill.' Casey brandished her phone. 'Look, *I'll be there in a minute.* Why would he say that if he was still in the flat?'

'You only live in Tufnell Park,' said Miranda. 'It's not exactly far.'

'It might be a figure of speech,' Dash murmured. 'He could have been delayed for any number of reasons.'

'But Ed was punctual,' protested Casey. 'It was me who was always late.'

'Maybe he had to go back to the flat? Forgotten something.'

'They were trapping me.' Casey stared at her phone again. 'Whoever it was. They used his phone to get me to wait at the top of Parliament Hill.'

'"Hampstead Heath robberies", Ross was reading aloud from the BBC website. '"Police launch covert operations after spate of muggings." That's from a month ago.'

'So someone might have seen this man,' said Casey defiantly. 'That's good. It wasn't a mugger. No mugger would chase someone like that, surely?'

As she spoke, an image flashed into her mind: Ed laughing over his shoulder as a boat raced over the waves. Her throat closed up. More images. Scarlet tulips, pattering rain and a city bright in the darkness.

You don't have to choose.

Cat's Cradle or Kissing Gate? I love you. Feather Pillow or Wood Smoke?

You do have to choose.

The tears were hot on her cheeks now, and Casey rubbed them furiously away.

'I'm fine.'

'You're not,' Dash said decisively. 'Go home, Casey. You're not to come back to the office until after the funeral. At the very least.'

Casey looked up and saw the blunt compassion in his eyes.

'Come on.' Miranda stood up. 'I'll take you home, Casey.'

The little flat was empty, cold. No parents to go home to, waiting with soup, a hug, a bunch of flowers picked from the garden.

The police had gone.

They think it's a heart attack, Casey thought despairingly. There would be no questions, no investigation.

The flat had barely been touched. Only a hall table shoved out of the way, a few scrapes on the wall. *To get the body out …* Casey's mind turned away firmly, closing the thought like a book.

As Miranda flitted about, turning on lamps, boiling the kettle, Casey wandered around the flat, touching a bookshelf, a painting, a vase.

'Someone killed him,' Casey said again. 'I know it, Miranda.'

Miranda moved her into an armchair as if she were a child, and put a cup of tea down in front of her. 'What do you want for supper, Casey?' she asked.

'I can't eat.'

Casey found that she was crying again, tears flooding down her face.

'I know it seems unbearable now, Casey. But you will get through this. You will.'

'But how?' Casey blinked up at her. 'How can I possibly?'

Miranda offered to stay the night, but Casey insisted on being alone.

'Call me,' Miranda urged. 'Any time.'

'I will,' Casey lied.

After Miranda had left, Casey roamed around the flat. All around, she could hear the noises of everyday life. A neighbour's television, the bang of a front door across the road, a peal of laughter from the street. The sounds echoed in her head. The night was warm, sticky, too close. Next door, people were sitting in their garden, smoking, quiet music playing. A last summer evening, and a comfortable sort of happiness.

Casey veered into the bedroom.

A shape on the floor.

She dodged back to the sitting room.

A copy of the *Evening Standard* lay on the table. Ed must have brought it home, and chucked it down.

She picked it up, anything to distract. The same headlines.

Tourists flown home after Anglo Air collapse.

Norovirus crisis: Hospital bosses warn 'Stay away from A&E.'

Casey looked closer at the headline. Two words were underlined. In biro, almost invisible.

Stay away.

Stay away.

Stay away.

8

She waited outside, scraping her toe backwards and forwards over a crack in the pavement. The security guard was watching her, half-worried, half-bored, so she moved down the drab street, out of his line of sight. She felt dizzy from a lack of food, her throat raw, nails bitten.

When Brennan came through the security gate, she hurried forward.

'Professor Brennan, I am sorry to bother you, but it is really important.' As Casey spoke, she felt the pain in her throat sharpen.

The professor flinched and half-turned as if to go back into the facility. But then he lifted his chin and hurried past her.

'I don't have anything to say, Miss Benedict.'

'Who called you when I was in your office?' There was a ringing in Casey's ears, a blur in her eyes.

'I don't know what you mean, Miss Benedict.'

'You do.' Casey fought down the desperation. 'I have to know, Professor Brennan.'

'You don't.'

'Listen,' Casey tried to shout, 'After I left you yesterday, I was attacked. And later my boyfriend … ' Her voice choked up. 'Ed Fitzgerald, my boyfriend. He was killed, Professor Brennan.'

Brennan turned towards her, a strange fear in his eyes. But he shook his head, and continued to stride towards the station. 'Leave me alone, Miss Benedict.'

Casey tried to follow him, and then doubled over, the pain searing down her throat, across her stomach. The world was fading into the distance. She staggered to a garden wall and sat down. Wiped a hand across her face, and tried to focus.

'Wait!' A last croak. 'Please wait … '

She had shown Miranda the copy of the *Standard*.

Miranda had touched the crumpled newspaper softly.

'You do believe me, don't you?' Casey had pleaded, and Miranda met her eyes calmly.

'I believe you were chased, Casey. And I know that it is extremely unlikely that someone as fit and healthy as Ed just died. But this … ' Miranda's fingers traced the faint biro lines as her eyes went to the pile of pens on Casey's desk, untidy in the corner of the room.

'You have to believe me, Miranda. You just have to. Why would I make it up?'

'There isn't anything linking the Colindale people to Noah Hart or the Royal Brompton,' said Miranda. She looked tired after a long day at work.

'There's me.' Casey's voice was thick. '*I* could be the link. I think it may have been because I published an article quoting Noah Hart. Then I could have been followed to Colindale. And someone could have … '

Spoken aloud, it sounded unlikely.

'Please get some rest, Casey.'

Miranda called a private doctor to Casey's flat, paid for by the *Post*. The doctor prescribed some pills, not too many, and Casey was left staring at the ceiling, her eyes occasionally drifting to the window. On the sill, there were a bunch of flowers, sent by the newsroom. They blossomed and faded, and Miranda swept away the shrivelled petals on one of her visits.

It was like being in a shipwreck, Casey thought. Plunged deep beneath the surface, and looking up at the roaring storm. Drifting below the flotsam and jetsam, and the rage. Because she knew that if she broke the surface, the storm would surround her. And she knew that she would be crushed, and torn, and ripped. That she could never survive.

It was far easier to stay down here.

My love. Beloved.

Far easier to stay down here, and drown.

One morning, Miranda picked her up and drove her to Wiltshire.

Casey sat in the church, the sunlight shining jewelled rainbows through a stained glass window. Ed's mother was white, frozen, snowed in by grief. His father shook hands, and nodded, his mouth a single line. Ed's brother marched to the front for the eulogy, chin up stern, and spoke to the back of the church, unable to look at anyone.

His voice broke on the last line: *my little brother.*

Afterwards, Casey stood on the vicarage lawn, a half-healed cut on her forehead, surrounded by Ed's friends and hushed voices.

That's his girlfriend.

The poor thing.

In black, although she might have worn a white dress once, in this garden.

'Dash says not to rush back to work,' said Miranda, as they drove back towards London.

Miranda had drawn her away as the crowd's conversation turned to chatter, as it always does. How are *you*? Haven't seen you for *ages*.

'I've got nothing else to do,' said Casey. 'Anyway, who'll write up the new breast cancer statistics?'

'Eric's covering health for the time being,' said Miranda. 'You're to take as long as you want.'

'But I'm bored,' said Casey. 'And I've got no idea what is going on in the world.'

She was reaching into the back of the car, where Miranda had abandoned a pile of newspapers.

'You won the sweepstake, by the way,' said Miranda, indicating as she joined the motorway. 'On Sophie and our esteemed acting health editor.'

'How?' Casey was startled.

'Well,' Miranda grinned, 'There was an exchange of emails. And I happened to bump into them at the Cirencester on a Tuesday evening, so they couldn't cross-ref too early on.'

'Miranda,' Casey smiled properly for the first time in days, 'I'm genuinely touched.'

'Thought you needed cheering up. The newsroom is awed by your foresight.'

Casey grinned again. 'What else is going on in the madhouse?'

'There was a total fuck-up on a story about that cyclist, Jed Naji.' Miranda rolled her eyes. 'Someone handed over a bunch of emails to Ellis – you know, that tall guy on the Sports desk – proving that Naji had been doping, and Sports cheerfully published a big article off the back of them. Of course, we all know Naji's been doping to the eyeballs for years. But it turned out those particular emails were faked.'

'Ouch,' Casey winced.

'Yeah. The guy who brought the emails to the *Post* used to train with Naji and knows – *knows* – that he's been doping. And the muppet thought he was being helpful by knocking up the emails and now the *Post* is going to have to hand over a fortune to Naji, even though we all know he's a fraud. And even worse, we're having to run a big cuddly interview with him, all about his brilliant training techniques.'

'Oh, dear.' Casey upended a packet of crisps.

'And now Ellis has been done over by Papercut too.'

'Poor Ellis.'

Papercut was an anonymous blog that published bitchy articles about various Fleet Street hacks. Ross had spent a sizeable chunk of time trying to unmask the individual behind the blog, to no avail. Papercut had responded with a couple of vicious paragraphs pointing out that Ross's wife had left him recently, and he hadn't even realised for three days. 'The thing is,' the home affairs editor had grumbled, lighting one cigarette from another outside the Plumbers, 'knowing that the person behind Papercut is someone who thinks Ross is a bellend doesn't exactly narrow the field.'

'The Papercut piece is a bugger for Ellis,' Miranda agreed. 'It's just all a bit embarrassing.'

Casey turned back to her newspaper then sat up straight.

'Oh, my God!'

Horns blared as Miranda swerved across a lane.

'Jesus Christ, Casey.' Miranda fought to get the car under control. 'What the hell … '

Casey was reading a small column in the *Argus*. 'Oh, god,' Casey was whispering, under her breath. 'Bloody, bloody hell.'

'What?' Miranda pulled into a petrol station and stamped on the brakes. 'Casey, you can't do that while I'm driving.'

'Look.' Casey brandished the *Argus*.

'"A senior scientist was killed in a cycling crash in north London"', Miranda read aloud. '"Professor Ernest Brennan, 64, died in a collision with a vehicle on Grahame Park Way, Colindale, early on Thursday morning. The vehicle failed to stop. Police are appealing for witnesses."'

'He's dead,' Casey was whispering. 'Professor Brennan … '

Miranda's face was serious. 'He's the man you went to see the morning Ed died?'

'Yes,' whispered Casey. 'And I went to front him up again the other day too.'

'Again? Dash told you to stop working,' said Miranda. 'And he told me not to let you do anything, Casey. It was a real order.'

'Brennan wouldn't tell me anything anyway.' Casey sounded despairing. 'It's too much of a coincidence, Miranda. You must believe me. You do, don't you?'

Miranda watched cars creep round the petrol station car park. The signs were garish, greedy, neon. The motorway dragon roared behind them.

'I'll ask Arthur to call the police about the Brennan incident,' Miranda allowed. 'See if they can shed any light on what happened.'

Arthur was the *Post*'s crime correspondent, and enjoyed popping out for drinks with chummy sergeants. He could ask a casual question without the ripples going far.

'Fine,' said Casey. 'But we also have to go back to Noah Hart. We have to find out what he knows.'

9

Tillie was charged with finding a way to talk to Noah.

'If,' Miranda said, 'and it's still a big if, Casey, someone is monitoring Noah, it's not fair to approach him at the hospital. The same thing goes for his home address. It's got to be discreet.'

A few days later, Tillie reported back.

'Noah goes to the gym most mornings, so you could bump into him there.'

'Tricky,' said Miranda. 'They're always crowded at that time in the morning.'

'Or he sometimes manages to grab a sandwich from the canteen and then goes to sit in St Luke's Gardens. But not always. And I suppose it probably depends on the weather, too.'

'Again,' said Casey, 'too busy, especially at that time of day.'

'What else?' asked Miranda.

Tillie brought it out like a prize. 'I happened to be behind him in the queue for the hospital cafeteria yesterday. We got chatting. He's going hiking this weekend, apparently. On Dartmoor, I think. Staying with his parents in a little village not far from Exeter. He hasn't been down there for months, he said. Looking forward to it.'

'He told you all that?' Casey looked surprised. 'He's usually quite cautious.'

'Noah mentioned he was going hiking and staying with his parents and that he hadn't had any time off for ages,' Tillie conceded. 'Then I tracked down the parents. They live right on the edge of Dartmoor, so it just makes sense that's where he is going hiking.'

'I suppose it might. How did you find them?'

'Fairly easily,' said Tillie. 'I got Noah's full name off the GMC register, then found his birth certificate, which meant I had his parents' full names too. John and Sally Hart. Not the easiest names to track down, right? The parents weren't immediately evident on the publicly available electoral roll or Companies House, but I managed to find a really old photograph of Noah on Facebook – one of his friends' pages, he's quite careful with the privacy settings – and you could just about make out the school crest on their blazers. They attended a school in Moretonhampstead, which isn't far from Exeter, so I guessed that the parents must have been based around there. Then I found out that there used to be a GP called John Hart in Moretonhampstead, and he looks very like Noah Hart, which was encouraging. After that, I found a birdwatching website – twitching, they call it, very popular, you know? – where people post snaps of birds they've spotted. One JHartDevon156 has posted lots of photographs from their garden, and some of the photographs have Dartmoor in the background. From analysing the hill shapes, you can work out that the photos were taken in a very small hamlet just west of Moretonhampstead. There are only four houses in the hamlet, two are holiday cottages. One of the houses is lived in by a woman who runs a business selling homeopathy kits, of all things. So I rang the GP surgery, to check whether I had the right address for old Dr Hart because I wanted to send him his university newsletter. Isn't it funny how people won't give out addresses, but they will confirm—'

'All right,' Miranda cut her off. 'Thank you, Tillie.'

'I'm sure there would have been a more straightforward way,' Tillie carried on, unabashed. 'If I'd had time to go down there and just ask, but you said you needed the information quickly. I could have checked the physical electoral roll down in Devon. Or if I'd been talking to people, I'd have got it straight away. You know how it is when you're actually face to—'

'Yes, thank you, Tillie.'

They all peered at a Google street-view image of the Hart family home. In the screengrab, it was a neat cottage, white-painted, with hollyhocks like pastel fireworks in the front garden. The hamlet was at the end of a long lane.

'You'd definitely be able to tell if Noah was being followed,' said Casey. 'It would be easy.'

'Once you're up on Dartmoor,' Hessa shuddered at the memory of a lengthy Duke of Edinburgh's Award trek, 'you can see for miles.'

'He might be going hiking with a friend.'

'No.' Casey thought about Noah. The sense of sadness, and the greying face. 'I think he'll go alone.'

Casey travelled down to Devon the day before Noah, and spent the afternoon wandering thoughtfully around the local village. She pottered into the little shops, meandered through the churchyard and ambled past the GP surgery.

On the Friday afternoon, Hessa loitered among the waiting crowds at Paddington, and then squeezed on to the train. She sat awkwardly in the aisle – 'I get all the best jobs' – and watched Noah as he stood a few rows away.

'What's Hessa up to?' Ross asked Miranda casually, as they queued for a stale croissant in the canteen.

'Up in Derbyshire,' Miranda yawned. 'A bit of light NHS fraud.'

At Exeter, Noah was met by a pretty woman in her sixties, with rosy pink cheeks, sensible grey-blonde hair and practical shoes. She smiled at her son, hugged him close.

From a patch of moorland far above the house, Casey watched as Sally Hart's car headed towards the little hamlet at a prudent speed, her indicators flashing at the last turn-off although there was no one to see for miles. The car disappeared behind the high green hedges that criss-crossed the valley, and Casey's thoughts drifted to the Marines, training up on Dartmoor's wild beauty. She had to force herself to concentrate again, sitting in the heather until she was sure no one had followed Sally Hart's car.

'Tiny bit paranoid?' Miranda asked flippantly when she called later. Casey was back at the little cottage she had rented for the weekend.

And then she regretted it when she heard a choke in Casey's voice.

'Maybe. But hopefully Noah'll realise that no one could ever know that we've spoken to him out here. And it'll catch him off guard. Plus he'll realise that we're completely serious, that there will never be an escape from us.'

The morning dawned, a sapphire sky with small puffs of cloud to the west. From a respectable distance, Casey watched as Noah set off up a narrow footpath behind the house. Small brown ponies cropped the turf, and the Harts' yellow Labrador bounded happily ahead, burying its nose in rabbit holes. No one else followed.

A few minutes later, Casey walked up the path, matching Noah's pace. The birds were shrilling and there was a smell of honey in the air. The last of the summer had bleached the moorland grass to blond, the same colour as the dog.

Noah strode along, apparently content in this familiar place and luxuriating in the sun after weeks in the hospital. He didn't look back. Casey waited until he had walked a couple of miles, past a stony outcrop. Then she jogged a few hundred yards, and caught up with him easily.

'Noah.'

He turned, his face twisting with fury as he saw her. 'What the hell are you doing here? Leave me alone!'

Noah pushed past her, and began hurrying along the track. Casey kept up with him effortlessly.

'We need to talk, Noah.'

'No, we don't. This is harassment.'

'Please, Noah.'

'Go away!'

'Professor Brennan is dead, Noah.'

He paused, bewildered, turned back to her. 'Who? Who the hell is Professor Brennan?'

'Brennan was a senior scientist at Colindale,' Casey said. 'He was killed not long after I spoke to him about antibiotic resistance. Not long after I met you and Flora Ashcroft, in fact.'

'I'm sorry,' Noah managed, still confused, 'to hear that.'

'And then my boyfriend,' Casey's voice choked, 'died too.'

Noah stopped, turned towards her. 'What? How?'

'They think it was a heart attack. A heart attack that happened a few days after I spoke to you. And all these incidents ... they all look like accidents.'

'They may be accidents, Casey.'

'Do you really believe that?' Casey pulled the copy of the *Standard* out of her rucksack. Noah reacted as if she had pulled out a gun.

'Get away from me.' It was nearly a scream. 'Stay away from me.'

He sprinted towards the house, but Casey stayed on his heels. Noah managed a few hundred yards, his breath getting heavier, and then his foot caught on a heather root and he slammed into the ground. Casey stopped, and stood over him. The doctor was gasping for breath, the eyes of a hunted animal.

'Abigail,' said Casey. 'Your sister, Abigail.'

Noah's face collapsed into tears. 'Stop it,' he said. 'Please.'

'I saw her gravestone,' Casey's face was full of compassion. 'I'm so sorry, Noah.'

10

The day before, Casey had stood in the churchyard for a long hour, staring down at the gilt letters and granite. The flowers were fresh: neat and gentle in a small blue vase.

In ever loving memory of Abigail Hart,
adored daughter, sister and friend

Dead for two years.

'I didn't realise she was so young,' she had said to the churchwarden, who was unlocking the heavy oak door.

'The old doctor's daughter.' The old man had shaken his head. 'A tragedy.'

'I know Noah,' Casey murmured. 'Are there any other brothers and sisters?'

'Anna and Julia. Lovely girls.'

'It's so sad.'

'It was a terrible thing.'

'What happened to Abigail? Noah never said.'

'A car crash, up on the moor. It was truly awful. John and Sally have never been the same since.'

Noah pushed himself upright until he was sitting on the stony path. Casey crouched beside him.

'No one,' she promised, 'will ever know that you've spoken to me.'

Noah stared across hundreds of acres of moorland. It was empty, the grass rippling in the wind. The weather was changing now. To the west, heavier clouds were gathering, a first band of rain rolling in off the Atlantic.

'I don't know,' Noah said stiffly, 'what happened to Abigail.'

'But you have your suspicions?' Casey prompted. 'Doubts about the car accident?'

'Abbie always drove like a madwoman.' Noah's face softened. 'She knew that road well. Too well. We think that she was probably driving too fast, racing back over the moor after an evening with some friends in Tavistock. There was no other car involved in the collision, as far as we know. The police checked for scrapes of paint on the wreckage, stuff like that. I asked them … Asked them specifically if something could have happened up there, but they said there was nothing … There was nothing … '

Noah broke off, stared at the horizon.

'But you weren't sure?'

'It was the middle of the night and it seems that there was no one else around. But it didn't make sense that she'd gone off the road at that precise place. Gone right over the edge.' Noah's voice broke, then went on more strongly, 'The police said she might have gone to sleep, just drifted off … But Abbie would have spent the night in Tavistock if she was tired. She'd done that before. Her friends all said she was fine, happy, wide awake. And she was well under the limit.' He looked at Casey. 'I know it sounds odd, but there are wild ponies up there. If someone had made them bolt into the road at exactly the right minute … Abbie always loved horses. She would have swerved. There were hoof prints near the crash. But of course there would be … There were footprints too. But then there were paramedics, firemen, any number of people up there that night.'

Casey thought of the small brown ponies she had seen that morning, and a ripple of blue lights in the dark. 'Why did you think it could be more, Noah?'

He swallowed, the fear returning in a flood. 'Just before it happened,' he forced the words out, 'someone left a copy of the *Standard* in my locker at work. There were two words underlined on the front page. "Last" and "chance". Last chance. The words weren't even next to each other, you had to look quite carefully. And I only looked carefully because I knew that I hadn't left a copy of the paper in my locker. But they were quite heavily underlined.'

'Do you still have it? The paper?'

'I threw it away.' Noah's mouth twisted with frustration. 'And then a few days later Abigail died, and everyone was – well, you can imagine.'

'What did you do after receiving that message? After being told it was your last chance?'

'I ... ' he stalled.

'You didn't tell anyone about the message at the time?' Casey doubled back. 'After the crash?'

'People would have thought I was mad. I've got two other sisters,' he cried. 'And my parents. If anything had happened to Julia or Anna ... My parents ... I didn't know what to do ... '

'What had happened?' Casey asked gently. 'After you got the warning in the *Standard*.'

Noah sat silently on the ground, looking at his walking boots.

'You promise no one will ever know I spoke to you?'

'Yes,' swore Casey.

'Never?'

'Never.'

Noah breathed out slowly, and began to speak.

'About three years ago, I went to work for a private company in the States. On a sort of secondment. I wanted time away from the NHS,' Noah spoke haltingly. 'Needed it, I suppose. My bosses approved anyway – they thought it might be useful.'

'What were you doing in America?'

'I was working for a company called Pergamex. A pharmaceutical company based in San Francisco.'

'I haven't heard of it.'

'No, you wouldn't have. It was small, and very secretive. I mean, a lot of pharma companies are secretive anyway, because some of the stuff is market sensitive, or there are issues with corporate espionage. But even by those standards, Pergamex was paranoid.'

'What were you working on?'

Noah hesitated. He looked up at Casey again. 'You promise?'

'I promise.'

'We were working on an antibiotic. A brand new one.'

A lark shrilled far overhead, and Noah flinched.

'I've been told that new antibiotics are very unusual,' said Casey.

'Exactly. And the Pergamex one – Corax, we called it – was really good. It was a whole new class of antibiotics, far better than anything we had seen before.'

'It sounds great.'

His face was alive. 'It was.'

'So what happened?'

Noah's smile faded. 'One evening, Pergamex just shut down operations. From one day to the next, we were locked out of the building, all our data destroyed, our jobs over. Everyone who had worked there had signed non-disclosure agreements, of course. Everything just disappeared.'

'Do you know why they shut it down?'

'No.' Noah stared at the larks, dancing high up in the air. 'No one would say anything about it at all.'

'Who wouldn't say anything about it?'

'Well, there was Garrick, who set up the company. He's an entrepreneur.'

'What's he like?'

'He grew up in the UK, but spends a lot of time in the US. He's charismatic, I suppose. Charming. A bit of a player. He's always got various girls on the go. He'd worked with lots of startups before, but Pergamex was his unicorn, he'd say. The one that would make the real billions. He'd already got a nice place in Pacific Heights, and he would go and stay in an amazing house up in Lake Tahoe too. He had money even before Pergamex.'

'Who else would have known about Corax?'

'It wasn't a very big team working on it. Zac was the doctor in charge of the technical side. He was English too, actually. But he was brilliant. Really brilliant.'

'And neither of them would say anything to you after it shut down? Neither Zac or Garrick?'

'No. I was angry about it. Very angry, I suppose. Corax could have been an incredible drug. It could have cured loads of different diseases, according to the early results. And among a lot of other things, it could have helped CF patients with abscessus.'

Flora Ashcroft.

'So what did you do?'

'I was only very junior on the project,' said Noah. 'They kept everything pretty siloed too, so I was only carrying out tests on bacterial samples. I would have broken my NDA, but I didn't know enough. I tried though. I went to Garrick and told him he had a moral duty to keep going with Corax.'

'What did he say?'

'He just ignored me. Walked straight past me in the street.'

'And Zac?'

'Zac?' Noah shrugged. 'After Pergamex shut down, Zac just took off.' He stared across the moor. 'I never saw Zac again.'

'Did you try and find him?'

'Yes, of course I did. I tried to find out where he was working, but he had just disappeared. He seemed to have stopped being a doctor, or doing research. And he'd been the very best.'

'What's he like?'

'Zac's an arrogant git,' Noah shrugged. 'Rude, too, at times. But he could be a laugh, in the right mood, and he was good at a lot of things. He plays the piano brilliantly, knew a lot about art. He was teaching himself Italian when we were in San Francisco. Sporty too. Annoying, quite frankly.'

It was starting to spit with rain, half the sky still blue, the other black clouds.

'So why do you think,' Casey asked, 'that you got that message in the *Standard*?'

'I'd come home to England by then,' said Noah. 'I went back to working at the Royal Brompton. But I was still furious, you know? I'd put a lot of work into Corax, and it was important. I was spending day after day in that wretched hospital watching people die when this drug might have helped them. And then one night, very late, I was at home, falling asleep in front of a programme about kiteboarding ... '

'Kiteboarding?'

Noah waved defeatedly at his hiking boots. 'I used to love it, but when do I get the time these days ... '

'What did you see on the programme?'

'I saw Zac. Right there on the beach. He wasn't featured or anything, but he was there, in the background. Hanging out. I'm not even sure if he knew he was being filmed.'

'Where was the programme based?'

Noah's face twisted into a rueful grin. 'Zac always fell on his feet. Mauritius. That bloody programme was filmed in Mauritius.'

Noah ducked as two hikers appeared on the horizon. The rain was pouring down now. Casey sat down beside him, pulling up her hood and fiddled with her shoe as she waited for them to pass. They were a couple, in their forties. Matching Berghaus fleeces and identical Karrimor rucksacks. Completely unthreatening, but Noah only breathed when they were past and Casey saw how distressed he had been, for so long.

'It's OK,' said Casey. 'It's all right, Noah.'

'But you don't know that,' he said.

In silent agreement, they began walking back towards his parents' house.

'What did you do after you'd seen that programme?'

'I was even more angry,' said Noah. 'There was Zac, living the life of Riley in Mauritius. And I'd heard that Garrick had moved into an even bigger place in the Pacific Heights, and meanwhile Corax had disappeared into the ether. I emailed Garrick, telling him I was going to go to one of the other pharmaceutical companies with what I knew. I didn't know much, but I might have been able to put them on the right path. It would have given them a start at least. And the very next day, that copy of the *Standard* was in my locker.'

'Then what?'

'I ignored it. I decided to go to Adsero. That's the company that makes zentetra.'

'The drug Flora's on?'

'Yes, and they're developing their new drug, saepio, too. That makes them one of the very few pharma majors still working in antibiotics. They've got big headquarters just outside Milton Keynes, so I got on the train and went up there.'

'And?'

'I was waiting in the queue for a taxi outside that huge station. And just as I was getting to the top of the queue, the man next to me said, very quietly, "I wouldn't if I were you." I wasn't sure what I'd heard. I turned towards him, and he gave me this polite look, and said again: "I wouldn't go to Adsero."' Noah shook his head at the memory. 'He looked friendly, you know. Affable. And then he smiled, and his whole face changed. His eyes went dead, and he just looked like pure evil. I panicked. It's pathetic, I know, but I ran to the platform. Got on a train and went back to London.'

'And two nights later … '

Noah's face crumpled again. 'Two nights later, Abbie died. It was my last chance, and I think just by getting on that train, I blew it.'

Casey gave him a moment. 'Why do you think they didn't just kill you?'

'In my email to Garrick,' Noah's eyes were distant, 'I threatened him. I said I'd lodged letters to be sent in the event of something happening to me. You know the sort of thing. Melodramatic, I suppose. But there was something about the Pergamex set-up. I don't know if that was what … Even before anything happened, I was scared.'

'This man you saw in the taxi queue in Milton Keynes. What did he look like?'

'Short dark hair,' said Noah. 'Caucasian. A bit taller than me. Brown eyes. They didn't really seem to reflect the light, if you see what I mean? Flat. I can't really describe them.'

'Hollow eyes?'

'Yes,' he said. 'Hollow.'

It might be the man who chased her on Hampstead Heath, thought Casey. But her own sighting had been so fleeting, as to be almost useless.

They walked along the footpath in silence.

'What was so special about Corax?' asked Casey eventually.

'It was a completely new class of antibiotics,' said Noah, a flicker of enthusiasm returning. 'That's what made it so extraordinary. Different classes of antibiotics destroy bacteria in different ways. The beta-lactams – like penicillin – block the bacteria's cell-wall biosynthesis, for example. The tetracyclines block the synthesis of protein, which means the bacteria can't grow. Bacteria have started to find a way around all those blocks, so they can carry on reproducing. But because Corax was a completely new class, the bacteria had no way of resisting it.'

'How did Pergamex find it?'

'I'm not sure,' admitted Noah. 'Finding new antibiotics is bizarre. You'd think it was all done in a laboratory, but you're basically looking for a quirk in nature. Something that has evolved a way of fighting bacteria for a specific reason. You always hear that they discovered penicillin in soil, for example. But what Fleming actually found was a fungus – Penicillium chrysogenum – that produces penicillin, probably to compete with bacteria for food sources originally. Today, scientists look all over the world for potential antibiotics. They've looked at Komodo dragons in Indonesia, and found a possible antibiotic there. They even looked at leaf cutting ants in the Amazon, for heaven's sake.

'They found that some ants keep a specific fungus in their nests, and bring leaves back to feed the fungus. Then the ants eat the fungus they've grown. They do that because the fungus is better at digesting the tough leaves than the ants. So they're working together. But in order to defend their nests – and their fungus – from other microbes, the ants produce incredibly powerful antibiotics. So it's a weird little miracle, right there in an ant's nest in the middle of the Amazon. Millions of years of evolution to produce one little quirk.'

Casey was struggling to keep up.

'So Corax could have come from anywhere?'

'I suppose so. But the low-hanging fruit in antibiotic discovery is very definitely gone. They're looking in volcanoes and glaciers, now. Or the very bottom of the ocean.'

'And you didn't know enough to just produce Corax by yourself.'

'No,' he said regretfully. 'Nowhere near.'

They said goodbye just above his parents' house, shaking hands with an odd formality in the middle of the Dartmoor wilderness.

'I'll call you if I can think of anything else,' said Noah earnestly.

'Thank you.'

'Good luck in finding Zac,' said Noah. 'I really tried. You may have other … techniques.'

The sun had come out again, the light gold heavy on the moor. Noah looked around the empty, rolling hills, and almost laughed. Then, for a second, they stared at each other.

You know, thought Casey. You know what it is to lose someone.

She thought about the doctor she had first met, in the beige of that Royal Brompton ward. She had thought he was drowning in the hospital sadness, but it was more. It was always more.

'Thank you, Noah. I will do my best.'

A brief nod. She watched him trudge down the hill, followed closely by the Labrador, before she turned and hurried towards her car.

11

'Mauritius?' Miranda laughed. 'I might have guessed.'

For years, as the nights lengthened into autumn, Miranda and Casey had brainstormed a reason to travel to the Caribbean. A dodgy hedge fund in the Cayman Islands. A doping scandal in Jamaica. Once they had headed for Australia to investigate a corrupt gold-mine owner. Dash always rolled his eyes. *This had better be worth it.*

'I know,' Casey admitted. 'And Zac might only have been in Mauritius for a week's holiday.'

'Nice place for a holiday, all the same.'

They both looked at a still from the television programme. Tanned dark brown, Zac had dark hair and scruffy stubble. He was leaning back on his elbows, bare chested, his eyes closed under the blazing sun. His kiteboarding kit was beside him, and he was laughing at someone to his left.

'That's Le Morne, at the southern end of Mauritius.' Casey pointed to a hunk of rock in the background, covered in lush greenery.

'Gorgeous. And Noah Hart didn't mention that Zac was extremely easy on the eye?' Miranda's eyes gleamed.

'No,' said Casey. 'I don't think Noah really notices that sort of thing.'

'But Noah is absolutely sure it is him?'

'He says he is,' said Casey. 'Although who knows?'

They were sitting in Miranda's kitchen. In the pretty house in Queen's Park that Miranda's husband had chosen. Tom, picking out curtains and wallpaper and the right sort of schools. A family home with no family, and it took them years to realise there never would be. Tom left one day, and whenever she thought about it, Casey was surprised that Miranda was still here.

'And you haven't been able to track Zac down anywhere else?' asked Miranda.

'Zac Napier,' said Casey. 'Zachary Napier. No. I've done every search I can think of. He's disappeared off the face of the earth, as far as I can tell.'

'Well, maybe he has disappeared off the earth. There's a lot of Indian Ocean around Mauritius, and it is rather deep.'

'Maybe.'

'Family?'

'No,' said Casey. 'His mother brought him up alone, no sign of a father. She died a few years ago, after a long illness. There are no siblings, no cousins, nothing that I could track.'

'Friends?'

'No one has heard from him in years.'

'So he can just take off for Mauritius?'

'Apparently.'

'And you think Pergamex bought him off?'

'Presumably,' said Casey. 'Hopefully, from our point of view. There's no money in Zac's background, and he worked for the NHS before he went off to Pergamex. But Mauritius is an expensive place to live, if you factor in a nice house, a bit of kiteboarding.'

'So you think Pergamex threatened some, bribed others, and if that didn't work ... '

'Something like that. Maybe Zac didn't look like he would threaten anyone, so they gave him a lump sum and told him to bugger off and park himself in paradise.'

'Why not just kill him?'

'I don't know,' Casey said wearily. 'Maybe they thought he might be useful at some point. Noah did say that he was very bright.'

'And why would they attack Ed?' Miranda's voice was cautious.

'I don't know that either,' Casey muttered. 'Maybe they meant to leave that copy of the *Standard* in the flat, but Ed just happened to be there. It was a mistake or bad luck. Or maybe they targeted him rather than me because killing off an actual *Post* journalist would be like kicking a termite nest.'

'Or they might have guessed,' Miranda said brutally, 'that you were known to be a bit of a loose cannon at the moment, and attacking him would push you over the edge.'

'And they had already killed him when the message from me bleeped in saying I had just been to Colindale. So they decided I was too much of a risk too …'

'Maybe.'

'And now,' Casey felt a flood of self-pity, 'there's no one left for them to threaten.'

'So what do you want to do?'

Casey looked around the kitchen. Tom's expensive saucepans were gone, she noticed. The lawn, overgrown. There was a picture missing from the wall, a patch of paint unfaded.

'Will Dash send me to Mauritius?'

'I don't know. I'll ask.'

'I have to go, Miranda. I have to find out what happened.'

12

Casey dipped her head beneath the surface, feeling her hair flow along her back. Down and down she dived, all the way to the rippling sand far below. For a few seconds, she looked up through the blue shimmer to the splinters of sunlight at the surface. Gasping, lungs burning, she burst back into the air, and swam slowly along the beach. The sea was cobalt, the sky azure. Palm trees fringed the ribbon of golden sand, and in the distance she could hear the ocean snarling against the reef. Inside the reef, the water was smooth, silky, tamed.

She hadn't found Zac.

She had hung out at Le Morne beach for days, watching the kites dance in the sky. She had smiled, chatted, flirted, and never caught a single glimpse of that dark hair, that scruff of stubble.

On the third day, she had tracked down one of the boys featured in the television programme. Parker, 22, with a big, easy smile.

You were on TV? That's so cool. Show me. Wow, look at those moves! Who's he? Pause it! He's so hot.

But Parker looked vacant, genuinely unsure. *I don't know him. Nah. Do you want another drink?*

But you're always round here? You must know that guy.

Nope. Sorry.

And her heart sank. In the evenings, she drove around the island, through the endless fields of rustling sugar cane. The names were an invocation. Flic En Flac. Poudre d'Or. Cap Malheureux. And everywhere there were honeymoon couples, laughing families, a faded sort of grandeur.

You would have loved it.

She dropped the name into conversation again and again. *Zac Napier said I'd enjoy it here, and he was right … You look so like my buddy, Zac Napier … Zac Napier recommended the snorkel trip?*

Not a flicker.

Scraping the barrel, she visited a couple of Italian restaurants, in case he had bothered to practise his Italian. *Zac Napier ha detto che la pizza qui è buona come quella di napoli.*

Nothing.

At night, instead of sleeping, she watched the programme repeatedly, obsessively. Zac had appeared a couple more times, always in the background, laughing, his kite a vivid scarlet.

'If he's here,' she grumbled on the phone to Miranda, 'he's using a different name.'

'Makes sense, I guess.'

'Shall I come home?'

'Dash says to stay out there.'

Keeping her out of the way, Casey translated sulkily. Even if her hotel room was costing a small fortune, it was easier having her several thousand miles away than weeping in the newsroom.

'Zac could be anywhere by now,' Casey moaned. 'He could have been here for a fortnight, just passing through.'

'But Mauritius is the only clue you have.'

'I'll find him,' Casey promised.

'If he's still there.'

Casey dived beneath the surface again. The problem was that she wanted to catch Zac unawares. If she wandered around the island showing people a screengrab of the laughing boy on a beach, it was too easy for people to alert, alarm, forewarn him. You could never guess at loyalties, like steel hawsers under the sand. That's if he was here at all. She kicked her legs sullenly.

A rim of seaweed lined this stretch of beach, like a dirty bath. Fragments of plastic – orange, green and blue – were tangled among the black strands. A gardener, bent double, was piling it all into a wheelbarrow.

In the evening, Casey made her way back to Le Morne, heading to a beach bar. She threw herself into a chair, and ordered a cocktail, and then another one. The sun was setting red, another wasted day burning to a cigarette stub.

On the edge of the lagoon, two small boys were skimming stones over the still water in a blur of speed. Hop, hop, splash and gone, hop, hop, splash and gone.

The sun slipped below the horizon.

This would be perfect if you were …

A physical pain.

Casey's phone buzzed. It was a message from Flora Ashcroft, and Casey managed a small smile.

I'm doing work experience at the Post next week! Thank you so much for putting me in touch with Ross Warman!

I'm so glad, Casey messaged. *Although you may revise your opinion once you've met him. I hope you enjoy it.*

She looked towards the kiteboarders. A few of them were still twirling in the safety of the lagoon as the sky darkened to indigo. But there was no red kite, no hope. Nothing. A young couple came into the bar, sat down, entwined like ivy. The candlelight flickered.

Hop, hop, splash and gone.

Another cocktail.

Why didn't we come here when …

Hop, hop, splash and gone.

All that time, we could have …

The night was closing in now. Maybe she would hop, hop, splash, and disappear beneath the surface forever. A blur of speed, and gone for good.

Beyond the lagoon, a few yachts bobbed, tied up to buoys. Their lights were brightening in the dark, and a dinghy puttered towards the shore, ready for dinner.

Suddenly, Casey was on her feet, throwing a few rupees down on the table. She ran for her car, paused. Gesticulated for a taxi and raced back to the hotel.

In her room, she restarted the television programme for the hundredth time, and there they were: the long tracking shots over the lagoon, so familiar now.

The programme makers must have sent up drones to film the kite-boarders, Casey thought. Zooming out to showcase the glory of the beaches, zooming in as a boarder somersaulted over a wave.

Frame by frame, Casey noted down the names of the yachts tied up beyond the reef. *Endless Summer. Andiamo. Serenity. Renaissance. Liquid Asset.*

Then she started researching. *Endless Summer* was being sailed around the world by a retired couple from Alderney. A small piece in a sailing magazine noted that they had been rescued by a trawler two-thirds of the way across the Indian Ocean after *Endless Summer* capsized. The yacht had been left to her own devices, currently believed to be floating somewhere off Sri Lanka.

Hope all OK? Casey was interrupted by a text from Hessa, kindly checking in.

I'm fine, thanks. Could you see if you can find out who owns this yacht? A snap of *Serenity*.

Sure.

Casey put her head down again. According to Instagram, *Liquid Asset* belonged to a Spanish banker who had done a couple of years for conspiracy to defraud. There were five children in the photos, and a third wife who looked as if she knew the fourth was in the wings.

Not *Liquid Asset*.

Andiamo was owned by a holiday company, and chartered expensively by the week. Casey crossed her fingers. Not *Andiamo*, please. Five oceans to search.

Her phone buzzed. *Serenity belongs to a member of the Alexakis family. Do you want to know more?*

Greek shipping billionheirs. *No, that's fine*, Casey tapped back.

Do you think there might be a link to the Alexakis family? It was Miranda. The investigations team must be working very late on something. Casey imagined them all sitting in the office, excited and gossiping, a team.

No, Casey messaged back to Miranda. *But I realised that if no one on the beach at Le Morne knew Zac, it might be because he had sailed down to the peninsular for the day? So that might mean that one of the boats tied up in the background could belong to him. And he came ashore only to kiteboard.*

That's possible, I suppose.

Casey looked at the footage again. In one shot, *Renaissance* was dropping her anchor, red sails lowering as she turned into the wind. She was one of the smaller Spirit yachts, with sleek golden wood and exquisite lines. A tiny figure crouched in the cockpit, staring up at the mast.

Renaissance, with her brave scarlet sails.

Renaissance.

13

Casey stood on a pier and looked out across the water. She was close to the Grand Baie Yacht Club, opposite the Pointe aux Cannoniers. Here, the ocean had taken a nip out of the island, creating a safe harbour for dozens of gleaming white yachts. Tied up to their buoys, the boats bobbed merrily in the breeze.

And there she was: *Renaissance*.

Earlier, she had messaged Noah Hart.

Did Zac ever use the phrase Renaissance Man?

Yes! How did you know?!

The doctor who played the piano, kitesurfed, knew about art and taught himself Italian …

Another text, a moment later: *As I said, he could be a bit arrogant.*

Casey had grinned, and peered closely at the smaller writing under the yacht's name. *Grand Baie*, in italics. As dawn broke, she headed for the sprawling seaside village to the north of the island.

Smiling sweetly, she managed to book a table at the yacht club for an early lunch, dragging out her meal with the help of a novel.

No sign of Zac Napier.

She made conversation with each of the smiling waiters. *Zac Napier mentioned he might go out for a sail today … I think Zac Napier is a member here? Has Zac Napier been in today?*

Until she was tired of the name, bored with the game.

The afternoon crawled by, the yachts drifting in lazy arcs as the tide ebbed.

A man sat down at the table next to her. Loud Yorkshire accent, sunburned, too many lunches. Casey smiled at him, and soon they were chatting. Within five minutes, the man had explained he was in Mauritius for tax reasons – 'CGT, not income tax' – and that his wife was an alcoholic so he'd left her in the UK. 'I'm with Elene now. She's from the Seychelles.' Pause. 'She's fucking gorgeous. Off somewhere else at the moment, though. Shopping, I think.'

'Sorry about your wife.'

'She was a fucking nightmare. I'm Martin,' he added, holding out a sweaty hand.

Casey smiled and pondered how long it would take her to become an alcoholic married to Martin.

Not long, probably.

They chatted, though, Casey ordering a coffee. Martin was delighted to talk. Bored, Casey diagnosed. Five years abroad to avoid capital gains tax: banished to paradise.

After a few minutes, she pointed at *Serenity*, bobbing nearby.

'That's gorgeous. Someone mentioned it belonged to Yiannis Alexakis?'

'Yeah, I know old Yiannis quite well. He's a mate.'

'How about that one?'

'Oh, that one belongs to Biggins.'

Not nicknames. Please.

'You know everyone!' – and he preened. 'How about that one?' She pointed to the *Renaissance*.

He peered at the yacht, and she was barely able to breathe.

'Nah,' he said. 'Don't know that one … ' Her fingers dug into her palms. 'Oh, no, wait a minute. I do. That's Daniel Richmond's.'

'Daniel Richmond?'

'Yeah.' Martin was looking round for a waiter, gesturing for another drink.

'What does he do?'

'This and that,' he grinned. 'Quite a few blondes. Spends a lot of time at the Robery.'

'By the way, have you ever come across someone called Zac Napier? I think he hangs out round here quite a lot.'

Martin gulped his drink, wiped his mouth. 'Zac Napier? Can't say that I have.'

14

The Robery was a beautiful old colonial house, built by some long-forgotten slave owner. It sat at the top of a small hill, a few hundred yards back from the beach.

'It was constructed in the nineteenth century,' recited a waitress. 'The main house of a vast sugar plantation.'

The waitress was Creole, probably descended from the thousands of slaves brought to Mauritius. Here, too, the injustices were embedded: an exquisite island with a vicious history. This elegant edifice balanced on foundations of unbearable violence.

The waitress wound up her speech with an efficient smile, and waved Casey to her table.

A wide verandah wrapped around the building, wooden shutters protecting the old rooms. A few tables and chairs were arranged on the gallery, and others dotted the lawn beneath big cream umbrellas. Bougainvillea and frangipani edged the grass, the jungle looming beyond.

Casey sat in the shade of the verandah. She placed her small handbag on the chair next to hers, and ordered fried squid. Wide ceiling fans turned idly as she got her novel out again, but her eyes kept straying across the lawn, to the path that led up to the house.

And as the light faded to gold, there he was. Tall and dark, in a blue linen shirt and shorts. Sunglasses on his head, and a restless pace. A small dog trotted behind him. Part terrier, Casey guessed. A mongrel's confidence. She breathed out the surge of relief slowly.

'Mr Richmond.' The waitress gave this man a genuine smile, 'Your friends are waiting for you.'

That evening, Casey sent a series of photographs to Noah. The small bag had contained a neat little camera, and the images of Daniel Richmond were sharp.

That's him! The encrypted message came back within seconds. *Where on earth did you find him?*

Do you know any of the people he is sitting with?

A wait. *No. Looks like a nice place though. A bit of a step up from the Royal Brompton canteen.*

Thanks, Noah.

Later, she messaged Miranda. She always did on the rare occasions she investigated alone. To show where her mind was wandering. In case she got lost, or was lost. Hansel and Gretel breadcrumbs, a sort of superstition.

This is where I was.

And this is what I thought.

Because I do want to be found.

I do.

Or I want the story to be found, almost the same thing.

In black, though she might have worn white.

I do.

She was woken by a knock on her hotel room door the next morning.

'That was quick,' Casey yawned.

'I was in Dubai anyway.'

'That time of year.'

'Exactly.'

Casey's balcony overlooked the beach, the ocean growling in the distance. Miranda threw herself into a seat, and looked at Casey.

'So what's the plan?'

'He's a doctor,' said Casey. 'And doctors like to save people.'

'You're hungover.'

'A bit. Dash didn't think I would find anything out here, did he?'

'He did not. You OK?'

'Zac's taking the *Renaissance* out today.'

That had been a bit of luck. She had watched Zac's group getting ready to leave the Robery, and walked out ahead of them. Then she had hovered unobtrusively as he walked past, laughing on his mobile phone. A pretty blonde had her arm around his waist, possessively. As he was getting in his jeep, Zac's friends called out an invitation for the next day, and he shouted back: 'Sorry, can't make it. Sailing.'

'I'm annoyed I can't come out with you,' the blonde had grumbled. She wore a short pink dress, diamonds at her neck and ears. Her sleek hair and high heels looked out of place in the jeep.

'You'd be bored.'

'So he's going alone?' asked Miranda.

'I think so. Or with a different blonde.'

'So … '

'Yes.'

15

The sea glittered, a million broken mirrors. Casey tipped her head back, enjoying the sun. Miranda applied suncream.

'Do you really think this is a good idea, Casey?'

'It's worth a shot.'

The little Wayfarer bobbed serenely. Just under sixteen feet long, the wooden sailboat was painted a dark green, with crisp white sails. *Pink Gin* was written neatly on her bow.

Miranda had convinced a cheerful hotel worker to rent them the boat for the day.

'I've sailed a lot over the years,' she had announced airily.

'Have you?' asked Casey, under her breath.

'Well, a few years ago now. I'm sure it's like riding a bike.'

Miranda had grown up with ponies and skiing and a mother who cried every evening. Yachts too, apparently.

'Stay inside the reef,' said the man firmly. 'In fact, you must keep away from the reef altogether. It can be very dangerous.'

But Miranda had managed the little boat efficiently. Now *Pink Gin* floated quietly, just inside the reef. On the other side of the black rocks, the waves boomed in percussive jolts of foam and spatter. Without the protection of the reef, the typhoons of the Indian Ocean would long ago have blasted away all the pretty beaches, and all the expensive houses. There were gaps in the reef here and there, however, where boats could make their way out to the open sea.

As soon as the little boat was bobbing close to one of the gaps, Casey and Miranda lolled back in *Pink Gin*'s awkward seats. Miranda adjusted her bikini, smiling up at the sun. Casey kept an eye on the yachts tied up inside the safety of the reef.

'Look,' she whispered.

A couple of hundred yards away, a dinghy was darting towards the *Renaissance*. A small dog had its paws up on the prow of the little inflatable.

'Zac is indeed alone,' Miranda grinned.

They watched discreetly as Zac prepared the *Renaissance* for a sail, fiddling with the ropes, checking the winches. Finally, he stepped forward, preparing to lift the anchor.

'Now,' murmured Casey.

It took only seconds to raise *Pink Gin*'s sails, and Miranda guided the little sailboat towards the gap in the reef.

The current gripped the boat immediately. The waves were far more powerful than Casey had realised, jolting the boat hard. It was as if the ocean had reached through the reef, and was playing with the little yacht. All at once, *Pink Gin* felt like a toy, bobbing at the whim of a giant.

'Go on,' said Casey.

'I'm not sure … ' Miranda was hesitating, hand on the tiller.

'Come on.' Out of the corner of her eye, Casey could see the *Renaissance* motoring towards the gap in the reef, ready for a day on the ocean. Zac was untying ropes with one hand, steering with the other, his eyes at the top of the mast.

'It's too dangerous.'

'Hurry.'

'No, Casey … Don't … '

And Casey let herself tumble overboard.

It was like falling into an explosion. The ocean seized her like a doll, the crests high above her head. The sea was alive: pulling, pushing, wrenching, jerking. Can't see, can't breathe. The waves came from every angle, all sense of direction lost. A wave swamped her, pushing her down and down. She battled to the surface for one gasp before the next wave smashed in, breaking over her head.

Casey struggled up again – a panicked animal in the wrong element – and another wave slammed into her. No heave of air this time, her lungs screaming. A battle up, a last desperate gulp of air, a churning shock, and as the wave swallowed her down, she felt the rip of a rock against her leg.

Deeper now, and she fought wildly, which way up? Everything was a swirl of water and foam and black. The world fragmented.

Another crash, crunching into the reef again. Her shoulder was gouged, and there was a searing pain as she was tossed upside down underwater.

Over time, the lungs may stop working properly.

Somehow she was at the surface, just for a second. Miranda shouting: 'Casey!'

Down again, down again, nothing but noise and saltwater. Water burning her eyes, her nose, her mouth.

Where are you?

I'll be there in a minute.

Were those even your words?

For a second, she caught a glimpse of a blue sun, through the scream of the waves. She couldn't fight her way up, not again. Couldn't be battered by the sea rage, not again.

Cat's Cradle or Kissing Gate? I love you.

It was far easier to stay down here, drifting, so gently.

Into a sort of peace.

My love. Beloved.

This must be drowning.

You don't have to choose.

The mermaid's song, you will be safe here.

You do have to choose.

And her legs kicked, just once.

An arm grabbed her shoulder.

'Come on!' The voice shocked her.

She felt a pull, a jerk, rough enough to hurt. Someone was in the sea beside her, a lifebuoy jerking orange in the waves. A man dragged her through the water. Casey struggled, and felt her arms lock mechanically around the lifebuoy. A white shape loomed above, and the demons of the sea fell away, defeated.

It was the *Renaissance*, bobbing obediently in the slack water just inside the reef.

'Here.' A ladder had been unfolded from the stern of the yacht, and the man boosted her up it unceremoniously.

Casey collapsed on the deck, choking and coughing, bleeding, utterly exhausted.

'You OK?' Zac clambered up the ladder with the ease of practice.

'I'm fine.'

'That was stupid.'

'I know.'

Casey rolled on to her back, looking up the mast. *Renaissance's* sails were scarlet against a silken blue sky.

'You saved my life.' Casey turned her head towards him.

A smile glimmered. 'I know.'

'Thank you.'

'A pleasure, Casey.'

'How do you know my name?'

'Your friend shouted it.' He nodded to his left.

There was Miranda, slightly shamefaced, with *Pink Gin* bucking like a naughty pony beside the racehorse elegance of the *Renaissance*. Casey waved weakly, her thoughts pulling together. She sat up, determined to smile.

The small dog regarded her suspiciously.

'Thank you—' she began.

'Is your shoulder all right?' he said. 'You must have really banged it on a rock. I could—'

'I'm fine,' she managed. 'You must let me buy you dinner. To say thank you.'

He grinned, distracted from her shoulder. 'Must I?'

Casey thought about the blonde in the jeep, sleek in her diamonds and met his eye firmly. 'Tonight?'

His mind was turning to the sea. 'Sure, if you're up to it. The Robery at 7?'

Miranda brought *Pink Gin* alongside, and Casey climbed carefully across, still shaking.

They watched as he brought *Renaissance* around, and then the yacht was away, flying over the sea. As Casey watched, Zac glanced back, with a fleeting salute.

'Well.' Miranda reached for the suncream again. 'That's certainly one way of doing it.'

16

She was a blank canvas with nothing to hide.

It worked best when they projected their thoughts on her, as if she were a screen just waiting for colour.

Blank, empty, hollow: bare.

Eyes, flecked with grey and green, blue and gold.

No.

She would keep him waiting, quite deliberately.

She was meticulous with her make-up. Pink blusher: here. Grey eyeshadow: there. Colouring in, staying between the lines. Smile, and smile, and ...

She would choose her clothes with care.

Cinderella's rags, a child in a dress-up box, slice your foot for the slipper.

She stood in her hotel robe, staring thoughtfully at her reflection. Skin bronzed from the sun, a healthy glow. It seemed unlikely, implausible, impossible.

The pain throbbed down her legs, her arms. A cut on her shoulder stung.

She reached forward, and touched the cool constancy of the mirror. In the other world, a pretty girl smiled.

Her face seemed to fragment, just for a second, and it was a room she didn't recognise, a face that wasn't hers.

Where am I? Oh, yes. Who am I?

She concentrated on the embroidery adorning the hotel robe. A flower twisting over her heart, so pretty, and then she shook her head, forcing the thoughts away.

She stared at the mirror again: back in the real world. Dried her hair, twisting it into a complicated plait. Steadier now, she painted on her eyeliner with a flick, and brushed on a curl of mascara.

Where am I? Oh, yes. Who am I?

A silence.

She clasped her hands as if to pray, crushing her fingers together until they hurt. Then she looked away from the mirror, picking through her lipsticks. A deep red curve for her mouth: yes.

This side of the mirror, or that. You can't be both, can you?

Can you?

Where am I? Oh, yes. Who am I?

I don't know.

Stop it.

Casey crossed the room with a determined step and pulled open the cupboard. Cotton florals? No. Red lacy flounces? No. She tried on a peacock blue playsuit, wincing as she pulled it over her head, and peered in the mirror again. Yes.

She stepped back. A huge bruise on her leg. No.

She put on a floaty yellow dress, silk with long sleeves to conceal all the scratches.

It would do.

It would have to do.

I wore this dress when we went to that funfair. Candyfloss and a thump of music and all the girls squealing in dodgems. The big wheel, higher and higher, and when it stopped at the top, you kissed me, and the yellow silk caught the breeze.

No.

A spray of scent. A bright smile in the mirror, clipped on like a rosette and not quite right. A shot of vodka from the minibar, and it tasted like a mistake.

A knock at the door.

'Are you all right?' Miranda's eyes were hard on hers.

'I'm fine.' A stammer. Then louder: too loud. 'I'm perfectly all right, Miranda.'

And the next time she looked around, she was in a taxi to the Robery, the warm summer night speeding past in a blur.

It was twilight when she arrived, candles burning in the hurricane lamps. Outside the Robery, she was pleased to see a large party arrive just before her, and head in just ahead. It gave her a few seconds to rally.

She could see Zac at a table beneath the verandah, but loitered behind the group, forcing herself to smile.

Usually, it was like pulling on a dress. Yesterday, I was cotton florals. Today, I am red flounces. Tomorrow, I am … She was an actress, inventing her own lines. Because isn't that what everyone does?

But tonight, she felt unmoored, adrift. There was no surge of adrenalin, no secret excitement, and as she waited behind the group, there was a flicker in the corner of her eye so that she almost flinched away.

'Are you enjoying your holiday?' The maître d' was jovial, and she blinked at him, and almost told him the truth.

'It's lovely, thank you' – and there was a hesitation in her voice.

The maître d' showed her across, and Zac half-stood. 'Good evening, Casey' – and he grinned.

At first, it was easier. As she sat down, she watched his eyes narrow appreciatively, and she smiled through her eyelashes while the waiter draped a linen napkin over her lap.

There was the babble of *bread water wine? The swordfish is a miracle*, so she could look round the restaurant and breathe.

But then the waiter was gone, and she was lost again.

Where am I? Oh, yes. Who am I? I don't know.

For a moment, it was as if her mind was caving in.

Green gold eyes, staring at nothing.

'It's gorgeous here, isn't it? Such a treat. The receptionist at my hotel said I *must* try the swordfish … ' Usually, her words were fluent: an actress, smiling, cued. But this was a splurge of words, rattling too fast. Then just as quickly, her mind went blank, the silence stretching out. The clean, crisp linen was incongruous, the tinkling music unbearable.

Zac smiled smoothly. 'So—'

'I realised that I never asked you your name this morning.' She interrupted him: that had been a mistake, too.

'Daniel Richmond.' There was no hesitation. 'Dan.'

'Thank you for earlier, Dan.' Too fast, again. 'I don't know what to ….' But he gestured it away. 'It'll make an excellent story, one day.'

She watched his mouth move and knew that she should smile. The words appeared slowly, floating to the surface of a dark pool, one by one.

'Are you on holiday in Mauritius?' she managed.

'I live here.' His voice was English, accentless.

Again, the words were there, scooped out of the blackness. 'I can't believe people actually live here! I'm so jealous. It's heavenly.'

'It is.'

'And what do you do?' Casey asked.

He smiled. 'This and that.' Martin's voice echoed in her head. *Quite a few blondes.* Then he softened, added a few words, 'I have a few investments. Some businesses in Dubai.'

'How long have you lived on the island?'

'A couple of years?'

'And where were you before?'

'What is this?' He was laughing. 'Twenty questions?'

She could feel the bruises from the sea, sharp beneath the fluttery yellow and leaned forward, gulping her glass of wine, weary to the bone.

'Sorry,' she smiled at him. 'About all the questions.'

As if she might lead him back …

One chance.

Now.

She lifted her head, to an inaudible battle cry, and all at once, the smile was real, and she was real, and she was the girl in the mirror.

'It doesn't matter.' Zac was smiling at her now, catching the change of her mood. 'What about you? How long are you here for?'

She shrugged. 'A week or so. I'm between jobs.'

'Sounds fun. What do you do?'

'I'm in marketing. Not very interesting.' It was fluent now. 'So where do you live in Mauritius?'

'Roches Noires, on the east side of the island.'

She nodded, remembering, the confidence still flooding back.

They had found the house easily once they had his name. *Parcel for Daniel Richmond? Not here, just along there. His place is* Ombres Paisibles. *Three houses down.*

Miranda and Casey had walked past *Ombres Paisibles*'s high walls, and the Armed Guards: Immediate Response sign, before strolling on.

There were narrow footpaths between some of the houses, running from the road to the ocean. Two houses beyond *Ombres Paisibles*, Miranda wandered down one of the paths to the beach, and looked back up through palm trees and hibiscus to glistening glass and steel.

'His house has steps straight down to the beach,' Miranda had reported back later. 'Very nice indeed.'

Now Zac poured her a glass of wine, and the words became easier again.

'That's delicious, thank you,' Casey giggled, and it was real, or the right sort of lie.

There was an odd feeling against her ankle, and she squealed.

'Stop playing footsie, Dodo.'

It was the little mongrel, peeking out from under the table.

'Dodo?' Casey asked.

'He was almost extinct when I found him.'

The dodo – clumsy, large and fatally edible – survived barely twenty-five years after the Dutch settled on Mauritius four centuries ago.

'Why was this Dodo almost extinct?' Casey fussed over the little mongrel.

'One day I had to go to the supermarket early one morning.' Zac was almost serious for a moment. 'The stray dogs used to hang around there. And they were catching them in big nets, to put them down. But I convinced them to give me Dodo.'

'That's awful. He's so lovely.'

The little dog panted up at her.

Zac laughed. 'He is some of the time.'

As the sky darkened, they chatted on. Zac was quick, charming, sharp. After three hours, she knew almost nothing about him.

When she stood up to go to the bathroom, the restaurant was too loud, the colours too bright. She realised she was drunk.

Casey stared at the girl in the mirror and watched, almost with interest, as tears filled her eyes.

Pull yourself together.

She checked the miniature camera robotically, although it had caught nothing of note.

You have to get him to talk. Have to.

And so she strutted back to the table, heads turning as she walked. Not invisible, not tonight.

'Shall we head off?'

She met his eye. 'Sure.'

He waved for the bill, gossiping briefly with the waitress. Casey messaged Miranda: *leaving soon.*

As they walked out of the restaurant, Casey meandered towards the cars. 'No.' Zac caught her arm lightly. 'The boat is this way.'

Casey hesitated. Miranda was in a hire car, near the entrance. She couldn't follow them on a boat.

'I can give you a lift back to your hotel,' Zac said. 'I sailed round the headland earlier. But I can call you a taxi if you just want to head home.'

She stood for a second.

You have to get him to talk.

But anything could happen.

I don't care.

'Sure,' she smiled. 'That would be lovely.'

It was a still night, the dinghy puttering through the ripples. The moon glowed, a long beam of light reaching across the sea. Sitting in the boat's prow, Casey trailed her fingers through the water. She had sent a message to Miranda, *going out to the Renaissance*, and then shoved her phone deep in her handbag.

'Who are you going to be?' Miranda had asked earlier, because Miranda picked characters as if she were picking a book off a shelf.

'I don't know yet.' Because it was easy, wasn't it? And it was, back then, all those hours ago.

Where am I? Oh, yes. Who am I?

But everyone had a weak spot. Everyone. Didn't they?

Maybe on the boat, in the house, there would be a clue. Maybe.

Anything could happen.

I don't care.

'Do you miss anything about England?' She looked back at Zac.

'St Paul's.' He surprised her. 'My favourite place.'

'Why?'

He was looking up at the incandescence of the moon. 'Because it's beautiful.'

It wasn't his fault that she thought of a magical dome, seen from the top of a hill. And scarlet tulips, and a pattering rain and a city so bright in the dark. And a kiss.

He helped her climb aboard the *Renaissance*, and swung up behind her. Dodo hopped aboard too, claws rattling on the deck. They sat on the deck, side by side, and he opened a bottle, poured her a glass of wine.

The wooden deck was still warm from the sun. Casey felt unstable, erratic, almost giddy. Too many drinks, and not quite enough drinks. She felt precarious, nervous, on the edge of tears.

'You're running away from something.' Zac's words startled her.

'I'm not.' A reflex.

'So why are you here?'

Ed.

'A holiday.' A forced giggle. 'I told you. I needed to get away for a bit.'

'So you are running away from something,' he said, with satisfaction.

'Aren't we all?' – and now her laugh wouldn't stop.

He turned to watch her, the boat rocking gently on the swell. And then he leaned across and kissed her.

For a second, Casey kissed him back. His body was solid against her, his arms oddly comforting. His hands were on her body, running up her back, pulling her close, and then he was stroking her face, kissing her again, harder now, and for a moment, there was only him, the world fading away.

Casey opened her eyes.

Not Ed.

'No,' she gasped.

'Come on.' He kissed her again, his mouth hard on hers, pushing her backwards towards the deck.

'No.' A surge of panic. No one knew where she was. And he was strong: far stronger than her. She felt as flimsy as her yellow silk dress.

'It'll be fun.'

'No,' louder. Both her hands on his chest, and she rammed him away. He pulled back, letting her go, and she felt a surge of relief that almost choked her. Lucky. Fool. What are you *doing*?

'All right, all right.' Zac was laughing again. 'You don't know what you want, Casey.'

Her name was a shock. She turned her face away from him, her eyes full of tears. 'I know. I'm sorry.'

She heard him refill their glasses, her eyes on the ocean. The sea whispered against the sides of the yacht, and it seemed as if the boat was drifting in some lonely, dark emptiness.

'Why are you really here, Casey?'

Casey forced her face to calm. She turned to Zac, and looked him straight in the eye.

'It's my sister.'

'Your sister?' Zac was baffled, still smiling.

'She's called Flora.' Zac waited. Casey took a breath. 'My sister Flora is nineteen years old, and she has cystic fibrosis.'

'I'm sorry to hear that.' Zac's voice was even.

'She has Mycobacterium abscessus,' Casey recited it, as if it were a scene she had seen once. 'It isn't looking good.'

'I am sorry.'

'Flora is a gorgeous person,' said Casey. 'She's clever and funny and generous and kind. Everyone likes her. You'd like her.'

'I'm sure I would.'

'So I came out here to find you.' Casey refused to look away. 'I know that your real name is Zac Napier, and that you used to be a doctor. I know that you were working on an antibiotic called Corax. And I've been told that Corax might work on Flora. It might cure the abscessus.'

Zac's face didn't move.

'Please,' said Casey. 'Please help us.'

Zac took a swig of his wine. 'I can't help you, I'm afraid.'

'Why?'

'I'll take you back to the jetty,' he said.

'Please, Zac. I know you were working on it.'

But he was standing up, moving towards the cockpit. 'Which hospital is looking after your sister?'

For a second, she hesitated. 'The Royal Free. Close to Hampstead Heath.'

He looked straight at her. 'Not the Royal Brompton?'

'No.' Too hasty, she almost kicked herself. 'Why?'

'I don't have any information on this Corax stuff,' Zac said. 'I'm sorry you've wasted your journey.'

He fired up the engine and the *Renaissance* started to move, slicing mechanically through the waves.

'I know you can help us,' Casey tried. 'We need your help.'

But it was like shouting at the ocean. The yacht churned through the waves, all her flying speed gone, and Zac sat in silence all the way back to the jetty.

17

Miranda was waiting at the hotel, taut with nerves. Casey had barely closed the door to the room before she exploded.

'You can't go off like that.' Casey had never seen Miranda so upset. 'Anything could have happened to you. Anything.'

'But it was fine.' Casey was swaying with exhaustion.

'I didn't know what to do. Who to call. You can't … You can't just *go.*'

'It was fine,' Casey repeated.

Miranda's relief was turning into anger.

'You don't know him, Casey. It's insanity. I have to be able to trust you not to … Not to do unbelievably stupid things.'

'I don't.'

'Twice in one day you could have been bloody killed.'

'Zac was hardly likely to murder me.'

'But you don't know that.' Miranda's hands were splayed with frustration. 'Dash thinks you're going to get yourself killed. That you almost *want* to get yourself killed.'

'And that's why he sent you out here, is it? To babysit me?'

'You know that's why.'

'He doesn't trust me any more, does he?'

'Not right now he doesn't, no. He wants you to take time off, Casey. Get your head straight.'

'Why doesn't he just fire me then? Because I know where all the bodies are buried?'

Miranda steadied, managed to smile. 'You buried most of them, to be fair.'

'It's not funny.'

'I know. But he wants you back to normal. We all do.'

'Normal? What the hell is normal now?' Casey felt the tears start again. 'I can't make sense of anything until I know what happened to Ed. I have to find out what happened to him.'

'But we don't know that anything happened to Ed,' said Miranda flatly. 'The post-mortem didn't show anything dodgy.'

'They weren't thorough enough. I *know* someone killed him.'

'You don't know that, Casey. You can't let yourself consider the possibility that he might just have died. That his heart simply stopped working one day. That's normal too, not being able to believe it.'

'It's not that.'

'People never want to believe it.' Miranda stopped. 'Are you all right?'

Casey had gone pale. Her hands were shaking, her legs quivering. She turned sharply towards the window, staring out over the sea. Standing there, she gripped the steel rim of the window frame, crushing her fingers against the metal until it hurt.

'What is it, Casey?' Miranda asked.

'Can't you understand that I would so much rather believe he just died?' Casey erupted. 'Don't you see it would be easier if he had simply had a heart attack?'

Miranda's eyes were wide.

'It's OK, Casey. It's all right.'

'I could almost bear it if it had been a heart attack,' Casey screamed. 'But don't you see that if someone killed him, it's my fault? If they killed him because of some stupid story, that means that he's only dead because of me!'

Casey's voice broke. She fell against the wall, sliding down into a ball on the floor. 'It's all my fault,' she said again and again. 'All my bloody fault.'

Miranda huddled down beside her. 'It's not your fault, Casey. You didn't know … Even if someone did kill him, no one could possibly have known then … '

'I made him ... ' Casey couldn't stop the tears. 'So many times ... I made him go to the Sahara. To Bangladesh. To help me. And he didn't want to. I made him, every time. I didn't make him happy, Miranda.' She looked up. 'Why didn't I just make him happy?'

'You did make him happy.' Miranda stroked her shoulder. 'Anyone could see that. He was always happiest when he was with you.'

They sat on the floor, side by side, watching the moonlight shimmer on the water.

'I can't believe he's gone,' Casey whispered. 'I'm surprised, every time I think of it. Every time something happens, I think *Ed never heard that joke. Ed would have loved this walk.* I can't believe that his life just stops, and I carry on, getting further and further away from him. How can that be?'

'It's normal,' Miranda murmured. 'It's normal to feel like that. And it will get better.'

'But I don't want it to get better. I don't want to wake up one morning, and not remember exactly what he looked like when he smiled. I don't want to forget how he would raise one eyebrow just a fraction when I was being ridiculous about something. I don't want to get used to him not being here.'

'You have to.'

'But what if I can't?'

After a few moments, Miranda stood and crossed the room to where a miniature kettle stood. A collection of teabags and biscuits sat on a doilied tray.

'What did you get out of Zac?' Miranda asked over her shoulder.

The change of topic calmed Casey. 'Nothing,' she said dully. 'I screwed it up completely.'

Miranda turned round with a teabag in her hand, eyebrows raised. 'You didn't get anything at all?'

'No.'

'What happened?'

'I couldn't think straight,' Casey admitted. 'I got everything wrong. I couldn't decide who I was, how I should play it, what I should do.'

Miranda sat down on the floor next to her again.

'Never mind. We all get things wrong at times.' She smiled. 'Even me.'

'I felt like I was watching myself fuck up from a distance,' said Casey. 'As if it was happening to someone else.'

'Yes, I can see that's not ideal.'

'I let him kiss me, Miranda.' Casey pulled a face. 'Anything could have happened out there. I was unbelievably stupid.'

Miranda contemplated her. Then she picked up the printed screen-grab of Zac laughing on the beach. 'Well,' she grinned, 'I've certainly made worse mistakes.'

'Shut up.' But Casey was smiling too. 'I ruined it. How could I do that?'

For a second, Miranda's face was serious. 'Dash isn't just being a pain in the neck, shifting you off investigations, you know,' she said. 'It's hard, what we do. And it can go very badly wrong, very quickly. You can't do it if your mind is only half on the job, and Dash thought you were struggling even before … You need time out, Casey. You need to sort yourself out.'

'It felt as if I had lost my nerve.'

Miranda looked down into her teacup. 'It can happen.'

'But what would that mean?' Casey's eyes were wide.

'It'll come back. You'll be OK.'

'But how?' asked Casey. 'And what if I can't?'

18

'Dash wants us back in the UK.' Miranda was bright-eyed, hair dripping from a dawn swim. 'They've booked us both on the flight home tonight.'

Behind Miranda, the sun was glittering on the ocean. In the distance, one of the hotel workers was raking the beach while singing tunelessly.

Casey was sitting on her bed, examining her bruises, plum and magenta.

'I don't want to go home.'

'It's an order, I'm afraid … '

Casey looked up. 'Did you tell him about … '

'No,' said Miranda. 'But he called me last night. While you were off. He asked where you were. Told me that you should ring him back within an hour. And, of course … '

'I'm going to go and front-up Zac before we go.' Casey's face was rebellious. 'Just this one last thing.'

'I can hardly stop you,' Miranda shrugged. 'But it doesn't sound like you're going to get anywhere.'

According to some old estate agent particulars, *Ombres Paisibles* was built around three sides of a square. The beach made up the fourth side of the courtyard, marble steps leading down to the sea.

In the photographs, cream deckchairs reclined next to a coppery green pool in the centre of the courtyard. Behind floor-to-ceiling windows were a beautiful sitting room to one side of the house, and a long dining space on the other. The black rocks that gave Roches Noires its name protected the sand from the crash of the waves.

From the beach, Casey could see that the house's security shutters had been opened by an invisible maid. *Ombres Paisibles* would still be bristling with alarms, though, with a hotline to a private security team. Almost all these beachfront houses had formidable defences. 'You don't want to be the obvious target,' someone had drawled in the yacht club. 'Always make your neighbour the easier mark.'

Mauritius, with its frill of wealth along the waterfront. A froth of luxury gift-wrapping around a far poorer centre. A silver lining, and a diamond edge. Money, an unyielding reef.

Casey walked along the beach, her footprints washed away by the sea. Tiny crabs scuttled over the black rocks. From a distance, she could see Zac standing by his pool. He was stretching, eyes on the horizon.

As she got closer, he smiled down at her, unsurprised. 'Good morning, Casey.'

'My name is Casey Benedict,' she called up. 'I work for the *Post*.'

'I know.'

A jolt. She raised her chin. 'People always say that.'

I was just testing you. I was only joking. I knew all along. The defiance always crumbled in the end.

'I'm sure they do.'

It'll make an excellent story: his words had made her hesitate, right at the start of the evening. She had convinced herself: no. But now she realised: he had known. He had known all along.

'Was that why you stopped?' she realised. 'You know … '

'No.' Mock appalled. 'I'm a gentleman.'

She glowered up at him. 'I want to know about Corax.'

He was smiling down at her. 'Yes. I guessed as much from your – err – performance.'

'Why did Pergamex abandon the work on Corax?'

Zac shrugged, hands wide. 'I have absolutely no idea.'

'You do.'

'Prove it, Casey Benedict from the *Post*.'

'How,' she gestured at the opulence of *Ombres Paisibles*, 'do you afford all this, Zac? You were an NHS doctor just a few years ago, and we know that you didn't inherit anything. I've seen your mother's will.'

He didn't rise to the bait. 'I'm a businessman. I have investments. They're all above board.'

'We can tell the world who you are: Zac Napier.'

He considered this. 'Not exactly a marmalade-dropper, is it?' He grinned down. 'A doctor no one's ever heard of, on an island no one can place on a map, who is using a different boring name. I'm not sure the *Post*'s beloved readers will be exactly fighting their way to the newsagents.'

'Won't your new friends in Mauritius be surprised?'

'Hardly.' He started to laugh. And she thought of Martin, just beyond the claws of the taxman. And the Spanish banker reunited with his elegant yacht after a mere couple of years. *Liquid Asset*: two fingers. Zac was right: no one in this little tax haven would be remotely interested in his name change.

'Then why did you change it?'

'There's no law against it.' He yawned, stretched a hamstring. 'Why don't you come inside, Casey Benedict from the *Post*? You're very attractive when you're angry.'

She ignored that. 'Doesn't it worry you that people connected to Corax seem to die unexpectedly?'

He grinned again at her. 'No. In fact, I can think of a specific set of circumstances where it might be viewed as a genuine positive.'

'But you were a doctor?' Casey almost pleaded. 'Don't you care about what Corax might be?'

'I'll tell you if you'll come inside.' He was laughing. 'I was most impressed by your artistry last night.'

She blushed, furious. 'I was told Corax could save thousands of lives. Surely you would rather do that, instead of rotting away on a beach in the middle of nowhere.'

Zac glanced at his reflection in the sparkling windows of *Ombres Paisibles*.

'Hardly rotting.'

'It took years of medical training to get to where you were. Why would you give it all up?'

'Is that what little Noah Hart asked?'

'How much did your silence cost Pergamex, Zac?' She ignored the mention of Noah.

'A kiss.' He glanced at his watch. 'If you really won't come inside, I must be going. Tennis, you know. Dodo likes being ballboy.'

'Tell me,' she pleaded.

Zac sighed, then leaned against the railings. 'It's nowhere near as interesting as you think,' he said. 'It was a patent infringement issue.'

'A patent infringement?'

'Yes,' he said. 'A boring old patent issue. Corax was too similar to an Adsero drug, and Pergamex got warned off.'

Pharmaceutical companies defend their patents with ruthless aggression. Every drug, as soon as it is created, is patented so that no other company can use the technology. For twenty years at least after its invention, no one else can produce a protected drug, and during that period the developer can name its price: whatever the market can bear.

More if it saves a life.

Most if it saves a rich life.

We have to protect our R&D, the companies will insist. *Market forces. Shareholders. Fiduciary duties.*

'A patent infringement?' Casey asked again.

'I know.' Zac lobbed a neon tennis ball towards the sea, and Dodo raced past Casey, yapping excitedly, snatching it just before it reached the ripples. 'Tedious, isn't it?'

'Adsero make zentetra, don't they?' said Casey. 'And they're developing another antibiotic too.'

'So I gather.'

'But Adsero haven't used the Corax technology for their new antibiotic. Saepio is just an enhancement of zentetra.'

'So?' He shrugged. 'They don't have to produce Corax.'

'But why wouldn't they? If it's so effective.'

'I have absolutely no idea.'

'I don't believe you.'

He shrugged again. 'Well, there you go.'

Casey knew she was getting nowhere. Her shoulders slumped. 'I hope you enjoy it all, Zac.'

'Oh, I will.' He was unabashed. 'I will.'

She turned away, plodding back along the beach. He watched her go.

'Casey,' he called after her.

She glanced back. 'What?'

'Leave Pergamex alone.' His face was serious. 'Find something else to investigate.'

'Stay away, you mean?'

'Yes, that's exactly what I mean. Stay away.'

19

Casey didn't sleep on the long flight home. Instead, she researched Adsero, reading everything she could find, which wasn't very much. She trailed through baggage collection behind Miranda, and waited impatiently while Miranda retrieved her car.

'I was driving back from Gloucestershire,' Miranda explained, 'when I was packed off to Dubai.'

'The problem is,' Casey began, when they were safely on the M4, 'that Adsero are notoriously secretive.'

'I know that.'

'I can't even find the name of someone who works in their anti-biotic division, let alone who is working on their new drugs,' said Casey. 'I suppose I could always go and loiter round the pubs in Milton Keynes.'

'How tempting. You have to give up on all this, Casey. You agreed.'

Casey ignored Miranda. 'On top of that, Elias Bailey is famously taciturn.'

Over the previous thirty years, Elias Bailey had built Adsero from minnow to behemoth. On the plane, Casey had pored over the only interview he had ever given: a slot in the *Argus on Sunday* reserved for the most successful tycoons. For this article, Bailey had chosen to meet the journalist in the staff canteen in Milton Keynes.

According to the interview, Bailey had spent part of his childhood in South Africa and part of it in England. He then studied natural sciences at Cambridge. After working as a research scientist for a few years, he seized control of Adsero in a particularly brutal takeover.

The city didn't like him, Casey extrapolated from catty pieces in the business columns, but it adored Adsero's booming profits. Despite the frugal staff canteen lunch, Bailey now owned several houses around the world, including a ski lodge in St Moritz. Controversially, he also owned a vast game reserve in northern Zimbabwe.

The interviewer noted that Bailey was fascinated by Zimbabwean wildlife, and especially dedicated to the conservation of the black rhino. The rhino herd was protected by armed gamekeepers.

Bailey took his privacy extremely seriously and flew around the world on his own jet. A 'well-known philanthropist', the paper called him.

Throughout the article, Bailey focused on the virtues of the modern pharmaceutical industry, extolling its 'visionary creativity'. A heart transplant, just over three years earlier, had only increased his enthusiasm for the industry.

Casey studied the photograph that accompanied the interview, and then tracked down three other pictures online. In his late fifties, Bailey's hair was grey, cut close and receding. His eyebrows had remained black, drawn together in a scowl. He had very dark brown eyes, and a lifetime under the African sun had left a few blotches on his cheekbones.

'Still attractive though.' Miranda peered over Casey's shoulder.

'Not my type.'

In one photograph, Bailey was talking to the head of the IMF at Davos. In another, the US president was smiling at him chummily.

'There is no way,' said Miranda, changing lanes as they passed the tower blocks at Brentford, 'that Elias Bailey will tell you anything about Corax. At his level, you only talk to very big cheeses. It would be impossible for us to fake that.'

The words hung unsaid: *and maybe you can't. Not again. Not ever.*

'I could ask to go round the Milton Keynes site,' Casey thought aloud, 'as acting health editor.'

She had already messaged Heather as she fidgeted at passport control. *Sorry to interrupt your maternity leave, Heather, but do you know much about Elias Bailey and Adsero?*

Interrupt away. I'm bored senseless. No, never got near them, I'm afraid.

'Bailey's private investigators are meant to be phenomenal, too,' Miranda added. 'They wouldn't let him go into a meeting with just anyone. They'd give whoever it was a proper background check first. Douglas – you know, that guy on the business desk – found himself dating one of Bailey's investigators within three days of writing just one page lead about Adsero. Poor Doug only guessed a month into it all. And even then it was only because he was on a night out with this girl at Gigi's, and they bumped into one of her other targets. Apparently, it was all a bit awkward.'

'Probably the only way Doug can get a date,' said Casey, 'if we're realistic.'

'Poor thing. He really liked her,' Miranda went on. 'I was talking to Delphine about Adsero, and I gather that the *Argus* said that Bailey only gave them that *Sunday* interview because halfway through their divorce his ex-wife gave them some dirt, which Bailey didn't want out there. So the *Argus* swapped the dodgy story for the interview, fair exchange.'

'What happened to the wife?'

'Very, very quiet in Cape Town. Signed a brutal NDA for a decent chunk of Adsero shares. Delphine said that there were public interest issues around the wife's story anyway, so the *Argus* were quite happy to swap it for a sit-down with Bailey himself.'

For a low profile individual like Bailey, the *Argus* would have to show there was a public interest in writing about his private life. Public interest and what the public are interested in aren't exactly the same thing.

'Could you find out what the story was?'

'Probably. Delphine would certainly be able to find out,' said Miranda. 'She's still buddies with them all at the *Argus*, especially Jessica Miller and that lot.'

Jessica Miller had taken over the investigations team at the *Argus* after Miranda joined the *Post*. Miranda and Jessica maintained a reasonably friendly rivalry.

'If it was anything good, they would just have run it, surely?'

'I imagine so.'

'He hasn't married again. And he never had any children.'

'Sensible man.' Miranda drove on.

'I'm going to head to the office.' Miranda yawned as they approached central London. 'Just for a couple of hours. Find out what Hessa and Tillie have burned down in my absence.'

'I'll head home then,' Casey mumbled.

'See you soon.'

'Sure.'

But when Miranda got back to Queen's Park five hours later, Casey was sitting on the doorstep.

'Well,' said Casey. 'You wouldn't want me to get rusty.'

'I might,' Miranda sighed, stepping over her.

'I got most of the way back to my flat,' said Casey. 'And then realised something.'

'You astonish me.'

'What exactly are you working on at the moment?' Casey asked, as she followed her into the kitchen.

Miranda eyed Casey as she sorted through her post. 'Are we pretending you're not still reading my emails?'

'As a sidebar,' Casey grinned. 'I think pissoffCasey is quite a rude password.'

'Not rude enough, evidently.'

'So you're investigating Ambrose Drummond?'

Miranda waited a beat. Then: 'Oh, I'm sorry, I thought you knew.'

Ambrose Drummond was a junior health minister. A long-time political fixer, he was the son of a former trade minister, and the grandson of a former chancellor. All three of his sons were at Eton, preparing for the family mantle. Drummond's seat in Gloucestershire had a 20,000 majority, and he only visited it for shooting weekends. His wife, on the other hand, was rarely seen in London. Drummond held directorships in London, Hong Kong and Singapore, and his register of interests – the list of financial information that all MPs have to disclose – revealed extensive shareholdings, not all of them inherited.

Widely regarded as the kingmaker behind the new Prime Minister, Drummond's influence reached far beyond the health brief. Most of his media profile revolved around his selection of gaudy ties, but he was sent out on *Newsnight* when the government was on the back foot. 'A safe pair of hands'. An operator.

Drummond had a booming voice, a florid face and a regular table at the Cinnamon Club, Quirinale and Russet. 'A wheeler-dealer with a finger in every pie,' the *Post*'s sketchwriter noted snidely. 'And the waistline to match.'

'What's the story about?' asked Casey.

Miranda sighed, switched on the kettle. 'Usual thing,' she said over her shoulder. 'Your common or garden conflict of interest.'

A conflict of interest: when an MP's personal interest collides – disastrously – with the interests of their own voters. MPs were always supposed to err on the side of their voters. Often, they didn't.

Several times in the past, Casey and Miranda had presented themselves as charming businesswomen, offering a small payment here, a generous fee there.

The requests were small: a question in Parliament, a small adjustment to a piece of legislation.

The headlines were big.

'What's the conflict for Drummond this time?'

'Hessa's running this one,' said Miranda. 'She's presenting as a company director from Hyderabad, asking Drummond to sort out a piece of legislation blocking the import of certain antibiotics to the UK.'

Casey nodded. The Indian factories produced tonnes of antibiotics a month. Cheap generics, out of patent mostly. As health editor, Casey had written about the antibiotics leaching into Hyderabad's rivers from the factories. In one analysis, the level of ciprofloxacin in factory wastewater was higher than it would have been in the blood of a patient taking regular doses of the drug.

'But Hessa's family's from Bangladesh,' said Casey. 'Not India.'

'Do you really think Drummond cares?'

'What does he want in return?'

'He wants a shareholding in the Hyderabad company – in a trust, obviously – and two weeks in the Maldives.'

'So he's going for it?'

'He is indeed. We thought we might front him up in the Maldives, just for a laugh.'

Casey imagined Hessa pursuing the rotund Ambrose Drummond around a five star resort in the Maldives.

'I'm not sure if the nation is ready for Drummond in his swimming trunks.'

'No, probably not.'

'When are you going to see him?'

'Next week sometime? We did the recordings in Dubai. Hessa and Tillie have been going through the tapes while I was in Mauritius.'

Going through the tapes, transcribing every word, was a tedious but necessary task. Once that was done, the reporters would put together a list of questions. Once everything had been checked over by the *Post*'s in-house lawyers, they would confront Drummond with the evidence.

'Was Tillie doing anything in the scenario?'

'She was Hessa's PA.'

It was always useful for one of them to play the PA role. Tillie would be able to smile, have it all explained, a useful idiot. *I don't understand how these legislations work at all! It doesn't make any sense to me! How* exactly *are you going to change it?*

And Drummond's own PA might always have something to moan about, to Tillie the friendly counterpart.

'Can you wait for a bit?' Casey asked. 'Before fronting up Drummond?'

'Why?'

'Well, you said it yourself,' Casey explained. 'Bailey will only talk to really big cheeses. So do you think he'd make time for a health minister?'

20

It wasn't easy to work out when Elias Bailey would next be accessible. His profile was deliberately low, few of his appearances announced in advance.

'We need to get him somewhere where he will have time for a conversation,' reasoned Casey. 'He'd be far too busy at something like Adsero's AGM. We need him and Drummond to meet in private.'

Business journalists often bought the single share required to access a company's annual meeting. 'But I'm a *shareholder*,' they'd announce proudly, marching unstoppably through the door.

'You can't go to sodding Davos,' Miranda said firmly. 'You've already turned over too many of the attendees. You'd be lynched. Stoned with canapés. Workshopped into oblivion.'

'Could we pack Drummond off to the Milton Keynes site? Bailey would probably turn up for a ministerial visit. Especially if Drummond dragged the PM along.'

'But how do we get Hessa into that meeting?'

'We have to hurry up on this,' Miranda warned Casey, a couple of days later. 'It's not fair on Hessa. It's her first really big story, and things always go wrong when we delay.'

They were in the investigations room, Casey sprawling on the sofa. It was late in the evening, the office almost empty.

'I know. And I am really sorry about that. But what could go wrong with Hessa's story now? Drummond doesn't seem suspicious at all,' said Casey. 'And he's so pally with Hessa now, that he's given her about fifteen other stories. Archie got the splash yesterday with something Drummond mentioned to her in passing.'

Dash had decided to run the story about class sizes under the political editor's byline, just in case Drummond got curious about Hessa Khan's sources.

'Drummond might get shuffled out any minute,' Miranda pointed out. 'The PM's under pressure to shake things up.'

Miranda had once had an excellent story about a defence minister held for several days, 'by an absolute tool of a lawyer at the *Argus*'. During the delay, the defence minister had been sacked. 'We ran the story anyway.' Five years later, Miranda was still cross. 'But who really cares about yet another dodgy backbencher?'

Casey was fiddling with Tillie's stapler. 'Drummond won't get demoted. The PM owes him.'

'Well, some other paper might do him over for something completely different.'

That was the nightmare. Miranda was often woken in the night by the thought of being scooped by another newspaper.

'It won't take much longer,' Casey promised. 'Do you want another coffee?'

She stood up and stretched. Most of the big newsroom was in darkness, only the night editor's desk a glow of light.

'Who's that?' Casey asked.

'That's AJ, the new night editor.' Miranda came to stand beside her.

'What happened to Aaron?'

'Oh. It must have happened while you were … ' Miranda started to laugh. 'Aaron resigned at 3 a.m. in the morning a few days ago. He updated the online splash headline to 'Ross Warman is a slave-driving fuckwit' and stormed out of the building. The headline was only changed back when Ross woke up at 5 a.m., because obviously the site is the first thing he checks every morning. One of the subs was moaning, saying they'd all hoped it would be up for at least another hour, given that Ross had rung in to scream at them at 2.30. He only left the sodding office at midnight.'

'Ross is deranged,' said Casey.

'He's even worse than usual at the moment,' Miranda yawned. 'Git.'

It was Flora Ashcroft who came up with the solution. She arrived for work experience, pale but determined. Eric and Sophie were on holiday together, so Flora sat at Eric's desk, next to Casey.

Flora delighted everyone by making buckets of tea, and even endeared herself to the home affairs editor by tracking down a terrorist's great-aunt in Bury.

'Although I'm not absolutely convinced the great-aunt isn't the bomb maker,' he said thoughtfully. 'So it might be best if that's not your first ever doorstep. Now, there's this Libyan chap ... Even Five haven't been able to ... '

Casey told Flora she was investigating Adsero, but left out the possible existence of Corax. It seemed too cruel.

And late one evening, Flora spun her screen towards Casey. 'Didn't you want to know where Elias Bailey would be appearing next? How about there?'

'The 14th Pharmaceutical Research and Development Symposium,' Miranda read aloud from her computer screen a few minutes later. 'It's as if they design the names to be dull.'

'I think they do, actually.'

Miranda looked up at Casey and Flora.

'How on earth did you find out, Flora? We couldn't see his attendance promoted anywhere. Well done.'

'Oh,' said Flora. 'I just trawled and trawled.'

'I've just rung the hotel to check,' said Casey. 'He's definitely going.'

Just checking that you knew that Mr Bailey prefers a room on the east side of the building.

Of course. I will make a note on his booking.

'Well done, Flora,' Miranda nodded. 'And where the hell is Wrocław anyway?'

'Poland,' said Casey sweetly. 'We drove past it once on the way to Katowice, if you recall?'

'How could I forget?'

'Anyway,' Casey smiled at Miranda as Flora headed back to her desk, 'Bailey is a keynote speaker at that symposium and I am sure the organisers would be delighted if a British health minister happened to be in town.'

21

The organisers were indeed delighted. Ambrose Drummond was swiftly inserted into the programme of the 14th Pharmaceutical Research and Development Symposium, and given a prominent billing.

'Wrocław?' Drummond had roared at Tillie, over a quick drink at his club. 'Never heard of it.'

'It's in Poland. Meant to be charming. And my boss would be so appreciative if I could have a meeting with Mr Bailey.'

Drummond scrolled through his diary. 'Meant to be in the constituency that weekend. Christ, I suppose even Wrocław will be better than that.'

'We'll organise everything. And I'm sure you'll get a most generous bonus.'

'All right. I'll mention it to the department. But make sure I get a decent bloody suite.'

'Of course, Mr Drummond.'

Tillie and Hessa coordinated Drummond's visit to Wrocław. Drummond ordered his special adviser to find a current email address for both Bailey and his executive assistant.

'Oh, I'm sure his spad loved that,' Miranda laughed, when she heard about it.

Serena Brackenbury, Drummond's elegant special adviser, was well known in Westminster for regarding her current role as a tedious stopgap before she stood for a safe seat and continued her inexorable rise. The MP in the constituency neighbouring Drummond's was 79 and rheumatic, and Serena spent most of her time on the rubber chicken circuit, flicking her poker-straight blonde bob and chatting up party members.

Once Serena had resentfully tracked down Bailey's email address, Drummond messaged the Adsero chief executive, copying in Tillie. 'Elias – it'd be good to catch up in Poland. My assistant Jilly will sort out all the details,' Drummond typed airily.

As far as Drummond was concerned, Tillie was Jilly. The rhyme was enough to make Tillie glance up.

'Maybe you'll be Dora, one day,' Tillie said to Flora, as they ran out to get a sandwich, and Flora's eyes lit up.

Bailey had responded within minutes, briskly ordering his assistant to fix a time and place for a meeting in Wrocław.

'It's all coming together,' Casey grinned. 'Good work, Jilly.'

'And now I've got to write a bloody speech for him,' grumbled Hessa later. 'He said he can't ask Serena to write it, because she'll ask too many questions about what on earth he's doing in Wrocław.'

'Well, at least you're not having to write stories about the crisis in mental health care and the meltdown in A&E waiting times,' said Casey. 'And for God's sake, don't accidentally change government policy with some random speech in Wrocław.'

The *Post* had been involved in an inadvertent switch of government policy at least once before. Two floors up from the newsroom, there was a boardroom where caterers served salmon en croute and strawberries and cream to visiting politicians or pop stars or minor royals. One or two of the *Post*'s favoured columnists – never the reporters, they were kept well away – would pop up for a jolly gossip, before the guest was given a congenial tour of the newsroom.

The ambitious leader of the then opposition had been visiting the *Post* for lunch three years earlier. Over coffee, after a couple of glasses of Sauvignon Blanc, the last editor of the *Post* had held up his hand, fingers spread out. 'There are five things you need to do about education,' he began, launching into a recital of one of the *Post*'s most recent leader columns, listing the points off his fingers.

'And then, bugger me, I couldn't remember the last one,' he told his giggling political team later. 'I was going to look like an absolute tit, so I had to make something up on the hoof.'

A year later, the new government solemnly voted through the changes.

'All right,' Hessa said gloomily, deleting a paragraph from her speech. 'No new government policies.'

Dash, busy with a terrorism crisis, waved through the budget for the Wrocław trip.

'I thought you said the Drummond sting was pretty much there?'

'When we checked the recording, the wording wasn't quite right. Too wink and a nod,' Miranda lied. 'He needs to really spell it out.'

'Fine. But that story is costing a bloody fortune.'

'Yes, sorry. Also, we think he may be about to drop Warwick in it somehow.'

This wasn't true, but it sounded plausible. Colette Warwick was the Health Secretary, Drummond's boss. Fiercely ambitious, she evidently irritated Drummond, Miranda had noted from the transcripts. Younger than Drummond – and significantly brighter in Miranda's opinion – Warwick was creeping closer to the overall crown, and Drummond resented it.

'Everything OK with Casey?'

'Oh, yes,' nodded Miranda. 'She wrote up a very interesting article on MRSA last week. Did you see it? All about how some staph infections become resistant to all the standard antibiotics.'

'Yeah, yeah.' Dash turned back to the big televisions that dominated the newsdesk. The Home Secretary was talking. 'Can you turn that up?'

Casey and Hessa flew to Wrocław the afternoon before Drummond arrived, with a couple of large boxes among their luggage. They checked into a big hotel that looked out over one of the pretty, pastel-coloured Wrocław squares. The Old Town Hall dominated the view, Gothic and forbidding. In the distance, church bells jingled merrily.

'It's very beautiful,' said Hessa.

They had booked two standard rooms, as well as the presidential suite for Drummond.

'He'll demand it anyway,' sighed Hessa.

They picked up two keycards for each of the three rooms, and as soon as the bellboy had disappeared, they went to work.

The presidential suite had two large bedrooms, each with superking beds piled high with cushions. There were grey marble bathrooms and a generously-sized sitting room connecting the two bedrooms. The sitting room had plump gold and silver striped sofas, gilt-edged mirrors and heavy walnut furniture. The wallpaper was gold damask, and the curtains a dark yellow velvet.

Within minutes Casey had fixed tiny microphones to the underside of the coffee table. As Casey worked, Hessa placed a small sculpture on a sideboard and a reading light on a desk beside the sofa. She tucked the hotel's own reading light neatly into one of the empty boxes they had brought with them. Hessa then took a small oil painting of a Russian grand duchess off the wall on the opposite side of the room, and hung a disapproving Polish count in her place. She stepped back to check that the portrait was level, then nodded with satisfaction.

Before flying out, Hessa had looked up the presidential suite on Expedia. The website fortuitously provided photographs of several different angles of the sitting room.

Hessa, Flora and Sagah – a surveillance genius who operated out of an attic in Holborn – had gone shopping on Tottenham Court Road for the reading light. The sculpture and the disapproving Polish count came from a cheap auction house in south London. All three items matched the decor of the hotel room perfectly.

'I even changed the plug of the reading light so it's compatible with Polish electrics.' Sagah had kissed his fingers. 'It's that sort of attention to detail that really makes me stand out.'

Flora had touched the Polish count with awe, Hessa watching her with a proud indulgence.

Now Hessa gave the room one more check. She doubted that the hotel's hurried housekeeping staff would notice the difference.

And even if they did, it was almost impossible to spot the tiny cameras buried carefully in the sculpture and the light. She peered closer. The pinhole in the Polish count's moustache was quite invisible; Drummond would never notice the wide-angle lens peeping through. The cameras were all motion-activated, working off Wi-Fi. Tiny infrared LEDs allowed them to operate in the dark.

'That Polish count matches the colour scheme even better than the grand duchess,' said Casey admiringly. 'You are clever, Hessa.'

'I was reading about theatre props,' Hessa grinned. 'About how sometimes a prop is designed to look more real than the actual item. Forced perspective, it's called.'

'Really?'

'Michelangelo's *David* was designed to be seen from below.' Hessa polished the base of the reading light. 'Because he was meant to be positioned on the roof of the cathedral, so his head is slightly larger than you might expect. Same thing for the *Statue of Liberty*.'

'I did not know that.' Casey stepped forward to nudge the Polish count a quarter of an inch to the left.

'And they used to build raked stages,' said Hessa. 'Stages that slope up from the audience so that when an actor was at the back of a set, he would be higher than the one closer to the audience. Quite literally upstaging him. It's all a question of perspective.'

'It must have been awkward to walk on them,' said Casey.

'It was,' said Hessa. 'You'd have to sort of limp along. They don't do it with modern theatres. They changed how the audience sits instead.'

Hessa was on her knees by the coffee table, checking the microphones again.

'Even if Drummond did spot them,' Casey said, 'he'd assume it was only the Polish secret services.'

'They're probably recording it all too anyway,' said Hessa. 'I do wish we could divvy up the transcribing.'

22

As Elias Bailey walked into the hotel suite, his two bodyguards took up a position outside the door. Drummond met Bailey at the door, all good cheer, guiding him towards the sofas. Can I get you a drink, tea, coffee? Good to see you, Bailey.

Bailey came to an abrupt halt as he saw Hessa, sitting in one of the big gold and silver sofas. Hessa rose to her feet and smiled, putting out her hand.

'Ah, yes,' Drummond was closing the door, 'Have you met Jessa Uddin, Elias? She runs StellaBiotics in India.'

'I don't think I have heard of it.' Bailey shook Hessa's hand. 'How do you do?'

In the room next door, Casey and Miranda were sitting in front of three laptop screens. The feeds were showing footage from the reading light, the sculpture and the disapproving Polish count. Casey felt like a theatre director, peering out from the wings, hoping – desperately – that no one would miss their cue. Sidelined, and she hated it.

'No,' Miranda had been firm, 'you can't.'

'But—'

'It's Hessa's story,' Miranda said. 'And after Mauritius …'

'But—'

'No.'

And Casey had nodded, defeated.

Bailey walked into the feed from the reading light, giving a close-up of his face. As Casey stared at the scowling eyebrows, she felt an uncontrollable rage, sharp as a stitch.

You.

You killed Ed. I know it.

I *know* it.

She sensed Miranda turn towards her.

'Casey … '

'I'm fine,' she spat out the words.

As Drummond completed the introductions, Bailey nodded curtly at Hessa. The chief executive of Adsero was a tall man, solid across the chest and shoulders. He gave no sign of being affected by the heart transplant. There was an impression of resilience about him, a robustness.

In fact, he dominated the room with an intensely physical presence. This man would not, Casey thought, be pleased to discover he was being manipulated. The puppet's puppet: it would trigger absolute rage.

On the laptop screens, Hessa looked small beside him.

'We operate out of Hyderabad,' Hessa was saying smoothly. 'We're not on the scale of Adsero yet, but we're working on it. It's an honour to meet you, Mr Bailey.'

Casey remembered the first time she had met Hessa, in the queue for the vending machine at the *Post*. She had been so shy then, a junior reporter ducking her head when she came up with a clever solution to a problem, almost inaudibly. Now Hessa smiled at the pharmaceutical tycoon with just the right balance of assurance and sycophancy, then turned to the Health Minister to say goodbye. In her smart tailored suit, spiky patent heels and sheer Heist tights, she was immaculate.

'Jessa was just leaving,' Drummond announced, as Hessa handed her business card to Bailey. 'But why don't you hang around for a bit, Jessa? I'm sure Mr Bailey has helpful words of advice for a young entrepreneur like yourself.'

On the screens, Casey watched Bailey's eyes go to Drummond, one eyebrow slightly raised. Then Bailey relaxed: he knew he was being set up to meet Jessa Uddin, thought Casey. But Hessa's real identity would never occur to him. Bailey tucked away her business card in an inside pocket.

'Of course. Where are you based in Hyderabad, Jessa?'

'We're actually up by Kazipally,' Hessa spoke fluently. 'Just off the outer ring road.'

Hessa had never visited India, but she had spent hours researching the Hyderabad antibiotics industry, gazing with horror at photographs of brown choking rivers, of toxic green lakes.

Casey crossed her fingers.

Bailey sat down in the middle of one of the sofas, while Drummond perched neatly in an armchair.

Drummond steered the conversation confidently. He was good, thought Casey. All those years of navigating the Parliamentary tea rooms showed. He was charming, entertaining, a couple of well-timed jokes. One crack at the PM's expense: a reminder of the balance of power in that particular relationship.

The steel was more evident in Bailey. Ignoring Hessa, he reeled through the issues he wanted to raise with Drummond. Tax breaks on R&D, data access, an upgraded road to one of Adsero's factories in Lincolnshire.

Drummond parried, nodded, promised to look into it and get back to you, I'll have a word with the PM. By the way, Elias, have you ever thought about making a donation to the party?

Hessa sat and smiled. Agreeing with Bailey, joking with Drummond.

And finally, Drummond moved on to antibiotics. 'When I was visiting a hospital in Carlisle the other week,' he said, 'they mentioned they were starting to see quite a lot of resistance to zentetra.'

'Yeah.' Bailey's South African accent grew stronger, 'Zentetra's been a great antibiotic for two decades or so, but the bacteria are starting to fight back now.'

'But you've got another one coming up?'

'Saepio,' Bailey nodded. 'Should be out soon.'

Bailey would be careful talking about any new drug. The information was highly market sensitive. A breakthrough would send Adsero's share price flying. Rumours of a duff drug – and millions of research dollars down the drain – would echo bleakly around the City. Although Bailey owned a huge chunk of Adsero, there were still rules, strict ones.

'So saepio's the next gen zentetra?' asked Hessa.

'It is. But saepio is a lot better than zentetra,' said Bailey firmly. 'We're very pleased with it.'

'I've heard that some of the new tetracyclines are performing really strongly,' said Hessa. 'It's an interesting area.'

'Exactly.' Bailey nodded at her.

Hessa took a breath. 'I was talking to someone the other day about a new Adsero antibiotic called Corax,' she said. 'They said it was a very exciting new drug.'

'Oh, yes?' the Health Minister asked. 'What's going on with – what's-it-called? – Corax, Elias?'

Bailey had gone still. 'Would you mind me asking where you heard about that, Miss Uddin?'

'I can't remember.' Hessa looked vague. 'It might have been at a conference in San Diego the other week.'

'Why?' Drummond asked, all geniality, 'What are you up to with this Corax stuff, Bailey?'

'Nothing.' The word was sharp.

'Really?' asked Hessa. 'Because I heard that there was some sort of patent dispute going on over Corax.'

Bailey was on his feet, convulsively.

'We haven't got any sort of patent dispute in our antibiotic division, Miss Uddin.'

'Oh,' said Hessa calmly. 'Right.'

'And you were speaking to someone in San Diego about this?'

'As far as I can remember. Mr Drummond, I—'

'I would be very grateful,' a barely controlled menace in Bailey's voice as he interrupted, 'if you could try and remember who you heard this from, Jessa.'

'I believe it was during a ten-second conversation in San Diego.' Hessa was glacial. 'I cannot recall who mentioned it.'

Bailey sat down again but leant forward until he was only a few inches from her face.

'Miss Uddin, I would like to know who told you about Corax.' The politeness of the words only heightened the sense of controlled fury.

'Mr Bailey—'

'Now steady on—' Drummond tried to smooth things over.

'Housekeeping!' It was Miranda, in a black tabard, with a copy of Drummond's keycard and a loud knock on the door. She bustled past the bodyguards, all efficiency, pushing a trolley she had swiped from a maid down the corridor.

'Hello, sir. Very sorry to interrupt. Won't be a minute. Toiletries, *tak*?' in what might have been a Polish accent.

The bodyguards hesitated behind her, caught on the hop.

'I must be going.' Hessa was on her feet. 'Mr Drummond, I'll catch up with you soon. Thank you so much for your time. Goodbye, Mr Bailey.'

And as Hessa hurried round the housekeeping cart and made for the lifts, Miranda solemnly upended a wastepaper basket.

Hessa took the lift down to the lobby, diving round to the back entrance of the hotel once she was sure she wasn't being followed.

'That was quite stressful.' Hessa threw herself on the bed in Casey's room. She had already switched off the tiny camera buried in the smart black suit. 'And I didn't get anything out of Bailey at all.' She thumped a pillow.

'You did,' Casey soothed. 'You proved that either Zac or Bailey is lying about the patent issue.'

'Does that really matter? Bailey was furious. He'll definitely blow my cover with Drummond.'

It wouldn't take long for Bailey's investigators to establish that there was no StellaBiotics in Kazipally.

'Don't worry,' said Casey. 'We've got more than enough on Drummond now. We'll go to him as soon as possible, and get your conflict-of-interest story out there. All that stuff he was saying to

Bailey was brilliant for your story anyway. And don't worry about Adsero. Worst-case scenario, they'll conclude you've just been doing a light bit of corporate espionage. That's why we got the business cards, remember.'

In the past, they might have chosen a random company in Hyderabad, and hijacked it. Hessa might have set up an email address, just one letter off, for communicating with Drummond. A Trojan horse, a parasite, long gone by the time anyone checked.

This time, however, there was a London address for StellaBiotics on the business card that Hessa had handed to Bailey. The address was in Ilford, an empty house that looked habitable from the outside. When Bailey's investigators googled the Ilford address, several websites would appear, pushed to the top of the Google rankings by Toby, the *Post*'s technology correspondent. Toby always enjoyed some mild skulduggery on the side.

Uddin Private Investigations, one website would blare. Uddin Risk Solutions, another. With the same phone number on every site. And if Bailey's investigators ever called it, Hessa would answer, 'Uddin Corporate Investigations, can I help you?' And so Bailey's people would report back. *Someone's taken an interest. No, they haven't got anything. Just some amateurs in east London, don't worry.*

And that would be the end of the hunt for Jessa Uddin.

'Drummond certainly won't rock the boat.' It was Miranda behind them, stripping off the tabard after dumping the trolley two floors away. 'He and Bailey will probably work out there was something a bit dodgy about Jessa Uddin, but that doesn't matter.'

Thanks to Toby's work, nothing would ever connect Jessa Uddin to Hessa Khan. The *Post*'s involvement would be completely hidden until Hessa sent the email to 'Dear Mr Drummond … '

They all turned back to the laptops. Bailey had recovered his equilibrium now, and was chatting calmly with Drummond.

As she listened to the men talking, Hessa reached for her burner mobile and typed out a message. *My apologies, Minister – I have to return to London urgently. Enjoy your time in Wrocław! All the best, Jessa.*

Casey watched as Drummond reached for his phone and read the message without reacting. He wouldn't try and track her down, she knew. The last thing he would want was an investigation into a Jessa Uddin. He would wait, and hope that it would all go away. Because, quite often, it did.

Now Bailey was leaning forward to emphasise a point. Finger jabbing, pugnacious body language, the mood only slightly leavened by his half-smile. He was a brutal businessman, Casey thought. Absolutely ruthless.

And she pushed another thought to the back of her mind. That at the moment when it was spinning out of control, when Jessa Uddin was pinned down with nowhere to go, it had been Miranda who leaped to her feet. Miranda who moved decisively and precisely. While Casey had sat there, frozen and terrified, her mind a whirling chaos.

23

Back in the office in London, Casey slumped into frustration.

'You haven't really got anything new on Corax.' Miranda was sympathetic. 'We know that either Zac or Bailey is lying, but that doesn't really help us much. And I don't think you're going to get anything more out of either of them now.'

Ross, at least, was delighted by the footage of Drummond asking Bailey for a donation to the party. 'The sting's sting. We should have got Drummond to offer pharma boy a peerage for a million,' he said. 'Lord Bailey. Baron Bailey. That would have put sodding Drummond in jail.'

Over the years, Ross had spent quite a lot of time trying to work out how he could manoeuvre a peerage out of Downing Street. 'We could send in Casey,' he would say wistfully. 'She could be Baroness Benedict of Fleet.'

'Fleet?' the home affairs editor asked.

'Well, Fleet Street would be a bit obvious, you goon.'

'I'm not,' Dash would shut down the conversation, 'handing over a million quid for that.'

'The thing is, I think they're both lying.' Casey had sidled into the investigations office after Dash had gone home for the evening. 'Zac's story doesn't make sense, because if Corax is a completely new antibiotic, why would there be a patent issue with an Adsero drug? And Bailey … Why the hell are they doing it? Why?'

She threw herself on the sofa and kicked out at the wastepaper basket.

'Never ask why,' Miranda said unexpectedly.

'What?' Casey looked up, mid-kick.

Who, what, where, when, why? The words were embedded in every journalist, like Brighton through rock.

'*Quis, quid, quando, ubi, cur,*' the *Post*'s deputy editor – who took his Oxford education seriously – would murmur in the morning conference.

'And I want the fucking answers in the first sodding para,' Ross – who didn't – would retort.

'It's what Delphine used to say,' said Miranda. 'You can never know why someone is doing something, unless they have specifically told you.'

'I don't … '

'You have to look at the facts, Casey,' said Miranda. 'And only the facts. You can't extrapolate why someone is doing something, and you'll look very stupid in court trying to defend it later.'

Casey sat on the sofa, processing this. 'Because they can just say, "no, that's not what I was thinking", and you can never prove otherwise.'

'Precisely.'

'Except,' Casey pointed out, 'when you're undercover, and then sometimes they do tell you what they're thinking.'

'Sometimes, they might.'

'So.' Casey went back to kicking the wastepaper basket. 'That's what we have to do.'

'Casey. Give up.'

'What are you working on?'

'Oh,' Miranda yawned, 'not much. The Treasury dumped thousands of pages on their website under Freedom of Information. And I know there is a story somewhere in here, but it's very buried. You know how they bury the good stuff in a million pages of dross.'

'A needle in a haystack,' Casey sighed. 'Thousands of pages of chaff.'

'Exactly.'

'But what if Bailey—'

'*Casey.*'

Later, Casey meandered back to her flat. She walked into the sitting room, and folded into the sofa. Clutching a cushion to her chest, she stared across the room, exhausted.

Four patches of paint slapped on the wall.

Cat's Cradle or Kissing Gate? I love you. Feather Pillow or Wood Smoke?

The patches of paint blurred.

She stood, straying towards the fireplace, which had been blocked up decades ago. There were a few cards on the mantelpiece, still. Condolences. Commiserations. Miranda had opened them as they arrived, and read them aloud as Casey stared into space.

There weren't many. And most of them had been sent via the Post.

She peered at them now. Several from Ed's friends, thoughtful.

Dear Casey, I was so sorry to hear …

Dear Casey, I hope that …

One from Delphine Black, Miranda's old boss.

It is a truly dreadful thing, Casey. For months after Finlay died, I couldn't feel a single emotion. Like a woman after one of those terrible bomb blasts, and she doesn't even realise that her arm is gone. She just wanders the streets, quite oblivious, covered in her own blood. Or one of those burns that is so deep that all the nerve endings are cauterised and obliterated and you can't feel anything at all. But you do survive, Casey. You do.

There was something pathetic about the letters. Pieces of card: twee pictures of daffodils, a sunny beach in Cornwall, some sad-looking teddy bears. Words, nothing more.

A life reduced to words.

Casey's eyes drifted to a photograph frame on the windowsill. Ed had placed it there, of course. Casey stared at it for a long time. The two of them, smiling at the camera, his arms around her. Wiltshire, and a glorious day in the sun.

One glorious day, a tiny stitch in a lifetime of happiness. One pretty bead on a necklace. And now the necklace was snapped. Junk, swept away.

I miss you, a whisper.

I miss you so much.

And I don't think I can do it without you.

Later, she found herself staring at one of the cards again.

A beach in Cornwall.

There had been a few days at the seaside, once.

A childish heaven of fish and chips and buckets and spades. A few pastel houses: a rosy pink, a sun-bleached turquoise, a faded foxglove purple. Their cottage was yellow. Primrose, her mother called it. With a golden thatch pulled down like a bonnet.

One day, he took her hand: we'll go fishing.

She remembered peering into rock pools as the seagulls bickered overhead. Barnacles and mussels and anemones shiny as tourmalines.

He had bought her new sandals, red and white, and most precious. She took them off to keep them safe as they clambered over the rocks.

'Wait for me, Daddy.' Those most treasured syllables. And there was that quick glance around, always.

He smiled at her though, fishing rods over his shoulder.

'We need bait,' he decided, as he put down the fishing rods. 'Limpets.'

He'd brought a little knife, a blunt one.

'The secret is,' he said, 'to get the blade under the shell before they clamp down. Once they've heard you coming, they lock up and then nothing will get them off. Nothing. It's one of the strongest things in the natural world, a limpet.'

She scrutinised them – drab brown triangles, boring – and watched as he wrestled them off, revealing a slimy underbelly: black and yellow and greenish.

'Yuk,' she said, and he laughed, gouging with the knife.

They didn't catch anything, the limpets dangling aimlessly on hooks, but she was perfectly happy, blissfully content. Hours, just the two of them, watching the waves dance and dazzle.

'Right.' He stood up in the end. 'Home time.'

It wasn't their home, but that didn't matter.

She held up her little blue bucket of limpets, most of them still in their homely brown shells.

'Shall we put them back?'

'You can't,' he explained. 'Once you've pulled them off, they can't go back on.'

'Oh.' She looked at her bucket of green and brown and yellow triangles. 'That's a shame.'

'We can't take them home,' he said. That word, again.

They threw them off the rocks into the clear blue water, and she watched as they sank down and down, watched until they disappeared.

Later she wondered if her mother had spent those days thinking: could this be real?

And, of course, much later she wondered what story he had told his family.

The other family.

The real family.

There must have been a story for those few days.

There must have been a story for everything.

She told only one person. At university, when he was drunk, tragic, reeling from a father admitting a twenty-year affair.

A childhood, in fragments.

'It's every memory,' he said. 'Every single holiday, he was waiting to see her as soon as we got home. Every birthday was a missed day for them. Every Sports Day, a lost afternoon. I see her in our family photographs, now, as if she was there all along. A shadow unseen. Every snapshot, a lie. Every memory, a lie.'

We only know snapshots.

'It probably wasn't like that, you know. Not for her.' And she told him some fragments.

'At least you had a sort of truth,' he said.

And she didn't tell anyone for years, after that.

She kept a few things. The red and white sandals. A pack of cards. Pocket chess, and a photograph of three children, found by mistake. A battered music box, with a name engraved. Cassandra, in lavender italics. Tenderness there, surely?

For a while, maybe.

She opened the music box one year, and almost cried at the cracked notes.

A limpet, torn away.

24

Casey woke up on the sofa, stiff and cold. Making a coffee, she rang Noah Hart.

'Are you calling about Flora?' Noah asked immediately.

A thud of apprehension.

'No,' said Casey. 'Why? She seemed fine a few days ago.'

She thought back to Flora in the office, delighted at tracking down those addresses, and laughing as she tried to remember all the tea orders.

'Flora's back in hospital,' said Noah flatly. 'An infection flared up suddenly. Give her a call? It's not looking ... Well. Call her, anyway.'

'I'm so sorry,' said Casey. 'I will ring her. Will she be ... '

'I don't know.' There was a long pause. 'So what were you calling about?'

'Corax.'

'Oh. Yes.'

'I was just wondering if you could think of anything else that might take us forward?' Casey could hear the hopelessness in her own voice.

'Sorry, no.'

'Anything at all?'

'I don't think I sh—'

'It might help Flora, Noah.'

'You could go and talk to Professor Jalali ... Maybe. Down in Tooting.'

Casey took care as she travelled to Professor Jalali's hospital from the *Post* office. First, she got on the Victoria line heading north before jumping off at Green Park. Then she took the Piccadilly line west for a couple of stops and trotted across the platform to the eastbound line. Finally, she climbed on the Northern line at Leicester Square and headed back south again.

Not ideal, she thought, for a health editor.

As she walked from the Tube to the hospital, she called Flora.

Flora answered with a gasp. 'Hello?'

'It's Casey.'

'Oh, hello.' Flora's laugh turned into a cough. 'How are you?'

'Are you OK?'

'Not really.' Flora didn't try to pretend. 'It's the abscessus. It's staging a bit of a comeback. Stupid thing.'

I can't help you, Casey thought in despair, I'm failing you day by day, and you don't even know it really.

'I gather you're back in hospital?'

'Room 23A,' Flora laughed. 'The apricot feature wall is going to finish me off altogether.'

'Oh, Flora.'

'I know. It's fine though, really.' A third laugh. 'Might repaint it when they're not looking. Undercover decorator. Not the original plan, maybe, but it'll keep my hand in.'

They talked, filling the air with nothing and everything. The leaves were falling now, fluttering into the road to be crunched by the cars. It looked like rain, the sky a dappled grey.

'So work experience at the *Post* didn't put you off altogether?' Casey asked.

'I loved it,' said Flora. 'I'll be on the investigations team soon.'

'Oh, god. I don't need the competition. But you will be great, Flora. I know it.'

And they laughed and said goodbye, and Casey wondered if she would ever see her again.

25

At the hospital, Professor Jalali was waiting for her, flanked by two nurses.

'I thought we would start in the NICU,' Jalali was brisk in her scrubs. 'That's the neonatal intensive care unit. Then we can move on to special care, which is where we transfer the babies when they need slightly less support.'

They proceeded smartly down a corridor.

'I gather you're interested in antibiotic resistance,' said Professor Jalali. 'As you probably know, babies are usually born at around 40 weeks. However, some of these very premature babies will have been born at 22, 23 weeks, so they are severely undercooked. They are moved to the NICU as soon as they are born and put on antibiotics immediately – gentamicin and penicillin – because they basically do not have an immune system at this point.'

'And they survive?'

'Many of them do.' A nod. 'There are often long-term problems, of course, but they do survive.'

The little group had paused outside a ward, peering in through a glass panel. The big room was claustrophobic with equipment, and there was a sink at each bed. A nurse was washing her hands at one of these basins, moving with rehearsed precision. Her movements were almost balletic: every gesture designed to reduce risk and increase the frail chance of life. The ward was quiet, the silence expectant.

'Four to a ward in intensive care,' said Professor Jalali rapidly. 'We used to have six babies on each, but we reduced it because of the infection risk.'

Casey stared through the glass panel, shocked. There were three babies in this room, each child just a few inches long. These were tiny scraps of humanity, clinging on to life. Little kernels of human beings.

In the bed nearest the glass panel, a couple was sitting beside the incubator. They were both grey with exhaustion, bent like trees in a hurricane. Two gloves, bulky and awkward, extended into the incubator. The mother was stroking the baby very gently.

'But they're so small,' Casey exclaimed.

The baby in the incubator was fragile and wrinkled, translucent as a baby bird. Not quite formed, but perfect. An impossibly miniature human being.

'Sometimes when the babies are born,' the nurse said quietly, 'the mothers are very ill too. The preemies are brought here, but the mother can't be moved. We take photographs, so the mothers can see their brand new baby. But we had to start putting biro pens next to the babies, because the mothers would see a perfectly formed child, and think there wasn't a problem. But with the biro in the picture, the mother can see that the baby is only a few inches longer than the pen.'

'We need to keep the parents informed,' said Professor Jalali. 'And we need to be realistic.'

Jalali walked on, passing the entrance to the special care unit. A baby was crying in special care, the sound a relief after the deadening silence of the NICU.

On the intensive care reception desk, Casey could see a white candle in a small jar. Beside the candle, there was a small sign.

If this candle is burning, parents are saying goodbye to their child. Please be quiet, so they can say goodbye in peace.

'Right.' Professor Jalali sat down at her desk. 'Do you have any other questions?'

She had dispensed with the nurse with a few crisp instructions, the nurse hurrying at her words. Now she sat forward, eyes on Casey.

Jalali was short with long black hair tied in a tight bun. Her hair was thick, shiny, a few wiry white hairs sticking out disregarded. In her sixties, her skin was a polished dark brown, and her intelligence almost visible, like a quiver in the room. She moved with economic motions, every action purposeful.

Jalali gave off an air of intense morality, thought Casey. Not puritanical, but profoundly principled.

'I'm actually interested,' Casey looked straight at the professor, 'in the work of Zac Napier.'

Jalali's eyes focused sharply. 'I haven't heard that name for a few years. You know he trained here, of course. I taught him for several years.'

'I'm interested in the work he was doing in America.'

Professor Jalali leaned back in her chair. 'I was also interested in the work he was doing in America. But then it all went quiet.'

'Do you know why?'

'No.' Jalali put her chin on her hands. 'Do you?'

'I do not,' said Casey. 'I am trying to find out.'

'I have not spoken to Zac for at least two years,' said Jalali. 'Have you spoken to him?' For a second, Casey was caught off guard. 'Interesting,' Jalali nodded. 'Where is he now?'

'Why would they have shut down work on Corax?'

'Is that what it's called? It could be any number of reasons,' said Jalali. 'Often with antibiotics, everything starts off looking positive, but then things go awry.'

'Why?'

'Well,' said Jalali. 'An antibiotic isn't much use if it kills Enterobacter, but also stops your kidneys functioning. Or if it fixes your UTI, but sends you blind. Or you may find that there will be insuperable problems in producing mass quantities of your new antibiotic. Then, of course, if it turns out that the drug has to be given intravenously rather than swallowed in pill format, you're looking at a hospital stay, and for billions of people around the world, that is simply not feasible.'

'Anything else?'

'Antibiotics are tricky things,' said Jalali. 'Another thing that Colindale has to check is whether a new drug will trigger resistance too quickly. Bacteria will inevitably find a way around a new drug, and if it will happen too fast, it's not a good idea to use it widely.'

'I see. Do you think that happened with Corax?'

'It's impossible to know.'

'And Zac never told you about it?'

'I know he was excited about his work,' said Jalali. 'But he had signed an NDA with Pergamex, and couldn't tell us anything. He enjoyed teasing us, I think. Have you looked into that Pergamex company?'

'Garrick McElroy, the chief executive, is based in the US.'

'You haven't got very far then.'

'No.' Resigned.

'The problem with the pharmaceutical industry,' said Jalali, 'is that it could be almost anything. It could be that another company didn't like what Pergamex was discovering, and incentivised them to stop.'

'That happens?'

'Oh, yes.' Jalali's eyes gleamed. 'If, for example, a young scientist is carrying out research on the material used to make artificial hips, and another company who manufactures their own artificial hips doesn't like the look of the new data emerging, the hip manufacturer might miraculously find the funding for the scientist to investigate something else. The original research is left unfinished, and that's that. It gets buried, essentially.'

'Could that have happened here? Someone said that Adsero might have raised a patent issue with Pergamex.'

'There is a link to Adsero in all this?'

'I think so. It's not clear.'

'They are known to be ruthless,' said Jalali. 'But brilliant.'

'So it might be a patent issue?'

'It is possible.' Jalali stared at her fingers. They were roughened from years of antibacterial handwashing. 'Patents are constantly being used to block research. It is a scandal.'

'It seems bizarre.'

'It is deeply frustrating for doctors. But then the pharmaceutical companies invest millions in research, so ... ' A shrug. 'We do know that there are major issues with resistance to Adsero's zentetra now. And possibly because of that, Adsero is trying to develop their new antibiotic. But I've heard there are problems with that drug too.'

'Saepio?'

'I think that's what they've called it.'

Casey thought about Bailey's instantaneous, uncontrollable rage. Maybe it was stress, she thought, over a failing new drug. And they'd interpreted it as anger.

'It could be almost anything then, Professor Jalali?'

'Yes, it could,' she said soberly. 'I am sorry I cannot be more helpful.'

'Did you try and get hold of Zac? After he left Pergamex.'

'Once or twice. But we are very busy here, Casey.' Jalali waved a hand around the sparse room. 'And the problems are only getting worse.'

As they had walked around earlier, a nurse had pointed out an empty ward, mothballed for lack of funding.

'I can ask around about Corax, if it would help?' Jalali offered. 'And Adsero.'

Casey looked straight at the doctor. 'Did you know Professor Brennan, at Colindale?'

'Yes, we worked together in Oxford for a while, years ago, and I always enjoyed his company. I attended his funeral, of course.'

'I can't be sure,' Casey said slowly, 'that Professor Brennan's accident wasn't connected to Corax. Or it might be connected to me in some strange way. I don't know, but it's important that you know that there may be a risk in asking questions about Adsero and Corax. That traffic crash may have been an accident – that is certainly what the police think – but they still haven't found out who was driving the car. It is possible, Professor Jalali, that just asking about Corax could be dangerous.'

Jalali gave her a long look. 'Are there any links between Adsero and Ernest Brennan?'

'Brennan and Bailey would have been at Cambridge at the same time,' said Casey. 'Brennan was a couple of years older, but they could have met there. And, of course, they've both been connected to the pharmaceutical industry for years.'

Casey remembered Brennan's face as he answered the phone. That avuncular smile disappearing.

'You could draw similar connections between Brennan and me, I suppose,' said Jalali. 'And Bailey and me. There aren't so many of us, working in this field.'

'Yes. I won't run any article about the neonatal unit until I am sure it won't put you at any risk.'

'I see.' Jalali's eyes never flickered. 'Do you have a phone number for Zac Napier?'

'I do. And he goes by the name of Daniel Richmond now.'

'Please give it to me.'

Casey read out the number. 'Did you like Zac?' she asked.

'He had an exceptional mind, and there was a lot of good about him.' Jalali allowed herself a small smile. 'But it was better for morale among the nurses when he left.'

'I can imagine.'

'As a doctor,' Jalali said slowly, 'every time you prescribe an antibiotic, you have to debate: is your moral duty to this patient or to future generations? The runaway train, and you're at the points.'

A buzzer rang, and Jalali stood up. Casey stood too. 'Thank you for your time, Professor.'

'A pleasure,' said Jalali. 'I will call you if I can think of anything else.'

'I'm very grateful.'

'I hope you find out what happened to this Corax,' said Jalali, abruptly serious. 'In a few years' time – not many at all – the world will be desperate for a new antibiotic. You need to understand that millions and millions of lives will depend on it.'

26

'How are you going to get to Garrick McElroy?' asked Miranda.

'It's certainly a tricky one.' Casey's eyes were glued to her screen. 'Hang on, just filing an interview with the Health Secretary for the Saturday paper.'

Casey typed a few more words and sent the article through to the newsdesk with a sigh.

'What are you going in on?' asked Miranda.

'I'm interested in the Right Hon. Colette Warwick's links to the City,' said Casey. 'But features have decided that the topline is her Juniper loyalty card. She's been photographed wearing a pair of red Juniper stilettos for the article. You can only imagine the excitement. Cressida is even doing a sidebar.'

Cressida was the fashion editor, who rolled her eyes at Casey's occasional requests for assistance.

'But of course.'

'It's all a question,' sighed Casey, 'of perspective.'

'Well, those stilettos are probably the only thing anyone will remember about Colette Warwick, anyway.'

'True.'

'So what are your options with McElroy?' asked Miranda.

'Garrick McElroy's got to come to me,' said Casey. 'From what Noah's told me, he prefers the chase.'

'So you're casting bread upon the waters.'

'Exactly.' Casey reached for her phone. 'Which reminds me.'

She sent a quick text message.

'Was that to McElroy?'

'It was. Garrick matched with Madison three weeks ago on Tinder,' said Casey. 'They've been chatting ever since.'

'And who,' Miranda sighed, 'is Madison?'

'Me in a blonde wig with blue contact lenses.' Casey showed Miranda a couple of photographs. 'And a lot of make-up. Photoshopped a bit by the picture desk.'

'I would not recognise you,' Miranda examined the screen in awe. 'Why don't you just go in as Madison?'

'I don't think Madison would get much out of McElroy,' said Casey. 'Madison just finds out where he's going to be and when. And what he's like. She's very useful at building up intel is old Maddie.'

'How did you get him to match with Madison in the first place? I thought Tinder operated off your location.'

'When Evie was up in San Fran,' Casey said airily, 'she logged into Tinder as Madison and went and stood outside McElroy's house in Pacific Heights till he logged in as well.'

Evie was the *Post*'s West Coast correspondent. She was based in Los Angeles, but flew up to San Francisco on a regular basis to report on the tech scene.

'How long did poor Evie have to stand outside his house?'

'About five minutes,' said Casey. 'Noah was right. McElroy is definitely a player.'

'But can't he tell you're logging in from London now?' asked Miranda. 'Doesn't Tinder show how far you are from someone?'

'Madison is in London for work now,' Casey explained. 'To be honest, that's how she's been able to keep chatting to McElroy for so long. It gives her an aura of inaccessibility that might otherwise be lacking, quite frankly.'

Casey's phone buzzed again.

'Garrick's going to be in Miami next week for another round of fundraising,' Casey read aloud. 'He's trying to raise money for some oil deal. I think it might be time for a few more breadcrumbs.'

A couple of hours later, Maurice Delacroix telephoned Casey, sounding almost angry.

'Casey, your wretched business desk is asking questions about my Monet.'

'Which Monet?'

'Don't play games with me, Casey. The one in the Freeport.'

'I don't know anything about the Monet in the Freeport.'

'Tell them to bloody stop.'

'I can't, Maurice. I don't have any control over what the business desk gets up to.'

'Casey.'

'It is odd that you should call, though, Maurice. I was just about to ring you. I wanted to ask a favour.'

'What a very fortuitous coincidence, Casey.'

'Just think how lucky it is that the business desk don't know about the Picasso, Maurice. Or the Van Gogh.'

'Casey.'

'Or even the diamond mine.'

Delacroix was a fixer. He had started trading in oil years ago, when the industry was based on a nod for a pipeline and a handshake for a cargo of crude. As he built his fortune, his business interests – and network – widened.

Casey had met him in Monaco, when they were both on the hunt. They had been friends immediately, and traded secrets like toys.

'What is this favour then, Casey?' There was a laugh now behind the slight French accent.

'It's not so much a favour, Maurice, as a little investment advice.'

'And you'll have a word with your business desk.'

'Well, they do sit directly opposite me.'

'By the way, Casey, I have a little property development in a ski resort in Colorado. It's about ready for a bit of publicity in the *Post*.'

'Of course, Maurice. But first … '

27

Now Delacroix prowled through the huge living room and out to the vast balcony.

'This is an amazing house,' said Casey.

'It belongs to a friend of mine,' Delacroix gestured. 'Moldovan.'

The waterfront mansion sat on one of the most exclusive islands in Miami, close to the golden sizzle of South Beach. Built in the art deco style, the sprawling villa mimicked Ocean Drive's knowing sparkle but included every billionaire requirement from cinema room to recording studio. Staff in white polo shirts and camel-coloured chino shorts darted about discreetly.

'They brought that sand in from the Bahamas.' Delacroix nodded down at the pink beach in front of the house. 'Christ, I hate Miami.'

Delacroix's deep-set black eyes glowered at the palm trees. He was tall, tanned, and always beautifully dressed. His voice was English public school with the occasional French syllable. Like Casey, he could draw the eye or fade into a crowd, depending on his mood.

'Don't worry,' soothed Casey. 'You'll be back in Lyford Cay soon enough.'

She had known that Delacroix retreated to his Bahamas home at this time of year. And also that he got bored easily. He would probably have flown the hour to Miami even without the mention of the Monet.

'Remind me who this man is again?' Delacroix sighed.

It had been easy for Madison to work out who McElroy was meeting in Florida. McElroy enjoyed boasting to pretty blondes, it turned out.

Delacroix had read through the list of McElroy's investors dismissively. 'I know him,' he sighed. 'And him. And he really owes me.'

A couple of phone calls later, one of McElroy's potential investors was putting a hefty sum into Delacroix's property development in Colorado. The investor had also promised to give Delacroix a heads-up if he heard about opportunities in energy or pharma. 'Give them my number,' Delacroix added. 'I'm stuck in bloody Miami for a few days anyway.'

When exactly, Casey wondered idly, listening in, did oil companies become energy companies?

Now Delacroix smiled at Casey. 'It sounds like your man has burned through any payout he got pretty fast, and he's on the lookout for investors. Idiot. It's easy to make money.' Delacroix lay down on one of the sunloungers and pulled his Panama hat over his eyes. 'The secret is to hold on to it.'

A couple of hours later, Delacroix's phone buzzed.

'Yes?' his voice was bored. 'Sure. Yes.'

Delacroix rattled off the address and hung up. He turned to Casey. 'Your man's on his way.'

Garrick McElroy sauntered into the mansion.

'This is a great place you've got here.' He waved at the panorama of downtown Miami, across the sparkle of the bay. 'And it's so great to meet you, Mr Delacroix. I've heard a lot about your work in Africa.'

'Thank you,' Delacroix nodded. 'Drink?'

McElroy was tall and blond and aware of his own good looks. The voice was English, an American twang overlaid. He had a slightly weak mouth, Casey thought. Laughed too often.

A flash of a thought: Ed, and a smile that glinted for an instant.

She forced herself to focus.

'A beer would be great,' McElroy nodded.

Delacroix had been sitting at a small table beside the vast swimming pool. Now McElroy threw himself into a chair opposite him, all athletic confidence.

Dressed in a white polo shirt and camel shorts, with a baseball cap pulled down over her nose, Casey brought them both beers. The rest of the staff had been given the day off. Casey then retired inconspicuously to the bar on the other side of the swimming pool, where she polished a couple of glasses before bending her head over the crossword in the *Miami Herald*. McElroy barely glanced at her.

'No cameras in this house,' Delacroix had said firmly before Casey even left for Miami. 'No recording equipment. Nothing.'

'OK.'

'You just listen to what he has to say. And none of this ever connects to me. You don't use anything at all unless it could have come from somewhere else, OK?'

'Of course not, Maurice.'

Within minutes Delacroix was grilling McElroy about his CV. 'My researcher looked into you,' Delacroix began, smiling thinly.

After ripping apart McElroy's first venture, a tech company based in San Francisco, Delacroix moved on to the two property businesses McElroy had founded in Canada.

McElroy was on the back foot now, trying to charm before being forced back again. He started to sound defensive, the voice almost a whine. From a distance, Casey admired Delacroix's onslaught. McElroy had arrived a glossy jock, but the insecurities were rapidly being laid bare. The players were always insecure underneath it all. Casey made busy notes around the crossword puzzle.

'And then,' Delacroix dropped both his palms on the table, 'we get to this little pharmaceutical company Pergamex.'

'Pergamex was really positive—'

'It wasn't,' said Delacroix flatly. 'It never did anything.'

'It did.'

'Where?' Delacroix threw his hands in the air. 'I can only see Pergamex losing money.'

'It was complicated,' said McElroy.

'Impossible.' Delacroix pronounced it the French way. 'I'm not going to invest in your company if I don't understand how you do business, Garrick.'

'You just have,' McElroy tried the charm again, 'to take my word for it.'

'I don't take anyone's word for anything,' Delacroix said darkly. 'Not these days.'

McElroy was silent for a few minutes, watching a yacht cruise past the island, music blaring.

'I'm sorry.' Delacroix made to stand. 'But I don't think I can invest in this venture, after all. I wish you all the best with it, Garrick. I think it has some exciting prospects, but … '

Standing at the bar, Casey pressed a button on her mobile. Delacroix's phone rang.

'One moment please.' Delacroix picked up his phone, and walked away from the table.

McElroy stayed at the table, his eyes on the Miami skyline. After a minute, Casey picked up a tray and walked over to the table. As she walked, she felt a surge of adrenalin.

What if he knows? What if he can tell you're a lie?

Don't be ridiculous. It was a scream in her head. *This is nothing.*

But the tray was shaking. Her feet were clumsy as if the ground were suddenly uneven: tripping on a raked stage. She forced herself to breathe slowly, eyes on the paving stones. Nearly at the table now.

'It's a beautiful day, isn't it?' Casey said quietly, as she approached.

The words sounded rehearsed, anxious. But it didn't matter. She was a white polo shirt, a pair of camel shorts. She was nothing.

McElroy looked up at her, almost surprised. 'It is.'

'Can I get you another beer, sir?' The adrenalin was easing now. She was deferential, forgettable: big sunglasses and dark hair tied up under her baseball cap. McElroy would never connect her to the bubbly, perky Madison.

'A beer would be great, thanks.'

Casey retrieved another bottle from the bar, and opened it. McElroy was still staring into space, dark brown eyes glazed over.

'He's a great boss.' McElroy looked up in surprise as Casey spoke.

'He's certainly quite a character.' McElroy was fiddling with the bottle, peeling away the label.

'He is. But he's also a great boss. He has our backs, always.'

Casey picked up the used glasses and disappeared back towards the bar. A couple of moments later, Delacroix reappeared.

'I am sorry to keep you waiting, Garrick. But as I said … '

'There was a side deal,' McElroy interrupted him. 'We had an amazing new drug, and we sold off the rights.'

Delacroix sat down again slowly. 'Sold them off to whom?'

28

'I can't believe you invested in McElroy's bloody oil company,' Casey stormed afterwards. 'I'm going to put him in jail.'

'Yeah, yeah,' Delacroix shrugged. 'I priced that in.'

'But the company will collapse when I do.'

'You may not manage to put him in jail. And the company owns some excellent rights in central Africa, either way.' Delacroix stretched. 'And my lawyers can make sure that if he goes to jail, someone ends up with those rights.'

'I hope you lose your money.'

'I won't, Cassandra.' He raised his glass to her in a mock salute. 'I never do.'

'Do you know anything about a company called Adsero?' Casey asked later, as they ate stone crabs by the pool.

'Elias Bailey?' Delacroix's eyes were sharp. 'A bit, sure.'

At a certain level, Casey thought, they all knew each other.

'What's he like?'

'Very tough.' Delacroix nodded appreciatively, 'And very clever. He made Adsero into what it is today. I heard that one of their heart drugs – they've sold millions of dollars' worth of it – came about because he had heart trouble, so he put every Adsero scientist on finding a cure, and they ended up creating a brilliant new drug. That's what he's like, I guess. Solves his problems *and* makes a fortune.'

'He had a transplant in the end, though.'

'Yes,' Delacroix said. 'When he needed it. He's known to be a ruthless man, Casey. I wouldn't cross him if I were you.'

Casey picked at the crab and changed the subject. 'How the hell did Garrick McElroy end up with a load of African oil rights anyway? It doesn't make any sense.'

'Apparently he bought them,' Delacroix shrugged.

'Thanks.' Casey gave him a quick grin. 'I'll give you a byline for all this.'

'Don't,' Delacroix shuddered, 'even joke.'

Casey flew back to London that evening. She hadn't asked Dash for permission to fly to Miami, just told Ross that as health editor she was going to a Wellbeing and Spiritual Wellness Conference over the weekend. Ross, in the middle of trying to recruit yet another night editor, had nodded vaguely. She hadn't mentioned that the conference was in Miami.

Delacroix gave her a lift to the airport.

'Remember,' he kissed her hand goodbye, 'to have a word with your business desk about the Monet.'

'Did you know,' Casey grumbled, 'that there is art worth $100 billion in the Geneva Freeport? It would be the greatest museum in the world, and no one ever gets to see a single painting.'

'It is a true tragedy.'

'Your ex-wife does seem quite interested in the Monet's whereabouts, by the way.'

'A wonderful woman,' Delacroix sighed. 'But she'll have to settle for the Bonnard.'

Miranda dropped her head into her hands.

'You went *where* for the weekend?'

'You knew Garrick was going to be in Miami,' protested Casey. 'Anyway, I needed some sun. Plus I got three decent lines out of the Wellbeing and Spiritual Wellness Conference. I even filed 700 thrilling words on numerology to Cressida.'

'Numer-what? You didn't do any undercover stuff, did you?'

'No,' Casey said aloud. Barely, she thought.

'You mustn't,' said Miranda. 'Not for a while, Casey. It's not good for you.'

'Sure.'

'And do consider my budget, please? Dash almost cried over last month's figures.'

'Yes, ma'am.'

'So the rights to Corax were transferred to some random British Virgin Islands company.' Miranda was reading Casey's notes again.

'Yes.' Casey bit her lip. 'Garrick really didn't seem to know anything else about it.'

'Can you find out anything more about this company?' Miranda asked. 'Slopeside Inc.'

'Slope side is a skiing term.' Casey made a hopeless gesture. 'Apparently. It doesn't mean anything to me, and I can't work out who any of the shareholders or the real directors are either.'

'Doesn't take you much further then, does it?'

'No,' Casey said. She was exhausted from the overnight flight. 'It doesn't.'

Ross appeared at the door. 'Casey, I need 500 words on that big medical trial in north London. The one that went wrong. Get on with it, yeah?'

'Sure, Ross.' Casey stalked to the door. 'Sure.'

The days rolled past. Casey ignored Christmas, barely aware of the glitter, the giggles, the fun.

To Wiltshire, her calendar announced a few days before Christmas, and she crossed it out until the square was a black blur.

The *Post* Christmas party was the usual disaster, enlivened by the new night editor getting off with one of the fashion writers.

'He's the most attractive man on the newsdesk,' said the fashion writer dreamily.

'Rarely have I heard fainter praise,' muttered the home affairs editor.

The next morning Eric, the junior reporter, was so hungover that he fell asleep on the Islington doorstep of an MP caught speeding after six glasses of mulled wine. Ross spotted him in the background of a BBC News live broadcast and took a taxi straight to Highbury.

'He didn't even stop the cab,' Eric said woefully in the Plumbers later. 'Just hurled his notepad at me as the taxi shot past.'

'Another mulled wine?' the home affairs editor asked, as he scrolled through the gleeful Papercut article. 'They've spelled your name wrong, Eric.'

'We have now been banned from every restaurant within a two-mile radius,' grumbled the newsdesk secretary. 'You can sodding organise it yourselves next year.'

Miranda came round to Casey's flat on Christmas Eve.

'I miss Tom.' Her husband: this Christmas, he was posting photographs of a pile of presents, matching dressing gowns, a pretty girl sitting by a fire.

Rebecca. *Becky.*

They peered at Instagram together.

'You don't miss him,' Casey said soothingly. 'You just worry that you should.'

'It's odd seeing her like that. Next to him.'

Early on in Miranda's suspicions, they had found the sleek grey website: Becky from business development, in pearl earrings and a neat black jacket. In the corporate photograph, she had looked up at the camera, so friendly. Tilted head, highlighted hair, coy little smile.

The same smile in every photograph, Casey noticed, as they scrolled. It made it look as if she had been superimposed on to a series of backdrops.

'She's like a doll brought to life,' Miranda snapped. 'Everywhere you look.'

'She's precisely the sort of person,' Casey zoomed in on Becky eating a cupcake, that same smile, 'who quotes *Love Actually* as the start of the grand romance.'

'Something, something, saying it at Christmas … ' And Miranda was laughing, at last. 'Yuk. And I never imagined Tom on bloody Instagram.'

She looks happy though, Casey thought. He looks happy.

'I'm sorry to go on about it,' said Miranda. 'When you're … '

'Don't be silly.'

But Casey heard the sadness roar, a wave crashing on the beach, again, and again.

'Are you OK?' Miranda's eyes were sympathetic.

'I don't know how to describe it,' Casey said quietly. 'It feels as if I am living the echo of the life we might have had. This is how it might have been. And this is how it is. Running in parallel, and it feels as if I am trapped in the wrong version.'

'Oh, Casey.'

Casey spent Christmas Day on the sofa, under a blanket, eating chocolate and biscuits and waiting for it all to be over. And she volunteered to work the night shift on New Year's Eve, as dawn chased the fireworks around the globe.

And then, one morning in early January, the phone on Casey's desk rang.

'Casey Benedict,' she said listlessly.

'Casey Benedict from the *Post*?' There was a laugh in the voice.

She sat up. 'Is that—'

'Yes.' He cut her off. 'Can you meet me?'

'Where?'

'My favourite place, of course.'

29

Casey walked cautiously down the aisle of St Paul's. Black and white, the aisle stretched out in front of her. The cathedral soared above with that strange, frozen majesty.

In black, though she might have worn white.

Casey walked on, and paused, walked on, and paused, peering around. Anyone would hesitate here, mesmerised by the baroque glory. Amid the bustle of the city, the cathedral was nearly empty. There was a scattering of tourists, a school group traipsing around, an elderly woman praying in a pew, a plastic bag at her feet.

Jewelled rainbows through a stained glass window …

Now Casey was beneath the dome, a gilded false heaven glistening far, far above.

No Zac.

She moved awkwardly to a pew, sat down.

She briefly considered religion as a pandemic. Touching, spreading, killing. And then from somewhere in the distance, she heard a scattering of notes, and a slow ripple of magic. Somewhere, someone was rehearsing on the organ.

No Zac. Casey stood up, and wandered around the great cathedral again. She looked into the little chapels. Nothing. She headed down into the crypt, a long-buried secret. Nothing. She stared up at the organ. There was a woman practising, head down, all her focus on the keys. No.

And at last, Casey saw a narrow flight of stairs, and climbed.

Quite suddenly, she was out in the daylight. A winter sun poured through the long windows, light on light, gold on gilt. All at once, the huge dome seemed close enough to touch, exquisitely painted and oddly intimate.

A gallery ran around the inside of the huge dome, the white statues gazing down blindly. Casey walked to the edge of the gallery, glanced over, and felt the void hook into her stomach. It was a hundred feet down to that black and white floor, but the view was almost hypnotic.

And there was only one figure up here, a tall, dark shape on the opposite side of the gallery. Relief flooded Casey.

Zac.

She stepped to her left to make her way around him, and he immediately stepped to his right.

A step to her right, and he stepped left again.

Stop playing games, she thought, irritated.

A step to the left, and another step to the right.

And then she heard it, the whisper.

'I knew you'd guess.' Zac's words reached Casey effortlessly.

They were in the Whispering Gallery, Casey remembered: an eccentric little quirk of the grand, old cathedral. By a fluke of physics, the tiniest sound travelled effortlessly around this round, empty space, the quietest whisper echoing from one side of the dome to the other. She almost laughed, then whispered back.

'It was obvious, you know.'

'I know. Did you come alone?'

'I did.'

'Good.' Across the hundred feet of nothing, she could see that he was smiling. 'Because anyone could be listening.'

She watched him waiting for her in the little park. He wandered around the small space, apparently aimlessly, and then sat down on a bench. Next to the bench, the snowdrops were tiny green knives, slicing up through the winter chill. For a moment Casey hesitated, feeling shy, awkward, almost embarrassed by her mistakes in Mauritius, but then she squared her shoulders and marched towards him.

'Very melodramatic,' she said. 'Back in the gallery.'

'You never know.'

Casey glanced around. This bench was in a corner of Postman's Park, just to the north of St Paul's. Whispering into the cathedral quiet, she had suggested they meet here in half an hour, both taking circuitous routes around the City.

'Did anyone follow you?' Casey asked.

'There definitely wasn't anyone behind me in the coffee queue.' He handed her an espresso.

'Can you stop taking the piss?'

'Probably not.'

She wondered how worried he was, really. He was impossible to make out.

'All right.' Casey put the coffee on the ground next to the bench. 'What do you want, Zac?'

And there it was, the flicker in his eyes. Not so relaxed after all.

'Have you … ?' He stopped.

'What?'

A robin was flitting round the bench, bobbing for the end of a sandwich. A larger bird landed next to it, and the robin squared up, tiny chest puffed out ludicrously.

Zac was staring across the little park.

'"The Memorial to Heroic Self-Sacrifice",' he read aloud. 'Not really my sort of thing, you know, Casey? Self-sacrifice.'

Casey had been five minutes late, on purpose. As she watched him, she had wondered if he was glancing at the Victorian tiles, sideways, fleetingly. The expression on his face was unreadable.

'"Harry Sisley of Kilburn, aged 10, drowned in attempting to save his brother after he himself had just been rescued May 24 1878."'

Mrs Sisley, and her howl of grief, echoing down the centuries.

'"Amelia Kennedy, aged 19, died in trying to save her sister from their burning house in Edward's Lane, Stoke Newington Oct 18 1871."'

A quiet, instinctive self-sacrifice.

For a moment, Casey's mind was full of Ed, the memory a burn.

We were in this field of maize. And I suddenly realised there were too many of them. Taliban. And I had to cover the others, my men, so they could get out. I had to stay behind. In this endless field of maize. And I just thought, 'I'm going to die. I am going to die now.' It felt so simple suddenly. I don't know … I still don't know how I got out …

He only spoke about it once. Never realised others mightn't. That others wouldn't.

'"Samuel Rabbath"', the cynicism in Zac's voice jerked her back to the little park. He was reading aloud from one of the ceramic tiles. '"Medical officer of the Royal Free Hospital who tried to save a child suffering from diphtheria at the cost of his own life October 26 1884". Is that what you're after, Casey Benedict from the *Post*? Your very own heroic tile on a wall?'

Casey turned towards his profile, raising an eyebrow.

'Is that what you're offering, Zac?'

The robin hopped nearer, all impudence. Casey waited.

'This lot would all be dead by now anyway.' He gestured at the wall. 'Years ago. Long gone, and forgotten.'

'But they're not forgotten, are they?'

'I suppose not. Can't little Noah Hart help you out then? He's always so keen to help. He's the classic teacher's pet, that man.'

'I'm sure Noah would.' Casey made her voice deliberately callous, 'But his sister was killed shortly after he left Pergamex, so he's not really in a position to help anyone right now.'

It silenced Zac, as she had intended. She heard him breathe out.

'This isn't about Corax.' Zac broke the silence. 'Me being here. I am never going to tell you about Corax, you understand?'

'OK. I'll probably still ask though.'

'Fine.'

'"Ellen Donovan of Lincoln Court, Great Wild Street"', Zac was procrastinating again, reading aloud from another tile. '"Rushed into a burning house to save a neighbour's children and perished in the flames."'

'Zac—'

'Adsero have two main antibiotics on their books.' Zac cut her off, as if it hadn't been him hesitating. 'Zentetra and a new one called saepio, that hasn't been released yet.'

'I know that,' said Casey. 'And hospitals are seeing increased resistance to zentetra. But they hope that saepio is going to plug the gap.'

'Indeed.'

'And, separately, as the coronavirus crisis proved beyond all reasonable doubt, a medical disaster that starts in one country takes exactly the same time as a flight to reach us. So a catastrophically resistant superbug in, say, Nairobi, is only ever just over nine hours from central London.'

'Zac,' Casey was growing impatient, 'what are you talking about?'

'"Thomas Simpson",' he recited. '"Died of exhaustion after saving many lives from the breaking ice at Highgate Ponds, Jan 25 1885."'

'Yes, Zac. I know.'

He turned to her, serious at last. 'But what do you know,' he said quietly, 'about drug dumping?'

30

'Drug dumping?' Casey blinked. 'I don't think I know anything about it at all.'

'Not many people do.'

Casey sat quietly, watching the robin and waiting. 'All right. What is it?'

'When there is a disaster … ' Once he started talking, Zac spoke fast, 'Anywhere in the world, you see appeals, right? On TV, in the newspapers. For earthquakes, floods, war, whatever. Starving children, huge eyes. Especially if it's happening in one of the poorer parts of the world, you see the big appeals everywhere.'

'Yes.' Casey nodded slowly.

'Well, quite often pharmaceutical companies will respond to those appeals,' said Zac. 'And send medicines off to the crisis. It looks good, after all. It looks public-spirited. It shows you *care*.'

'Sure.'

'You can see how it made sense originally,' said Zac. 'Pharma companies have got the medicines to hand, and someone else needs them desperately, so why not encourage them to donate drugs in times of disaster? Plus it's often difficult to manage cash donations in a crisis situation, for all sorts of reasons. So if there is a need for a certain product, why not just take donations directly from the drug companies?'

'Why not, indeed?' said Casey.

'Quite,' Zac said. 'The drug companies get the good publicity and the photogenic earthquake victims get the drugs.'

'Everyone's a winner.'

'Well,' said Zac, 'not exactly.'

'Why not?'

Zac paused again, watching the robin scuffle a crisp packet. Casey waited.

'The thing is,' he said slowly, 'that for years, US drug companies received tax breaks for those donations.'

'What do you mean?'

'Pharmaceutical companies work out how much a drug costs to make, and how much it would theoretically have cost on the open market,' explained Zac. 'Then a proportion of that amount is knocked off the company's tax bill. Quite a big proportion, actually. And if you don't have to pay $10 million in taxes, that's basically the same as an extra $10 million in profit. The bottom line doesn't care where the money actually comes from.'

'And so what happens? With the dumping?'

'Well, pharmaceutical companies started sending stuff in response to the appeals, and then they immediately claimed the money back off their tax bill. Sometimes, they were really sending stuff that was desperately needed on the ground, but quite often, they sent whatever they had to hand. Unfortunately, that meant that mountains of drugs and equipment were dispatched for years, and tonnes of it was completely useless. Breast implants were sent to Malawi. After the huge tsunami in 2004, Indonesia was left with tonnes of cough syrup. Slimming products were sent to Sudan, for God's sake, in the middle of a famine. And all along, the companies were claiming the tax breaks.'

'But that doesn't make any sense.'

'It is madness. And on top of that,' Zac said, 'for years, there were no checks on the use-by dates of the drugs at all. So millions of doses of these drugs would be sent off when they were already past their expiry date, and that freed up lots of nice, expensive warehouse space back in the States. The added beauty for the drugs companies is that it costs money to dispose of even useless drugs properly. You can't just pour them down the drain. But all of a sudden pharma companies could pack them up and send them off, and claim the tax break. During the Eritrean war of independence, it apparently took six months to burn all the out-of-date aspirin sent by donors. And on top of all that, because of the rules around transporting drugs, once the useless pills have been dispatched from the US, you can't send them home again. During the nineties, 17,000 tonnes of useless drugs were sent to Bosnia.'

'But … ' Casey was lost for words.

'And furthermore,' Zac's mouth twisted ironically, 'the drugs would be shipped off with no instructions in the relevant language, no packaging, nothing. Aid workers, who were already up to their eyeballs in chaos, would then have to decide whether or not to try and use the drugs. A sort of pharmaceutical Russian Roulette. At one point, eleven women in Lithuania were temporarily blinded because a doctor guessed what a pill was, and it actually turned out to be something that was meant to be used on animals.'

Casey found that her coffee had gone cold. 'That's insane.'

'I suppose the thing is,' Zac said, 'it's easy to convince yourself that something is better than nothing. And no one in the real world understands tax breaks anyway, because your readers just glaze over and go on to the next thing.'

'Maybe.'

'The other thing is,' Zac was watching the robin, hopping to and fro, 'it wasn't just implants and slimming pills they were packing up.'

'What else were they sending?'

'They also sent antibiotics.'

31

Mary Rogers Stewardess of the Stella, Mar 30, 1899, self sacrificed by giving up her life belt and voluntarily going down in the sinking ship.

Henry James Bristow, aged eight – at Walthamstow, on December 30 1890 – saved his little sister's life by tearing off her flaming clothes but caught fire himself and died of burns and shock.

'Which antibiotics?' Casey asked quietly. 'And where were they sent?'

'It happened a few times.'

'Tell me.'

'Well, back in 1994,' said Zac, 'there was the genocide in Rwanda. Hundreds of thousands of women were raped. Family after family massacred. There were probably a million dead.' Zac stared across at the old memorial wall. 'And the world did nothing until it was far too late.'

He stopped. The air was an icy blue, the rumble of the city all around them.

'I remember.'

'And after that, the war sprawled into what was then Zaire. The First Congo War.'

'What happened with antibiotics?'

'You'll have heard of Swann Hopkins?' Zac waited for Casey's nod. 'One of the biggest pharmaceutical companies in the world. And it happened to have millions of capsules of Garso parked in a warehouse. Garso's a second-generation ciprofloxacin and for whatever reason, Swann Hopkins had made 8 million doses of Garso with a different strength to their usual one, assuming that the FDA would wave through the new version. But as it turned out, the FDA was slow to approve the new dosage. So Swann Hopkins had this mountain of Garso just sitting in a warehouse in Idaho or wherever, getting closer and closer to its expiry date.'

The robin was hopping between the snowdrop blades now. 'Then what?' Casey asked.

'The war rumbled on. Millions of people ended up stuck in refugee camps, in absolutely horrendous conditions. As usual, an appeal went out, and at that point, Swann Hopkins got in touch with a charity, offering $50 million worth of Garso. Naturally, the charity bit their hand off, and off went the antibiotics.'

'Could the charity actually use Garso on the ground?'

'No, not really. You tend to use really basic antibiotics in refugee camps, because the testing facilities are either limited or completely non-existent. Ciprofloxacin isn't something you can just hand out randomly, either. You're meant to be really careful using a drug like Garso. And you can create antibiotic resistance quite quickly if you don't.'

'So what happened to the Garso that Swann Hopkins sent to the Congo?'

'A lot of it had to be destroyed, they think. But how do you ensure the security of millions of doses of an antibiotic in the chaos of a Congolese refugee camp? Especially when lots of the people stuck there would desperately need antibiotics, anyway.'

'And if you need antibiotics, and you've got antibiotics to hand ... '

'Exactly. And a few months later, Swann Hopkins got tens of millions of dollars back in tax rebates for its unuseable, unused Garso.'

They sat side by side on the bench. Casey's feet were blocks of ice.

'So how does all this connect to Adsero?'

Zac's eyes roamed around the park. His hands were fists on his knees.

'A few years later, a cyclone hit the east coast of Africa. Massive floods. Catastrophic flooding. Hundreds of thousands of people trapped in refugee camps, again. All the crops, everything washed away, again. The appeal went out, once more. And this time, Adsero responded.'

'What did they send?'

'Adsero sent millions and millions of doses of zentetra down to Mozambique. Apparently, there had been some deal to export it to the Middle East but that collapsed, so Adsero's US division was stuck with loads of this drug, and it was heading towards its expiry date. When the cyclone hit, they just loaded the zentetra on a plane and sent it off to Africa.'

'So tonnes of zentetra arrived in a refugee camp?'

'Yes, and then Adsero lost control of the shipment. Now the drug's turning up all over southern Africa.'

'And now what's happening?'

'I don't know,' Zac said bleakly. 'I have absolutely no idea. But I don't think it's good.'

32

'Hang on,' said Miranda. 'What does any of this have to do with Corax?'

'Zac won't talk to me about Corax,' Casey explained patiently. 'But he will talk more broadly about Adsero.'

'Why won't he talk about Corax?'

'I don't know.' Casey bit her lip.

'But he's saying that we can hit Adsero a different way?' said Miranda. 'By targeting them on dumping tonnes of zentetra into Mozambique?'

'I think Zac definitely wants to take out Adsero,' said Casey. 'But for whatever reason, he won't tell me about Corax. And presumably, he can't be linked to the zentetra problem in Africa, so he knows he can't be blamed if that ends up in the *Post*.'

'How much do these companies make out of the tax breaks?' asked Miranda.

'Millions,' said Casey. 'The taxpayer essentially funded these companies to dump their junk medicines into struggling countries. It was all out in the open, but because tax breaks sound tedious, no one pays them any attention. The WHO pushed back on it all, and the charities have got wiser to it all now, but it used to happen a lot. And in Adsero's case, the zentetra dumping seems to be triggering serious antibiotic resistance.'

Miranda shook her head slowly. 'How bad is the resistance in Africa now?'

'Antibiotic resistance is the silent pandemic,' Casey recited. 'That's what one of the doctors I spoke to called it. In his research in Zimbabwe, he found that 50 per cent of children in a hospital were carrying ESBL-producing bacteria. In the UK, those kids would be off in a side room, safely away from everyone else, with the doctors and nurses in full PPE. Over there, they're barely tested. Zentetra triggers the same sort of resistance to lots of antibiotics. Pan-resistance, they call it.'

'But they wouldn't do that on purpose ... '

'Wouldn't they?' snapped Casey. 'Look at what these companies get up to that we already know about. Cranking up the price of insulin. Cranking up the price of cancer drugs. Decades of promoting opioids, although they knew about the addiction risks. God knows what else. These companies are giants, and they make billions more every year. They're hugely powerful and they are absolutely ruthless.'

Miranda pondered. 'So what's the plan?'

'I'll try and convince Zac to fly out with me, to find out what is going on. The science is complicated, and he knows what he's looking for.'

'Will he go with you?'

'I don't know yet. But he could have just rung me up from Mauritius and told me this stuff. He says he was coming to London anyway, but I think he wants to get out there.'

'Casey,' Miranda said slowly, 'I really don't think it is a good idea.'

'It'll be fine,' said Casey. 'I'll be fine.'

'You don't know—'

Ross stuck his head around the investigations room door.

'Any chance of you filing any time soon, Casey?' The sarcasm was heavy. 'An extra 300 words on the care home crisis if it wouldn't interrupt your day too much.'

'You only need the extra words because you cut out the reference to DartCare,' Casey said pertly. 'They own over 400 homes and they've just cut the hourly rate for their care workers while paying out a massive dividend to the shareholders.'

'Yup,' said Ross. 'But then again, the chief executive is a very good friend of our owners, and I simply can't be arsed to start World War III for 800 words on CQC reports. Focus on Brightweather, OK?'

'Ross—'

'Get on with it, Casey.'

'This is a lovely reverse ferret on the Naji doping story, by the way.' Casey waved that day's *Post* at Ross rebelliously. The front page was a big photograph of the cyclist hugging his baby son. 'A real classic of the genre, I have to say. I so enjoyed hearing about his favourite cycling shorts and his lucky shamrock necklace. Heart-warming stuff. Really cutting-edge journalism.'

'Shut it,' Ross advised amiably.

He disappeared across the newsroom, pausing only to bawl at Eric. 'Unless you've got today in that sweepstake, you can stop dicking around too.'

'What sweepstake?' Eric stared at Ross's departing back. He glowered around the room. 'Is this about that Islington fuck-up? Are you bastards actually betting on when I'm going to be sacked? That's not bloody fair.'

'Oh, don't worry,' the home affairs editor said soothingly. 'It's not as if we're letting Ross get involved. That,' he finished primly, 'would be insider trading.'

'Git.'

'Shh,' said the home affairs editor. 'Can you at least *try* and hang on until a week on Thursday?'

A thought struck Eric. 'What day has Sophie gone for?'

The home affairs editor checked his notepad.

'Three weeks on Friday.'

'But that's so … ' Eric searched for the word, '*disloyal*.'

'Oh, I don't know,' the home affairs editor consulted his notepad again. 'All things considered, I'd say that was fairly devoted really.'

'Arse.'

'Fancy a bet yourself?' the home affairs editor asked chummily. 'There's still a couple of days available.'

Casey turned back to Miranda. 'I have to go.'

33

The pickup swerved around a pothole.

'Sorry,' Kizzie grinned back at them unrepentantly. 'Not far now.'

'You always drove like a lunatic,' Zac grumbled, clinging to a handle.

They were speeding down a wide street, past sprawling houses just peeking out over high crumbling walls. Wide verges – the patchy grass bleached by the sun – lined the road. The scale of these streets was spacious, generous. Elegant, even. But everywhere, there were signs of disintegration.

A collapsed road sign here, a gate dangling off its hinges there. On one corner, a burned-out house turned blind windows to the world. Jacaranda trees twined overhead, the branches tangling like dreams. In October, they would be a haze of purple, street after street of violet magic. These were the bones of a beautiful city.

'Welcome to Harare.' Kizzie dodged another pothole. 'Welcome to our chaos.'

Casey and Zac had abandoned the English winter for the Zimbabwean summer, stepping out of the plane into a muggy heat. Kizzie had met them at the airport, wrapping Zac in a hug. A doctor at one of the local hospitals, her pass and lanyard still dangled around her neck.

'Most of these houses have gardens of two or three acres.' Kizzie pointed, as she accelerated round a man pushing a handcart. 'And they're almost all a complete mess. That one there was seized by a government minister for his mistress.'

As Kizzie spoke, she veered to the right, pressing a button on the dashboard as she braked hard in front of tall electric gates. The gates creaked open unwillingly. They had been painted black, once, a long time ago. But the paint had peeled away, showing first a coat of dark green, and then a layer of maroon. On either side of the gates, eight-foot walls looked to be embedded with broken glass, and topped with razor wire.

'And here is Kewlake,' said Kizzie, as the car bounced down a narrow track, bushes scraping the paint. 'Lovely, lovely Kewlake.'

Kizzie parked the car under three huge mahogany trees that soared to the sky. Stepping out of the car was like tripping into an aviary, dozens of birds chirping, warbling, trilling. As Kizzie slammed her car door, an emerald turaco squawked away towards the gates.

The house lay beyond a wide stretch of what must once have been a lawn. Now it was a sea of grasses, layers and shades and ripples of a thousand different greens. The delicate msasa trees hesitated, like ballerinas posing at the end of a dance. To the left, Casey could see a termite nest, six feet high and seething with activity.

'Be careful that way.' Kizzie waved to the right. 'There's a swimming pool somewhere in the grass. God knows where.'

They walked up a stepping stone path that picked its way through the grasses, studded by giant marigolds. Kewlake itself was a long, low house, peering out from behind a row of cassias, its name in curlicues over the door. A wide verandah, held up by colonial pillars, wrapped itself around the house. The roof sagged.

'It's beautiful,' said Casey.

'It was, once. My boyfriend's parents lived here for years,' Kizzie explained. 'But they left a decade ago. They just locked it up one day, and headed back to England.'

'They never sold it?'

'Property in Harare isn't worth much,' said Kizzie. 'And it's almost impossible to get capital out of Zimbabwe, anyway. I suppose Oscar's parents like to think that they might come back one day. They won't, though.'

Kizzie bounded up shallow steps to the front door, and it opened with a screech. The hall was wide, the ceilings high and cool. There was a smell of cinnamon and mould. Kizzie led them into a drawing room, with huge velvet sofas and lots of heavy brown furniture. Five full-length windows looked out over the wilderness of the garden. Kizzie leaned over and switched on a table lamp, crystal, with a fringed shade.

'Miss Havisham in the colonies,' she laughed. 'Your rooms are down that corridor, by the way.'

'Thank you,' said Casey.

'So.' Kizzie threw herself into a dusty armchair. 'Where do you want to start?'

34

Casey had sent Kizzie her research on zentetra before they got on the plane. Now Kizzie sat in front of Casey's laptop, reading aloud from an old newspaper article.

"'We are very happy to be able to assist with this shipment,' said a spokesman for Adsero. "We are proud to be able to support millions of refugees during this terrible conflict.'"

'It's the quote from the charity that coordinated that cargo,' said Zac, 'that really completes it.'

"'The wonderful thing about this is everyone has done the right thing for unselfish reasons". Kizzie rolled her eyes. "'It's something that everyone should feel good about.'"

'No mention anywhere,' Casey said, 'of tax breaks.'

'Nope.'

Forced perspective, Casey thought to herself. It was all a question of perspective.

'I was talking to Professor Jalali about the problems around here with zentetra,' Kizzie said, pouring glasses of lemonade. 'I speak to her every so often, run ideas and thoughts past her. I trained under her, like Zac.'

'And then Jalali called me,' sighed Zac. 'I wonder how she got my new number?'

He looked sideways at Casey.

Casey kept her eyes firmly on Kizzie.

After their meeting in Tooting, Professor Jalali had contacted dozens of her former students, talking for hours about developments in antibiotics around the world. When Kizzie mentioned the problems with zentetra and Adsero in Zimbabwe, Jalali had contacted Zac and talked to him about the growing antibiotic resistance crisis.

Zac, Casey guessed, had seen an opportunity to attack Adsero without any reference to Corax – his strange code of honour satisfied – and had agreed to help Casey with the story after Jalali insisted she was far too busy working on an upcoming conference in Sydney.

Jalali, Casey thought, would have made a hell of a journalist.

After the meeting in St Paul's, it had been fairly easy to convince Zac to fly to Zimbabwe.

'What else are you going to do?' Casey had fixed him with a stare. 'Scoot back to that blonde in the little pink dress?'

'Good point.' Zac reached for his phone. 'I totally forgot to call her.'

'But what will you actually *do* on that little rock? While away a lifetime with a bunch of people whose only common denominator is a wish to avoid tax?'

'It does bring people together, though,' Zac mused. 'It really unites them.'

'What else will you do out there? Bob around on that boat a bit more? Have a few long lunches with Martin?'

'Martin?'

'I met him in the yacht club. Dumped his alcoholic wife for the fucking gorgeous Elene?'

'Oh, Christ, yes, he's awful. I honestly think I'd rather be gunned down by Adsero's goons.'

'This,' Casey had promised, 'will be an adventure. Plus you know what you're looking for, and I don't.'

'All right.' A long sigh. 'Fine.'

Still avoiding Zac's eye, Casey leaned forward and took a biscuit. 'Where's Oscar at the moment, Kizzie?'

'Oscar comes and goes, hey?' Kizzie's words rose at the end, turning sentences into questions. 'There's basically no point in him working in Zim at the moment, but he goes abroad, works for a bit, comes back again for a while. He's in Spain right now.'

Zimbabwe had been crippled by decades of disastrous inflation. For a generation – almost two, now – everyone who could get up and go had got up and gone. Almost no one had brought hard currency into Zimbabwe for years, ever since the government started confiscating businesses, houses, farms.

'So what did you tell Professor Jalali?' asked Casey. 'About zentetra?'

'Well.' Kizzie jumped to her feet, endlessly energetic. 'It's probably easier if I just show you.'

35

It took twenty minutes to drive from Avondale, the elegant old suburb in the north of Harare, to Mbare Musika market in the hectic south of the city.

As she drove, Kizzie pointed out the local sights. 'Belgravia, Kensington, Alexandra Park,' she recited. 'You recognise all those names, don't you?' A quick smile. 'For years, only white people owned houses in the northern suburbs. And they brought their place names with them.'

Kizzie smiled again. Her skin was dark brown, hair twisted into short braids. She had high cheekbones and a big, generous mouth. Early thirties, Casey guessed, and a naturally buoyant personality, dragging everyone up with her. Able to enjoy life, even when surrounded by tragedy. Not because she lacked compassion, but because she was instinctively, intuitively resilient.

She had an innate glamour too. Even in the dusty pickup, her make-up was immaculate. She was wearing a tea dress, nipped in at the waist, vivid with a red-and-orange butterfly print.

'And now?' Zac asked.

'That's all changing,' Kizzie shrugged. 'The Avondale Curtain may be rising, but everything else is going to shit.'

They passed a petrol station, the queue stretching for a quarter of a mile down the street.

'They must have managed to get a tanker through from Mozambique,' Kizzie said. 'I have to tell Zira. She's completely out of petrol.'

The men in the queue were pushing their cars slowly down the road towards the station. No one could wait with their engine running, not here.

Kizzie clicked her tongue in disapproval, and then accelerated down the road, shooting past a huge power station that was sitting idle. She cornered hard and pulled the pickup to a halt.

'Here,' she said. 'Mbare.'

The Mbare market was vast, sprawling over several acres. As Casey climbed out of the car, the noise hit her: shouts from the market traders, the blare of music from street stands, the hoot of the car horns. There was a smell of smoke and hot dust and dirt intermingled with a waft of watermelon, a whiff of cabbage. The crowd swirled past in an endless flow of laughter and gossip and bargaining.

In front of Casey, vegetable and fruit traders lined a track, squatting on the ground in the searing heat. One woman was selling a small heap of tomatoes, another, eight bruised mangoes. A man stopped his handcart, piled high with cucumbers, and waited for Casey to move out of the way.

Beyond the small-time traders were rows and rows of the bigger market stalls. These stalls were a scramble of corrugated iron, crumbling breeze block and tattered tarpaulins, all lashed together. Here and there, a tulip tree or a phone mast poked up over the stalls.

Three women bustled past Kizzie's car, each with a baby tied to her back. A small girl followed a few paces behind the women, a little doll strapped to her back in turn.

As well as being the market, Mbare was Harare's main bus terminal, and endless dilapidated buses and battle-scarred kombis were inching their way through the chaos of the crowd.

A violet kombi stopped next to Kizzie's car, and it seemed to Casey as if dozens of people climbed out of the little minibus. Once everyone was out, a pile of luggage almost the size of the kombi was passed out, the biggest bags unstrapped from the roof. 'No seatbelts' noted a sticker on the back window. 'We die like men.'

In quick Shona, Kizzie commandeered a small boy to stand guard over the pickup. 'He'll keep an eye on it,' she said. 'This way.'

Part of the Mbare market was covered. In other areas, scrappy tarpaulins were tied together in a sort of roof and underneath this it was cooler, and even noisier. Casey, Zac and Kizzie jostled past women bartering over fish and beans and onions, the stallholders cooking over open fires as they waited for business.

There seemed to be little organisation in this market. One stall would be piled high with old mobile phones, the next with dried caterpillars. At a tight bend in the passageway, Casey had to squeeze past two men playing checkers; their checkers were bottle tops, the board painted on to a splintery piece of plywood.

'Here.' Kizzie came to an abrupt halt in front of one of the smaller stands. A smiling woman sat behind a table, neat in a turquoise dress and a magenta headscarf. The stall counter was covered in white packets, and Zac jerked in shock. A jumble of drugs, so casual.

Casey forced herself not to stare. At the front of the table, she could make out antacids and painkillers. Behind them were anti-inflammatories and skin-lightening creams. In a creased cardboard box by the woman's feet, there were antiretrovirals for HIV, and three different types of birth control pills.

And there were antibiotics too.

Piles of them.

Some packets held only a few pills, others dozens of tablets. A few of the cartons had been opened, one or two capsules popped out. Many of the packets were dog-eared, the corners torn. Casey could make out brand names, warning symbols, colourful logos.

Kizzie was talking quickly, joking with the trader in Shona. She held up one packet of painkillers, haggled, then handed over a few bond notes, Zimbabwe's flimsy, largely useless currency. Next, she picked up a box of antibiotics. Amoxicillin, read the packet: a cheap generic antibiotic that could have been produced anywhere in the world. The woman named the price, and Kizzie handed over the money.

Then Kizzie spoke again. Casey heard the word zentetra.

This time, the woman shook her head, and Casey felt a slump of disappointment. But the vendor began to talk again, pointing down the row of stalls.

'This way,' Kizzie said over her shoulder as she walked.

'Are there any regulations at all?' asked Casey.

'The market does get raided every so often,' said Kizzie. 'So they can be a bit cautious at times. But they don't get raided very often, and she says this guy has loads.'

'They're not exactly that cautious,' said Zac. 'In the UK, you'd need a prescription for almost everything that woman was selling,' he added to Casey.

'When I've been here before, the traders were keeping empty boxes on the counters,' said Kizzie. 'One of the kids would run off to get the drugs as soon as they've made a sale. But they're obviously feeling fairly relaxed at the moment.'

Zac was turning over the box of amoxicillin. Some of the words on the packet were printed in Chinese. 'It's so easy,' he sounded shocked. 'I can't believe it's this easy.'

'Sure,' said Kizzie. 'The usual smuggling route for these drugs is over the Zambezi from Zambia. They bring the boxes across in canoes. But they come from all over the place. The DRC, Tanzania, everywhere. The generics are mostly produced in India or China.'

'As far as we know,' said Zac.

'And we'd have to check that the amoxicillin is actually real,' said Kizzie. 'There are fake drugs all over this continent. So you're giving your kid what you think is Malarone, but then the child drops dead of malaria. They reckon between 30 and 60 per cent of the drugs sold in Africa are fake.'

'It's so depressing,' said Casey.

'Sure,' said Kizzie. 'And, of course, the whole thing is funding organised crime, anyway. Because you invest a hundred bucks in white boxes and whatever random chalk-dust pill you can find, and then those little white boxes can bring in a cool half million.'

Now they were passing a huge pile of spoiled fruit and vegetables. Small children were digging through the heap, looking for an edible mealie head, a bruised cauliflower.

'Of course, the other problem with out-of-date antibiotics,' Kizzie carried on, 'is that they start to degrade. So people are getting a lower dose of the antibiotic than they think, and that makes it's even easier for the bacteria to bounce back.'

'Having learned how to resist that particular antibiotic,' said Zac flatly. 'It's a system basically designed to create resistance. And we still think it's someone else's problem.'

They could see another stall, this one also piled high with small white boxes.

'You wait here,' Kizzie ordered, and Zac and Casey stopped, examining a stall of small toys made from chopped-up drinks cans.

Kizzie was back within minutes, carrying three packets of zentetra. The boxes had the neat Adsero logo bold on the carton.

'He had loads of it,' Kizzie said bleakly. 'He had piles of the bloody stuff.'

'The thing is,' Kizzie said, as she led the way back towards the car, 'if your son is ill, and you can't afford to take him to a clinic because it's five bucks to see the doctor, and you're living off the proceeds of selling six mangoes a day anyway, then – sure – you're going to be buying antibiotics off a market stall in Mbare. *Ndatenda*.' This to the small boy waiting patiently by the pickup. 'At least the car is still here.'

'I know,' said Casey. 'Anyone would do the same.'

'One of Professor Jalali's colleagues was working for an NGO in Mozambique after those floods,' said Kizzie. 'She saw the zentetra arriving there. Truckfuls.'

'All paid for by the taxpayer,' said Zac.

'It wasn't hidden,' said Casey. 'Adsero announced the fact they were sending it out there, for heaven's sake. Their PR team put out press releases, the whole thing.'

'Hidden in plain sight,' said Zac.

'Yes.'

They climbed into the car. 'Right,' Kizzie said. 'And now I will show you the consequences.'

She chucked the zentetra on to the dashboard, and handed round a bag of oranges she had bought from a woman squatting at the side of the track.

'Let's go.' Casey leaned forward, 'Please.'

'This is my first day off for months,' Kizzie said to herself. 'I can't believe I'm spending it in the wretched hospital anyway.'

'Thank you.'

With the car key still in her hand, Kizzie fixed Casey with a stern stare. 'I'll take you to the hospital, Casey. But you have to promise me you won't write anything bad about it. St Agnes caters to some of the poorest women in Zim. We are doing our best, but it is an impossible situation, you understand?'

'Yes,' said Casey. 'I do see that.'

'Good.' Kizzie brightened, 'I've told the matrons that I have two visitors coming. Wealthy philanthropists who want to see the work of St Agnes's Hospital first hand.' She looked Casey up and down, and laughed. 'I suppose you'll have to do.'

36

There was a piece of paper sellotaped roughly to the end of each cot. Each torn page had a rough scrawl: a name and a weight.

Fadziso, 2,156g.

Precious, 1,982g.

Tawana, 1,763g.

The babies were wrapped in unmatched blankets, and they were so small that each cot appeared to hold only a little heap of rags. As Casey watched, the blanket nearest the door began to wriggle, and a small brown arm reached out and up to the ceiling. The baby started to cry, a thin, lonely wail, and then stopped again.

The white cots were less than a foot apart, standing in rows of fifteen. There were dozens of babies in the room, and only one nurse.

'It is very basic,' Kizzie had warned them beforehand. 'It is hard in these hospitals.'

The nurse stepped across to the cracked basin by the door and turned the tap. She made a gesture of frustration.

'The water must be out again,' Kizzie murmured. 'That happens all the time here. She can't even wash her hands.'

In silence Casey walked slowly down the long corridor. No one asked what she and Zac were doing there, the few doctors and nurses hurrying from room to room, too busy to glance up.

On either side of the corridor, there were five big rooms. Each of the ten rooms had a large window from the corridor, allowing Casey to stare at the rows of small, bewildered babies. The corridor was hot and airless, the half-hearted air conditioning humming away somewhere in the background. Sunlight seared through the external windows into the wards. The floor was a peeling grey linoleum and the paint on the door frames was flaking.

Two incubators were parked in the corridor, and even Casey could tell they were broken, random wires sticking out.

'The equipment here is rubbish,' said Kizzie. 'A few weeks ago, we had twins with jaundice. We put them under a heat lamp. It's completely standard. The sort of thing you'd do without thinking in the UK. But the lamp malfunctioned … and both the babies burned. They burned and they died.'

Kizzie turned away sharply.

Casey looked through the glass into the second ward. In this room, a doctor had his head bent over a tiny baby, hands moving quickly, precisely. The baby screamed and screamed. In the cots on either side, the babies wriggled miserably, distressed by the howls.

'A minor procedure,' said Kizzie. 'The mothers can't afford scans, so they don't pick up congenital disorders until the babies are born.'

'Where are the mothers?' Casey asked.

'They have to stay in the wards downstairs,' said Kizzie. 'They're allowed up every three hours to feed the babies.' Kizzie made a face. 'The women have to walk up four flights of stairs to get to their babies, even if they have just had a caesarean section. Then they have to carry those wooden benches into the wards, and sit there, on those hard benches, trying to get the babies to feed. Then they have to carry the benches out, because there's not enough room otherwise. I've tried to get them to change the rules, but … '

She shrugged.

Halfway down the corridor, a girl – maybe fourteen – was sitting on one of the benches that lined the corridor. She was wearing a rough brown gown, and looked utterly exhausted. The girl had leaned her head back against the glass partition, her eyes closed. Tears were trickling down her face, and her lips moved as if she was praying.

The nurse came out of a ward and muttered a few words. The girl stared at the nurse as if she had been punched, her eyes desperate, pleading: But this is my baby. My *baby*. Mine. You can't say that my baby is *dead*. It *cannot* be. My *baby*. How could the world continue to turn if such a thing were true?

The nurse stood there implacably. The girl dropped her head into her hands and started to scream, a rising howl of agony. She rocked to and fro, her fingers tearing at her face, her wails echoing down the corridor.

Moving briskly now, the nurse forced the girl to her feet and marched her along the corridor towards a flight of stairs. The girl could barely walk, doubled over with grief. There was a dark stain on the back of her gown.

If this candle is burning, parents are saying goodbye to their child ...

The staircase door slammed, and the babies' cries filled the air again.

Casey peered into the room that the nurse had just exited. In one corner, there was a row of babies, separate from the rest. A woman was bending over one of the cots, picking up a small covered body. She moved quickly, tenderly.

'What's happening to those babies?' Casey asked.

Kizzie's eyes were dark. 'That row of babies ... '

Kizzie stopped. 'What?' Casey persisted.

'If a baby is born in this hospital and he or she weighs less than a thousand grams,' Kizzie said quietly, 'there isn't much we can do here. We make them comfortable, try to let them know they are loved, but ... '

Kizzie folded her arms firmly. Casey stared at the little row of babies, the little row of lives. Tiny babies, left to die.

For a moment, Casey thought of Professor Jalali marching down the corridor in Tooting, looking on death as merely a challenge. Fiercely, ruthlessly, wilfully determined to keep every one of her small patients alive, regardless of the odds. Deploying every known medicine, and commandeering every piece of hugely expensive, impossibly complex equipment in that quest.

Casey thought about the nurse in that London ward, moving in that balletic routine just to wash her hands. As single-minded as

Jalali in her focus on protecting her charge, and defending the infant from an unseen enemy. And that nurse in Tooting had been looking after one, maybe two, babies. Not dozens.

In America, they had saved babies weighing less than 300 grams, Casey knew. She looked at the small doomed row, and imagined the mothers trying to feed these tiny babies every three hours. Not knowing they were already condemned. Not knowing it was hopeless. Like trying to hold water in cupped hands, impossible, watching those little lives ebb away. Her throat closed up.

'Surely there must be something … '

'These babies won't survive here,' Kizzie said evenly. 'Not in St Agnes. And even if they made it through these early weeks, they wouldn't survive life in the extreme poverty of this bit of Harare. We can either throw all our resources at that row of babies, or we can help dozens of children with a real chance of surviving. It is that simple.'

Kizzie spoke firmly, coolly, but Casey saw her eyes flicker. Impossible choices, every day. 'So they're all going to die,' said Casey simply.

'Yes,' said Kizzie. 'They are all going to die.'

Casey turned towards Zac. He had his forearm up against the glass partition to the ward, his forehead leaning on his arm as he peered into the ward. His face was only a couple of inches from the partition, so she couldn't see his expression. But his fingers were a fist, as if he might punch through the glass.

'Zac.'

When he looked towards her, his face was devoid of cynicism for once.

'What, Casey?'

'I suppose this is all quite a long way from the *Renaissance*,' Casey said pointedly. 'A long way from the beach bar at Le Morne.'

His eyes sharpened. 'Yes, Casey Benedict from the *Post*. It most certainly is.'

But as he moved away down the corridor, his face was still turned towards the rows of tiny babies.

The nurse who had escorted the young girl away was trotting down the corridor towards them. 'Good morning, Anenyasha,' Kizzie said brightly. 'How are things going today?'

Anenyasha was short, with over-plucked eyebrows and a wide face. She was in her forties and she looked shattered.

'It's not good, Doctor. It's not good at all.'

'What happened to that girl's baby?'

Anenyasha turned to look into the ward. Her elbows were bent, hands held stiffly in front of her, instinctively trying to minimise the risk of touching anything.

'That girl's baby was born late last night,' the nurse said quietly. 'The little one fought. She really tried. But it was hopeless. You could see it. And we don't have … We don't have *anything*.'

'I know,' said Kizzie. 'I am sorry, Anenyasha. We are really struggling with infections at the moment.'

'We are,' said Anenyasha. 'I don't know what we can do any more. I don't know what … '

'We keep trying,' said Kizzie. 'It's all we can do.'

'But it's the babies,' Anenyasha said. 'The babies are dying.'

37

'Bacteria are complicated little buggers.' The three of them had squeezed into a small, shabby office at the end of the ward, and Kizzie was making tea as she spoke. 'One of the ways bacteria spread antibiotic resistance is by transferring DNA between themselves. That's called conjugation, and it means that bacteria can pass on resistance to different antibiotics – in the form of DNA or plasmids – to other bacteria. Do you see? Essentially, bacteria can pass on genes. Mutate.'

Casey nodded uncertainly.

'The plasmid carries the code for blocking antibiotics,' explained Zac. 'So for example, you have your Mycobacterium abscessus – the one your beloved sister Flora suffers from – and by conjugation, that bacterium can pick up a plasmid that makes it resistant to, for example, clarithromycin.'

'I'm sorry to hear about your sister,' Kizzie said to Casey.

'I don't have a sister called Flora.' Casey glowered at Zac.

'OK.' Kizzie rolled her eyes at them.

'I was seeing quite a thick girl in my first year of medicine,' Zac reminisced. 'And back then I explained it by saying, basically, your bacteria can put on a blue coat, and that protects it from, say, vancomycin. And then it can put on a red rain hat, and that protects it from tetracycline. And then it can put on yellow wellingtons, and those protect it from zentetra. And, given the right conditions, at any time it can duplicate the yellow wellingtons or the red rain hat or the blue coat and hand them over to another bacteria to let them do the same thing. Mind you, she flunked out at the end of the first year. God, she was dim.'

'In so many ways,' said Casey.

'The problem now is that in St Agnes,' Kizzie said hastily, 'we are seeing a massive rise in resistance to zentetra.'

'Zentetra is a crucial antibiotic in hospitals all the way around the world,' Zac explained to Casey. 'When you're treating bacterial infections, you have your first-line antibiotics – that's the first line of defence. Those antibiotics are usually cheap, easy to give to patients, and because they have low toxicity it means there isn't much in the way of side effects. The amoxicillin we just bought at the market is a typical example. Then you have the second-line antibiotics. Doctors move on to those after the first-line drugs have failed. Then there are third-line antibiotics and lastly, there are the drugs of last resort. The drugs of last resort are precisely as bleak as they sound. After you've tried those, there isn't really anything else left. Those are drugs like colistin. And now we're even starting to see plasmids that carry colistin resistance.'

'So bacteria can transfer resistance to these antibiotics between themselves?' Casey felt as if she was wandering in a fog.

'Yes,' Kizzie said with satisfaction.

'And now you're seeing resistance to zentetra in the hospitals?'

'Exactly,' said Kizzie. 'And the problem is that the plasmid that carries resistance to zentetra – your yellow wellingtons – seems to be excellent at transferring itself on to other bacteria, and it also blocks a whole range of antibiotics.'

'Like cephalosporins?' Casey remembered a part of her conversation with Brennan.

'A bit like that, yes. So suddenly all the diseases that we would have been able to deal with using zentetra are unstoppable. And we dealt with a lot of things with zentetra.'

'Is it only affecting the babies?' asked Zac.

'No.' Kizzie looked bleak. 'We had a nurse come down with a bacterial pneumonia last week. It was resistant to everything, including zentetra. We've informed the authorities, but …'

'What happened to her?' asked Casey.

A pause. 'She died.'

'It's going viral,' said Casey quietly.

'Well,' Kizzie put on a schoolmarm voice, 'it's going bacterial, really.'

In a hospital, thought Casey, which didn't even have any water. She reached into her bag, pulled out a bottle of hand sanitiser. It seemed puny.

There was a knock and Anenyasha put her head round the door. 'That man you were asking about, Doctor,' she whispered. 'That man is here.'

38

'He has been coming for weeks now,' said Kizzie.

They were sitting on the wide old daybeds on the verandah at Kewlake. All around them, the garden was darkening, the shadows swallowing the marigolds, the msasas, the cassias. The drowned magic swirl of a nightjar floated through the trees.

Kizzie had left the office door open as she walked out to meet the man in the long grey corridor of the St Agnes neonatal unit.

'Can I help you?' Kizzie spoke in brusque tones, in English not Shona.

'I'm here to pick up the samples.' As Anenyasha headed back to her ward, Casey had watched through the hinges of the office door.

The man was slight, forgettable, wearing neat little glasses. Around forty, he had a high forehead and wide cheeks, giving the impression that all his features had gathered together at the centre of his face. His skin was dark brown and his eyes were bloodshot, whether from exhaustion or illness, Casey couldn't tell. He wore a neat white coat and in one hand, he was carrying a medical cool box, dotted with gaudy stickers.

'What samples?' Kizzie demanded.

'It's part of the Black Heart Fund's work.' The man gave a small smile that didn't show his teeth.

'I have not heard of this Black Heart Fund,' Kizzie said briskly.

'Everything we do has been approved by the medical director of St Agnes.' The man allowed himself some hauteur. 'Thank you for your time, Doctor.'

And with a brisk nod, the man had headed for the double doors at the top of the ward.

'I don't know what he wants with those samples,' said Kizzie now, lighting another candle as a mosquito whined closer.

'What,' asked Casey, 'could he be doing with them?'

'Who knows?' Kizzie stretched out her arms, palms turned up. 'The medical director is off sick, so I can't check with him easily.'

Kizzie had asked around the ward afterwards. The other doctors were too busy, too exhausted to do more than shrug. One nurse, looking thoughtful, thought the man came every three or four days. 'He's interested in samples from the babies with the zentetra-resistant bugs,' said the nurse. 'But those bugs are just bouncing from baby to baby anyway at the moment … It's a nightmare, the whole thing.'

'Do you often get people coming on the ward like that?' Casey asked now.

'No,' said Kizzie. 'Not often. I know St Agnes looks like chaos, but everything has to be signed off, and the matrons are stri-ict,' she elongated the word, 'so he must have got permission from somewhere.'

'So what do we know?' said Zac. 'We know that Adsero sent millions of doses of zentetra to a refugee camp in Mozambique during a flooding crisis. And we know that Adsero and the aid workers lost control of the shipment, and that the whole lot probably just disappeared into the black market, and it is still floating around. We've seen zentetra for sale on a random stall in Mbare – and that situation is probably being replicated all over this part of Africa – and now there is a major spike in zentetra resistance emerging in Harare.'

'We are seeing a zentetra-resistant form of several diseases,' said Kizzie. 'Which leads to pneumonia and catastrophic damage to the liver in healthy individuals, among other things.'

'Although these diseases would never normally cause serious infections in a healthy patient,' added Zac. 'They usually only cause problems for immunocompromised patients.'

'Alcoholics,' Kizzie explained to Casey, 'Diabetics. CF patients. The very old. Loads of people carry these bacteria anyway. In their mouth, on their skin, in their intestines. It's when it gets into your bloodstream or lungs that it's a problem.'

Like Flora's disease, thought Casey. Just about survivable when it was in her lungs; a killer in the bloodstream.

'Have you reported it?'

'We have,' said Kizzie. 'But after Covid-19, all they're interested in is viruses, not antibiotic resistance. Even though we know that antibiotic resistance has the potential to be far worse. And the authorities here … Well … '

'They won't be able to do routine operations anywhere in the world in a few years' time,' said Zac bleakly. 'At the moment, you're given antibiotics if you have a minor operation on your knee, right? But with antibiotic resistance, we'll get to the point where any operation would lead to an insuperable risk, like before penicillin. We'll be going back to the Dark Ages. You'll have to hop your way through the rest of your life because no one will pick up a scalpel unless it's life or death.'

'The Black Heart Fund.' Casey was searching on her laptop. 'It's registered as a charity in the UK, but I can't find out much about it. It's run from a lawyer's office in Somerset, of all places. The trustees all look like reputable citizens. I could try ringing a few of them?'

'Where is this guy taking the samples?' asked Zac, not expecting the question to be answered.

There was a silence.

'We could follow him,' said Casey eventually.

'We could wait in St Agnes's car park,' Zac agreed. 'See where he goes.'

'But you have to be careful,' Kizzie warned. 'Really careful. For weeks now, that man has been building a collection of some of the worst bugs I have ever come across. That man could be doing anything.'

39

Casey hired an old jeep with dark-tinted windows and one of Kizzie's friends managed to track down a few jerrycans of diesel for it.

Kizzie went back to work, late into the night every evening.

'I'll call you as soon as he turns up,' she promised.

The hours drifted past slowly in the heat of the car park. 'Who's looking after Dodo?' asked Casey.

'My neighbour,' said Zac. 'He's a mad Italian. He rang up yesterday to say that Dodo was going through his bins every night and eating all his cushions.'

'Old habits die hard.'

Sitting in the back of the car, legs stretched out, Casey rang round the trustees of the Black Heart Fund, eventually getting through to a spry retiree in Taunton. 'We don't do anything in *Zimbabwe*.' Mrs Winnett sounded bewildered, 'We give books to local schools. We do fundraising for libraries, that sort of thing. In Bridgwater, though, mainly. Not *Harare*.'

'They must have hijacked the name,' Casey said, after she'd said goodbye to Mrs Winnett. 'They can't have expected anyone ever to check.'

A text arrived from Miranda. *Is everything OK?*

Fine, Casey tapped out.

And a message from Noah Hart, a flood of foreboding as his number flashed up. *Flora is really starting to fade, Casey. The abscessus is out of control. Have you found out anything more about Corax? We are getting desperate.*

And she found that she couldn't answer.

The hours crept by. Zac moved the jeep with the shade, like the yachts in Grand Baie bobbing in half circles with the tide. They played cards, talked, gamed out the possibilities.

As she ate some crisps, Casey thought of all the times she had waited. A van parked in a dreary back alley in Poznań. A car, its motor turning over quietly, somewhere in Pristina. Long hours outside a chief executive's townhouse halfway down Pont Street.

Patience is a virtue.

And slow days in a dusty hotel in a scruffy town somewhere in southern Algeria, once. Strong Arabic coffee and shisha smoke drifting, and Ed laughing as the pink bougainvillea petals swirled in the breeze.

Don't.

A message from Miranda interrupted her thoughts. *Dash is telling Hessa to front up Ambrose Drummond. I suppose we might as well crack on with that story.*

Do we have to? Why now?

Hasn't got a decent splash for Saturday, I guess.

They threw people to the wolves on a strict schedule.

Casey stared at the dusty rows of cars. She couldn't think of any more reasons to delay the Drummond story. And it wasn't fair on Hessa. *Fine.*

'Is it always like this?' Zac asked, as she put down the phone. 'Hours of invisible work.'

'Often, yes,' she said. 'And then this tidy little story appears, all the loose ends tucked in. Black and white and easy to read. We even clip out all the long words so it fits neatly on the page.'

'You only ever see the top of the iceberg with the media, I suppose.'

It was more like looking at a dark pool of fish, thought Casey. Fish in a feeding frenzy, a maddened swirl of black, glistening scales breaking the surface for a second.

'Yes,' she said. 'It's a bit like that.'

When she looked up next, Zac was reading something on his phone.

'What are you reading about?' she asked, bored.

'Cupid and Psyche.'

'What?' Bemusement.

'Psyche was so beautiful that even Venus became jealous of her, and sent Cupid to make her fall in love with an ugly monster. But Cupid accidentally scratched himself with his own arrow, and fell in love with Psyche. He became her secret husband, a mysterious figure visiting her only under the cover of darkness. Until one night, Psyche lights her lamp and steals a glimpse of him, and he flees, abandoning her.'

'OK.'

'It's about how we punish female curiosity.'

Casey was watching a car edge into a tight space. Distractedly, fretfully: 'What do you mean?'

'Eve tastes the apple, and is banished from paradise. Lot's wife glances back, and is turned to a pillar of salt.'

'Pandora opens the box, and unleashes the deadly sins.' Casey picked up the baton. 'Bluebeard's pretty new wife finds only the bloody corpses of his wives, dangling from hooks on the wall.'

'And then there's Psyche and her lamp,' said Zac. 'Sneaking a look at Cupid. *Love cannot dwell with suspicion.*'

'How cheering it all is.'

'But it is fascinating, isn't it? For millennia, women have been punished for curiosity. For investigating. For sticking their noses in.'

Casey peered moodily through the smeary windscreen, and then gave Zac a sideways glance. 'Historically, curiosity's been pretty mediocre for cats, too.'

Suddenly, they were both laughing, overwhelmed by the ridic-ulousness of the situation. Casey doubled over, cackling until her stomach hurt.

'What the fuck are we doing here?' Zac's face was creased with laughter. 'A few days ago, I was on my beautiful yacht in Mauritius.'

'I don't bloody know.' Casey wiped away a tear. 'A few months ago, I was … '

Just then, a navy blue Hilux appeared on the road leading past the hospital. It was moving fast, but took a sharp right into the hospital car park, skimming to a halt close to the hospital entrance.

'Look,' Zac murmured, hilarity vaporising immediately. 'What do you make of that, Psyche?'

A man climbed out and walked round to the back of the pickup. He pulled out a cool box and disappeared towards the hospital.

'Now what,' Casey muttered, 'the hell are you up to?'

They waited, and a few minutes later, Kizzie rang Casey. 'The Black Heart guy's got the samples. He's heading back out.'

Face blank, Zac started the jeep. He headed towards the exit of the hospital, turned left, drove a hundred yards and pulled into a small street leading off the main road. They waited. A few minutes later, the Hilux emerged from the hospital, indicated left and accelerated down the road, past the small street.

Zac followed.

The man headed west through the city. He drove patiently, skirting the northern suburbs before taking one of the roads west again out of Harare. Casey and Zac trailed behind, just a few cars back.

Now they were driving through the countryside, through the millions of acres of Zimbabwe's abandoned farmland. After the rains, everything was green, lush, glorious. Bright pink flowers billowed on both sides of the potholed road, and flame lilies dotted the grass. As they got further from the city, the scenery became wilder. Scrappy miombo trees spiked the blue sky, the grasses and shrubs sprawling as far as the eye could see. The earth here was red, scorching in the sun. As they reached the hills, the kopjes – vast granite boulders – began to dominate the landscape, a giant's full stop on the skyline.

All along this dusty road, there were collections of little shacks: just mud and thatch patted together. The women walked in groups, large sacks balanced on their heads. Men crouched by stalls, selling a few vegetables. Poverty lined the roads, so it was as if the beauty of the country was stitched together by long seams of hardship.

Here and there were the big tobacco barns, ugly brick buildings where the leaves were cured for weeks on end. Tobacco: almost the only thing to escape Zimbabwe into the big hungry world beyond.

Zac drove for almost two hours. Occasionally, they passed opulent gates or a long avenue of jacarandas or flamboyants that looked as if they might lead to some magnificent farm or some proud, elegant house. But there was nothing in the distance. The avenues never led to anything but a bleakness, an emptiness, a burned-out memory.

The traffic thinned out gradually until Casey started to get nervous. 'He'll see us if he looks back,' she murmured. 'We've been following him for too long.'

'Do you want me to stop?'

'No.'

'Well, then.'

A few minutes later, they passed a grand old country club, the squash-court roof gaping to the open air. Ornate gateposts had been pulled down and the guards' hut torched. A cheery red sign, 'Members Only', sagged to the ground.

And just as Casey was going to ask Zac to stop, be careful, we've gone too far, the Hilux pulled over on to a narrow gravel track a few hundred yards ahead of their car. There was nothing to do except drive on, cruising past the Hilux as slowly as they dared.

Glancing across as they drove by, Casey caught a glimpse of big red gates – not burned these gates, not damaged in any way – and a guard in a navy blue uniform hastening to raise a car barrier. The guard had his arm lifted, his hand in a near salute. Behind him, the red gates were tall, with a starburst design. They made up a formidable obstacle. As they watched, the first gates were opening to reveal a second set just behind.

'And what,' Zac drove on smoothly, 'do we think is going on in there?'

'So where were you exactly?'

Kizzie was standing behind Casey as she opened up a map on her laptop. Zac and Casey had driven back to Kewlake, and Kizzie was just home from a long shift at the hospital.

'Here.' Casey pointed to a spot over a hundred miles west of the capital. 'There were big red gates,' she said. 'And a guard.'

Kizzie stared at the screen, eyebrows drawn together.

'Are you sure that is where you were?'

Casey glanced at Zac for confirmation, and he nodded.

'Huh,' Kizzie said slowly, 'I think that is the entrance to the Njana reserve. I believe that is the massive game reserve that belongs to Elias Bailey.'

40

'The Njana ranch used to belong to an old arms dealer called Jacques van de Berg,' Kizzie explained. 'Back in the seventies, van de Berg managed to sell guns to not one, but both sides of the Bush War, which required a certain dispassion.

'Then he got out of the country altogether for a few years when things got too lively. He managed to hang on to Njana for all that time though, God knows how. He used to do business all over Africa, and eventually he came back to Zimbabwe. I don't know when, but things didn't go so well for him after that. He was too old school. Couldn't keep up when the world went electronic and no bad thing, as far as I am concerned.'

'What happened to him?'

'The van de Bergs ran out of money pretty fast,' said Kizzie. 'Jacques van de Berg held on to the ranch until he died, but only just. The son sold it as soon as the old man journeyed on. Maybe five, six years ago? Not for much, although Bailey probably paid a bit more into some overseas account that the Zim authorities couldn't track. It's meant to be beautiful, Njana. All the land up there is stunning, hey?'

'Do you know how much time Bailey spends at the reserve?'

'No idea,' said Kizzie. 'Van de Berg was certainly a big deal in Harare for a long time. I think Oscar knew his son. Not especially well, but Harare is not a large place, as you may have noticed, so they would have crossed paths a lot as they were growing up. I could ask Oscar if he knows anything?'

'But Bailey isn't the same presence locally as the van de Bergs?'

'Not at all. Bailey's ex-wife is South African, lives down in Cape Town, and even when they were married, she had zero interest in Njana, by all accounts. Presumably he must spend a lot of time in Europe and the US too?'

'Yes,' agreed Casey. 'Being the boss of Adsero can't leave much spare time on his hands.'

'Sure.'

'What's he doing up there?' Casey was almost speaking to herself. 'He's having lots of samples taken there. He could be testing them … '

'There might be some sort of facility,' Kizzie murmured.

The thought hung menacingly in the air.

'What's it like,' Casey asked. 'The Njana ranch?'

'I'll call Oscar.'

A few minutes later, Oscar was on speakerphone. He sounded as if he had just woken up, but glided easily into memories of the old game reserve. His voice was deep and slow, the strong Zimbabwean accent never far from a laugh. Casey could see how he and Kizzie made a good team.

'The van de Bergs used to have parties,' Oscar said. 'Such parties, my friend. They were held in the main house, right at the top of a hill, looking straight across at the sunset. Then in the daytime, we'd go on game drives, and they were just amazing. Old man van de Berg used to collect black rhino, as well as giraffe, sable, eland, zebra, so it was incredible. And then in the evening—'

'OK, OK,' interrupted Kizzie.

'Did you all stay in the main house?' asked Casey.

'No, there were smaller lodges all over the reserve,' said Oscar. 'Off down little tracks. Beautiful places too, hey? The drivers would pick us up, and take us to the main house for lunch, dinner, whatever. There's a big reservoir at the bottom of the hill in front of the main house. One night, we all got steaming drunk and went for a swim. The next morning van de Berg absolutely bollocked his son. Arno had forgotten that there were crocodiles in the river above the dam.'

'So how would we go about getting on to the ranch?' asked Casey.

'I would *not* recommend it,' Oscar said with heavy emphasis. 'Njana is not the Masai Mara, sure, but there are lions on that reserve. Van de Berg collected black rhino too – about the only good thing that man ever did – so the guards will be properly armed. Poachers are a real problem in Zimbabwe. They gun down the animals and take the horns. There are very few black rhino left now, hey?'

'But we have to get in,' Casey fretted. 'We need to find out what that man is doing with those samples.'

'I will have a think,' promised Oscar. 'But that reserve is a big one, hey? It must be a hundred thousand acres, at least, and it is wild country up there. Blundering around on the Njana ranch would be pretty close to suicide.'

Zac's eyes met Casey's. 'I see,' said Casey. 'Thank you, Oscar.'

And Kizzie shook her head.

Early the next morning, there was a bang on Kewlake's dilapidated front door.

'Henke.' The voice was gruff. 'Oscar called me.'

As the man held out a huge hand, Casey's phone bleeped.

Don't ask me how I know Henke, Casey read Oscar's message. *But he should be able to get you into Njana.*

Still half asleep, Casey stared at the man. He was about 6'5", she guessed, with a mop of shaggy red-gold hair. She couldn't make out much of his appearance, but guessed that the African sun had been brutalising his skin for fortyish years. A huge beard covered the lower half of his face, and reflective sunglasses his eyes. He was the sort of man who still called the country Rhodesia, Casey thought, and the capital Salisbury. Behind him sat a battered Mitsubishi pickup, one silver wing stoved in.

'Casey?'

'Hello.' She shook his hand automatically. 'How do you know the Njana ranch, Henke?'

'Well … '

A poacher, she thought. Thanks very much, Oscar.

Her phone beeped again. *I can't think of a single other way of getting you in (and out, crucially) of Njana. Good luck! O.*

Casey looked up at the stony-faced giant. 'It would be great to have your help, Henke.'

41

They left Harare just after darkness fell.

'You don't have to come,' Casey had said to Zac again, as they waited for Henke's pickup outside Kewlake.

'But you don't know what you're looking for,' Zac answered, and it was true.

Car headlights bounced down the road towards Kewlake, and the battered Mitsubishi ground to a halt beside them. Henke was smoking. He waited impassively as they climbed into the car, then accelerated hard.

'It'll be cold up in Njana, hey?'

Both Zac and Casey wore warm coats, long trousers. Even at this time of year, Harare – right up on the Highveld plateau and 5,000 feet above sea level – got chilly as night fell.

'We're not sure what we're looking for in Njana,' Casey admitted, as they raced down the empty roads. 'It could be something in the main house. It could be somewhere else.'

Henke nodded, but didn't speak. Without the sunglasses, Casey could see his eyes, pale brown and bloodshot.

'I don't think Elias Bailey is staying on the estate at the moment,' said Casey. She had looked up the Adsero private jet on one of the flight tracker sites that afternoon. The day before the plane had flown from Cincinnati to Frankfurt and it was still parked up in Germany. 'But presumably, he leaves some of his team behind in Zimbabwe when he travels?'

'I guess so.'

'Bailey just flies in and out of Njana, doesn't he?' said Zac. 'He doesn't come into Harare at all.'

'*Ja.*' Henke sat in silence for a moment. 'It was van de Berg put in an airstrip, not far from the reservoir. It's about the only bit of flat land in Njana. The rest is all hills.'

It was very dark on the road west of Harare. Few of the shacks had electricity at night, and most of the roads were empty. A half moon rose slowly.

Staring out of the window, Casey tried to make out where they were. She thought she recognised the ruined country club, and a few minutes later, Henke pulled off the main road. Now they were bouncing down a dirt track, the potholes deep and wide. Henke barely slowed, and Casey almost hit her head on the roof of the car.

After a couple of miles of dirt track, Henke slammed on the brakes, bringing the car to an abrupt halt. He switched off the headlights, and for a moment, they sat in the dark. Slowly, their eyes acclimatised and Casey started to make out trees, shrubs, a chain-link fence.

'That's the fence around Njana,' grunted Henke. 'Are you sure you want to do this? It could be …'

A shape on the floor.

'Yes. Yes, I'm sure.'

Henke started the car again, headlights still off, and headed further down the track. The fence was eight feet tall and topped with barbed wire. The brush had been cleared for ten yards on either side of the barrier. A mile later, the chain-link fence disappeared to the right, up a small hill, while the track continued to the left. Henke drove a few hundred yards further, then pulled into a small thicket.

'Now,' he said. 'We go.'

He pulled a rucksack out of the back of the pickup, and began walking back towards the fence without another word.

By the time Casey and Zac caught up, Henke was at the fence. He had pulled a pair of wire cutters from his rucksack, and was clipping a neat hole in the fence.

'Won't they see that?'

'This fence runs for miles,' Henke muttered. 'They check it maybe once a week. We'd be very unlucky.'

A few seconds later, he was pulling back the wire. As soon as they had climbed through, the fence sprang back into place behind them, the sound loud in the dark. Henke twisted a few pieces of wire together.

'Don't want all the animals making a break for it.' Almost a smile as he headed off across the grass.

It was strange walking through the moonlit darkness of the reserve, falling in behind Henke. Casey sensed rather than saw the animals hidden in the dark. There was an occasional slither in the grass, a hiss in the distance, a black shape whipping away faster than sight.

Following in Henke's silent footsteps, Casey felt crashing, obvious. Henke moved fast across this country, his pace barely changing whether he was walking up a hill or pushing through a boggy patch. Now and again, Casey had to break into a jog to keep up with him. She could smell leaf mould, damp dirt, the occasional tang where an animal had marked its territory. Once, she saw a gleam in the corner of her eye, and turned sharply.

'Hyena,' Henke murmured. 'They won't hurt us.'

But a moment later, he came to a sharp halt, his hand directing them urgently to the left.

'What is it?' Casey gasped, after they had scrambled down a small dip.

'Nothing important. A kill.'

A few minutes later, she found she was walking on gravel – oddly civilised – and a small house loomed up in front of them.

'Wait here.'

Henke dissolved into the dark. Casey and Zac crouched by the side of the road, Casey abruptly aware: *what if he didn't come back?* But he returned within minutes, unseen until he began speaking.

'That's one of the guest houses that van de Berg had built on the property,' Henke muttered. 'There's a man sleeping in the main bedroom, and another in a second bedroom. But I couldn't see a laboratory in this house, nothing like that.'

'How many of those guest houses are there across the whole estate?'

Henke counted. 'Six, I think. We're about a mile from the main house now.'

'Six? We'll never be able to check them all in one night,' hissed Zac. 'Not on foot.'

'Probably not,' said Henke, with all the patience of the hunter. 'We'd have to come back tomorrow evening.'

'Let's keep going for now,' Casey said hastily. 'Where do you think they would be most likely to do any testing? Is there anywhere on the reserve where it would make sense?'

In the moonlight, she could just make out Henke considering the question.

'There is a big enclosure for the rhino about a mile away from here,' Henke said at last. 'It's not far from the main house, or the airstrip. The animals in this reserve aren't completely wild, you know? They get fed, if it's a bad year. And if something like a giraffe has an illness or an accident, they might bring in a vet. The rhino in particular are kept fenced in. They have a big enclosure, sure, but it is fenced. It's just above the dam.'

'And are there any buildings in that area?'

'That's why I'm suggesting it, isn't it?' Henke sounded annoyed. 'A couple of years ago, they put up a building there. Just shipping containers, all knocked together from what I could see. But that building wasn't there back in van de Berg's day.'

'OK,' said Casey quietly, trying not to think about why Henke might have been surveying the rhino enclosure. 'Let's try that.'

'This way,' Henke said. But as they turned, Casey heard an odd, dry coughing noise in the distance.

'What is that?' she asked, just as the lion's roar ripped through the air.

42

'He's at least a mile away,' Henke shrugged.

'Oh, excellent,' said Zac. 'Perfect. Wonderful.'

'Come on,' said Casey.

They hurried along. 'Our problem,' Henke warned as they walked up a rise, 'is that there is a team patrolling the rhino enclosure and those guards are some tough bastards, let me tell you.'

'Good,' said Casey briskly. 'They keep the poachers out, don't they? And it means that if there was something you wanted to keep safe in Njana, you would put it there. It might even have been why Bailey bought this place. Somewhere hard to access, with built-in security.' She saw the corners of Henke's mouth turn down, as he nodded thoughtfully.

In the end, they had to walk further than a mile, skirting a small herd of buffalo. 'We don't want to annoy those buggers,' Henke said firmly. 'They can be pretty nasty.'

But finally, he indicated they should drop to the ground, and they crawled forward silently. The ground was still warm from the sun, the grasses dry. Casey could sense insects rustling away as she crept forward on hands and knees.

'This enclosure is only about a hundred acres,' whispered Henke. 'The rhino get fed every evening. In the old days, van de Berg used to bring visitors down to watch. There's a big tree house, where everyone would have a nice gin and tonic while the sun goes down. I don't know if Bailey does that any more. Probably not.'

'Sounds delightful,' said Zac.

'The rest of the time, the guards use the tree house as a lookout post,' said Henke. 'They have a little guardhouse too. And right next to that is the new building.'

'OK,' said Casey. 'Let's go.'

Henke looked at her. 'If the guards spot us, they will shoot first and not ask many questions later, *ja*? And these boys shoot to kill. No one will mourn a few poachers.'

'I understand,' said Casey.

'And the rhino themselves can be vicious,' Henke went on. 'Don't be taken in by their size; they move faster than you can believe. I've seen one attack a Land Rover once. He threw it right over, again and again. Gored in all the windows. The people inside ended up in hospital, and they were in a very bad state. If one comes over to us, you stay very still. You're not going to outrun him, you understand?'

'OK.'

'Are you sure you want to do this?' Henke asked again.

'I'm sure.'

An elaborate sigh from Zac.

Casey couldn't see Henke's expression in the dark. 'Follow me,' he whispered.

The rhino fence was less of a barrier than the main Njana fence, Casey saw. It was only designed to keep rhino in, rather than everything else out. Tall and solid, it was constructed out of pieces of timber the size of telegraph poles. They crawled under it easily.

Henke led the way, slithering effortlessly along the ground. Casey could feel her knees beginning to bruise, her arms aching. It was very dark, the Milky Way glowing overhead. Zac was last, and Casey could hear him swear as he scraped over a rock.

'Quiet,' hissed Henke.

They scrambled on, and as they emerged from another patch of scrub, Casey realised she could make out the glimmer of water.

'The rhino fence runs all the way down to the reservoir,' whispered Henke, turning back towards her. 'The guardhouse is over to the left.'

'How far?'

'Couple of hundred yards?'

'Fine.'

Henke turned to move forward, and froze. A few yards away, a huge black shape was shifting in the dark. Casey heard the animal inhale loudly, scenting out the intruders. The rhino started to scuff the ground, letting out a rumble that sounded as if it came from the middle of the earth. Casey could only make out the animal's outline as it pawed the ground: its massive shape, the spike of its horn just visible in the dark. Now it was edging closer, lowering its head, getting ready to charge.

Casey felt the fear surge through her body. Lying on the ground felt impossibly vulnerable, pathetically exposed. *You're not going to outrun him.* But she couldn't stay still. Couldn't. She would be crushed, mangled, disembowelled.

There was another blast of noise and the vast bulk moved even nearer, tossing its head and tearing at the ground. She could see the rhino quite clearly now, in all its awkward, almost alien shape. A few more steps, another bellow, and she was bracing herself for the attack when the animal abruptly turned away, trotting into the bush with a surprising nimbleness.

'One of the young ones.' Henke seemed casual, 'They're more curious.'

Casey let her head slump forward, forcing herself to breathe evenly.

'Won't the guards have heard all that?' asked Zac from somewhere behind her.

'Oh, the rhino square up to each other all day, all night,' said Henke. 'That amount of noise won't worry the guards. They'd be listening for a rifle shot.'

Slowly, Casey felt her heart rate ease back to normal.

'How many rhino are there in here?'

'Fifteen? Maybe twenty? Let's keep moving.'

Across a stretch of grass, Casey could make out a large tree house with a wide balcony, high up above the ground. A couple of human shapes sat on the deck, and a cigarette glowed in the night. The guardhouse was off to one side, and beyond – about quarter of a mile away – Casey could make out an ungainly mass of shipping containers.

Henke gestured and they began to crawl in a wide arc around the guard shack, keeping far away from the tree house.

Finally, they were creeping up to the shipping containers. There were four of them, Casey could see, welded together. The main door had a padlock on it, but Henke was going for his rucksack again, pulling out a bolt cutter. It took him only moments to hack through the lock.

'I guess this location is normally security enough,' he murmured, and he was through the door.

Zac pulled the door closed behind them before Henke flicked on a torch. And there it was: a laboratory gleaming, all steel and shining glass.

'Fuck.' Zac took it all in. 'What the hell are they up to?'

43

The laboratory was both sophisticated – with glistening rows of machines – and basic. The tables had been knocked together out of rough boards and scaffolding poles bolted tight, while gleaming equipment lined the sides of the room. Big bottles of chemicals were neat on shelves.

Casey could see test tubes, agar plates, beakers. The smell reminded her of an office block in Colindale, a lifetime ago. That public health facility, and Professor Brennan's face changing as he spoke on the phone. For a moment, she was in another place, another world.

'They've brought in a lot of kit, hey?' Henke's words snapped her back to the present. 'Must have flown it in bit by bit. What does it all do?'

'I'm not sure.' Zac was prowling around the shipping containers. He and Casey pulled out small torches.

The containers had been opened up to form one big room. There were long tables down the middle of the space and biosafety cabinets around the edge. At one end of the room, someone had installed a wall of wooden cupboards that looked as if they had been ripped out of a kitchen during an upgrade. A stack of grey files rested on the cheap plywood countertops. There was another row of cupboards at eye level. Zac prodded an empty flask thoughtfully.

'We need to hurry,' said Henke. He had taken up a position by the door, peering through a crack.

'Here.' Zac had stopped by one of the cabinets. 'Look at this, Casey. They're definitely working on antibiotic resistance.'

Casey moved to where he was pointing and saw several rows of agar plates, with grey-green smears of bacteria growing patchily. On each plate, someone had placed a series of small discs, the circles carefully numbered.

'What are those?'

'Each disc will be soaked in a different antibiotic,' explained Zac. 'Look. Right there. You can see the bacteria has stopped growing in that disc. That means that this antibiotic can kill, or at least slow, that particular bacteria.'

Casey peered at the discs.

'Most of these antibiotics seem to be doing pretty badly.'

'Yup.'

'But how do we know which is which?' Out of habit, Casey started photographing the agar plates, before taking a series of shots of the whole room.

Zac switched on a laptop that was lying on a table. 'I don't know. Everything on this computer is password-protected,' he said. 'Can you do anything with it?'

But Casey had picked up a file lying on the end of one of the long tables.

'Look,' she said.

It was a long list of medical terms. Zac joined her, reading over her shoulder.

'That's referring to pseudomonas,' he said. 'Acinetobacter. Klebsiella. C. diff. MRSA.'

'All the greatest hits,' said Casey. 'Presumably those are all samples from the hospital?'

'Presumably. But we don't know for sure.'

'But which antibiotic is which? Could one of them be Corax?'

Zac's eyes gleamed with annoyance. 'No, none of them is Corax, Casey.'

'Why not?'

'Because in every single tray, the bacteria is showing some resistance to the discs. That means none of them is Corax.'

Even in the gloom of the laboratory, Casey felt the burn of frustration.

'Why won't you just—'

'Not now, Casey.'

'But—'

'I said not now,' Zac's voice rose.

'Shut up.' Henke's whisper was urgent. 'You bloody idiots.'

'Could we grab some of the agar plates?' Casey forced herself to be calm. 'And get them tested somewhere else to try and work out which antibiotics they are researching?'

'You want to shove a few samples of MRSA in your backpack?' asked Zac, incredulous. Then he softened. 'I don't think it would survive the trip back to Harare and then God knows where we would get it tested.'

'Damn.' Casey was leafing through the file, but it was pages and pages of closely typed words. She looked closer, almost forgetting where she was.

'Switch off your torches,' Henke hissed. 'There's somebody coming.'

Zac and Casey raced to the door, clumsy in the sudden darkness. Casey was still carrying the file, and Zac slapped the laptop closed as he passed.

Henke pointed silently through the crack in the door. Casey could hear men calling to each other. The shapes on the tree house balcony had gone. The two men were somewhere between there and the laboratory, she realised. *They were coming.*

'Quick,' murmured Henke. He hurried down the laboratory to the bank of kitchen cupboards at the end of the room. 'Get in.'

Casey yanked open the first cupboard. It was crammed full of box files, and came only to waist height. She pulled open the second: it was full of random pieces of equipment. But the next cupboard was empty, and Zac pushed her roughly inside. She crouched down in the dark, and Henke closed the door.

As she squatted in the dark, the back of her head bumping against the top of the cupboard, Casey could hear other cupboard doors opening and closing quietly. Please find a place to hide. *Please.* The room fell silent. Huddled down, Casey felt her legs start to hurt.

Stay still. Be quiet. Don't move.

There were loud shouts from the guards as the door of the laboratory crashed open. The neon ceiling lights flickered sharply then settled to brightness. Doubled over, Casey could see a glow all the way round the cupboard door, the light like an assault. Pressed against the top of the cupboard, she felt her throat close up, the claustrophobia a hand over her mouth.

They're coming, ready or not.

She was trapped like a rat.

They're coming. They're coming. They're coming.

Casey tried to make herself breathe smoothly, her ragged gasps too loud. Shivers ran over her scalp. The back of her neck felt fatally defenceless, a bowed head waiting for the axe.

Footsteps.

One man had made his way into the shipping container, and was pacing beside the tables. The footsteps stopped. Casey listened frantically, trying to deduce his position, her thoughts pinballing chaotically. The guard moved again and then stopped: he must be listening, peering around, searching. Huddled over, Casey's legs burned, and started to shake.

A flurry of words she didn't understand.

Casey could hear the man breathing now. She tried to force her legs to stillness. The man took a few more steps, and he must be right beside the cupboard now, just a few inches away from her, nothing but a layer of plywood between them. She held her breath, waiting for the door to be flung open. Waiting to be dragged out, kicking and screaming and desperate. Waiting for the bullet …

Another flood of words.

A different man – further away, by the door maybe? – was speaking now. This voice was calmer. But the man in the room became more jittery. She could hear him moving from foot to foot, almost bouncing, and her legs were shaking again and surely he could hear? Surely he would sense her presence, smell the fear?

The man at the door spoke again, and there was a long silence. And then she heard the footsteps moving away, pacing unwillingly. A couple more words and the light clicked off, the darkness a benevolence.

The door slammed.

It might be a trick.

Casey stayed still, swallowed by the blackness. Slowly, her breathing returned to normal. She was a wild animal, hidden by the night, somehow safe in the dark.

Or a child, closing her eyes: *if I can't see you, you can't see me.*

Pathetic.

A new movement close by sent prickles down her spine. *They're coming, they're coming.* All the fears blazed up again, and she almost screamed as someone pulled open the cupboard. But it was only Henke, a rough hand on her shoulder, and a minute later Zac was climbing out of his cupboard.

'I definitely,' he muttered, 'want a sodding tile on that wall after all this.'

'One of the men has gone to get another padlock.' Henke's whisper was nearly inaudible. 'I put the padlock in my rucksack when I chopped it, so they're not sure whether someone just forgot to lock it last night. He's gone to ask. They've been told not to touch anything in the laboratory on pain of instant dismissal, so that's why they didn't search it. That's what that older guy by the door was saying.'

'We've got to run,' whispered Casey. 'Now.'

'We can't,' Henke muttered. 'The younger one, he's still guarding the door. He's right the other side,' he paused. 'And he has a gun.'

Casey could just make out Henke's face in the room, illuminated by the computer displays and digital clocks. He looked stern and determined. Quite ruthless.

'We'll have to try and run anyway,' Casey decided. 'We can't stay here. We have to—'

She stared around the room, trying to work out an escape route. But there were no other doors, and the floor and walls were a smooth, unyielding steel. The panic surged up again.

'Fuck it.' Zac made a furious gesture. 'We're completely trapped.'

'We'll think of something. We'll—'

In the glimmer of light, she could see Henke opening his rucksack, ignoring her pointless gush of words.

Henke was pulling out a gun.

'No.' Casey felt her vision blur at the edges. 'We can't, Henke. These men are just a couple of guards, out in a safari park. We can't kill them. We just can't.'

She watched Henke's eyes narrow.

'If those guys find us in here, they will kill us,' he hissed. 'These aren't nice people, Casey. These guys are hardcore.'

'I don't care.'

'You're going to die then. And I'm not going to die along with you. That's not the deal.'

Zac started to say something, then stopped.

'You don't know that these men are bastards,' Casey insisted. 'They could be anyone. They could be boys from the next village, who just need a job.'

Henke let his breath out, almost a hiss. 'You're crazy, missus.'

The room filled with silence.

'We don't have much time,' Zac spoke quietly. 'What are we going to do?'

For a moment, Casey wished that Ed was there. Ed, always brave, his eyes calm in the chaos.

Then she turned sharply towards Zac. 'What would explode, Zac? In here?'

'What?' Casey could just make out Zac's eyes as he blinked at her. 'We can't blast our way out of here, Casey. It's made of steel. We'd all be killed.'

'I know.' Impatient. 'But this is a laboratory, Zac. Can't you make something like – I don't know – a Molotov cocktail? Anything to push them back a bit, confuse things? Create smoke, maybe?'

'Right.' He looked around. 'Probably.'

Zac moved fast then, hurrying towards the shelves of chemicals. He was back within seconds, carrying a few large bottles, and enveloped in a smell that made Casey's eyes water. A taper smouldered.

'OK,' Henke said appreciatively. 'You two sling those in all directions, and I'll lay down covering fire. We can make it tricky for them at the very least.'

'Shoot over their heads,' Casey demanded.

'Yeah, yeah. I will.'

They crowded at the door, almost as if it was the start of a race.

'I'll go first,' said Henke.

'I should,' Casey insisted. 'It's dangerous.'

'No.' Henke spoke as if he was slapping away a fly. Then he paused, and handed her his rucksack. 'The car is about two miles south-west of here. There's a compass in that bag. Keep going that way, and you'll come to the fence. If you can't find the hole in the wire, just make another one.' The briefest of smiles. 'Make that the least of their problems, *ja*?'

'Henke … '

'We have to give it a go,' he shrugged. 'If these bastards get their hands on us, they'll … I'll lay down fire as you run for it, OK? And then I'll run for it too, and … '

'I'm sorry, Henke—'

'Go left, and keep running. And don't stop, no matter what happens.'

Casey looked him in the eye. 'I won't stop.'

'They'll know who I am,' Henke said, 'if they get me. With any luck, they'll think it was just a gang of poachers, who thought they'd take a look and see if there was anything else worth stealing.'

'You won't—'

Henke's hand moved towards the latch.

'I'll hold them off.' There was arrogance in Henke's voice.

He stood by the door, and then he threw it open.

44

Afterwards, Casey could only remember a blur of shouts and gunfire and crashing explosions. She and Zac burst out of the door, hurling the bottles wildly as Henke blasted a hail of bullets across the clearing. As they sprinted up a tussocky hill to the left, she caught a glimpse of the guard. Younger than she'd thought, clinging to his gun and firing randomly, panicked and hysterical. She heard bullets zing past her head, ricocheting off the steel sides of the shipping container.

And she heard the coughing choke as Henke was hit.

She didn't turn back. She didn't even look.

'Come on, Zac!'

She sprinted up the hill, faster than she'd ever run, hearing shouts behind her and more gunfire, and then a final, deathly silence.

They didn't stop at the top of the hill, just kept running through the brush, dodging past crumbling grey rocks. Then it was down a gentle slope and *there* was the rhino fence and its heavy timber. They scrambled under the barrier and set off again, racing through the wilderness.

They'll have cars, Casey thought. Land Rovers, able to bump across this terrain, pickups able to go anywhere.

She ran until her lungs screamed, and her eyes filled with tears.

'Stop,' Zac shouted, in the end. 'We have to check the compass. We'll get lost.'

The sky was beginning to lighten. Casey slowed, chest heaving. She scrabbled through the rucksack. There was the compass. She stared at it, adjusted their direction slightly, and they were on the move again.

'Remind me,' Zac was almost laughing, 'where were the lions hanging out again?'

The light was pink now, the landscape coming to life. A herd of zebras trotted ahead of them for a few steps, before breaking to the right. Duikers watched them pass, jaws moving placidly.

'We must be nearly there,' said Casey. 'It can't be much further.'

'Unless we're lost.'

And finally Casey saw it, the wire fence a gash across the grassland.

'There, Zac. Look. We're nearly there.'

The growl of a motor splintered the silence. Casey spun round. Two safari trucks were racing across the savannah.

'Run!' she screamed.

They sprinted.

'Where's the gap?' shouted Zac. 'I don't see it.'

They crashed into the fence, frantically staring up and down the line of wire.

'That's the little track we drove down with Henke,' Casey pointed, 'isn't it?'

'It has to be,' said Zac. 'So the gap would be that way?'

The roar of the trucks was getting closer. Too late. Casey yanked out the wire cutters.

Her fingers were trembling, and clipping the wires was almost impossibly fiddly. Zac was trying to help by pulling at the wires. 'You're doing fine, Casey. Keep going.'

As the last piece of wire snapped in two, the truck was nearly on them, crashing through the brush as Zac yanked the fence apart.

'Go, Zac,' screamed Casey. 'Go!'

Zac scrambled through, Casey on his heels, the sharp ends of the wires tangling in her clothes for agonising seconds. Ripping, snarling, she tore off her jacket, far beyond thought.

The guns blasted. Zac and Casey sprinted down the road, guessing the direction: one chance, their only chance.

The trucks roared to a halt beside the fence, unwilling to ram it, and it was that moment of hesitation that let Casey and Zac escape. There were shouts and a couple of men threw themselves out of the vehicles and forced their way through the gap after them. But they hadn't seen Henke's pickup, sitting patiently in the thicket. Casey sprinted towards it faster than she had ever run. With shaking fingers and exhausted legs, she scrabbled in the rucksack for the key.

And then Henke's pickup was thundering down the road. Bouncing over potholes, smashing past trees: gone.

45

'Jesus.' Kizzie tugged the door open. 'What the hell happened to you?'

They had abandoned Henke's pickup a few streets away. Kizzie's grin evaporated as Zac and Casey scrambled into the hall at Kewlake.

'Henke,' Casey gasped, too shattered to soften the blow. 'I think he's dead, Kizzie. I'm so sorry. I'm so sorry.'

Kizzie's face sagged in shock. 'Come in,' she said automatically. 'It'll be OK, Casey. It'll be all right.'

Later, they sat wordlessly in the sitting room, perching on the uncomfortable ginger sofas as the morning light flooded through the long windows. Kizzie was crying, rubbing away each tear with a swipe of her palm.

'I'll have to tell Oscar,' she said in the end. 'I never especially … But he and Henke, they went back a long way.'

'Henke was great,' said Casey. 'Without him … '

'If I hadn't asked Oscar to call Henke … ' Another tear ran down Kizzie's face.

'I'm so sorry, Kizzie. He was so brave at the end. If it hadn't been for him … '

'I should never have asked him. Never. I knew the risks of Njana … It's my fault.'

'It's not your fault,' said Casey. 'Not at all. I let Henke take us up there, and I should have guessed how dangerous it might be. It was my mistake, Kizzie. I shouldn't have … '

'I can't believe it,' Kizzie whispered.

'I'm sorry.'

Zac was leaning back against the sofa, arms crossed, staring blankly out at the garden.

After a long pause, Kizzie sat up and took a deep, ragged breath. 'So what are they doing up there exactly?'

'They've got a laboratory.' As soon as Casey started to speak, she felt a wave of exhaustion wash over her. 'They're testing antibiotics, probably on the various samples of bacteria that man is getting from the hospital.'

'And why are they doing that?' As Kizzie concentrated on the new problem, she stopped crying. 'Creating some monster superbug?'

'I don't know.' Casey pulled the file out of her rucksack. 'We got this.'

They all examined the file in silence.

'There.' Kizzie pointed. 'That date's three weeks ago, and it's when Maita – the nurse who died – got it.'

They read across. The sample had been tested against several antibiotics, overcoming most of them, only being defeated by one.

'This antibiotic is performing well,' Zac nodded. 'It's taking out all the zentetra-resistant strains. So that's something.'

'And it's definitely not Corax?'

'No.' The impatience flared again. 'Whatever antibiotic this is, it doesn't perform well against that strain of MRSA, for example. Corax would destroy that sample.'

'Well, then,' Casey said. 'What is it?'

Kizzie went through to the ramshackle kitchen and returned with a battered cafetière and several rounds of toast. Casey and Zac were still poring over the file, occasionally referring to the photographs Casey had snapped with her phone. Then Casey sat up sharply.

'Oh, God.'

'What is it?' The other two stared at her.

'What if the antibiotic that they're testing is saepio?'

'Saepio?' Kizzie looked confused.

'Saepio is Adsero's new drug,' Casey explained. 'They've been developing it for a few years now. It's meant to replace zentetra.'

Zac leaned forward, peering at the file again. There was a long silence.

'It might be,' he said. 'It very definitely could be.'

'But … ' said Kizzie.

'It would be unorthodox,' Zac said slowly. 'And illegal. Not to mention unethical. But I suppose it is just about possible that Adsero could have set up an off-the-books lab down here. Running it in parallel to their operation in Milton Keynes.'

'But why … ' said Casey, then answered her own question. 'A few years ago, Bailey realised that by losing control of millions of doses of zentetra near here, they would inevitably have caused resistance. So for some reason, he sets up a secondary operation in Njana to test his new drug against the various new resistant strains of these diseases.'

'Why's he doing it?' asked Kizzie. 'Because he wants to make a nice profit out of this new drug?'

'He certainly would know that the market was going to be there shortly,' Casey thought aloud, 'because he created it. Either by accident or completely on purpose.'

'Could he have done it deliberately?' asked Zac. 'That would be … '

'Who knows?' Casey was fiddling with her silver necklace.

'Bailey knows that the world is going to need a new antibiotic soon,' Zac spoke slowly. 'So he's making sure that Adsero is ahead of the game.'

'What a bastard,' murmured Kizzie. 'He created the problem, and he's going to cash in with the solution.'

They stared out into the garden. Two sunbirds were ducking and diving through the verandah uprights.

'But the other option is that he is doing all this as a way of quietly fixing his own mistake,' Casey said soberly. 'By buying Njana and setting up a subsidiary lab to carry out the research, he might actually be finding a way to fix the problem. I don't know. We don't know. He could be doing it for any number of reasons.'

'So is he saint or sinner?' asked Zac.

'Or a mix of both?'

Who, what, where, when, why?

'It would only truly fix the mistake,' said Kizzie angrily, 'if he made this new drug available to us in the hospital. For free.'

'And we can't know yet if he will or not,' Casey said. 'I can't write something saying that he won't. Because he might.'

Why? The shout echoed in her head.

They sat in silence in the old sitting room. A bougainvillea branch scraped against the window in the breeze, making them jump.

'So what next?' asked Zac wearily.

'I don't know,' said Casey. 'It's certainly interesting that Adsero may have some sort of shadow operation running out of Njana, but it's not a massive story.'

The story, the story, always the story.

'Great,' said Zac. 'So we just give up and go home?'

'You can,' Casey said defiantly. 'But I have to find out what happened to Noah's sister, and Professor Brennan. And Ed.'

'You don't know,' Zac thumped the arm of the sofa, 'that anything happened to them at all. Their deaths could just be accidents.'

'I know something happened to Corax,' said Casey truculently. 'And that they're doing something weird in Njana too. I have to find out what Adsero is up to, even if you won't help me.'

'Well, you've made sure that I have to, haven't you?' Zac's eyes were hostile.

'What?' Casey stared at him.

'When we were escaping the guards,' Zac said, eyes hard. 'Twice, you shouted, "Come on, Zac!", "Go, Zac!" And I don't have any way of knowing if they heard you or not. And that means I have to assume that they did.'

Casey thought back to the blur, the chaos. 'Did I?'

'You know you did. You did it on purpose, Casey.'

'No.' But all at once she wasn't sure. 'I'm sorry.' It sounded weak.

Zac glowered at her.

'So what,' he asked, 'do we do next?'

'I don't know.' Casey threw her head back. 'I don't have a bloody clue.'

Kizzie drove them to the airport.

'Stay for the night at Kewlake at least,' she had said. 'You must be absolutely knackered, both of you.'

'I'm worried we might have put you in some risk,' said Casey. 'It's best if we just get out of the country altogether.'

Kizzie stared through the windscreen. 'The police aren't exactly going to kill themselves trying to work out what happened to Henke. That's if the Njana lot ever even tell the police he was there in the first place. It's a big ranch, that one. And those animals wouldn't leave much, anyway.'

'But his car … '

'You left it half a mile away from Kewlake,' said Kizzie. 'And Oscar called Henke from his foreign cell, which he does all the time anyway. The police aren't going to guess that Henke came to this house to pick you up.'

'But Henke's family … '

'There isn't much family any more,' said Kizzie sadly. 'I'll work out what to tell them.'

They sat in the airport, dispirited. Zac scanned the departures board. 'Where are we going next, my little pillar of salt?'

'I'm thinking.'

'In your own time then.'

'You don't have to come, Zac.' Casey's temper flared. 'You can get the next flight back to sodding Mauritius if you want. You'll be back on your bloody yacht in time for sundowners. You can sit there and have a glass of champagne, and watch the sun go down. But then one day, maybe, you'll start to hear about some horrible diseases making their way around the world. And those illnesses will get a little bit worse, and a little bit worse, and no one will quite know how to cure them. And then, maybe, the people you love and care about – if there are any, that is – will start to get ill. And you'll always wonder, could *I* have made the difference? Could *I* have helped? Those tiny babies in St Agnes … Those patients in the Royal Brompton … But don't worry, Zac, it probably won't ever affect *you*.'

She subsided into silence. Zac opened a packet of crisps, and crunched one thoughtfully. 'I'm still here, aren't I?'

'What?'

'I mean, yes, I could be back on the *Renaissance* in a few hours, looking forward to a night with … ' He paused contemplatively, 'Tasmina, I think. But I'm here, aren't I? I just wouldn't mind knowing where we're going next. Plan my wardrobe, that sort of thing.'

'Oh, shut up, Zac.'

'Order up Dodo's next truckload of dog food. And a few more cushions to munch his way through.'

Casey stared at the neon blinking letters. There weren't many flights taking off from Harare's threadbare airport. Bulawayo. Johannesburg. Nairobi. Lusaka: cancelled. Lilongwe: delayed. Windhoek. Addis Ababa: delayed. Cape Town: boarding.

Cape Town.

Casey messaged Miranda: *That story Bailey's ex-wife tried to give to the Argus. Did you ever find out what it was?*

Nothing interesting, Casey read a few minutes later. *Delphine says Bailey was cheating on the wife. Same old, same old.*

Casey stood up. 'I'm off to Cape Town,' she said. 'You coming?'

46

Mrs Bailey, the butler said stiffly, was very busy and not to be interrupted.

'It's important,' said Casey. 'Tell her it's the London *Post* about an article that didn't appear in the London *Argus*.'

The butler was too good at his job to express confusion, but he vanished again, this time for a longer period. Casey fidgeted in the hall, surrounded by marble and chandeliers and perfect arrangements of freesias and hyacinths. She caught a glimpse of herself in a mirror – tired, smeary, grubby rucksack – and looked away.

They had checked into a hotel close to the beach at Clifton. 'I'll try on my own first,' Casey had said, and Zac had nodded, exhausted.

Mrs Loelia Bailey's house was on one of the best streets in Constantia, on the inland side of Table Mountain. Huge houses sat in spectacular gardens. The Bailey house looked as if a small French chateau had landed gracefully in the middle of this plush Cape Town suburb. Neatly trimmed lavender bushes lined the path to the front door, while a row of cypresses softened the high walls around the property. The garden sloped down towards a swimming pool, just visible through big glass doors at the back of the house. Blue hills loomed beyond.

The butler reappeared. He was carrying a small stack of notepaper.

'Mrs Bailey is busy,' he repeated. 'But she says you can leave a note, setting out your request.'

Casey grimaced. 'Thank you so much.'

She scrawled a quick note, with her name and number. She would have to think of another way of getting to Mrs Bailey. And that, Casey glanced at the high walls around the house, would not be easy.

Casey placed the note on the polished elm hall table, earning a brief nod from the butler. He opened the front door, and Casey felt him keeping an eye on her as she walked back down the lavender-lined path. The front door didn't close until she had clicked the heavy side gate behind her.

Standing out on the road, Casey felt defeated. Loelia Bailey was the only lead she could think of right now. She had flown all the way to Cape Town on a hunch, and it had been a complete waste of time.

The streets in Constantia were not designed for pedestrians. Casey stamped along the side of the road, leaping out of the way of the cars that powered along the winding roads.

As she walked away from Loelia Bailey's house, the street's proportions reminded her of Harare. Wide roads, grassy verges, all edged with lush, glossy greenery. But unlike Harare, the wealth glinted everywhere in this expensive suburb. It motored down the road. It peered out coyly from behind the tall gates. It echoed in the hush of the streets after the last Defender had roared off.

Just a few miles away were the squatter camps: Cape Town's bleak townships that sprawled for acre after acre. Thousands of shacks built from scraps of corrugated iron and scraps of wood, plastic sheeting and cardboard, despite all the promises. But here in Constantia, it was immaculate, only the rolling power cuts hinting at the struggles beneath the surface.

Casey tried to work out what to do next. Her rucksack was heavy on her shoulders, and she would need to get a taxi back to the hotel. She began to walk past rows of houses, gardens so big that you could only tell you were outside a different property because the wall design changed. Grey stone here, fifteen-feet-high painted white there.

As she walked, she rang Arthur, the *Post*'s crime correspondent.

'Any news on Brennan? That bike accident in Colindale, remember?'

'Soz, babe. Nada.'

'When did you last speak to the police about it?'

'Yesterday.' Arthur sounded hurt. 'I know how to do my job, OK?'

'Thanks. Sorry.'

'Where are you anyway, Casey? Haven't seen you for weeks.'

'Bit busy, Arthur. Got to go.'

Then she rang Miranda, bracing herself.

'Where are you?' Miranda demanded.

'Cape Town.'

A short laugh. 'Right time of the year for it.'

'Loelia Bailey won't talk.'

'She didn't exactly fit the profile for telling all, did she? But that's a bugger about Njana, isn't it? If it's just saepio they're working on out there.'

Casey had emailed Miranda her notes about Njana from the plane. Hansel and Gretel breadcrumbs, just in case.

'It is.'

There was a silence.

'Miranda—'

'Casey—'

There was an awkward sprawl of words, and then Miranda was speaking. 'Don't you think you should be coming home, Casey? You know I'm all for wild goose chases, but isn't it time—'

'Miranda, I've got to go.'

'Casey—'

'I'll call you later, OK? Bye.'

Ahead of Casey, a group of women were spilling out the doors of an expensive-looking gym. They all wore the same self-satisfied glow, a lustre to their toned limbs. There was a cacophony of goodbyes and *see you next weeks* and the chirrup of lavish cars being unlocked by key fobs.

As Casey waved wildly, one of the women stopped sharply.

'My god! What on earth are you doing here, Casey?'

They hurried towards each other, broad smiles on their faces.

'Delphine!'

'It's so nice to see you, Casey!'

They hugged, laughing. The other women were disappearing behind blacked-out windows, pulling away in an expensive flurry. Delphine was wearing yoga pants and a bright blue sports top, her short dark hair pulled back by a wide sweatband. She looked relaxed and happy. A good advertisement for abandoning journalism, Casey thought ruefully.

'What are you doing down here, Casey? Is Miranda with you?' Delphine's eyes were alive with excitement.

'She's not,' said Casey regretfully. 'She's back in London.'

'That's such a shame. I miss her so much.'

'Me too,' said Casey. 'Me too.'

'But what are you doing here?'

'I ... ' Casey couldn't think where to start. 'It's lovely to see you, Delphine. Do you live around here?'

'Just around the corner. Now, where are you going, Casey?' As Delphine spoke, she was chucking an exercise mat into the back of the car. 'It's far too hot to walk around here. Where do you need to go? I'll drive you.'

'Oh, thank you.' Casey realised how overheated she was. 'But I'm staying all the way over in Clifton.'

'It's not a problem, really. It'll be nice to catch up. Get in.'

The Volkswagen pulled away from the kerb smoothly.

'So, Casey. Who have you just been doorstepping?'

'How did you—' Casey stopped, laughed, answered her own question. 'What else would I be doing somewhere like Constantia?'

'Well ... ' They grinned at each other.

'I was just back there.' Casey waved over her shoulder. 'Actually, I was trying to speak to Loelia Bailey.'

'Loelia Bailey!' Delphine raised perfectly shaped eyebrows. 'What do you want with her?'

'Oh.' Casey felt too tired to explain. 'It's complicated.'

Delphine stopped the car abruptly.

'What are you doing?' Casey asked, as Delphine shifted the car into reverse.

'I'm taking you back to Loelia's house,' said Delphine cheerfully. 'We go to the same yoga class on Wednesdays. I'll have a word.'

The butler looked positively friendly when he opened the door this time. Delphine had grinned down the camera at the security gate. 'Horton, it's me, hey? Delphine.'

'I'll go and talk to Loelia first,' said Delphine when they had been ushered in. 'Smooth the way a bit. Wait here, Casey. I won't be a minute.'

Casey sat on a gold silk sofa, avoiding the mirror. 'Thank you so much, Delphine.'

'It's really no problem.'

Delphine reappeared in a few minutes, a wide smile on her face. 'She'll talk to you. She's not delighted at the idea, but she'll give you a few minutes at least. But don't screw her over, Casey. She's a friend of mine.'

'I won't push it,' said Casey. 'I just want to ask her a few questions.'

'Cool,' said Delphine. 'I must dash now. Have to pick up one of my boys from rugby practice.'

'Thank you,' said Casey, meaning it. 'Thank you so much, Delphine.'

47

The gardens were exquisite, the grass defying any drought. Mrs Bailey was waiting for Casey beside the swimming pool. She was wearing a silvery kaftan, and smoking a cigarette.

She hadn't been sunbathing though, thought Casey. Not with that carefully protected pale skin. Behind Mrs Bailey, a novel lay spine up on a padded sunbed. Next to it sat a small table bearing a bottle of white wine in a silver cooler. Not a bad life, all things considered. And not *that* busy.

'Can Horton get you anything?' Mrs Bailey asked as they drew closer.

'Just water would be lovely,' said Casey, and the butler disappeared, still disapproving. 'You have a beautiful home, Mrs Bailey,' she added.

'I know.'

Mrs Bailey waited until the butler had moved uphill out of earshot, then she crossed the marble paving stones to a more formal table and chairs placed on the other side of the pool. She carried her wine glass and the bottle with her, settling under yet another sunshade.

Delphine hadn't softened her up very much, thought Casey. The atmosphere was glacial.

'I received your note,' Loelia Bailey said. 'And, of course, I like Delphine. She's had a very difficult time, poor girl, since her husband died. But can I ask you … ' Her tone was balanced precisely halfway between polite and menacing, 'why you are here, Miss Benedict?'

As Casey sat down, Loelia Bailey regarded her coolly. The older woman's make-up was applied impeccably, the pale grey eyeshadow expertly blended. Casey had seen an old photograph of this woman, and knew that she had worn her silver blonde hair pulled back in a dancer's bun for at least two decades. A staggering beauty back then, icily elegant now. She was roughly the same age as her ex-husband, thought Casey, although she looked a good ten years younger: a rich South African divorcee.

'I wanted to ask you a few questions about Elias Bailey,' Casey said.

'I have nothing to say about Elias,' Loelia said briskly. 'I haven't laid eyes on him for almost five years, and do not expect that to change any time soon.'

There was a hint of bitterness in the woman's face at the mention of Bailey, but the anger was too carefully contained to exploit.

Casey mentally ran through what she knew about Mrs Bailey from Delphine's quick description in the car. A bright child, Loelia Colvile had grown up in the Cape, the only child of two besotted – and well-off – parents. At eighteen, she had travelled back to England – the family had only been in South Africa for one generation – to go to university. It was while Loelia was up at Cambridge that she had met Elias Bailey, a fellow South African.

Elias had been studying chemistry, Loelia law. After Cambridge, he had reached for the stars, while Loelia gave up her plans for a legal career in order to run their home. At some point, she had returned to South Africa full-time. It was unclear to Delphine which came first: the cracks in the marriage or the move. Either way, Loelia had kept the Constantia house after the divorce, and Bailey had bought a new place in Llandudno, an expensive little seaside village just south of the centre of Cape Town.

All that bright promise wasted on housekeeping; no wonder there was a severe twist to her mouth.

'How do you know this much about her?' Casey asked Delphine.

'Cape Town,' Delphine gestured, 'is a very small place.'

'We're interested in Mr Bailey's work up in Zimbabwe.' Casey tried now. 'What he's up to in Njana.'

'I don't know anything about that place,' Loelia Bailey shrugged.

'You never visited the reserve?'

'I went once or twice.' Loelia's mouth turned down at both ends. 'But I couldn't see the point in it. There was nothing to do up there. Nobody we knew.'

She glanced around the manicured beauty of the garden, a certain complacency in her eyes.

'Mrs Bailey—'

'What is this all about?' Loelia Bailey asked abruptly. 'What do you actually want, Miss Benedict?'

Mrs Bailey was bored, Casey diagnosed. Bored enough to let the pesky journalist in, just to see what she wanted. Lonely, too. Abandoned in this beautiful memory box, with no one to share the memories. Delphine's intercession had opened the door, but it was boredom and loneliness that was keeping Casey by the swimming pool.

'Mrs Bailey, could we possibly talk off the record about the Njana ranch? My colleagues and I are investigating Adsero's work in the antibiotic sector, and it would be very helpful to have a proper chat with you about it all.'

'I don't know much about anything,' Loelia Bailey said moodily. 'I was never told what Adsero was doing. And Elias would hate me talking about the little I knew with anyone, least of all a journalist …'

'But I know you did talk about it, once,' said Casey. 'You spoke to journalists at the *Argus* about his activities.'

There was the flicker of worry in Loelia's blue eyes. 'Those journalists also said that I could talk to them in confidence. They promised that they wouldn't publish anything, not unless we agreed. Such crooks.'

'I am sorry about that,' said Casey. 'I suppose it must have been that Elias Bailey offered them a good interview, and they just went with that instead.'

The blue eyes sharpened. 'Is that what happened? I guessed it was, given the timeline, but I wasn't sure.'

Miranda would kill her: better a white lie. 'I'm not at all sure about the sequence of events, Mrs Bailey. But I heard what happened, and saw the interview, and wondered if Elias Bailey had …'

Mrs Bailey's eyes narrowed. 'Elias was always manipulative.'

Casey sat in silence. The butler appeared with a glass of water, lemon floating, ice tinkling. They waited until he had gone again, proceeding back up the hill with imperious disapproval.

'I was in a state of some distress at that time,' said Loelia Bailey. 'I would never normally speak to a journalist. I was quite distraught.'

'I am sure,' said Casey. 'And I am aware that I am invading your privacy even further by coming out here today, but I hoped … '

Casey knew these steps of old. Loelia Bailey wanted to be convinced that she wasn't the sort of person who would talk to the press by the journalist to whom she was speaking. And she was nodding now, mollified.

'But it would be so helpful for my piece,' Casey nudged her a bit further, 'to get a sense of what Elias Bailey is like as a person. You really know him the best of anyone.'

An appeal to pride. *You're the expert.* Because what is the point of a secret unshared?

Mrs Bailey's eyes were tracing the vines that tangled along the wall. Casey waited.

'All off the record? Delphine said I could trust you, but … ' Loelia Bailey waited for Casey's nod. 'In that case, I can tell you. Elias Bailey is one of the biggest shits to walk this earth.'

The swear word reverberated in the air, a shock beneath the elegance of the periwinkle blue sunshade. The two women shared a small, conspiratorial smile.

'You understand, Miss Benedict, that I can't be quoted in any article,' said Mrs Bailey. 'During my divorce, I signed papers … '

'I understand completely.'

'And I don't know much about Adsero's work,' said Mrs Bailey, looking down at her hands. 'I never did.'

Loelia still wore her wedding ring, Casey noticed. And a sapphire circled by engagement diamonds, heavy on her finger. She was very definitely Mrs Bailey, not Ms Colvile. A Mrs Bailey clinging to a happier past.

'We're looking into an antibiotic that Adsero was researching,' said Casey. 'The drug is called Corax.'

But Loelia was shaking her head. 'Elias never discussed these things with me. I never even knew what all his drugs were called.'

'So why,' Casey pivoted, 'did you go to the *Argus*?'

'It was because I was so angry,' said Loelia. 'I was absolutely furious at the time.'

'Why?' asked Casey. 'Why were you so furious?'

Loelia Bailey stared at the blue of the mountains, far in the distance.

'It was that little bimbo,' she said. 'It was that little slut, Jeanie.'

'We couldn't have children.' Loelia Bailey stood and walked over to the sunbed, skirting the swimming pool. She picked up the bottle and poured herself another glass of wine. She stood, framed against the beautiful house. 'Back then, the science – it wasn't where it is today.'

'That must have been hard, Mrs Bailey.'

'Loelia, please. And it was,' she said. 'It was very hard for both of us.'

'When did it start?'

'His affair with Jeanie? I don't know precisely. I suppose I never really wanted to know. It must have been a long time ago, though. We married young, Elias and I. Not long after we left university. And after a few years, it became clear. It wasn't going to happen for us.'

'But you stayed together.'

'We did.' Loelia stared intensely at her wine glass. 'That was why I was so *angry*. We had decided to stay together. To build a life so that it didn't matter if we couldn't have children. We spoke about it, and we decided that is what we wanted to do. We had everything else. Everything we could ever possibly need.'

Loelia walked back towards the table where Casey sat.

'I'm sorry,' Casey punctuated the monologue.

'If he'd told me, I could have moved on years ago.' The sense of grievance bubbled up again. 'I would have lived a very different life.'

'It's all very unfair.' Although Casey wondered if Loelia would have, really. Maybe. Maybe not. Probably not.

'I wish it had been different.'

'How did you find out about the affair?' Casey asked.

'It was so stupid,' said Loelia. 'The school got in touch. About a scholarship. They were wondering if Elias might want to fund one.'

'The school?' Casey was lost.

'Oh, yes,' said Loelia. 'I assumed you knew about that. Jeanie McElroy had a son. With Elias.'

48

'A son?' Casey felt her mouth go dry. 'I didn't know that.'

'We didn't,' Loelia said sourly, 'exactly take out billboards.'

'That must have been very difficult to accept, given your circumstances.'

'It was.' Loelia stared at the sky, refusing to let the threatening tears spill down her cheeks. 'I was devastated.'

'Can I ask?' Casey said slowly. 'What is his name?'

Loelia Bailey's mouth curled. 'Garrick McElroy. Stupid name. She didn't have the nerve to give him the Bailey surname, thank God.'

Casey felt as if her stomach had been punched. Garrick McElroy, the golden boy in Miami, still occasionally flirting with Madison on Tinder.

She forced herself to stay still, to smile blandly.

'Garrick McElroy is the son of Elias Bailey?' she repeated.

'That's what I've just said, isn't it? Why? Do you know him?'

'No,' Casey said hastily. 'I've met him briefly, once. He wouldn't remember.'

'I see.'

Casey sat back in her chair for a moment.

'When did you find out all this, Loelia?'

'Five years ago,' Loelia said precisely. She stared at her wedding ring again. 'Evidently, Elias had been paying Garrick's school fees back in England, for all those years, and God knows what else. The boy went to Drewsteignton school in Norfolk. It costs something like £40,000 a year. But Elias must have known that I would get to hear about it if he was sent to school in Cape Town. I know the McElroys, of course. Not well, but enough. So Jeanie … ' Loelia hesitated at the name, not wanting to say it aloud, 'went to England to bring up the boy.'

'Did Elias see much of Garrick as he was growing up?'

'He says not. Elias and Jeanie—' Loelia broke off, eyes wet for a second. 'I hate saying their names together like that. Hate it.' She cleared her throat, went on, 'As far as I know, Elias didn't see Garrick at all while he was growing up. I guess what might have happened is that Jeanie gave Elias an ultimatum: if he wanted to know the boy, he had to divorce me. Be a proper father.'

'Maybe.'

'And once she had given him the ultimatum, Jeanie decided to stick by it.'

'Yes, that seems plausible,' Casey sounded sympathetic.

'But I suppose it's also possible,' Loelia nodded an unwilling acknowledgement, 'that Jeanie didn't want her boy growing up knowing that he was a secret. Decided to protect him from that, at least.'

It was a blade, running gently over the skin.

'Yes, that might be it.'

'Or maybe,' Loelia's eyes hardened to spite, 'Elias just got bored with her. There was never very much to Jeanie McElroy.'

'Did you know her well?'

'No.' Loelia shook her head, rejecting the idea. 'Not at all. She was a pretty little thing, sure. But … '

She flicked her hand dismissively, then lit another cigarette too quickly. Casey thought of Loelia Bailey speculating over the possibilities for hundreds of hours, too proud to ask, too angry to move on.

'And then … '

'Five years ago, someone from Drewsteignton rang this house.' Loelia took another sip of wine. 'Fundraising for some science block. I can still remember the woman's voice. All bubbly and friendly, probably reading from some script. Working her way down her list to the fiftieth call of the day. Ringing round all the old boys, all their parents.'

Loelia paused, ground out the cigarette.

'What did she say?'

'She was all jolly and happy.' Loelia made her face into an ugly caricature of gaiety. 'Asked how Garrick was doing? What was he up to these days, because he'd left a few years ago now, hadn't he? "Garrick who?" I asked. "Oh, sorry, wasn't I the mother of Garrick McElroy?" And then she must have noticed the surnames or something. Maybe there was a note on the file. I don't know. And her chirpy little voice changed so fast. I beg your pardon! Wrong number! Down went the phone. But I'd heard the name of the school, hadn't I? And I started researching.'

Casey could imagine Loelia Bailey making her way slowly to her desk. There must be an office somewhere in this pretend fairy castle. Rarely used, dusty even, but there all the same. Clever Loelia, with the wasted mind. All there, ready to go. Casey could just see her putting on her unfamiliar reading glasses, firing up the computer, and then starting to search: picking at the scab.

'What did you find?'

'I couldn't find anything online,' said Loelia. 'So I contacted the local photographer in Norfolk and ordered all the school photographs from the time. Using Elias's name, of course. They posted copies down to me a few days later. Including a photograph of Garrick in a rugby team. Drewsteignton's first fifteen, or something.'

Of course, Casey thought. She remembered the blond jock bounding into that mansion in Miami, with all that ebullient self-confidence, that self-assurance so easily pierced.

Because now she considered it, she could see the similarities between Garrick and Elias. Jeanie McElroy must be blonde, she thought. Elias had dark eyebrows to Garrick's gold. Garrick had a mop of blond hair, while Elias's had been clipped short as it retreated. But they had the same brown eyes, the same distinctive shape to their jaw and a particular tilt to the planes of their cheekbones. Elias was older, tougher, wearing the carapace of success, where Garrick was oddly brittle. But the resemblance was clear.

Casey imagined Loelia staring at that photograph, and coming back to it again and again, the next day and the next. Seeing the smile, the eyes, the mouth. She wouldn't need a photograph of Elias Bailey to compare, of course. One face known for every day of her adult life, the other seen for the very first time. One face more familiar than any other in the world, and one that should never have existed.

'What did you do next?'

'There's a private investigator,' Loelia said. 'He works here in Cape Town. He was good. Very efficient.' She shrugged. 'You know, some days I wish I had just ignored that phone call. We were happy, Elias and I. Most of the time. I could have forgotten about it all, couldn't I? Just got on with life.'

The genie back in the bottle, thought Casey. It rarely worked.

'But you didn't?'

'The PI got everything I needed,' said Loelia. 'He'd done it before. Will do it again, no doubt. We're his bread and butter, I suppose, us embittered wives.'

'And then you confronted Elias.'

'I did.' Two small words, the wreck of a marriage.

'What happened after that?'

'Elias left,' she said. 'He flew back to England. Adsero was going through a rough patch anyway, and he was very stressed about the business. And he was not well, don't forget. He'd been struggling with his heart for years. I guess the stress of it all didn't help that either. But I was angry. So angry. I filed for divorce while he was still in England, and we never spoke again.'

'He didn't fight it?'

'No.' Loelia poured another glass of wine. 'He did not. Maybe with his heart problems, and the difficulties with Adsero, he just couldn't. Or maybe he just didn't care enough. Who knows? Either way, later on I found out that Garrick went to work for Adsero around that time. So Elias must have got to know him, and quickly too.'

'Garrick went to work for Adsero?' Casey felt the gears shift again. 'When?'

'About four years ago?' Loelia was less certain. 'Not long after I started divorce proceedings. But it didn't work out, I don't think.'

'Do you know why?'

'I do not. Garrick left the company about the time that Elias had the heart transplant.'

'Oh, yes.' Casey thought back to the article she'd read on the flight back from Mauritius. 'Where did he have the heart transplant?'

'He had it back here,' Loelia said. 'At Groote Schuur.'

Groote Schuur, Casey remembered from the article Ross had ordered her to write, all those weeks ago. Groote Schuur, the world-famous South African hospital, where the first ever heart transplant had taken place back in 1967.

'Did you see him then? When he was here for the operation.'

'No.' Loelia's mouth was a thin line. 'He never asked for me, as far as I know. Maybe Jeanie was by his side. He was very ill before the operation, by all accounts. But the operation went well, and he was back to work at Adsero long before the doctors recommended, certainly.'

'And when did you go to the *Argus*?'

Loelia blew out his cheeks. 'It was after the heart transplant, and that was just over three years ago. I was still so furious at him. It was while we were negotiating the divorce. He is a tough negotiator, that man, hey?' There was the hint of pride again. Pride in her husband, before it disappeared like a trapdoor snapping. 'I just saw red one day, and rang the *Argus*. Elias never even mentioned the call to me. But in the next version of the divorce papers that my lawyer received, there was an NDA attached. A non-disclosure agreement. So Elias must have known about me going to that journalist.'

'Mrs Bailey.' Casey leaned forward through the haze of cigarette smoke. 'This is an odd question, but I have to ask. Were you ever scared of Elias Bailey?'

Loelia blinked at her. 'Scared of Elias? No, he never hit me, or anything like that.'

'I don't mean that,' said Casey. 'But he is a very ruthless businessman. Did you ever feel threatened by him?'

'No.' Loelia was still confused. 'What do you mean exactly?'

Casey took a sip of the iced water, watching Loelia carefully.

'People linked to Mr Bailey,' said Casey. 'They have accidents. Several people connected to Mr Bailey … Well, they are dead now.'

'Dead?' Loelia Bailey looked across at the hazy blue of the mountains, as if she was hearing a voice far in the distance. 'No,' she said. 'I was never scared of Elias.'

49

'Did you know?'

Zac had his eyes shut and his face tilted up to the sun. He was sitting in the hotel courtyard, a small fountain tinkling beside him. Pale pink roses bobbed their heads in a raised flower bed next to the fountain.

'What?' Zac's eyes snapped open to find Casey standing over him. 'Did I know what?'

'That Garrick McElroy was the son of Elias Bailey?'

'What?' Zac blinked very slowly, a flurry of emotions crossing his face. 'No, of course I didn't. Is he?'

Casey stared at him in a fury. 'Why else would I ask?'

There was a long pause. Zac folded his arms and looked up at her, his eyes slits against the sun. 'Has anyone ever told you that you're very attractive when you're angry, Casey Benedict from the *Post*?'

He was laughing.

'Stop playing bloody games, Zac! I've had enough, and I know you're lying. Tell me what you know about Garrick McElroy and Corax and sodding Elias Bailey. Tell me, right now.'

Zac glanced at his watch. 'He can tell you himself.'

'What? Who can?'

'I told Garrick we had to work out what was going on with Corax. His plane landed an hour ago.'

They met at Camps Bay, just to the south of Clifton, as the afternoon began its surrender to the evening, the blue of the sky slowly deepening.

As Garrick jogged down the beach towards them, a small group of women turned to watch him.

'Zac!'

'Garrick!'

Even in the circumstances, Casey could see there was a genuine affection between the two men.

'And this,' Zac waved towards her, 'is Carrie.'

'Can we trust him?' Casey had pressed Zac beforehand.

'Yes,' Zac was confident. 'I've known Garrick for years. He hates Bailey.'

'Why?'

'He can tell you himself.'

'And he never mentioned Elias Bailey was his father? That's quite a thing to not mention.'

'But Loelia told you that Elias Bailey and Jeanie McElroy kept their whole affair a secret,' said Zac. 'When something's been a secret since you were a child, it becomes a habit.'

'You can break it.'

'Can you?'

'I don't like it, Zac. We don't know anything about Garrick's loyalties. And don't tell him my name.'

'Casey—' Zac had laughed at her.

'Not my name.'

'He'll have to know,' Zac said reasonably, 'that you're a journalist. You don't have a choice about that. Why else would you be asking all these questions?'

'Just call me Carrie.'

'You,' he said pointedly, 'were quite happy to call me Zac.'

Now Garrick bounded forward with a broad grin, but as he shook her hand, he hesitated. 'Have we met somewhere before, Carrie?'

'I don't think so,' Casey said briskly. Madison had hastily deleted herself from Tinder a couple of hours earlier, and Casey had decided against trying to explain the Miami escapade. 'I can't think of anywhere we would have met.'

'Great to meet you anyway,' Garrick nodded.

237

'You too,' Casey said automatically.

Garrick was nervous, she could tell. He was edging from foot to foot, and glancing round at small groups of teenagers, as if they might be spies. There was a screech of brakes up by the waterfront, and Garrick jumped, too late to hide his fear. Casey smiled at him, trying to calm him down.

The three of them turned to walk along the beach, Zac in the middle. The north end of the bay was dominated by the jagged shape of Lion's Head. To the west, Table Mountain stood proud, picture perfect, green slopes sweeping nearly to the ocean.

Huge rollers crashed into the bay, blasted all the way across the south Atlantic just to smash into this golden sand. In the distance, at the north end of the beach, a scattering of surfers were bobbing, splashing, waiting for a wave. Occasionally, Casey could make out a shout, a laugh, a hello. Garrick stared at them longingly.

Casey looked down at her flip-flops, sinking into the sand, and couldn't think where to begin. But as she debated, Garrick began to speak, the words tumbling too fast from his mouth.

'I should have told you, Zac. About Elias. I'm sorry … I should have—'

Zac kicked at some sand. 'It certainly puts a different flavour on things, you git.'

'What?' asked Casey. 'What did Garrick tell you before?'

'I didn't tell him much at all,' admitted Garrick. 'I could never tell him about how I had found Corax, for example.'

Corax. Casey forced herself not to rush, not to pounce on Garrick and demand he tell her everything he knew.

'Didn't you wonder?' Casey turned to Zac, taking the pressure off Garrick for a moment. 'Where Garrick had found out about it?'

'Of course I did,' said Zac. 'But I wanted to work on the drug, and Garrick wouldn't tell me where it came from, so what else could I do?'

Casey crushed the furious words back down into her throat.

'I stole the Corax information.' The words spilled out of Garrick, as if he couldn't keep them in. 'I stole it from Adsero.'

He stopped, almost shocked by his own words, then glanced around, automatically checking for danger. He took a few more steps, gouging his feet into the sand, then came to a halt again.

'How?' asked Casey, after a short pause.

'Elias Bailey,' said Garrick slowly. 'He just appeared out of thin air one day, and turned everything in my life upside down. You have to understand ... ' Garrick hesitated, then carried on, his voice slightly lower, 'When I was growing up, my mother wouldn't ever say who my father was. She refused to talk about it at all.

'When I was little, I would pretend he was someone famous. Or a soldier who had gone off to war. Or an astronaut, even. Stupid stuff like that. And then as I got older, I assumed it was a one night stand or something. You don't really want to think about that sort of thing – not about your mother – so you don't.'

One of the surfers had caught a wave, and was arrowing over the ocean in a bright flare of speed. Garrick's eyes followed the trajectory of the surfer until they reached Casey's face.

'You didn't wonder about the money for school fees or anything?' Casey failed to stop herself sounding accusatory. 'A school like Drewsteignton doesn't come cheap.'

'No,' Garrick sounded apologetic, 'not really. You don't question that sort of thing when you're a kid. Well, I didn't, anyway. We'd come back to Cape Town in the holidays, and my grandparents – my mother's parents, that is – lived in a perfectly nice house in Claremont. I didn't really ask.'

'But your mother was living in England at the time?'

'Yes,' said Garrick. 'She would turn up for things like Sports Day or the school play, and I would be so proud of her. She was so much more beautiful than all the other mothers ... '

Casey could just imagine. Jeanie McElroy, the gorgeous blonde South African, all long legs and white teeth. A daffodil on a grey day in Norfolk. Pretty little Jeanie. Pretty Jeanie McElroy.

'And then what?'

'I wanted to be a success,' Garrick said flatly. 'My mother was living in a rented house in Sussex while I was at school. She never said anything when I was growing up, but I knew that she didn't have much in the way of security. And I was starting to realise that things weren't quite … I wanted to make us more secure.'

'How?'

'I went into business,' said Garrick.

Maurice Delacroix's research floated across Casey's mind. The tech company in San Francisco. The property companies in Canada.

'What sort of business?' Casey wanted to hear his version of events.

'I needed to make money,' said Garrick. 'But I also wanted to make the world a better place too.'

His eyes were pleading. We all, thought Casey brutally, want to make the world a better place.

'But you're working in oil now?' she asked. 'I googled you,' she added quickly.

'I am,' said Garrick. 'I am now.'

'And how did that come about?'

'I—' Garrick stalled.

'Where were you when Elias Bailey came into your life?' Casey took him back.

'I was working in Toronto at the time,' Garrick said. 'I was running two property companies I'd set up. They were going … OK.' The pause told Casey everything she needed to know. 'And then one morning, I got a call at work. It was this voice I didn't recognise. A man's voice.' Garrick stopped, running through that day again. 'It was Elias Bailey, and he said he wanted to meet me. He didn't say why at first. But I'd heard of him and his business, and I was curious, so I was happy to meet up. We had a coffee down on the waterfront the next day, and he told me who he was: my father.'

For a second, Casey's throat closed up. Zac was watching her out of the corner of his eye, a flicker of curiosity. Casey stared at Lion's Head, and ignored Zac.

'What was he like?'

'I had done some more research before I met up with him,' said Garrick. 'So I'd read about everything he'd done with Adsero. He is an impressive businessman.' This, defiantly. 'And we got on fine at first. Better than fine.'

'Then what?'

'We got to know each other bit by bit,' said Garrick. 'I liked him. He was tough, but he could be fun. Adsero have a big factory in Pennsylvania, so he was over fairly often. And he did a lot of business in New York. And each time either he would come up to Toronto or I would go down to New York. We got to know each other quite well.'

Garrick went down to New York more than Bailey went to Toronto, Casey guessed.

'It sounds as if Bailey made an effort to get to know you,' she said.

'He did.' And for a moment, Garrick's face lit up. 'We'd go for drives near Toronto. We sailed in the lake once. It was great. He could be great …'

His voice trailed away. 'What happened next?' asked Casey.

'Things started to go wrong with my property companies,' said Garrick. 'I was trying to make them work, but they just didn't. Eventually, I decided that I needed to shut them down.'

'You didn't ask Bailey for investment?'

'No. But I told him I was wrapping them up, and a week later he suggested I come and work at Adsero for a while.'

'Did you have any experience in the pharmaceutical industry?'

'No,' Garrick admitted. 'But he put me to work on their CSR programme.'

'CSR?' asked Zac.

'Corporate social responsibility,' recited Garrick. 'You know, the sort of thing that big companies do to show they *care*.' He emphasised the word with a twist of cynicism. 'Donating to charities, supporting local groups, telling their staff to volunteer in the community.'

'Would Adsero donate drugs?' asked Casey. 'In a big international crisis?'

'Yes,' said Garrick easily, not thinking about it. 'Adsero would definitely do that sort of thing.'

Garrick didn't know about zentetra, thought Casey. Not even a hint.

'Did you enjoy working for Adsero?'

'I did at first,' said Garrick slowly. 'But things started to go downhill with Elias.'

Elias, Casey noted: not Dad. Not Bailey, either.

'How?'

'He was having difficulties with his heart,' said Garrick. 'Everyone could see it. Everyone who worked closely with him, that is. He was breathless, and he would have to sit down, and then it got worse suddenly. But he hated anyone mentioning it. Absolutely hated it. I remember one secretary asking if he wanted a chair, and he basically fired her on the spot.'

'And it affected your relationship?'

'It made him very short-tempered. He became very controlling,' said Garrick. 'Or maybe he always had been and I just hadn't known him for long enough. And he was utterly ruthless when it came to Adsero.'

'How?'

'Early on, just after I had started working at Adsero, he decided he needed to close one of the factories in the US. It was a small one in Ohio, and he worked out that production could be done more efficiently in the Pennsylvania factory. So he decided to sack everyone right before Christmas. I was saying that we should wait and see if there was any way of saving the factory in the New Year, but he just ignored me.' For a moment, there was a hint of petulance in Garrick's voice. 'Everyone was laid off the week before Christmas. And it was in one of those bits of Ohio where there aren't any other jobs.'

'Brutal.'

'Yes. He never listened to me. He treated me like a child.'

There was too wide a gap between the son Bailey had wanted, thought Casey, and the reality of Garrick. If Bailey had spent those years watching his son grow up rather than just imagining him, it might have been different.

'What happened next?'

'In the new year, we travelled down to Cape Town,' said Garrick. 'We often travelled together back then, and it was fun. We were staying at his house in Llandudno. He'd bought it right after his divorce. It's a beautiful place.'

The three of them were down by the ocean's edge now, the roar of the waves blotting out the noise from the city. Casey let the water splash over her feet. As the waves rushed in, she winced. For all the golden beauty of the day, the water here was icy. Over on the other side of the Cape, the Agulhas current brings a flood of warmth down from the Indian Ocean but on the western side of the continent, the Benguela current rushes cold water up from the Antarctic in an endless, relentless flow.

'What happened at the house in Llandudno?' Casey asked.

'He has an office there,' said Garrick. 'It's right at the top of the house. Massive, with huge windows looking out to sea. You feel like you're in a ship. There's a balcony running all the way round, and during the summer he opens it all up.'

'Does he work up there alone?'

'Yes,' Garrick nodded. 'He has a PA, of course, but she has an office in a different part of the house. He's always working. Always.'

The sea was navy now, reflecting the sky. Two children – maybe eight and nine – were playing in the sea, daring each other to stand firm as the waves crashed in.

'Watch out for the rip,' their mother called out. 'It's very dangerous along here, sweethearts.'

'He was working from home though?' Casey asked.

'Adsero is his company, but it also isn't, if you see what I mean. The board has to OK everything. He has shareholders. He shouldn't even use the jet as much as he does. He was secretive about his work, though. He's always kept a small team slightly separate from the company. They're his people, not Adsero people.'

Casey wondered if the Adsero board even knew about the Njana operation.

'I was up in his office one day,' Garrick went on. 'He's got shelves and shelves of files up there. I suppose you'd expect it, but, still, hundreds of files. And I saw that one of the files was just marked "Garrick". Elias was off somewhere, so I didn't ask, I just opened it. And it was Corax. There wasn't much information, but enough for me to know what it was. I'd listened in to a lot of meetings about antibiotics by then. I knew enough to see that this one was important.'

'So what did you do?'

'I asked him about it,' said Garrick. 'At dinner, that evening. He was absolutely furious. Apoplectic. Told me I must never go into his office again. Told me I must never mention Corax ever again. I've never seen him so angry. And the file had *my* name on it.'

'But you carried on working for Adsero after that?'

Garrick paused. A cargo ship was tracking across the horizon, and Garrick's eyes followed it. 'For a while. And then I decided to stop. I decided to go and set up Pergamex, swiping the information from the file, and see if I could get Corax to work. I know it was wrong, but … '

'But something else happened first.' Casey was watching him closely. 'What happened to make you finally decide to leave?'

50

Garrick's eyes met hers for a second. 'I can't … ' He was almost pleading. 'He's my *father.*'

'What did your mother think about Elias reappearing in your life?' Casey decided to come back to Garrick's departure to set up Pergamex later.

'She didn't like it,' said Garrick. 'Whatever there had been between the two of them once, it was long gone by the time I was in my twenties. She was young when she met him, you know? And after she had me, I don't know … It knocked her out of the life she ought to have had. She was on a track going one way – a happy family, a nice home, a nice life – and suddenly she was right off that path. I remember her talking about growing up in South Africa. She loved it here, absolutely loved it. She always adored the outdoors, and she'd talk about riding on the beach at Noordhoek, swimming in the sea at Hermanus, driving to Knysna for a weekend of parties. She was at her happiest here, and then she had to give it all up.'

Pretty little Jeanie.

'What is she like?' Casey was curious.

'She's a golden person,' said Garrick. 'Whenever I think of her, I think of her laughing. She's generous, kind. But she always worries about what people think of her. And she worries about letting people down. I don't know … She's always been a bit fragile.'

Insecure, Casey diagnosed. Looking for someone to look after her. But also adept at making men feel as if she needed looking after, especially her son.

'What is she doing now?'

'She was with a nice guy for a bit,' Garrick's face clouded over abruptly. 'But he died.'

'Oh,' said Casey. 'I'm sorry.'

'She was very upset about it.'

'What does she do for work?'

'This and that,' said Garrick. 'She teaches Pilates a bit. She never really got into a career.'

'And she didn't like Elias coming back into your life?'

'Not at all. I rang her after I had met him for the first time, on the waterfront in Toronto. And her voice just went flat.'

'But she didn't put you off getting to know him?'

'She never mentioned it again,' said Garrick. 'That's what she does when she doesn't like something. She doesn't mention it at all, just acts like it isn't there.'

Garrick was thinner round the face than he had been in Miami, Casey thought. There were two lines down the middle of his forehead, between permanently anxious eyes.

'So after you left Adsero, you moved back to San Francisco,' Casey prompted him.

'I knew people in San Fran,' Garrick explained. 'I could get investors. I needed capital to start working on Corax.'

'And I moved out there not long after,' said Zac. 'I started working on Corax too, so we could get more money into the business.'

'Then we recruited more people,' said Garrick. 'We put together a really great team.'

'Including your little doctor friend,' Zac smirked at Casey.

She ignored him, speaking directly to Garrick. 'What happened then?'

'A few months later, Bailey found out that we were working on Corax.' Garrick's face tautened. He paused. 'What are you actually going to do with all this information?' he asked Casey. 'I don't even know who you are, not really. What is your plan?'

Casey stopped walking and met Garrick's eyes. 'I'm not sure,' she said. 'I think Bailey is doing something odd in Zimbabwe with

246

saepio, but I can't prove that it's actively malignant. And separately I can't work out what happened with the development of Corax.'

'Then what are you doing here?' Garrick sounded impatient. 'What do you want?'

Casey sat down on the sand. Zac dropped down too. A moment later, Garrick threw himself to the ground beside them.

'People close to your father.' Casey looked Garrick straight in the eye. 'People linked to Corax. They die, Garrick. Too many of them have died.'

Garrick jumped to his feet. 'You can't prove that.'

Casey stayed on the sand, staring out at the sea. 'I know I can't prove it, Garrick. Not yet. But I just know it. I know that it's true.'

'Who died?' Garrick took a few steps down the beach, moving convulsively. 'When?'

'A scientist in London. A young woman in Devon a few years ago.' Casey's throat closed up for a second. 'An ex-Marine, a few months back.'

'And why do you think it is Corax that links them all?' said Garrick. 'Maybe it's you who links them all. Have you ever thought of that?'

Casey closed her eyes. 'Yes,' she said quietly. 'I have thought of that.'

'We have to get to the bottom of all this,' Zac interrupted Garrick's rising hysteria. 'You know that. And this is the only way, Garrick.'

Garrick was pressing his palms against the back of his neck, fingers interlinked, all the muscles in his shoulders tensed.

'What happened?' Casey couldn't contain herself any longer. 'In San Francisco. What did Bailey say to get you to back off, Zac?'

Zac met her eyes coolly. 'You already know, Psyche,' he said. 'Bailey wrote me a cheque. A very big one. And I went off to Mauritius, to live happily ever after.'

'It wasn't just that though.'

'No.' He spread his hands wide. 'It wasn't quite.'

Back in the beautiful Constantia house, Casey had looked at the photograph for a long time. Stared at it just as Loelia Bailey must have once gazed. Calculating, deducing, guessing.

In a rage.

'You can have that one if you want,' Loelia had said casually, as she flipped through the stack of photographs in the shade of the periwinkle parasol. 'I've got copies.'

Because there he was. Three across from Garrick, standing to attention in the back row: the dark hair, the eyes slanting against the sun, that sardonic smile.

Zac.

'You were at school together,' said Casey now. 'Both of you, at Drewsteignton's.'

'I knew you'd get there in the end,' Zac grinned. 'It took you bloody ages though. You must be losing your touch.'

'You went there on a scholarship, Zac?'

'Yes. A teacher steered me that way when I was twelve. Odd how one person can change everything.'

Drewsteignton – school to a dozen foreign princelings – had nothing visible online. Everything digital was swept clean, so carefully. So there was no photograph of the head boy, a line of badges neat on his blazer. There was no photograph of the hockey team grinning in tidy rows, those loyalties like steel hawsers under the sand. And there was certainly no photograph of the first fifteen, nearly twenty years on. Not with the treasured son of a Gulf sheikh right there, next to Garrick.

For all her hours of searching, Casey could never have tracked down a young Zac Napier in Drewsteignton's impeccable uniform. That had required Loelia, working angrily, fiercely, from the opposite direction.

'They must be just delighted with how you've turned out.' Casey smiled thinly. 'And how about you, Garrick? How did Bailey buy you out?'

Immediately, she knew she had said the wrong thing. Garrick's face crumpled like a paper bag.

'I can't … '

'You can,' Casey snapped, the frustration biting hard. 'Of course you bloody can, Garrick. And if you don't, you'll have to be scared of him forever. And scared of what I'll find out too, because I will get to the bottom of this, Garrick. I will. And when I do, you'll be right in the heart of it all.'

'She's right, Garrick.' Zac dropped the cynicism for once. 'I'm pretty sure that Adsero know that I am talking to Ca— And if they do … '

'But—'

'She's dug into too many things.' Zac's eyes bored into Casey's. 'Couldn't keep her sodding nose out. And I've spent enough time with her now to know that she won't stop either.'

'No,' said Casey. 'I won't. I'm going to get to the bottom of all this, Garrick. And you can either help me, or … '

The words hung in the air, thunder in the distance.

'But … ' Garrick turned towards the mountain, as if he might find comfort there.

Casey and Zac waited.

'Come on,' Casey was impatient, 'We don't have time—'

She stopped talking at a small gesture from Zac.

'It's time to end all this,' Zac spoke straight to Garrick. 'Now.'

Garrick's eyes were still on the green skirts of the mountain, as if he might wish himself there, far away from this beach.

'Elias threatened me.' As he started to speak, Garrick's voice was almost a whisper. 'When he came out to San Francisco. He said he would destroy me if I didn't shut down the whole Corax operation immediately.'

'How did he say it? In those exact words?'

'He came to my house in Pacific Heights,' said Garrick quietly. 'The house that he had bought me. That's how he started it all off. By pointing out that he had given me everything. *Everything*.'

'He hadn't given you everything,' said Casey. 'You'd have been fine on your own, Garrick. You already had your own businesses before you met him.'

'Maybe,' said Garrick. 'Maybe not. But he listed it all, bit by bit. Drewsteignton. The job at Adsero. Even renting my mother's house in Sussex for her. Everything.'

'That was his choice,' said Casey. 'And by renting her house, he kept her dependent on him.'

'That's sort of what I said.' Garrick kicked at the sand. 'I said I'd pay him back, move out of the Pacific Heights house. Return it all, somehow. But that's when he got really angry. He said if I didn't do what he wanted, it would be my mother who suffered.'

Garrick stared at Casey, half-pleading.

'Jeanie?'

'Yes.'

'What did he mean by that?'

'I didn't know.'

'How did you know he was serious? He might have just been trying to scare you.'

'I knew that he meant it. His face … I knew it. I decided we had to shut down Pergamex. I didn't know what Elias might do, but he scared me. And Adsero had more than enough to take down Pergamex anyway. They're a multinational, for God's sake. They can do whatever they want, just using lawyers.'

'Yes.'

'Zac went mad when I told him we were shutting down Pergamex,' said Garrick. 'He was furious. Said that we were doing crucial work, and that we couldn't stop just like that. He said we were going to carry on, and I was being crazy. And he said I couldn't stop him anyway, that he would just take the formula somewhere else. It wasn't like I could have fought that, given that I had stolen it in the first place. Elias had gone up to Vancouver for the day, but when he got back to San Francisco, I told him I couldn't control Zac, and I didn't know what to do … '

Garrick stopped, remembering.

'What did Bailey do then?' asked Casey.

'He just shrugged,' said Garrick. 'We'd met in a hotel lobby, for God's sake, with people all around us. He was staying in the most expensive hotel in San Fran, of course. He just stood up and said he had a meeting in ten minutes.'

'I remember you calling me afterwards,' said Zac. 'Saying he seemed fine with it all.'

'But then my phone went at 4 a.m. the next morning,' said Garrick. 'My mother, and she was screaming. Completely hysterical. It was

Frank, her boyfriend. He'd gone out for a walk that morning. They had two little dogs. Pomeranians. Stupid things, but she loved them, and Frank had taken them out … '

'What happened?'

'Frank was … Frank was dead.'

51

'What happened to him?' Casey asked urgently.

'He had a heart attack,' Garrick faltered. 'Out walking in the woods next to their house. He'd had a heart attack and died.'

A shape on the floor.

'A heart attack?' Casey could hear her voice had roughened. 'Your mother's boyfriend died of a heart attack?'

'That's what the doctors said,' Garrick said miserably. 'Afterwards. After the post-mortem, and all that. They said he'd had a huge heart attack out on the walk, and that there had been no way of saving him.'

'A heart attack … ' Casey put the heels of her palms to her eyes, ramming them into the sockets.

My love, beloved.

'My mother was screaming down the phone to me,' said Garrick. 'No words, just this awful wailing. A policewoman took the phone, and said if there was any way I could get home, it would be for the best. Now, please.'

'You flew back to England?'

'I got the first flight,' Garrick said. 'But before I headed to the airport, I went to the hotel where Elias was staying. That stupid, swanky boutique hotel. It wasn't even dawn yet, but I got reception to ring his room. Made them. And when he answered, I shouted: "Did you do this? Did you? Did you?"'

'What did he say?'

'Nothing,' said Garrick. 'He just sat there in silence, and then just as I was putting the phone down, he said – very quietly, so I almost didn't hear it – "Worse things can happen, Garrick." And then the phone went dead.'

Casey was watching Garrick's mouth move, forcing herself to concentrate.

'What did you think he meant by that?'

'He was threatening my mother,' Garrick spoke confidently, for once. 'And me. I know exactly what he meant.'

'Did you tell the police?'

'Tell them what?' Garrick said bleakly. 'How?'

The tide was rushing in now, the waves splashing higher.

'Could they cause someone to have a heart attack like that?' Casey asked Zac. 'Could someone make a murder look like a normal heart attack?'

'Bailey runs a pharmaceutical company,' Zac shrugged, 'He was a NatSci at Cambridge, too. An excellent one. I'm sure there are all sorts of ways he could have done it, with that background, and with access to Adsero's stock of chemicals. It could be something as simple as injecting someone with a massive dose of insulin; it would be incredibly hard to trace it because your blood sugar levels go haywire after you die anyway. I imagine there are all sorts of other things, their anaesthetics … '

'Bailey certainly didn't do it himself,' said Casey. 'He was safely in San Francisco. But he has people around him.'

She thought briefly of the man who had scared off Noah Hart in the taxi rank outside Milton Keynes station, the man who chased her through Hampstead Heath.

'No,' agreed Zac. 'It wasn't Bailey himself.'

'Frank was cremated,' Garrick looked gaunt. 'I never said anything to my mother. She was in such a state, anyway. And I didn't want her to be even more upset.'

Casey wondered if Bailey could have given the order to kill Jeanie. Ordered the death of a woman he must have loved once. Garrick hadn't risked it, though. Garrick, who knew Bailey well.

'And then you got a payout from Bailey?' Casey heard the accusation in her voice.

'Yes,' Garrick wilted. 'I did.'

'He had to really,' put in Zac. 'We had investors. We couldn't just shut the whole thing down overnight. People would have asked questions.'

People like Noah Hart, thought Casey.

'Elias bought the rights to Corax through a British Virgin Islands company,' said Garrick. 'We did it formally. The investors got enough to keep them quiet.'

'How convenient.' Casey was glacial.

Zac met her eyes evenly. 'I believed he would kill Jeanie. And probably Garrick. And me too, critically. There was a carrot, but there was a bloody big stick too.' He shrugged. 'Not everyone spends their whole life looking for a hill to die on.'

'I don't … ' She turned away from him.

'So.' Garrick sat down on the sand again. 'What on earth do we do now?'

'We need to prove it,' said Casey firmly. 'Everything is circumstantial at the moment. When we go for Elias Bailey, we're going to have to be sure.'

'You can't prove he is doing anything catastrophically wrong with saepio,' Zac began. 'Abigail, down in Devon, she may have just driven off the road, and there is no evidence to suggest otherwise. Then there is Ernest Brennan. Still nothing to suggest that incident was anything other than a bike accident.' He raised his eyebrows at Casey.

'One of my colleagues is monitoring that in London,' said Casey. 'There were no witnesses, nothing.'

'Then there's the ex-Marine.' The casualness of Zac's words felt like a blow.

'Ed,' she said. 'There's Ed.'

'Sure. And finally, there's Frank. Both Ed and Frank died of heart attacks, which may be a coincidence.'

'Was Frank healthy?' Casey turned to Garrick, unable to bear Zac's nonchalance.

'Yes,' Garrick nodded confidently. 'My mother does Pilates, everything like that, and she got him into it too. She and Frank walked the dogs together, went jogging, all sorts of stuff. Frank must have been in his sixties, but he was fit.'

'How do we prove anything?' Casey fretted.

'Could you ring up Bailey?' Zac asked Garrick. 'Or just confront him? With a wire, or a camera.'

'Bailey is too careful,' Casey said. She thought of Hessa facing down the Adsero chief executive in that hotel room in Wrocław, the force of his rage. 'And he probably doesn't trust Garrick.'

She sensed Garrick flinch, but he stayed silent. It was true.

Loelia? Casey wondered. Then rejected the idea. She wasn't sure of Loelia's loyalties either, even though she had spoken freely, and handed over the photographs. Loelia hadn't even seen Bailey for years, and any reunion would be too freighted with emotion. She couldn't imagine Loelia getting Bailey to drop his mask.

'Where is Bailey at the moment?' asked Zac.

'His jet is still in Frankfurt,' said Casey.

'There's a factory near there,' Garrick agreed. 'He quite often spends time in Germany. He likes it there.'

'Well,' said Zac. 'Garrick, could you get us into the Llandudno house? To see the files he keeps there?'

Garrick hesitated, and Casey could see the tension across his shoulders.

'Could you?' she pushed.

'I don't know,' he said. 'I know the staff there, of course. I spent enough time there that they would recognise me.'

'Right,' said Casey briskly. 'Well, we'll try that.'

'They might check,' Garrick said doubtfully. 'They might ring him up.'

'How did you leave it with him?' said Casey. 'The last time you saw him.'

'I told him he was a bastard.' There was a glint in Garrick's eye. 'I told him never to come near me or my mother ever again.'

'Never mind,' said Casey cheerfully. 'He probably didn't spell all that out to his Cape Town staff.'

52

'Mabel!' Garrick threw his hands wide, too wide for sobriety. 'How the devil are you?'

The housekeeper regarded him solemnly. 'Good morning, Mr Garrick.'

'Would you believe it?' Garrick swayed artistically. 'We've been bloody mugged! All our things stolen!'

'Mugged!' chirruped Casey behind him. 'Bloody mugged.'

Casey wore a short black dress, and was carrying a pair of six-inch heels in one hand, and a big sequined bag in the other. The bag glittered in the light of the dawn. Barefoot, she teetered awkwardly on the gravel, cackling as she clutched at Garrick's arm. Last night, she had plastered on her make-up and then forced herself to sleep in it for a few hours. Before leaving the hotel room, she had backcombed her hair wildly and pinned it into place with a couple of diamante clips. Now Casey giggled again, a high-pitched sound ebbing away to drunken sniggers.

Mabel's eyes swept over her, the disapproval not quite hidden.

Garrick wore dark trousers, the suit jacket abandoned. His shirt buttons were undone, and his fuchsia-pink tie loosened. There was a smudge of Casey's scarlet lipstick on his collar, and she had chucked a shot of vodka over his blue shirt. The stench of stale spirits was a smear on the bright blue morning, clashing with Casey's perfume and the choke of cigarette smoke.

'Mr Elias is not here,' Mabel said uncertainly.

The housekeeper was standing at the side gate, her body tilted back towards the main house. This was not a house people walked up to, thought Casey: this side gate was barely ever used. Mabel was used to people driving up to the house, and the big electric gates deciding who entered, and who didn't.

Security cameras – several of them – peered down blandly. A few yards from the gates a guardhouse squatted.

'I know, Mabel,' Garrick said cheerily, too loud. 'Dad's in wretched Germany. But I need to call a driver, the police, everything. The bloody bastards pulled a gun on me, can you believe it? A gun! They stole my car, my cell, Carrie's handbag. This country, dude … Still, at least we're OK. Lucky, hey?'

As he spoke, they were bustling through the gate past the housekeeper.

'We were at a party in Llandudno,' Casey tossed over her shoulder, as she reeled past a marble fountain topped by a pouting cupid. 'It was such fun! Such great people! And then we thought we would drive up to the lookout, and there … Bloody bastards.'

'We had to walk,' Garrick spoke as if surprised by the notion. 'All the way here. Took fucking ages!'

'These shoes!' Casey trilled. 'Agony, I tell you … '

Delphine had driven them from Camps Bay to the seaside village of Llandudno, just south of Cape Town's central business district. Racing past the Twelve Apostles, severe in the dawn, then parking the car by the beach.

'I'll wait here,' said Delphine, and Casey nodded, tense.

They walked up through Llandudno to the long driveway that led to Bailey's house. The house stood alone, in the hills just outside the little town. The sun had risen as they walked, the fynbos – low scrubby bushes, small scrappy shrubs – rolling away on either side of the track. Far below the house, the sea glittered white and blue in the new day.

'I've got no idea how they managed to get permission to build this place,' Garrick had muttered.

As they got nearer to the house, Casey had felt the fear surge again, and turned away so Garrick couldn't see her face.

It feels as if I have lost my nerve.

It can happen.

Stage fright, on a raked stage.

'Don't worry,' Garrick said, almost as if he had read her thoughts. 'I've known Mabel for ages. It'll be fine. And his bodyguards only stay up at the house when he's in the country.'

And they walked on.

'Mr Garrick … ' The housekeeper tried again.

But they ignored her, strolling up the white steps to the huge entrance hall.

'What a gorgeous place,' slurred Casey, crossing the lobby. 'You were right, G. It is absolutely stunning.'

The house was built along sleek lines and geometric angles, almost every room opening out towards the sea. A wide spiral staircase curled up from the entrance hall towards the first floor, with a gallery running right the way around the enormous room. Beyond the huge windows, Casey could see a vast infinity pool twinkling in the sunlight.

'I need a sodding coffee,' shouted Garrick. 'Mabel, can you get me one?'

'Breakfast!' gloated Casey. 'Yes! Oh, I'm starving!'

Mabel hesitated.

'I suppose I had better call Dad! Tell him about the car.' Garrick clapped his hand over his mouth. Then he peered vacantly at his watch. 'Better leave it an hour or so. He'd be well and truly pissed off if I called him right now.'

'I can't wait to meet your father,' Casey squeaked, the smallest emphasis on the last word. 'It's such a shame he's not here!'

'And you're wearing just the right outfit to meet him.' Garrick grabbed her waist. Then he turned, abruptly peremptory. 'Where's that coffee, Mabel?'

'Or maybe just one more glass of champagne?' tittered Casey.

'And that,' Garrick bowed deeply, 'is why I love you.'

Mabel gave the smallest sigh, and walked off towards the kitchen. As the double doors swung closed behind her, Casey's eyes met Garrick's. Upstairs, Casey indicated with her chin. *Now.*

'I'll show you my old bedroom,' Garrick shouted loudly, and they ran up the spiral staircase.

'This way.' Garrick turned right as they reached the gallery. There was another staircase ahead, this one narrow, climbing up towards a long window. They sprinted up it, as quietly as they could.

Bailey's office was just as Garrick had described. Beyond the wide balcony, Casey could see Llandudno's beach and the enormous granite boulders that divided the earth from the ocean here.

The sea looked stormy now, gusts of wind sending the buddleias in the garden dipping and swaying. Close to land, the water was a chilly turquoise, a rim of white marking the breakers. Further out, the water darkened to indigo. It was a beautiful but oddly bleak view.

For a moment, Casey felt a surge of euphoria. They were *in*. And then she halted, taking in the enormity of the task. The cream walls were almost completely covered by shelves and shelves of files. Hundreds of them, all a serviceable grey.

'Where do we start?' asked Garrick.

'I don't know.' Casey felt blank.

Lurching forward, she began reading the labels on the back of the files. The tags were written in a neat black script, unremarkable. Odd names jumped out at her: Pittsburgh. Frankfurt. Valladolid. Epping. Were those all Adsero factories? Garrick was staring round the room, looking equally bewildered, and Casey felt the frustration boil up.

'Where did you find the original file?' she asked quickly. 'The one with the Corax information?'

Garrick pointed vaguely across the room, close to a window overlooking the hills behind the house. 'There. On the shelf closest to the ground.'

Casey hurried over and dropped to her knees. There was no file with Garrick's name now. It must have been removed. She photographed the shelf of files, then pulled out a file and opened it at random. Pages and pages of small type: Adsero's research into the role of clozapine in the treatment of schizophrenia. The trial had been carried out in Slovakia, it seemed. She slapped the file closed. On to the next one. Clinical trials on an experimental drug for rheumatoid arthritis. Trial completed in Belgium two years ago. Next was an Adsero heart drug tested in Cape Town, just under four years ago.

A shiver at the time ticking away, and she shoved the file back on the shelf, jumping to her feet.

'This is all information about Adsero drug trials,' she said to Garrick. 'I don't know enough to know if any of it is useful. This one's about a heart trial in Cape Town, for God's sake.'

A needle in a haystack, thousands of pages of chaff.

'I didn't think they even did trials in South Africa,' said Garrick pensively. 'Only in Europe.'

Casey slammed another file back into place. 'It hardly matters, Garrick. We need to find something that proves ... '

'He's probably being more careful nowadays,' said Garrick. 'Once bitten.'

Casey roamed around the room, reading one line of file labels, then another. She felt like a wasp, battering itself pointlessly against a sheet of glass, and then a blaze of anger. *Stupid girl. Come on.*

'Mr Garrick?' Casey jumped at the sound of Mabel's voice, unsure, on the landing just at the bottom of the stairs.

'I'm just showing Carrie the view from up here,' Garrick called down. His voice was a mistake, thought Casey. He was justifying himself to the housekeeper, which he wouldn't do normally. 'Is breakfast ready, Mabel?'

'Nearly, Mr Garrick.'

The footsteps receded haltingly.

Casey glared at Garrick, then ricocheted around the room once more, stopping by another window, this one overlooking the drive and the courtyard at the back of the house. Here were more rows of files. More neat black script. There was only a tangle of letters on the back of these files. ASF, KJT, FBT, BHF, WGF. Gibberish. She felt as if the maze was closing in around her: the dark yew hedges fairy-tale flourishing even as she hesitated. And any minute, the blackness would enclose, enfold, engulf.

Casey yanked out the WGF file blindly. The Wheaton Gulati Foundation, according to the first page in the file. She flicked through it mindlessly, then stopped sharply, going over the last few words again in confusion.

The Wheaton Gulati Foundation had been set up to pay for scholarships, Casey saw. It had been established to select ten high achieving girls from sub-Saharan Africa and send them to European universities. The sums were not small either. Casey looked closer, intrigued. Forgetting her surroundings, she started to read through the funding agreements more carefully. They had all been initialled by Bailey, with a neat E and a distinctively rounded B.

'Did you know your father was funding scholarships?' Casey asked over her shoulder. 'To universities in the EU.'

'No.' Garrick came to peer over her shoulder. 'He never mentioned it. How odd.'

Casey pulled out the next file along. ASF. The Almond Sheehan Foundation. This fund had been set up to pay for cataract operations for refugees in southern Asia. Fascinated despite herself, Casey flicked through the pages.

'What the hell is Bailey up to?'

'I have no idea,' Garrick said.

Casey shoved the ASF file back on the shelf, knocking another file off the end.

'Damn.'

As she bent to pick up the file, there was a distant roar out on the road. Casey looked up and felt fear slap her.

A black pickup was roaring up the narrow track towards the house.

53

'Garrick,' she whispered.

He was across the room in a flash, still clutching a file. 'Oh, no,' he said. 'Oh, God.'

'Who is it?'

The electric gates were swinging open long before the car could reach them. The pickup was kicking up a trail of dust as it tore up the hillside, screeching round the switchbacks.

'Quickly.' There was panic in Garrick's voice. 'We can't be caught up here. We have to get downstairs to my bedroom. It looks fine if we're caught there. Just about.'

'But who is it?'

'I don't know. Elias has bodyguards.' Garrick's eyes were wide, haunted. 'They must be his Cape Town people. Mabel must have called them ... Oh, God ... '

Garrick gripped Casey's hand and started dragging her towards the staircase.

'Hurry.'

She pulled back for a moment. 'I have to ... '

Casey grabbed the file that she had knocked off the end of the shelf. The file had flipped open as it fell, and as she closed it, Casey caught a glimpse of the front page of the notes.

The Fitzgerald Brennan Trust.

'Wait.' Casey jerked her arm out of Garrick's reach. 'Wait. I have to look at this.'

'What?' Garrick turned terrified eyes on her, his panic raw as meat. 'We have to go. We have to go right now!'

Out of the window, Casey could see the black pickup race into the last stretch. There were four men in the car, big, tough-looking men. As the pickup driver accelerated, he looked up, and for a split second his eyes met Casey's.

'We have to get downstairs.' Garrick yanked at her arm. 'Don't you see? If they catch us up here, they'll know … He'll know … '

'It's too late,' Casey said hopelessly. 'They've seen me. And Mabel knows we've been up here anyway … '

'Shit.' Garrick clutched at her forearm again. 'We have to get out of here. We have to … '

But Casey was pulling away from him. The Fitzgerald Brennan Trust. *The Fitzgerald Brennan Trust.*

She ripped open the file.

'What are you doing?' It was almost a howl. 'We've got to run!'

'But don't you see?' Casey shouted over him. 'Ed Fitzgerald. Ernest Brennan. This trust was set up in *their* names.'

'What?' Garrick stared at her.

Below the window, the pickup had screeched to a halt by the pouting cupid statue. The men were spilling out of it fast. There was no pretence here. No polite we-just-thought-we'd-stop-by-for-a-check. As Casey looked down, a man sprang out of the car and pulled out a gun.

Garrick glanced out of the window and Casey heard a shout that was almost a scream.

'They're going to kill us,' Garrick gasped. 'They're really going to kill us.'

'They won't kill us.' Casey wasn't at all sure if she believed that.

Moving quickly, she ripped a few pages out of the file she was holding. She yanked open her foolish sequined bag and pulled out a pair of trainers. She put them on, shoving the papers into the bag.

'Don't … '

'It's too late, Garrick,' she said. 'They know we've been up here.'

Garrick stumbled towards the staircase. 'They know … They know … ' It was as if his mind had jammed.

'Don't, Garrick … '

But there was nothing else to suggest.

There were shouts from below. The men were in the house now.

'Garrick!'

He looked back over his shoulder. 'I'm sorry.'

'Don't!'

There was a look of sympathy in his eyes, a glimmer of apology, and then he took the first step down the stairs. She heard his voice, loud and confident. 'Guys, guys. I'm Mr Bailey's son, hey? Chill out.'

There was a brief pause, then a rough voice with a strong Afrikaans accent, 'Put your fucking hands up, mister.'

'Sure, sure.'

'Where's the fucking girl?'

'The girl?'

'We've seen her on the security video, dude. We know she's here.'

'Hey, you don't need to be rough.' Garrick's voice pitched up sharply, 'My father wouldn't like it—'

'He's given us the fucking orders, buddy.' A scuffle, the sound of a punch. 'Now where the fuck is she?'

A silence, stunned, and Casey could almost see Garrick nodding towards the stairs. *That way.*

Casey scanned the office, a rat in a trap. The room was at the top of the house, and there was no way out, no escape anywhere. Beyond the French doors, the sea sparkled. Casey dashed across the room, slamming into the double doors. She tore at them frantically, but they were locked, solid, not giving an inch. A key? On the desk maybe? She was across the room in a bound, but the desk was bare. She yanked open the desk drawers. Notepads, pens, a hole punch: no key.

Casey looked back at the windows. A heavy green lamp sat on the desk, its solid bronze base gleaming. Casey grabbed it, tore it from its socket and raced across the room trailing wires. She hurled the lamp hard against the glass. The window shattered, still too small a gap. Casey snatched up the lamp and battered the window again and again, glass flying through the air.

Someone was racing up the stairs, footsteps loud on the treads. There was no time to look around, no time to … Casey forced her way through the gap, glass ripping her clothes. She felt an edge slice down her leg, pure agony, and screamed. But she was through.

Casey darted to the polished chrome railings. There was no staircase down. Nothing. Behind her the men were trying to force their way after her through the big French windows.

There was the blue of the infinity pool, wide and glittering. The water was perfectly flat, not even a ripple. There was no thought, just a scramble up the railings. Up, and over, and off.

For a split second, it was as if she was barely falling, the world frozen, the horizon oddly steady.

You'll smash into the bottom of the pool, spine shattering into a thousand pieces.

You'll be unable to escape, unable to swim, drowning as those men look down with a laugh.

But it was too late. She was falling, and it was as if she was falling forever, a bird shot out of the sky.

54

The water slapped her face and swallowed her up. There was an explosion of aquamarine. Her feet slammed hard into the bottom of the pool, and her legs folded up with a searing pain.

She was stunned for a split second, floating almost peacefully in that blue, blue water, and then she was moving awkwardly, her limbs spasming, her lungs starting to scream *now*. And then she was fighting her way to the surface, her legs still able to kick.

Casey broke the surface, looking up. Three men were on the edge of the balcony, staring down. As she scrambled to the side of the pool, she saw a movement, heard the curt shout, 'Get her.'

A gun.

Casey fought through the water, struggling and desperate. The water was so heavy, so placid, absorbing all her panic and deadening her frenzy.

There was a silver ladder fixed to the side of the pool, picture perfect in the blue, and she got a hand on it just as the gun went off, the bullet smashing into the marble side of the pool and sending up a shock wave of water.

Casey scrabbled to climb the ladder.

Another bullet, this one blasting into the paving stones around the pool, sending up splinters of marble.

But she was out of the pool, and she ran, half crouched, leaping over the bank beyond the infinity pool, and tearing away down the hill, leaving the house behind. The earthworks for the infinity pool helped her, creating a solid barrier between her and the house, and then she was racing through the garden, out in the open, back tensed for a bullet.

She ran and ran, waiting for the blast of the gun. The ground was powdery and steep, splinters of rock sliding away. Casey skidded and slipped all the way down the hill, the earth crumbling away beneath her.

Bailey's land ran down to the sea, she realised. On both sides of the property, there was a high barbed-wire fence. Ahead there was a fringe of greenery above huge granite rocks that dropped straight down into the sea. There was no beach here, no softening of the landscape. A narrow path led through the shrubbery, and beyond the wind-blasted trees, she could just make out a small jetty.

As she ran, Casey assessed the barbed-wire fence. There was no way she could climb that. Red caught her eye: blood running down her shin from her sliced leg, and she could feel a sharp pain.

Behind her, she could hear shouts. The men must have sprinted through the house, and now they were chasing her, hunting her down. She glanced back and caught sight of three men. Tall and fast, two of them holding guns.

Casey ran.

Ahead of her, the sea glimmered. She could see the white buildings of Llandudno far along the coast, glimmering in the early morning sun. But they were an impossible distance away.

The men were gaining on her, far faster down the crumbling hillside. They were wearing proper boots, proper shoes, not a stupid black dress and trainers. *Stupid girl.*

Casey reached the narrow path that twisted through the greenery, and didn't slow down. Branches whipped at her face, catching her hair and tearing at her dress. As she reached the open air again, she could almost feel the waves pounding at the rocks. The sound swallowed her up. These waves were huge, six foot high maybe, and relentless, inexorable, grinding into the crags of the granite.

A toy soldier trapped …

There was a boat tied up to the jetty. A silver speedboat, maybe twenty foot long. Casey glanced at it, assessing and rejecting. No key.

No time to untie the boat, no time to start it, and take the risk. No time … She scrambled out over the rocks.

The waves filled her world, crashing and roaring, the spray sharp in the air. Behind her the men had reached the jetty and were bounding on to the rocks, almost enjoying this pursuit. Casey leaped from rock to rock. Jumping, eyeing the next move, throwing herself into the air. Any slip, any missed step, that would be the end. An ankle sliding into a crack, a leg snapping like a wishbone. It would be over. The gun fired again, and they were so near, so close.

Casey was at the ocean's edge now, the waves crashing into the rocks just below her feet. Beyond the blast and the spray, the water was a filigree of blue and white, heaving up and down as if the sea were breathing. Seagulls shrieked overhead, buffeted by the wind.

Casey clambered on, scraping her knees and elbows. The blood was running down her leg, spattering red as she ran.

A few more steps, round yet another boulder, and she halted with horror. A jag of granite stuck out into the sea, smooth and sheer. The boulder was thirty feet high, unclimbable, the sea thundering at its base.

She was trapped.

'Get her!' The first man was less than twenty feet behind her now, springing from rock to rock.

It was impossible. There was no way forward, no way back. A seagull was hovering just a few yards out to sea, screaming into the wind.

Casey hesitated, staring down at the roiling water, and then she threw herself into the void.

55

The water was icy and Casey felt the ocean grip her instantly. There was a whirl of currents tugging her this way and that. She surfaced for a gasp of air and dived down again, swimming as deep as she could, knifing her way through the water.

The ocean roared. But this time she was ready for it. Not battling the power of the ocean, but slicing through it, letting the rip tide carry her along.

She had to get round the base of that promontory. Had to.

Casey surfaced: another gasp of air. She turned back instinctively, looking round for the bodyguards.

One man was standing on the edge of the rocks, and the other two had nearly caught up. It was the other two who had the guns. They had been slowed down by their weapons. Casey ducked her head underwater again, and swam as hard as she could, the taste of salt in her mouth.

Ahead was the jag of granite, the seaweed waving almost lazily. And now she was fighting the water, too desperate to let the rip carry her along. *Come on.*

To the surface: an ear-splitting bang and she dived down again. Up again. An explosion shattering the air. Down again. Last chance, raging against the might of the ocean. She swam and swam, until her lungs felt like they would explode.

To the surface. To the surface now.

Up again, her head jerking round to look back. And at last all she could see was granite, beautiful, solid granite. She had made it round the jag of rock sticking out in the ocean.

She had made it to cover. She had made it out of sight.

She was safe.

The tide yanked at her, the granite boulders gazing down bleakly.

No, not safe. Not safe at all.

Casey swam through waves, suddenly ice cold. It was that sweep of the Benguela, up from the Antarctic, bringing the current of ice. The sun was warm now, hot on her face, but the water was leaching away her energy, wave after wave after wave.

She was swimming with the tide, it was impossible to fight it. Desperately looking for somewhere to come ashore, to scramble up into the hills. But the granite boulders were huge, and the waves were breaking white over rocks hidden just beneath the surface.

A deep breath, head down, onwards. She had kicked off her shoes somewhere, and the sequined bag was long gone.

What would those men do to Garrick? He had trusted in a father's love, almost sweetly, but that might not be enough. Bailey might decide the Corax theft had been Garrick's only chance. Once bitten ...

In her mind's eye, she saw those men again, holding the guns with the ease of familiarity. Bounding over the rocks so effortlessly. They weren't the usual Armed Guards: Immediate Response. Those teams could be idle amateurs, cigarettes dangling as they hopped in their pickups, cruising easily across town to switch off the shriek of a malfunctioning alarm. These men were professional, ruthlessly so.

She remembered Noah's fear of the man in Milton Keynes, the determination of the man on Hampstead Heath. Bailey had assembled a formidable team.

Casey's legs were getting heavy, slow, her leg was throbbing where she had sliced it. She remembered a sign she had seen back in Cape Town. *Great Whites! Cage diving! Out in the wild!*

And here she was, swimming with a trail of blood following her in the sea.

Her breath caught in her throat. It was hopeless, all of it. She would never escape.

A wave washed over her face, and then another, and she felt the sea pull her down, as it had so many. She felt the yawn of nothing beneath her. She was a speck in the vastness of the sea, and what would it matter if she stopped and let the ocean take her … What would it matter …

Light-headed.

Casey shook her head, forced her arms through the water. *Keep going.*

She was further from the shore now. The tide must be drifting her away from the land, inch by deadly inch. Casey tried to correct her course, legs kicking slowly. Kick, and kick, and kick again.

Debbie and Marcella and a galleon, on a hospital wall. Tony and Lauren and sea monsters, swirling through the magnolia.

Delirious.

There was a yacht, far ahead of her. Another speck in the immense expanse of this ocean. But the sailors would never see her, a small, dark head, bobbing in the sea, just another piece of jetsam. And she could never reach them: that yacht floated in another world, untouchable.

Keep kicking.

A sort of peace.

Keep trying.

This must be drowning …

Casey kicked again.

I'll be there in a minute.

She kept her eyes on the yacht, counting the strokes in her head for something to do. The hills wavered. They seemed nearer for a moment, then further away, then closer again. The yacht was tacking now, catching the wind. She thought of the *Renaissance*, flying over the waves. Those people were having a perfect day, right there, just out of her reach. They would live, and she would die, and that was all there was.

A wave caught her by surprise, swamping her, filling her eyes and her mouth with salt and water.

Maybe it was time.

Cat's Cradle or Kissing Gate? I love you.

Another kick.

You don't have to choose.

Another kick.

You do have to choose.

And behind her, she heard the scream of an engine.

It was the silver speedboat, searing over the waves. Casey turned her head almost dreamily, too tired for fear. The boat was bouncing from crest to crest, spattering spray and froth. In the blue of the morning, it looked almost beautiful.

There were three men on board, searching.

They saw her easily. She knew that they would. She might have been just one tiny dot in an endless surge of waves, but they were hunting her. She couldn't dive down out of sight. Not again. If she let go of the air, she would sink down and down, and never resurface.

She couldn't.

The speedboat was hurtling straight towards her now, its prow leaping out of the water as it powered along.

The shriek of the engine filled the air. Casey was hypnotised by the thud of the boat skimming over the waves towards her. It was less than a hundred feet away now.

You do have to choose.

Casey dived beneath the surface, forcing herself deep into the clutches of the ocean.

The boat stormed over her, the propellers ripping through the water just a few inches above her feet. There was an underwater howl, a comet trail of foam, and then the boat was out of sight, disappearing into the blue haze of the sea.

Casey's lungs burned.

Stay down.

I can't.

Stay down or you'll die.

But I can't.

She surged to the surface. In the distance, the speedboat was turning sharply. She could see the men's eyes raking the surface of the water, scanning, hunting: *there.*

The speedboat accelerated towards her again.

Casey imagined the propellers slicing through the water towards her. Those steel blades would churn blindly through the ocean: savage, indifferent killers. They would bite into her, carving through flesh and bone without hesitation. There would be a short, sharp scream absorbed by the water. An eruption of blood in the ocean. A few lumps of meat floating.

The sharks would deal with that.

The speedboat was coming back again, rearing up out of the water, and Casey dived down again, down again, deep into the strange world below.

She didn't make it as far down this time. She felt the punch of the water swirling just below the boat, and when she bobbed awkwardly to the surface, she saw one of the men at the front of the boat, pointing straight at her. That's what they did with a man overboard, wasn't it? That was one person's job: their only task. Point and point and point, so the ship didn't lose sight of a tiny black dot in the waves. Point and point, so she couldn't be lost. Point and point, so she could never survive.

The motor screamed again, faster this time. The big double propellers would be blurring round, too fast to see …

Down again, down again, down and down.

They must have decided that a battered, dismembered body would raise fewer questions than a bullet-ridden corpse. Must have decided not to bother with a gun. And it was fun, this, too.

Up again. A pathetic attempt to swim a few strokes to the left, to try and escape the man's gaze as she came up. But his eye was on her as soon as she surfaced: it was hopeless. You can't hide in an ocean. For a moment, Casey trod water, rising and falling with the waves.

Waiting.

The speedboat was turning, glittering in the sunlight.

Any second now, it would accelerate again. Any second now.

There was a burst of sound, somewhere off to Casey's left. A loud-speaker, far away. She was so focused on the speedboat at first that she barely noticed.

But the pace of the speedboat slackened, the motor dropping quite suddenly to a purr.

Casey turned her head with an agonising effort, startled to see the yacht far closer now. The yacht was moving rapidly, closing the gap with a surprising speed. Casey kept kicking, keeping her face just above the waves. Now she could make out a man in the prow of the yacht, and a few seconds later she could see a lifebuoy in his hands. The loudspeaker echoed over the water again.

'We'll get her, mate.'

The speedboat had come to a bobbing halt.

'We were trying to grab her,' one of the men shouted across, as the yacht drew nearer.

'Sure you were.' The tone was equivocal.

It was Zac, she realised. Zac, sailing the yacht with a careless ease.

He didn't wave, just set his jaw. Not engaging with the men on the speedboat as he concentrated on Casey, daring them to interrupt him. It was a big yacht, she could see. There was at least one other shape in the cockpit, and there might be any number of people below decks. Too many witnesses. Zac threw the lifebuoy to Casey, a bright orange splash in the water.

'She'll be fine now,' Zac shouted. 'You lot can head off.'

They hesitated, the speedboat's engine grumbling in neutral.

'Everything OK?' the second man was swinging forward from the yacht's cockpit, moving easily up the shifting deck.

'Everything's fine.'

Zac was leaning down to the water, and Casey felt only sheer exhaustion as she reached up with her last scrap of energy, grabbing for his hand.

'We have,' he murmured, 'to stop meeting like this.'

The next minute she was sprawled on the deck, gasping for air, unable to move. Somewhere far in the distance, she heard the speed-boat rev up, and then it was racing away over the waves, leaving only a hint of petrol fumes in the air.

Casey lay on the deck, watching the lowered sails flap aimlessly in the wind.

Zac passed her a Coke, and after a while, she struggled up and took a swig.

'Thank you.'

She was still wearing the black dress, soaked through and snagged in places. She examined the cut on her leg. The broken window had sliced deep. The blood was trickling down her leg, mingling with the seawater and dripping on the deck. Robotically, she assessed her other injuries. She had gashed her elbow, the skin torn and bruised. There was a deep graze on her shin that she didn't remember getting. As she stared at the graze – a shocked purple red, the shape of the rock scored deep into her skin – the leg started to throb.

'We're heading back to the harbour, so you'll be able to see a doctor soon,' the other man said. She assumed he was the yacht's skipper.

'Thank you. Thank you so much.'

'We could see,' the skipper said slowly, 'that the speedboat was moving about oddly.'

'Yes.'

'They did a right number on you. Do you want me to call the police?'

'No,' she said. 'No. I'm fine.'

He gave her a disillusioned look and made his way back to the cockpit. Zac threw her a towel, a big sweater and an old pair of board shorts, and she put them on, gratefully.

They raised the sails again, and tightened the sheets. And as they turned back towards the harbour, Casey watched the faraway hills, a million thoughts racing through her head.

56

Zac had chartered the yacht for a day's sailing, Casey deduced as they headed to the port. All the way back to the port, he gave no indication that he had met Casey before, busying himself with the sails.

At the harbour, the skipper summoned a taxi.

'She should get checked out at the hospital,' Zac said, as Casey limped towards the car. 'I'll take her.'

And the skipper nodded, waving them off.

Casey slumped in the back seat as the car weaved through the Cape Town chaos.

'Delphine saw you run from the house,' Zac said. 'She was watching with binoculars. She told me where to go.'

Casey nodded at the taxi driver. *Not now.*

'Jesus Christ, Casey,' Zac muttered.

He messaged Delphine though, showing Casey the screen. *I've got her. Speak later.*

A pause, and then he added a couple of words.
Thank you.

At the hotel, Casey hobbled through the courtyard. With the board shorts reefed around her waist and the oversized jumper reaching halfway to her knees, she knew she must look strange. Her hair had dried in the sea breeze, stiff with salt. The cut on her leg was still bleeding, and she was covered with scrapes and bruises. She felt the hotel staff's eyes land on her and flutter away again.

In Zac's room, she took him through the events in staccato sentences.

'What happened to Garrick?' he asked at the end.

'I don't know.' She knew she sounded cold.

Zac turned away from her, stepping towards the window, looking out at the brightness of the day. Casey watched his back, too tired for emotion.

'I'm sorry,' she added, unable to cover the insincerity in her voice. 'He may be all right.'

'And he may not be.'

Zac was tracing shapes on the floor to ceiling window, pushing his fingertips hard against the glass.

'I know you want to trust Garrick, Zac,' Casey said. 'But he hadn't even told you Bailey was his father.'

'I'm aware of that.' Zac sounded as if he was gritting his teeth.

He was silhouetted against the brilliance. Casey had to squint as she looked towards him.

'What version of events did Garrick tell you in San Francisco?' she persisted. 'When he said you had to stop developing Corax? Why didn't he just tell you Bailey was his father?'

'He told me that Bailey had threatened his mother,' said Zac. 'And that Frank was dead. I had known Jeanie McElroy for years, don't forget. She had always been … kind to me.'

Zac's mother had been ill, Casey remembered. Jeanie McElroy must have stepped into the breach when Zac and her son were at school together.

'So you agreed to go off to Mauritius and forget all about it? Take the money and run?'

'Not everyone wants their name on a plaque in a crappy park in London, Casey.'

'It was quite a big part of the story for Garrick to leave out though, wasn't it?'

'Yes.' Zac turned and met her eye.

She saw the hurt, for a split second, and didn't care. Pressed down harder on the bruise instead. 'Presumably Garrick will tell

Bailey that you're involved in getting to the bottom of whatever happened to Corax.'

'Presumably, yes. If he's still alive. Which he may not be judging by the state of you.'

'Why did Garrick stop working at Adsero?' Casey asked, the questions spiralling up endlessly. 'What happened to make him leave and set up his own company?'

'I don't know.' Zac sounded weary. 'He never said.'

'We have to … ' – but she ran out of words.

'So what now?' Zac turned back to the view. 'What now, Psyche?'

'I don't know.'

Casey staggered back to her own hotel room. The Fitzgerald Brennan Trust, she thought. The Fitzgerald Brennan Trust. *The Fitzgerald Brennan Trust.*

She dragged off the board shorts and the sweater and dumped the remains of the sparkly black dress in the wastepaper basket.

The papers from the office had been lost with the sequined bag. Her camera, too. Casey vaguely remembered the bag's strap snapping as she threw herself off the rocks and into the water. For a moment, she was furious with herself, but then she forced away the anger. No, you would not have made it if you had turned back for the bag. No, you couldn't go back. This was the only way.

She imagined the bag sinking down in the ocean below Bailey's house, the papers blurring and disintegrating, the camera snuffed out.

Everything was gone.

Casey threw herself on the bed, exhausted.

The Fitzgerald Brennan Trust, like a burr in her mind.

She sat up and reached for her laptop, searching for the name over and over again. Nothing came up.

Nothing.

Someone knocked on her door. She ignored it. Then her phone buzzed. *Let me in, Casey.*

Wearily, she stood, and opened the door.

Zac was carrying a paperback and a comprehensive-looking first-aid kit. Without a word, he gestured towards the bed. Feeling like a child, Casey sat on the edge of the bed, watching tiredly as he unpacked the small bag, laying out the contents neatly on the carpet. He dressed her wounds, one by one.

Antiseptic, *this'll sting, sorry*, and bandages, several of them, smoothed on so carefully.

It was easy to forget that he was a doctor, Casey thought blearily. And a good one too, once.

When he was finished, he looked up at her, not having to repeat the words. *What now?*

I don't know, thought Casey. I just don't know.

'I'll be outside,' said Zac.

He stood up and stepped out on to Casey's small balcony. He looked at the view, the blue of the sea so gentle from here, and then he sat down in a deckchair, opened the paperback and began to read.

Oddly comforted by his presence, Casey reached for the laptop again, scrolling through her notes.

She ignored a one-word message from Dash – *Budget??!* – and read through her notes on Flora Ashcroft once again. Then her notes on Colindale, and the transcript of the conversation with Noah. Fitting the jigsaw together, piece by piece. Does this fit here? No. Here? Definitely not. Start with the corners, then: what are you sure about?

Nothing.

She clicked open her file on the Njana visit. Here was the list of diseases. Here were the photographs of the agar plates.

Click, click, click. She checked through the photographs, one by one.

A biosafety cabinet. Rows of beakers. Tables made of scaffolding and planks. A wide shot of the laboratory.

Casey stopped, looking again at the photograph of the laboratory.

At the far end was the wall of cheap kitchen cabinets. And a stack of files.

Casey peered closer, zooming in. A stack of files. A stack of *grey* files. A stack of files just like the ones in the house in Llandudno.

'Zac,' she called out. 'Look.'

She enhanced the photograph as much as possible.

'What?' Zac was beside her. 'What am I looking at, Psyche?'

'There.' Casey pointed. 'Look there.'

'FBT,' Zac read aloud, 'ASF, WGF. What the hell does that mean?'

'The Fitzgerald Brennan Trust,' Casey spelled out the names. 'The Almond Sheehan Foundation. The Wheaton Gulati Foundation.'

'But what are they? I don't understand.'

'I don't know,' Casey said. 'I don't know, precisely.'

'You don't,' Zac corrected her, 'know at all.'

'It's a bit of a coincidence,' said Casey, 'that Bailey set up a foundation named after Ernest Brennan and Ed less than a month after they both died. What if he sets them up as a sort of … I don't know. A sort of atonement? A form of penance.'

'Expiation,' said Zac slowly. 'A stab at redemption.'

'It might … '

'But who is Almond then? Who is Sheehan?'

'I don't know,' said Casey.

She had trawled through dozens of websites as she sat on the hotel bed. Could see no suspicious deaths, and certainly nothing that tied them into Bailey.

'When was that foundation set up? The Almond Sheehan one?'

'Five or six years ago?' Casey tried to remember the panicked moments in the Llandudno office. 'Brennan was scared of Bailey. I saw it when he answered the phone in front of me. Maybe Bailey spoke to him again later. Maybe … '

She stared at the photograph of the laboratory. She had hidden in the cupboard directly under that stack of files, she thought, burning with frustration. She had been just inches away from the stack of information.

'Well,' said Zac. 'It doesn't really help us, does it? There's no way we can get back into Njana. Not now.'

They sat in silence, remembering the sprint out of the laboratory, the terrified dash to Henke's truck. And Henke, abandoned somewhere out in the reserve.

'We can't get back into the house in Llandudno either,' Casey said. 'I imagine that the posse of bodyguards will stay there now, with their guns and everything. I don't think we can risk it … '

'We certainly bloody can't.' Zac was firm. 'Absolutely no way.'

'But what do we do?' Casey cried out. 'How do we work it out?'

57

It seemed impossible that it was only lunchtime. Zac stood and walked over to the minibar. He pulled out two tiny bottles of vodka, grimaced and shoved them back into the fridge.

'Wait there.'

He was back a few seconds later with a large bottle of rum, still in a garish duty-free bag.

'Enough,' he said, unwrapping it. 'That's enough for today.'

They sat on the balcony, enjoying the heat of the sun. Casey could feel her limbs stiffening up, the cut on her leg throbbing.

'They both so desperately wanted it to be real, didn't they?' said Casey. 'Garrick wanted a father. And Bailey … Bailey wanted a son.'

'I know,' said Zac. 'I can see that now.'

'Bailey couldn't just cast Jeanie to one side, either. Not out here. Her parents wouldn't have put up with that.'

I know the McElroys, of course.

'No. So she was half protected, half punished.'

'What was she like?' Casey asked. 'Jeanie.'

'She was sweet, kind, wore great clothes. I thought she was wonderful. A crush, I suppose. But it's odd, isn't it? The difference between a child's perspective and an adult's,' Zac said slowly. 'As a child, I just knew that Jeanie was a single mother, trying to make it all work. I suppose I knew that she didn't have a job, so there must have been someone somewhere paying for the house and the school and all the rest of it. But I didn't really *think* about it.'

'And you didn't question it as you grew up. But when you stop and think about it as an adult, it looks different.'

'Yes.'

'And now?'

'Now I look back and wonder,' said Zac. 'Whether it might have been better for Jeanie to fly the gilded cage?'

'Elias encouraged a dependence, you mean? From both her and Garrick?'

'Subconsciously in Garrick's case, but, yes, Jeanie always shaped herself to other people's lives rather than forge her own way, and I suppose that is what Garrick does too. He tells you what you want to hear. And if you do that long enough … '

'Half truths,' said Casey. 'The worst sort of lie.'

'But we were friends for so long … '

'Yes. Friendship, a sort of habit.'

'You get used to being friends,' he said. 'That shared history. The jokes that were funny twenty years ago, and told a thousand times since. Friendship is idealised, isn't it? And then one day, you stop and think: what do we actually have in common? French lessons with Mrs Thomson and that time we hammered Ipswich 66–9.'

'Maybe.'

'Garrick was the only person who came to visit me in Mauritius,' said Zac. 'He was the only one who could, of course. And when he was out there, it just struck me how different we were now. We started off in the same place, but we'd gone off in different directions. I was enjoying my life in Mauritius, of course. But … '

Drewsteignton's scholarship boy, Casey thought. Zac had gleefully snatched up the yacht, the house, the dream. The trappings everyone else had all along. But by the time Professor Jalali had called, perhaps it had started to pall.

'I never meant to stay out there forever,' said Zac. 'A few years maybe.'

'A few years can become a lifetime.'

'Not for me.' He was certain, shaking his head. Then his face lit up with a smile. 'I was bored.'

The last word was almost a shout.

'Not bored now.'

'No. I think Jeanie convinced herself she was doing it all for Garrick,' said Zac, taking another swig of rum. 'But it might have been better for Garrick if she had struck out on her own.'

'Maybe.'

'My mother,' Zac laughed, changing the mood, 'always fought her own battles.'

For a second, there was an old photograph, clear in Casey's mind. The beach in Cornwall on a hot summer's day. A primrose cottage, thatch a sunbonnet. Ice cream: scoops of pistachio and strawberry and mint choc chip. Sticky trickles of pink and green and brown.

Red and white sandals, a little blue bucket and two figures, smiling at the camera, eyes screwed up against the sun.

Her mother, overexposed in the sunlight, with her arm around a small girl.

There had never been a photograph of the three of them, she realised. He took all the photographs, always.

But her mother was *smiling*.

Smiling at the person behind the camera.

A happiness so close she could almost touch it.

But still: that smile, almost forgotten.

She must have fought so hard, Casey realised, quite abruptly. A pupil in one of the grandest barrister's chambers, awed by the QCs. Especially back then: thirty years ago and coming from nowhere.

She must have clawed her way up, tiger-eyed. Because no one would have made it easy. Not for her. Not then.

And one day ...

And there was no one to catch her, either.

'What did your mother do?' Zac interrupted the silence.

'She worked,' Casey said quietly. 'She worked very hard.'

Punctual. Good typing speeds. Neat sandwiches packed every day. And a smile lost somewhere in Cornwall.

But she survived, Casey thought, with a sudden pride. On her own. And that must have taken a sort of bravery.

'She fought for you.'

'Yes,' said Casey simply. 'She did.'

58

Zac leaned forward, pouring her another drink. When he looked up, his face was just a few inches from hers, and for a second, they stared at each other.

Then the phone beside Casey's bed rang, loud and demanding. She stood up, walked back into the room and answered the phone wearily.

'Hello, Casey.' Miranda sounded bouncy, energetic, normal. 'We've fronted up Drummond.'

Casey fought to remember: the health minister, a gaudy range of ties, and *have you ever thought about making a donation to the party*?

'Oh, yes,' Casey managed. 'What did Drummond have to say?'

She turned away from Zac, trying to concentrate on Miranda's voice.

'Are you OK?' Miranda asked. 'You sound … knackered. And your phone is dead.'

'I'm fine.' Casey shoved away the exhaustion, the injuries and the rum. 'I'll have to get a new phone. What was that about Drummond?'

'He wouldn't say anything over the phone.'

'Oh.' That was normal. *You'll hear from my lawyers* before the phone was slammed down. Some cried. Others begged. Casey dreaded that, always.

'Drummond's coming into the office.'

'He's what?' Casey thought that she had misheard.

'I know. All a bit odd. Anyway. We'll meet him in the little conference room upstairs. Keep him away from the newsroom. Do you want to watch?'

Casey's mind was moving slowly. 'Sure. That's weird though, no?'

'I certainly can't remember it happening before. Although I suppose Drummond's probably been here for lunch quite a few times over the years. He was quite matey with the last editor, wasn't he?'

'Yes, he was. And yes, I want to watch.'

Since the coronavirus crisis, video technology was installed as standard in the *Post*'s conference rooms. During the morning editorial conferences, the US editor or the Beijing editor, or whichever reporter happened to be in a key hotspot, dialled in.

'We'll leave the screens off,' said Miranda. 'He doesn't need to know you're watching at all.'

'Great.'

Janice, the editor's secretary, showed Ambrose Drummond to the upstairs conference room. He ignored her offer of a cup of tea, coffee, a glass of sparkling water, closing the door in her friendly face.

In Cape Town, Casey was crouching over her laptop. Zac had gone back to his room, understanding without being asked that Casey needed to be on her own.

In London, Miranda, Hessa, Dash and Ross were arranged round one end of a long polished pine table. There was a bank of black screens behind them, and a perfunctory plate of shortbread on a side table.

Drummond strode to a chair at the far end of the table, without the usual nods and handshakes. Casey saw the minister's eyes shift to the wall of technology behind Dash and Ross. The camera was so sharp that Casey could see every detail of Drummond's face. She could even make out the rows of blue horses cantering across Drummond's scarlet Hermes tie. Drummond's eyes rested on the screens momentarily, but then he looked away, unworried.

In fact, Casey thought edgily, Drummond looked buoyant, relaxed: remarkably unruffled by the severity of Hessa's letter. Casey's mind started to tick over, running through the options.

As he sat down, Drummond nodded to Hessa. Even from Cape Town, Casey sensed Hessa's squirm. She didn't envy the young reporter.

'Dash Bishop,' the head of news introduced the table, 'Ross Warman, Miranda Darcey and Hessa Khan.'

'I am quite sure I was introduced,' Drummond gave half a smile, 'to a Ms Jessa Uddin.'

The minister leaned back in his chair. He was wearing a three piece suit, and as he stretched out his legs, Casey caught a glimpse of bright red socks.

'It would be helpful,' Miranda said smoothly, 'if you could respond to the questions raised in Hessa's letter.'

'Ah, yes.' Drummond pulled a couple of sheets of paper out of his bag. 'This letter. From Miss – ah – oh, yes, *Khan*. She makes some interesting points, certainly.'

Drummond wasn't remotely intimidated by the four journalists, Casey thought with a certain grudging respect.

'We would like to reflect your response in any article the *Post* may publish … ' Dash recited the words Casey had written in a thousand right-to-reply letters. Balance, fairness: they had to promise it, at least.

'It is certainly quite a forceful letter,' Drummond continued. 'Especially after the *Post*'s efforts in Bangladesh last year. And the subsequent events, of course.' Casey grimaced. The *Post* didn't necessarily need the authorities going over the Bangladesh story with a fine tooth comb. 'And then there's all the Leveson stuff that was never quite resolved,' Drummond put the letter down on the boardroom table, and contemplated the journalists thoughtfully.

Was Drummond trying to blackmail the *Post*? Casey wondered incredulously. He must know such a manoeuvre could backfire. It would be an act of sheer desperation, and Drummond didn't look desperate.

Ross glanced at his watch ostentatiously, then leaned forward.

'Is there any specific point you'd like to make, Mr Drummond? Otherwise I'll be getting back to my newsroom. Busy time of the day and all that.'

'I assume this is all off the record?' said Drummond.

There was the briefest of hesitations.

'It can be,' said Dash. 'Although, of course, we will need a response to all the points raised in that letter before publication.'

'Of course,' said Drummond. 'Naturally, I would give you a full response within the quite draconian timeframe Ms – ah – Khan specified. So, to clarify: we are off the record?'

A small nod from Dash, and then a grudging 'yes'.

'The thing is,' Drummond made a flicking gesture with his fingers, 'I'm such a minor player in the world of Westminster. I'm a junior health minister. A mere nothing.'

They waited. Ross broke first. 'And?'

Casey and Miranda would have waited all day.

'I suppose that I just thought you might have bigger fish to fry,' said Drummond sleekly. 'Than little old me.'

The Prime Minister? wondered Casey wildly. Was Drummond's loyalty running out?

'Colette Warwick?' Miranda's voice was even. 'Your boss.'

'In a manner of speaking,' said Drummond.

'Not really. She *is* your boss.'

'Well,' said Drummond. 'I just thought you might be interested in some of her … activities.'

'What activities?' Ross, again.

Drummond peered thoughtfully at his scarlet socks.

'They're not exactly her activities, I suppose,' he said, as if speaking to himself. 'They're her husband's, to be precise.'

Colette Warwick's husband ran a hedge fund, Casey remembered. One of the very highest of flyers. The couple managed the shaming scale of their wealth by donating large sums to charity. A small percentage of their fortune, but generous enough to neutralise the rage, more or less. The tax of philanthropy, driven down as low as possible.

'Get on with it,' Ross snapped.

'How would Colette Warwick's husband affect her role as Health Secretary?' Miranda asked.

'It's not about her time in Health,' said Drummond smoothly. 'It's about her time in the Treasury.'

Warwick had been economic secretary to the Treasury, Casey remembered, a couple of years back. An anachronistic title for one of the stepping stones on her path to the cabinet.

'What happened?'

'Well,' said Drummond. 'You'll remember that there was a,' he paused, choosing his word carefully, 'hoo-ha about Mr Warwick's fund shorting banks.'

A couple of years ago, Aymen Warwick had made a fortune by betting against bank stocks twenty minutes before they plunged when the government announced aggressive reforms. The *Post*'s business editor had been delighted with her team for landing that scoop.

'We broke that story,' Ross shrugged, 'Two years ago. It was embarrassing for Warwick, because the government was making a big deal about cracking down on the finance sector. Making them pay their way and all that. She weathered it, though.'

'You broke half the story,' smirked Drummond. 'Or a quarter of it.'

They waited.

'What if,' Drummond asked casually, 'Aymen Warwick knew to short the stocks because he had read his wife's confidential emails?'

That would mean Colette Warwick's head on a plate, thought Casey. And if it was one point for a backbench MP and three for a junior health minister, a cabinet minister must be worth – what? – five? Like children, trading marbles: *I'll swap you.*

Casey stared at Drummond's smooth, smiling face, and knew exactly why he was being sent out with this offer. Colette Warwick was riding too high in the polls, the surveys the party tracked every single day. *Who do you think should be the next Prime Minister? Who would you like to see lead the party into the next election?*

Dangerous questions, asked chattily.

This would be a win-win for the Prime Minister. Protect his kingmaker and take out the threat, all in one seamless manoeuvre. If he fired Colette Warwick fast enough, they could even spin it as *decisive*.

And Dash would bite: of course he would.

'You can't prove it.' But a continent away, Casey could hear the hope in Ross's voice. 'Did she know?'

'She did,' Drummond smirked. 'And I can. You don't really want me anyway, old boy. I'm just a minor pawn in all this. A nothing. An irrelevance. A bagatelle.'

And this queen, thought Casey, had got too strong, too ruthless. Sliding across the board unrestrained, too aware of her power.

'No.' Dash surprised her. 'I've seen the footage from Poland, Ambrose. It's damning. We're running the story.'

Dash stood up, Miranda and Hessa leaping to their feet.

'But—' Ross couldn't help himself.

'Ross!' Dash barked the name. 'Come along. Good day, Ambrose. It's been a pleasure, but we would like your response by 5 p.m. tomorrow—'

'You're interested in Corax, are you not?' Drummond was still sitting, unflustered.

In Cape Town, Casey pounced on her phone.

Dash hesitated, turning back towards Drummond. 'Why?'

'Jessa Uddin.' Drummond hadn't moved, still lolling back in his chair. 'Miss Uddin seemed very interested in the esteemed Elias Bailey.'

Dash moved slowly back towards the table. He had been bluffing, Casey realised. Dash had been a news executive for so long that she had forgotten his reporter past. But it was there, always.

'What … ' Dash sat down and stared hard at Drummond, 'do you know about Elias Bailey?'

59

'Harare?' Drummond laughed, the next day. 'I'm not going to bloody Harare.'

'You are.' Miranda sounded stern. 'In fact, you're flying via Johannesburg, in a couple of hours.'

'But … Zimbabwe? What if someone finds out?'

Zimbabwe was subject to sanctions, the curt tactic the international community used to telegraph extreme disapproval. British ministers visited the country occasionally, but it was still a pariah state, and the brief burst of optimism after Mugabe stepped down had been rapidly extinguished.

'Tough,' Miranda said to Drummond. 'No one said this was going to be easy.'

'Yes, but … Harare?' Drummond was still disbelieving.

'And Casey Benedict will meet you there.'

'What?'

Drummond had known relatively little about Bailey, it had emerged. Dash and Miranda had fired dozens of questions at him in the *Post*'s conference room, until even Drummond's composure started to thin.

'You're not really adding much,' Ross said, deliberately brutal, 'to what we already know.'

'We'll think about it.' Miranda had ended the meeting tersely. 'I'll call you tomorrow.'

And it was Casey who rang back a few hours later with a plan.

Miranda and Dash listened to Casey's plan with matching disapproval. The Adsero jet had left Frankfurt, Casey pointed out, less than an hour after she had fled Bailey's house in Llandudno. She glossed over the details of her escape.

As Casey had been listening in to Drummond's meeting at the *Post*, she had simultaneously tracked the plane. The Adsero jet had headed south from Germany, its tail number just clipping Niger as it cruised over the Sahara.

A few hours later, the jet had touched down at Cape Town International, but the plane only sat on the airfield for a few minutes before taking off again, this time arcing north-west towards Zimbabwe.

'That's madness,' said Miranda, when she had finished.

'I know,' said Casey. 'But it might just work.'

'Well, hello,' Zac greeted her at the Camps Bay hotel a couple of hours later.

'Hands off.'

'But … '

After speaking to Dash and Miranda, and picking up a new phone, Casey had spent the rest of the morning at the most expensive hairdresser in Cape Town.

Delphine had advised her, laughing.

'I'll come with you, Casey. I need a cut anyway. And Cristiano is fabulous.'

'Could you blowdry it smooth?' Casey had asked as one of Cristiano's assistants wrapped her in a long black robe.

'I'll make you look glorious,' the hairdresser promised, wincing at her split ends. 'Just ravishing, hey, my darling?'

And Casey had buried her head in magazines, refusing to look up at Delphine's grin.

'Thank you,' Casey said later, as she paid, 'for telling Zac to sail down the coast.'

'It was nothing.' Delphine peered in the mirror. 'I enjoyed it. Sitting in a car at dawn, gaming out all the possibilities. I don't get to do that any more. I'm a no one now. I'm a mother.'

The insecurity startled Casey. 'You're brilliant, Delphine. Miranda always says so.'

Delphine waved her words away. 'Anyway, apart from you almost dying, it was fun.'

'Apart from that one little thing.' Casey rolled her eyes, and they both began to laugh.

'You look *different*.' Zac grinned now as Casey stood in the middle of the hotel room, feeling ridiculous.

'You would go for blondes,' Casey aimed for crushing. 'It's so clichéd.'

'I,' Zac was unabashed, 'go for anything.'

Hessa had organised blue contact lenses to be delivered to the hotel room. Opening the little packet shortly before she left for the airport, Casey put the contacts in and stared at herself in the mirror. For a moment, she had the oddest feeling that Madison was staring back.

But Madison from Tinder had bouncy blonde curls, bright pink lipstick and sparkly blue eyeshadow. Whereas Casey had made herself up with utter discretion, in shades of tan and fawn and sand. After the visit to the hairdresser, she had gone shopping, picking out ecru linen and taupe silk, neat skirt suits and elegant shift dresses.

And when he arrived at Kizzie's house, cross off the overnight flight to Harare, Drummond stared at her in bewilderment.

'But you look just like her.'

'She looks just like who?' asked Kizzie, baffled.

'Serena,' muttered Drummond. 'She looks exactly like Serena Brackenbury, my special adviser.'

60

It hadn't taken long for Casey to arrange a meeting with the Zimbabwean health minister. They would be *delighted*. First thing the next morning, Drummond grumbled his way to an ugly government block in downtown Harare, and smiled through gritted teeth as the minister earnestly discussed vaccinations and the effects of coronavirus and the constant, unending battle against HIV.

At the end of the meeting, Drummond posed momentarily for a grip and grin, and then he and Casey headed out into the dusty heat of central Harare.

'Now what?' Drummond asked bleakly, as they waited for one of Kizzie's friends to pick them up. 'You know it's a sackable offence having off-the-books meetings with foreign government ministers, don't you?'

'No one will ever notice back in the UK,' Casey soothed. 'You lot spend half your time trying to get these meetings into the paper. Now send that email. Say you've flown down here for a meeting with that minister and you're stuck here for the night and bored senseless.'

Grousing, Drummond tapped his phone. 'Right,' he grumbled. 'Let's get back to that God-awful house.'

'Kewlake is lovely.'

'It really isn't.'

Back at the rambling house, Drummond stamped off to his bedroom.

Casey wandered out to the verandah where Kizzie was sitting on one of the daybeds, enjoying the peace of the garden on her few hours off. It was still early, steam rising off the termite heap in the cool of the morning. Kizzie poured her a coffee, and for a while they chatted about nothing important. It might have been any beautiful day.

But finally, Kizzie stood. 'I must get to the hospital.'

'By the way, have you heard anything about Henke?' Casey asked quietly.

'Nothing.' Kizzie looked grim. 'Not one word.'

'They didn't even report him dead?'

'No. He just completely disappeared—'

Kizzie was interrupted by a bellow from inside the house: 'For God's sake, even this spider's legs have legs!'

Kizzie smiled, and headed off to her car.

An hour later, Drummond came bounding into the sitting room, where Casey was sitting on one of the velvet sofas.

'He's answered,' he chortled. 'He's asking if we want to come over.'

As they waited in the hotel reception, Casey forced herself to concentrate on the comings and the goings of the bellboy.

The bellboy wore a threadbare green uniform and roamed around the echoey hotel lobby, too energetic, too animated, too alive to stand and wait politely at the door. He looked about seventeen: loose-limbed, tall, good-looking.

As Casey watched, the boy washed up beside the welcome desk, half-monitoring the revolving door for the arrival of a guest, half-gossiping with the receptionist. There were a couple of laughed whispers, a sly grin, and then the receptionist rolled her eyes and feigned a slap. A burst of giggles, and a shifty glance round from both, in case the manager had noticed. Probably the same joke, every day, edging incrementally towards a date.

The bellboy was called Justice, Casey read on his nametag, the receptionist Shine.

Casey forced herself to concentrate on the bellboy as he veered around the hotel lobby again, bored as a bluebottle. She concentrated on his gossiping, his ramblings, his occasional dance steps practised half-heartedly.

She concentrated because she knew if she thought about what lay ahead, she might scream, might cry, might run out of the hotel and never stop running.

'Are you sure it's safe?' Back in the hotel in Cape Town, Zac had stood, both hands on the door jamb, as she peered into the bathroom mirror, trying on her unfamiliar bright blue eyes.

'No.' Flippant. 'I'm not sure.'

'But Garrick might have—'

'I know.'

'He certainly won't expect an attack from this angle, that's for sure,' Zac nodded approval at her eyes. 'Because it's utter madness.'

But now all the false confidence had ebbed away. Now Casey sat staring across the hotel lobby, her nails gouging white half-moons in her forearm.

It feels as if I have lost my nerve.

It can happen.

What if he guessed? What if he knew?

And what if I can't?

Drummond was tapping his feet and picking at his cuticles. He was nervous too, Casey thought, quite reasonably. A civilian, after all. And then she realised he was looking at her, concerned.

'Are you OK, Casey? I mean … Serena.'

Men running up the stairs, their footsteps loud on the treads.

The bellboy was flirting with the receptionist again, *Mukadzi akanaka.*

Clothes ripping, a gash of agony and a man looking down as she drowned.

'I'm great!' Casey knew her smile was too big. 'Absolutely fine!'

Drummond gave her an uneasy look, and Casey turned back to the fidgetings of the bellboy.

You'll worry him, she thought. Pull it together, or you'll rattle Drummond too.

But I can't.

I can't.

You must.

She dug her nails into her palms and turned back to Drummond, the broadest smile plastered to her face.

'I'm sure they won't be long.'

The bellboy ricocheted over to the revolving doors again, with a shout across to the receptionist, *Tarisa mota iyi*. And Casey stood, smoothed down her clothes and waited for Drummond to stand.

'They're here.'

Casey had booked a room at the hotel – five star, approximately – so that they could be picked up at a safe distance from Kizzie's house. As the big black Overfinch Range Rover pulled up outside the hotel, Casey felt the shudder ripple down her spine again. The interior of this car was black leather, the walnut dashboard inlaid with mother of pearl. The bellboy slammed the car door and tapped the roof with one last smile before turning back to the receptionist.

The engine growled, and Casey felt as if she had been swallowed by some ravening beast.

'Bailey might have a word with the Zim health minister,' she had said airily to Drummond. That was before, when they were safely back at Kizzie's. 'That's if he checks anything at all. You are a government minister, after all.'

But this car was an ostentatious display of Bailey's wealth and power. Not a man who left things to chance. Again, Casey thought of the aggression of the men in Llandudno. The ruthless determination of the man on Hampstead Heath.

And the shape on the floor.

She felt her nerves boil up again, her legs trembling against the smooth seats.

The car accelerated away.

61

The Overfinch cruised through Harare's streets, purring smoothly. The chauffeur glanced back. 'Can I get you anything? Chocolate? Peanuts?'

'We're fine.' Drummond barely glanced at the man, pointing out of the window at an ox cart. 'Look at that, Serena.'

Casey smiled, and looked towards a woman carrying a sack of maize on her head, and slowly she forced the nerves away.

Drummond could be engaging company, Casey decided, as the Overfinch reached the Zimbabwean countryside. In the absence of anyone more important, the practised charisma that had lifted him up through the political ranks was being deployed entirely on her. He could be funny, perceptive, sharp. She didn't like him, all the same.

As they drove, Casey thought of Colette Warwick marching around the department of health back in London, quite unaware that the last few strands holding up her private sword of Damocles were being carefully unpicked by Hessa.

It was an email that had caught the Health Secretary out. After realising what her husband had done, Warwick had sent him a furious message. Too enraged to think straight, Casey thought. Hammering out an email in a fury, the outrage clear in every line. But there was despair in Warwick's words, too: she knew what it meant.

She must have regretted those angry sentences the moment she had sent them.

She hadn't reported her husband, though. Because to report him would have been to jail him.

And, somehow, Drummond had got hold of a copy of that email.

'You could have faked that email.' Back in the conference room, Miranda had tried to stare Drummond down.

'Yes. I didn't though.'

'Prove it.'

'You'd have to go to Warwick before publishing anything,' said Drummond. 'And she won't be able to deny it.'

Ross had leaned forward. 'If you're lying to us, Drummond … If these emails turn out to be fake, I'm telling the whole fucking world that you gave them to us, and running every minute of the Poland tape to boot. You'll be finished either way.'

And Drummond had stared Ross straight in the eye. 'Deal.'

Casey wondered what she would have done in Warwick's position, faced with the knowledge of her husband's deceit. Probably the same thing, although she could never imagine Ed …

No. Don't think of him now.

Casey realised they were passing the ruins of the old country club. And then the driver was braking, turning sharply towards the red double gates with the big starburst design.

'Look,' Casey said brightly to Drummond. 'This must be it!'

Bailey was waiting for them in front of the main house. As she saw the tall shape, Casey felt the tremor in her legs start again.

But she straightened her back, dropped her shoulders.

You've done this a thousand times before.

And you can do it again.

You must. You must.

It is time.

The main house at Njana perched on the top of the hill, the verandah looking out over a vast grassy basin. From here, Bailey and his guests could see for miles. Herds of antelope meandered across the landscape, wandering through thousands of acres of scrub. Fat zebras nibbled at the grass, moving forward in an idle formation. To the north, a couple of giraffes, beautiful in their freakish clumsiness, ambled along, tearing at branches as they passed.

One man, thought Casey. One man owns all this.

'Quite incredible,' she murmured aloud. 'They don't look real.'

It was early evening. Bailey had greeted Drummond chummily as they arrived, and Casey had managed to breathe again.

'Excellent to see you, Ambrose. We rarely get the likes of you visiting this crazy old country. It's a real treat.'

'What a beautiful place you have here, Elias. Quite remarkable.'

'I do hope you'll stay,' Bailey had gestured, 'for a couple of nights at least.'

'Very kind, old boy. And this,' Drummond drew Casey forward, 'is Serena, my special adviser. Poor girl, she gets stuck travelling with me a lot. Didn't think it was fair to abandon her in Harare.'

'Of course not. There's plenty of room, as you can see.'

The small talk was oddly comforting, and Casey's smile was almost real.

'It's always a joy.' Casey found Serena Brackenbury's cut-glass vowels easy to imitate. 'All the travelling. It's fascinating to see so much of the world.'

'Well, we're delighted to have you to stay, Serena.'

They were in the main house. Adjacent bedrooms with an interconnecting door, Casey noted. Most discreet. She checked that the door was locked.

The main house was large, breezy, all on one floor. The rooms opened up on to a verandah that ran right the way round the building. She had hoped they might be in one of the guest houses out in the grounds, easier to wander, but this would do.

After Casey and Drummond had settled in, the three gathered on the gallery. Bailey poured gin and tonics – Drummond making predictable jokes about quinine and malaria – and they sat on rattan and teak chairs, looking out over the wilderness.

'What a wonderful vista,' said Casey, sincere as Serena.

'It's stunning,' said Drummond.

To the south-west of the house, Casey could see the reservoir, with the rhino enclosure just beside it. Just past the reservoir was the airstrip, Bailey's private plane sitting on the gravel.

Beyond that, Casey knew the Njana fence threaded its way through the savannah, a strip of emptiness shaved on either side. A narrow track ran along that fence, and Casey remembered sprinting for her life, desperate, panicking, terrified. And somewhere out there, somewhere in this beautiful panorama, Henke …

Casey shut the thought away, and turned towards Bailey with a smile.

'Do you spend much time in Zimbabwe, Mr Bailey?'

'Elias, please. And no, not enough,' he smiled at her.

'I'm sure a lifetime could never feel like enough.'

One of the housemaids emerged from the house, walking along the verandah towards the small group, and Casey felt her heart rate surge. Every time someone appeared, there was that moment of panic. Had this person seen her before, in that terrified dash from the laboratory? And would they know her again?

Bailey's men must be trawling Cape Town for her.

Logically, rationally, she knew she couldn't be identified. Her long brown hair was clipped into a smooth blonde bob. In her black silk shirt and dark green capri pants, she was unrecognisable from the maddened figure racing from the shipping containers with Zac. But you never know, a small voice insisted.

You never know.

The housemaid was checking their drinks, handing around pistachios.

'They'll be feeding the rhino any minute.' Bailey looked at his watch. 'Shall we go and watch?'

'Sounds delightful.' Drummond drained his gin and tonic.

Drummond was drinking fast, thought Casey. Nerves, probably. But then she didn't know what was normal for him.

She turned to Bailey with a big smile. 'Let's go!'

62

The herd of rhinos roared and stamped, sending up huge clouds of dust. They shouldered each other, barging casually with a strength that would crush a man.

'Blimey.' Drummond clutched the edge of the tree house, peering down over the balcony. 'Quite lively, what?'

One of the guards was pouring food out of the window of a slow-moving pickup. The rhinos followed the vehicle, rumbling and bellowing, each trying to jostle their way closer to the sack of food. When one of the vast animals got too close to the car, the pickup driver accelerated, keeping just ahead of the tossing horns.

'I'm not sure it would pass British health and safety standards,' Bailey grinned. 'But we've never lost anyone yet.'

As they watched, the matriarch jerked her head sideways, thundering at one of the younger males who had come impertinently close to her dinner. The younger animal hopped out of the way and the huge female – nearly a tonne of muscle and bone – lowered her head again, her calf following close behind.

With their awkward outlines, the animals looked as if they had been drawn by a child, but they moved with an extraordinary speed and agility.

'Remarkable creatures,' murmured Drummond, taking a swig of another gin and tonic.

'They really are.'

The sun was a molten sliver behind a fretwork of branches. The reservoir gleamed in the last light of the day.

To her right, Casey could see the guardhouse and, in the far distance, the bulk of the shipping containers.

'What's that?' She couldn't help herself.

Bailey glanced across. 'Just storage.'

The urge to run the quarter mile to the containers was almost overwhelming. Casey felt as if her legs might take the decision for her, marching across the clearing in front of all the guards, and Bailey himself.

I have to know.

Not now.

Half desperate to hunt, half desperate to hide.

'How long have you worked for Ambrose?' Bailey asked Casey, interrupting her thoughts.

'Only a few months,' Casey answered smoothly. 'I was with the home secretary before. That was a more junior role, of course.'

Casey had trawled over Serena's CV, double-checking everything with Drummond. Serena herself had been ordered to take a holiday. *I absolutely insist, dear girl. You've been working yourself to the bone. Take a few days off, it's an order. Cancel my appointments. It's recess, for heaven's sake.* And as a would-be MP, there would be no drunken photographs of Serena Brackenbury in Ibiza, no ostentatious shopping trips, no #wishyouwerehere and champagne.

'Because you weren't in Wrocław,' said Bailey. 'For that symposium.'

'No, I missed that trip,' Casey smiled. 'Jilly handled that one.'

'Ah, yes, Wrocław.' Drummond looked up from his drink. 'We'll have to talk about that, old boy. When we're ... '

Drummond nodded heavily at Casey, and she gazed out at the rhinos, pretending not to notice.

Later, when they were back up at the house, Casey glanced at her phone. 'Would you excuse me?' An effacing smile. 'I must just respond to these messages.'

Bailey was pouring yet another gin and tonic with a smile and a nod. Casey stood, crossing the verandah. She walked through an elegant drawing room, leaving the door slightly ajar behind her.

A few minutes later, she pushed the drawing room door again and edged her way back in. She sat down in an overstuffed racing green armchair concealed from their view and pulled out her phone.

If they hadn't heard her come back in, it was hardly her fault.

Out on the verandah, Drummond was talking, his voice quieter now.

'It was all a bit strange, old boy … I don't mind telling you … Still not quite sure what she was after … Or who she was working for … Could be a honeytrap … ' A sharp yelp of laughter from Drummond, 'Or could always be something to do with the Chinese, of course.' Drummond's voice rose slightly, 'Did I ever tell you? Last time I went to Beijing, my bloody charger disappeared on the flight and I was so knackered from the journey that I just borrowed another one from the hotel receptionist without thinking. And as soon as I plugged in my sodding phone, everything on my phone was downloaded instantly! Bloody everything!' A rumble from Bailey. 'Oh, yes, of course. Anyway, as I say … I have no idea who that bloody girl is … ' Drummond's voice dropped again, barely audible now. 'But I know where she is staying right now … And I thought you might be … Well. Interested.'

Casey listened as Drummond recited an address – a neat house in Buckinghamshire – while Bailey sat in silence.

Casey waited for a couple more minutes before walking out on to the verandah.

'I just love these gorgeous, warm evenings. It's never like this in England, is it? And, oh, look, what a glorious moon … '

They chatted until Casey yawned.

'I do beg your pardon.' Casey smiled round the room, a prospective candidate's gleam. 'But I think I'll have to go to bed.'

'Of course.' Bailey was on his feet. 'You know where everything is?'

'Yes. Thank you *so* much.'

Casey lay under a billowing mosquito net, watching the mahogany ceiling fan revolve.

Fear swirled through her, pulsing like blood.

Clothes ripping, a gash of agony and a man looking down as she drowns.

She forced herself to listen to the house settling to sleep. Doors closing, quiet feet pattering down a corridor, a brisk *goodnight* from Bailey.

She could hear the floorboards creaking as they eased into the cool of the night. One cracked so loudly that she sat bolt upright, her throat closing up. Her pulse roared, and it felt as if her blood had been replaced with a thin metallic flow of terror, adrenalin oozing from her pores.

And then she was falling, and it was as if she was falling forever.

Casey made herself lie down again. Drummond was pottering around his bedroom now. She could hear him clearly through the locked door, fidgeting with his laptop. There was a squeak of springs as he climbed into the bed.

Any minute now.

I can't.

You can.

You must.

She jumped as her phone lit up. A message from Miranda. *You all right?*

Not really.

A sort of vertigo. *I might step over the edge.*

The answer came straight back. *You can do this, Casey. You've done it a thousand times. You can do it.*

A long pause and then another buzz. *I trust you.*

Casey read the message again and again.

I trust you.

It was like a dam across a river, the reservoir slowly filling. Casey lay on the beautiful bed, and breathed in and out.

Not broken, no.

And now she had to force herself to stay still. Force herself to lie in the bed, and force herself to wait until the house was fast asleep.

63

She sat up.

The house was still.

Moving quietly, Casey slipped on her trousers and the black silk shirt. She grabbed her handbag and slid open the French doors that led out to the verandah.

The house was silent.

It was lucky, Casey thought, that her room was on the south side of the house, looking down towards the reservoir and the rhino enclosure.

She trod lightly over the boards of the gallery, and jumped down the steps, landing noiselessly in the grass. There was a breeze coming from the west and the garden was a mass of shadows and whispers.

Casey skirted the large swimming pool and hurried down the slope towards a fence. Bailey's voice echoed loudly in her head. 'The last owners had to have a big fence built around this house, right? After they ended up with a zebra in the swimming pool ... '

But there was no lock on the gate, and it took only a second for Casey to nip through and sprint down the hill towards the enclosure. Her handbag – one that Serena would carry – bumped against her hip.

She almost laughed aloud. The evening was warm, the moon shone down peacefully, and in her black silk shirt, she disappeared into the night.

Her feet flew. And *there* was the fence with the heavy telegraph poles. It slowed her only briefly, scrambling under. Then she was slipping through the enclosure, barely making a sound.

Casey crept around the clearing, edging nearer to the shipping containers. From here, she could see the guards high up in the tree house, idling the night away.

Now she was at the door to the laboratory, the padlock gleaming in the moonlight. She dug into her handbag for the tiny hacksaw, and it took only minutes to cut away the padlock. And then she was into the containers, moving quietly down the jerry-built room towards the old kitchen cabinets.

There it was: FBT.

Casey grabbed the file, fingers shaking.

She edged the laboratory door back open, pulling a brand new padlock from her bag. It snapped into place with the tiniest of clicks, and she turned towards the house.

A torch glowed, close by.

Without thinking, Casey was flat on the ground. The torch was between her and the tree house, bobbing briskly in her direction.

A guard? Doing an hourly check?

Casey lay on the ground, trying to estimate the distance to the bushes. She started to crawl, moving as quietly as possible. The grass crackled beneath her, every sound a roar in her ears. The guard was marching towards her, hurrying down the track towards the laboratory. She had to get off the path. Had to be hidden in the grasses before the torch lit her up, before the scurry of motion gave her away.

There was no time for caution. A jerky scramble, a hurried scuttle, and she was deep in the long grass.

The torch's movement stopped.

Casey became aware of a terrible smell. The stench coated the back of her throat, a putrescence enfolding her. She gagged.

The torch swung around.

She had to get deeper into the thicket. Had to bury herself in the dark. She wriggled forwards.

An eruption of flies filled the air, buffeting her eyes, her nose, her hair. One found its way into her mouth, and she retched instinctively, jerking forward.

Henke, she realised, the revulsion flooding over her. Henke slung into the brush like a sack of old rubbish. He was just a few feet from her, blackened, bloating, oozing.

For a second, Casey was oblivious of her surroundings, trapped by the horror. Then the torch flickered behind her again. She threw herself to one side just as the torch gleamed brightly on Henke's body.

The corpse was caught in the beam of the torch, reeking and rotting. There was an exclamation of disgust from the guard, and the torch glinted away again.

The man must have thought she was an animal feasting on the body, Casey realised. The rustle, the urgency, that sharp burst of panic.

The torch was bobbing away again. It rested on the laboratory door, found the neat padlock, and then jounced away, further along the edge of the reservoir. Casey lay on the ground, enveloped in the fetor of decay.

It took longer to climb back up the hill to the house. She was tired now, the adrenalin draining away. She squeezed through the gate, creeping up through the garden, and she was nearly there, nearly safe. She patted her hair smooth, brushed away a few blades of dried grass.

Henke filled her mind.

Chucked into a thicket, and left to rot. A man, abandoned.

And she was the only reason he was out here in Njana. She was the one who had led him here, urging him to his death.

Now he would lie there forever, picked clean slowly under the vast African sun. Because she'd abandoned him too, of course.

While every day, just a few hundred yards away, Bailey would smile, entertain his guests, pour another gin and tonic.

Just far enough away that the stench didn't quite reach, and even if it did, it might be a duiker, a rotting zebra: just another death in Zimbabwe.

She wondered if Bailey would ever even think about it, the corpse slung into the bushes, festering in the dark.

And it was all her fault.

Nearly at the house now. Nearly. She stopped short, all the air rushing from her lungs. There was a shape sitting on the verandah.

Bailey.

Back away?

No.

Hide?

Impossible. He had seen her, standing up with a gesture that might have been a wave.

And there was nothing to do but wave back and walk towards the house, and hope.

'Good evening, Serena.' Bailey's face was in shadow, but the lights in the drawing room behind him glowed. Casey knew that her face was lit up, spotlit, every movement clear. From his stage, he could see everything.

'Hello, Elias.' Casey somehow managed to smile. She scrambled for the words, scrabbled for the excuse she had practised earlier. 'I was just having a chat with my boyfriend.'

She climbed the stairs to the verandah, steps to the gallows.

'You must miss him. With all your travelling.'

'Oh, I do,' agreed Casey. 'Very much. But I enjoy working with Ambrose Drummond too. I'm so lucky to work for him.'

'I'm sure.'

'Everyone reckons he'll be in the cabinet soon,' Casey emphasised. The small talk seemed impossible. Henke lay just over there, rotting under the light of the moon.

'And what are your own plans, Serena?'

'I'm going to be an MP.' Casey dredged up Serena's icy self-confidence. 'And I would love your support in that, Mr Bailey.'

Bailey laughed, and it sounded appreciative, but Casey couldn't be sure.

'I'll be interested to watch your career, Serena.'

'Thank you,' Casey smiled.

She made as if to sit down in the chair opposite him, but as she stepped forward, she tripped and her handbag crashed to the ground, spilling its contents across the verandah.

'Oh, dear.' She rushed to grab her purse, her eyeshadow, her foundation.

Bailey bent down to help her, handing her a lipstick and a compact mirror, her phone and the contents of her handbag.

'Here.' He shoved them at her.

'Thank you so much,' she beamed at him. 'I must get some sleep.'

And she was away, hurrying back towards her bedroom.

All she could do was hope that he had been reassured there was nothing in her handbag. With an agony of relief, she thought about the little hacksaw and the buckled padlock buried in a shallow grave not far from Henke's body. And with any luck tomorrow they would think they had just misplaced the key for the padlock, hanging new and shiny, on the door to the laboratory.

But she couldn't be sure. Couldn't be sure that they might not come for her with an efficient brutality. And as she lay down to sleep, all she could think of was Henke, and thousands of crawling flies.

64

The next morning, Drummond bounded into the dining room, a grin on his face.

'You are looking … ' He posed in the doorway, 'at the new Secretary of State for Health.'

Casey let out a squeal. 'How on earth … What happened to Colette?'

'Congratulations.' Bailey was pouring himself some orange juice. 'A cabinet minister. Very impressive, Ambrose.'

'Colette Warwick has been sacked.' Drummond was reading aloud from his phone. 'The *Post* broke some story about her husband last night. Bloody vultures.'

Drummond wasn't really acting, thought Casey. He was genuinely delighted, forgetting it was all a set-up. A reward, and she had helped him.

'Poor Colette.' She made a face.

'Yes, well.' Drummond sat down at the breakfast table. 'It'll mean a promotion for you too, Serena, my dear. Now, Elias, I'm afraid the PM needs me home as soon as possible. We'll have to make tracks, Serena.'

'Of course, Ambrose, of course. Duty calls. You could always fly home in the jet, if you need to.'

For a moment, Drummond looked tempted. Then his eyes met Casey's. 'Better not, old boy. I'd have to declare it. Stupid bloody rules, but there we go.'

'Then I'll tell them to get the car ready to take you back to Harare.'

'Thank you.' Drummond sounded brisk, as if he was already settling into the trappings of his new role. 'Thank you, Elias. Most kind.'

The Overfinch took Drummond straight to the airport.

Serena, back in London and coolly efficient, pulled strings and scrambled Drummond on to the first flight out of Harare. Oblivious to Casey's existence, Serena made only one booking, and the rest of the flight was full.

'Fairly reasonable,' Drummond laughed as he peered up at the departure boards. 'Can't really blame old Serena.'

Casey felt twitchy, wanting to get back to the UK.

Miranda called her. 'I've checked and you can fly back via Nairobi tomorrow morning, Case. There isn't any mad rush. Hessa's story's running well, so we want to give that a bit of space, anyway. The political team can handle most of it.'

'Miranda, I don't think Hessa should … '

'It's OK, Casey. We've got it all covered.'

'But, Miranda … '

'It's fine. Everything is under control.'

And Casey couldn't explain the feeling of dread that descended.

She didn't go back to Kizzie's, but checked into a basic guest house as close to the airport as possible. Her room was on the first floor, opening on to a steel walkway that ran the length of the building before a flight of stairs led down to a dingy swimming pool. The place seemed to be almost entirely empty, just a couple of jet-lagged travellers confining themselves to their rooms.

The rest of the day crawled past, the hours bleeding into each other. Casey sat in her room, head down, typing up her notes. She edged the laboratory documents out of the secret compartment in her handbag, and looked at them with satisfaction. Then she sent photographs, notes, thoughts to Miranda, as she always did. Hansel and Gretel; a superstition.

Work done, she sat by the swimming pool. It was a dank spot, the high, blank walls of the guest house too close to the edge of the pool.

The space felt hemmed in, the sun never reaching this scummy water. The tiles were white, cracked, utilitarian. Big cartoon signs banned running and petting and shouting. Casey looked at the insects floating on the surface of the water and decided: no.

She stayed on the white plastic chair for a while – the seat an awkward basket weave design that left diamond shapes on her legs – thinking and fretting. Her legs hurt from the escape through the ocean, the bruises aching, the cuts throbbing. When night finally fell, she lay in the dark, listening to the sounds all around her. The room was hot, a small fan on a table spinning erratically. The mosquito nets pinned over the grimy window frames had split, and there was a smell of old cooking oil.

Is everything OK? she messaged Hessa.

It's fine, Hessa answered. *Go to sleep. It's all OK.*

Casey lay awake for hours and was only woken from a half-sleep by the jangle of her phone. She reached out, blinking at her watch, and stared bleary-eyed at the screen. Not a number she knew.

'Hello?'

'Good morning, Casey.' She didn't recognise the civil voice.

'Who—' Casey sat up.

'I have something … ' The words were silky smooth, oddly polite, 'that I need you to do.'

65

Casey reached convulsively for her recorder. It wasn't on the bedside table. It wasn't on the desk. Where was it?

'Why are you calling me?' Her voice rose.

'Listen to me, Casey.'

'Who the hell are you?'

It was Hessa who had identified the house in Buckinghamshire on Airbnb.

It's perfect, she had messaged Casey.

Casey had looked at the screenshot of the house as it flashed up on her phone. Four bedrooms, she read. Detached. Generous private garden. Stylish integrated appliances. Available by the week.

Fine. Go for it.

After publishing the first day of stories about Colette Warwick, Hessa had hopped on the train to Amersham. She walked down the leafy roads to the house and spent the night in executive luxury. The next morning, she got back on the train and carefully evaded any trackers as she stepped on to the Tube. Once she was sure no one was following her, she headed to the office for the second day of stories about the Health Secretary Scandal.

After another long day in the office, she hopped back on the train to Amersham, neat amongst the commuters. Walking slowly, she made her way to the house, which looked as if it had just been plopped out of its mould into a row of identical homes.

'You mean I'm a tethered goat?' Hessa had laughed when Casey first laid out the plan. 'Bait?'

'Drummond told Bailey you were investigating Corax,' said Casey. 'And we know that Bailey moves fast and aggressively to shut down any whisper about Corax. Drummond has spelled out where you'll be tonight, and on his past form, Bailey will strike fast.'

'So they'll track me to and from to the train station,' Hessa mused. 'And then ... '

Limpets dangling, black, yellow and green.
Torn away to die.

'You'll be quite safe.' Miranda had been firm. 'You'll have a security team with you all the time. They'll be with you all night, every night, while you're staying there. They'll be a few steps behind you on the way to the train station, with panic buttons and everything. You'll be safe as houses.'

'No problem.' Hessa's eyes sparkled.

'If Bailey's guys try anything at all, we'll have about fourteen cameras on them at all times,' said Miranda. 'We'll finally be able to prove it. Prove that he got your address from Drummond, and immediately sent round his thugs.'

Casey had felt misgivings almost at once. Wished she could retract the words, such casual words, the words that spilled so easily. *We could try this ...*

'You don't have to do it, Hessa,' Casey said urgently. 'I'll think of something else. It's too—'

'Bleat,' Hessa had giggled, pretending to nibble some grass. 'Baaaa.'

And now Casey clutched the phone to her ear in a seedy Harare guest house. 'Who is this? What's happening? What the hell do you want?'

The voice was polite, emotionless.

'There is a swimming pool outside your room. A telephone has been placed on the diving board.' The words were deadpan. 'Swim across the pool and wait for the phone to ring.'

'What?' Casey's brain was moving slowly, an ant sprayed with poison. Was the recorder in her handbag? *There it was.* Her fingers wrestled with the small black device: *nearly there*. 'You're saying I have to swim across the pool?' *Almost*.

'Goodbye.'

The phone went dead.

Casey stared at the phone in bewilderment, her recorder dangling uselessly. She stood in the middle of the room, thoughts rattling. Then she scrambled to ring Miranda's number.

No answer.

Hessa's phone: no answer.

Hands clumsy, she tried Miranda again. But the numbers rang out, the dial tone echoing round the streaky walls of the guest house.

Casey walked slowly to the door. Stepped out on to the steel walkway and peered over the edge.

There was the shabby swimming pool, grey scum floating in one corner. And there, on the diving board, was a small, incongruous object.

As Casey looked down, the telephone's screen lit up. Someone was calling.

Casey sprinted down the staircase, her feet clattering on the steel treads. The phone was vibrating on the plastic diving board, pulsing closer to the edge.

Swim across the pool.

She didn't hesitate. She jumped straight into the water. The pool was deeper than it looked, and she was out of her depth by the time she reached the diving board, awkward in her haste. Clinging to the edge of the swimming pool with one hand, she reached up to snatch the phone off the diving board.

'Hello?' Breathless.

'Hello, Casey.'

She knew the voice immediately. It was Bailey, clinically polite.

'You?' Casey shook her head, shoving wet hair out of her face, trying to avoid submerging the phone. 'What the hell do you want, Bailey?'

'I think you know, Casey.'

Clutching the phone, Casey scrambled along the side of the pool, making for the steps.

'I don't know.'

'Don't mess around, Casey. Don't mess around, or people will die.'

She reached the steps and leaped up, her only thought to reach her room, grab her recorder.

'Why is that, Mr Bailey?' *Keep him talking.* 'What do you—'

He interrupted her sharply. 'Don't move from the pool area, Casey. Stay exactly where you are.'

Casey stopped short, sliding on the slimy tiles.

That was the reason for the swim through the pool, she realised. So that he knew she had no recording devices with her. This was a conversation that didn't exist. The leap into the ocean at Llandudno had had the same effect, wiping everything. And now Casey glanced around, wondering if there were spies in this grimy hotel, if there were men watching from the shadows.

Yes. Someone had placed the phone carefully on the diving board. She sat down on the white plastic chair.

'What do you want, Mr Bailey?'

'I want the documents.'

'What documents?'

'The documents you stole from the laboratory.'

The morning was cool. Casey had slept in just a T-shirt and shorts, and she was soaked through. She started to shiver.

'I don't know what you mean.'

'You're wasting my time.'

'What if I say no?'

'Then people will die, Casey.'

Casey jumped at a sound behind her. She leaped to her feet and spun around. A man was watching her impassively.

'Who will die?' She didn't take her eyes off the man. 'You're bluffing.'

'I never bluff, Casey.'

'Who? Hessa?' Casey's mind was frantic. She thought of Hessa, sleeping peaceably in that Lego house with its *generous garden*, its *stylish appliances*, its *off-street parking for two cars*. Magnolia walls, and blood spattering. 'No, please …'

'I think you can guess.'

And she knew, like missing the top stair and falling, falling, fallen. 'Not Miranda. No. You can't … You mustn't. I—'

'I can. And so I suggest, Casey, that you do precisely what I ask.'

66

It was the chauffeur, she realised. The man waiting patiently by the side of the pool. He had driven the Overfinch out to Njana. She had seen only his shoulders, his hands, the back of his head. His profile, as he asked: *Chocolate? Peanuts?* But it was him, she was sure of it. Tall and powerful, with gym-built shoulders. He had large, capable hands and moved fast. And now he was moving closer, just a few feet from her table.

Casey could hear Bailey's voice on the line, but it was as if he was talking in the far distance. She couldn't make out the shape of the words any more.

'You can explain to your team, but no one else,' Bailey was saying. 'And that's only because your team will wonder, and because they will have to know what to say. But you don't tell the *Post* news editors. You don't tell anyone else at all.'

The words wavered again, like a radio losing its signal. She could hear disconnected syllables, but the sentences made no sense. Until one word jerked her back.

Miranda.

'You can't … ' she muttered.

'I can. Do you understand?'

'Yes,' Casey said quietly, not quite sure what she was agreeing with. 'Yes.'

The line went dead.

Casey stared down at the phone in her hand. It was one of the old Nokias, she saw dreamily. A long battery life, but basic. No capacity to record.

She looked up. The man was waiting for her, eyebrows raised. He nodded towards the steel stairs.

'Come,' he said. 'Quickly.'

The man stood beside her as she deleted all the photographs and all her notes. Then he picked up her laptop and searched it fast, his fingers quick over the keypad. He knew what he was doing, this man. Knew how to check.

His eyes narrowed as he found her emails to Miranda.

'Delete them.' There was a heavy Shona accent to his voice. 'And the emails in her account.'

'But I can't. I can't access her email.'

His face twisted into a smile. 'I think that you can.'

'I can't. Not from here.'

The movement was so casual that her eyes couldn't process it. But now he was holding a gun, the muzzle pointing inexorably at her forehead.

'I don't want to shoot you, but if you don't get rid of those emails, you will die.' His voice was quite calm, as if explaining to a child. 'And your friend, she will die too.'

It was the nonchalance that convinced her. His eyes were steady, dispassionate. She knew, with certainty, that he would kill her.

'No. Please. I'll try.'

The shock made her ungainly, her fingers sliding incompetently over the laptop keys.

'Hurry up.' The gun nudged closer. 'Do it now.'

It took her four attempts to get into Miranda's email account, cursing under her breath each time the computer froze, rejecting her guesses. But finally she was in, and the man looked over her shoulder as she searched and deleted, searched and deleted.

Miranda hadn't checked her emails for hours, Casey saw, with a shudder of despair. She hadn't read the emails Casey had sent the night before. And she always checked her emails. Always.

When Casey had finished, the man took her laptop and her phone, checking all the caches, all the possible hiding places. It took time, but he didn't hurry. Casey stood beside him, her mind filled with Hessa and Miranda. Finally he stood, holstering the handgun, still entirely relaxed.

'The papers?'

'I don't—'

'The papers.'

Unwillingly, she pulled them out of her bag. He read them briefly, counted the number of pages, then stepped out on to the steel walkway, pulling a lighter out of his pocket.

It took only a few minutes. The papers flared bright in the early sunlight, and crisped to a fragile grey ash that he dusted away with his fingers. Casey sat on the bed and watched through the open door as the cinders blew away on the morning breeze.

'Now,' he said. 'I will go.'

'But I thought … '

'No.'

He left then. As if a spell had broken, Casey scrambled to her laptop, flicking it on and checking everything again and again. But there was nothing to be done. It was gone, all of it: everything she had worked for. He had been thorough, wiping everything, overwriting all the data, deleting not just her emails but her accounts too. Her phone had been wiped. Her laptop was encrypted, of course. Backed up in the cloud. But its security depended on her. She had never imagined that she might be sent in, her own electronic Trojan horse. Washing away her own footsteps, destroying her own proof. She burned with fury.

Toby might be able to get it back, she thought desperately. Maybe. The *Post*'s data whizz, with all his recovery software: he might be able to perform some sort of wizardry.

But then she remembered Dash, after the Naji story. When the emails about the marathon runner were faked, and everything got a bit blurry.

Dash wouldn't rely on some document Toby managed to extract from somewhere deep in some Internet hole, not for this. He would need proof, proper proof to go up against the might of Adsero. He would need the physical documents she had hunted down, risking everything. And now they were gone.

Casey slumped against her pillows, exhausted for a moment.

Hurry.

She sat up, ringing Miranda – the only number she knew by heart – again and again.

Call Dash: *no.*

And just as she was about to scream, pick up the little Nokia and hurl it at the wall with a crunch of cheap plastic, the screen of the phone lit up.

'Hello?' Miranda's voice was faint. 'Casey?'

'Where are you?' Casey almost screamed.

'I don't know.' Miranda sounded hazy, confused. 'I'm in my car. I don't know … '

There was a long pause.

'Miranda?'

'I must have gone to sleep.' Miranda was louder now, more like herself. 'I'm near that house in Buckinghamshire. How odd.'

Miranda had gone to keep an eye on Hessa, Casey realised with a thud. Unable to trust anyone else to look after her team. And that meant …

Casey found that her eyes were wet. 'You didn't,' she said. 'You didn't go to sleep.'

'Well,' Miranda said slowly, 'What the hell happened then?'

'They must have used some sort of anaesthetic drug,' said Casey. 'Knocked you out as you sat in your car. Adsero would be able to get hold of those, easily.'

'What happened? Tell me quickly, Casey.'

And because it was Miranda, and because she always demanded precision and a clear, dispassionate accuracy, Casey managed to find the words.

'They must have tracked you down,' said Casey. 'God knows how. Knocked you out. And then injected you … '

'Injected me with what?' Casey could hear the fear electric in Miranda's voice.

'It's one of the samples,' she said. 'Bailey said it was one of the samples they took from the hospital in Harare.'

67

Casey hadn't been able to speak as Bailey set out his demands. There had been a loud buzzing noise in her eardrums, a sense of having too much blood in her veins.

But she had understood enough.

A sample from St Agnes. An injection. Corax is the only thing that will cure it. Listen very carefully, Casey, or she will die, do you understand?

She had stared blindly at the cream walls of the guest room.

'Where do I get it? Where do I get the dose of Corax?'

'I've got it here.'

'Where is here?'

'Cape Town. You can have it in a few days.'

'A few *days*?'

The Adsero plane, she had seen on her laptop, was down in Cape Town now. Garrick must have told him, she thought.

'You have to go to Cape Town,' Miranda was speaking again.

'Go to a hospital, Miranda. Now.'

'Why?' Miranda almost laughed. 'We know that none of the standard antibiotics will even begin to touch the sides of this bug.'

'Oh, Miranda.'

'It will be fine, Casey,' Miranda insisted. 'I feel fine right now. Just hurry, Casey.'

'I will,' Casey promised. 'I'll fly straight down to Cape Town now and I'll be back in the UK before you know it.'

'I'll tell Hessa what's happened.'

'But don't tell Dash. Promise me? I can't bear—'

'I won't.'

'I don't know what to do when I get—' Her mind felt tangled, twisted, the knots tightening with every attempt to unravel. 'They've deleted everything. Everything. Even my contacts.'

'I'll tell Delphine to meet you in Cape Town,' said Miranda. 'I'll send you her number. She'll help. And I'll send you as many contacts as I can, so you can reboot your phone.'

'Can we tell her what's happened? Bailey said only the investigations team could know.'

'She is investigations.' Miranda sounded firm, more like herself. 'And you can't do this by yourself.'

'Miranda—'

'I'll drive back to my house,' Miranda said. They all knew how to isolate, after corona. 'I'll wait for you there.'

'It could be a lie, Miranda. He may not have given you anything.'

'Yes. It could all be nonsense.'

'I'll be as quick as I can.'

'Great.' Somehow, Miranda managed to sound chirpy. 'I can't wait to see you.'

Casey waited at the airport. It felt safer. Once she was through security, she collapsed in one of the hard plastic seats and sank her head in her hands.

It was gone. Everything was gone.

She felt empty, weightless. What was the point in any of it?

After a few minutes, she forced herself to sit up, checking her emails out of habit. Miranda had managed to send her her contacts list again, so she reloaded her phone. She glanced at her text messages without reading them, except one. *Call me. MD.*

Exhaling, she rang the number. 'Maurice? It's Casey.'

'Good evening, Miss Benedict.' His voice sounded light-hearted, cool, jarring with her surroundings. He must be in the Bahamas, thought Casey, a few time zones behind Zimbabwe.

'What's up?' She had to delve for the words, stumbling awkwardly.

'Is everything all right?' His voice sharpened.

'Oh,' she said. 'Fine.'

'Sure?'

'Yes.'

'I just thought you would be interested.' He brightened again. 'You remember that company that bought the rights to Corax?'

Casey tried to think. 'Slopeside Inc.? The BVI company?'

'Exactly. Well, I've just come across them again.'

'How?'

'That oil deal I went in on with Garrick McElroy? In central Africa.'

'Yes.' A faint spark. 'I hope you're losing money on that, by the way.'

Maurice Delacroix laughed. 'Never, Casey, never. But I was going through the documentation on the oil rights, and it turns out Slopeside Inc. used to own them. I saw the name on some old loan agreements.'

Casey shifted forward on the hard plastic, forcing herself to concentrate. 'When?'

'Slopeside owned the rights just before they were transferred to Garrick,' said Delacroix. 'You know how these rights bounce around for years before someone actually starts drilling. So I called my Moldovan friend. You remember him? You were a guest of his in Miami. He does a lot of business in that part of Africa. Knows all the players. I asked him if he knew who was behind this Slopeside company.'

Delacroix stretched out the silence.

'Who is it?' Casey cracked.

'He didn't know,' Delacroix said idly. 'Never tried to track it down.'

'Maurice ... '

'But Slopeside is also connected to a certain ranch in Zimbabwe,' said Delacroix smoothly.

'The Njana ranch?'

'I knew,' he spoke with satisfaction, 'that you would know about it. You're really not bad at this job, Casey.'

Slopeside, Casey realised, van de Berg. The old Dutch name for a family who came from the mountains. It made a sort of sense.

'I don't know what you are working on, Casey,' Delacroix went on. 'And I am not even sure why you are so interested in this Garrick McElroy. But it is clear: whoever owns this ranch also used to own the oil rights. And now this company owns the rights to Corax, too. A sort of swap, if you will.'

Elias Bailey, Casey thought. Elias Bailey had snapped up the Slopeside holding company in the fire sale after Jacques van de Berg had died. The oil rights must have been part of a job lot of African assets held by Slopeside Inc. Piled high, sold cheap. Just a small fraction of the billions of pounds' worth of African natural resources traded like playing cards by rich men who rarely even saw the diamond mines or the oil wells or the vast tracts of timber, slashed and burned.

And Bailey had handed the rights to his son like pocket money, to see if the boy could make something out of them. Something for Garrick to do. She wondered when exactly Garrick had warned his father about a Carrie asking too many questions. Bailey's men had approached the Amersham house with enough care to identify Miranda, so they knew by then.

They must have found the new padlock on the laboratory door the next morning, the suspicions sparking to a blaze in the hot savannah. The sting's sting.

'I see,' said Casey.

'I'm glad it makes sense to you,' said Delacroix.

'I could never understand,' said Casey, 'how Garrick had come to hold those rights. It wasn't his field at all.'

'No,' he said.

Those loyalties, thought Casey. Invisible, and enduring. Garrick half-hated his father, but he hadn't been able to walk away. And Bailey had taken him back into the fold after Pergamex, tying Garrick close again. That dependence, encouraged.

She had assumed the Llandudno break-in would be the final straw for Bailey. But he must have controlled his rage somehow, buried his fury.

But when they found the padlock, Bailey knew his errant son held the secrets. And when Bailey needed to know, Garrick had told him everything. The whisper travelling around the emptiness, so much further than anyone could know.

Casey couldn't sit any longer. She strode round the airport, past the tired passengers, past the bored men, past the big windows looking out over the runway. She needed to get to Cape Town. Needed to get out of this dusty building.

She wondered if Garrick had told Bailey everything before she and Drummond had even left the reserve. Probably not, otherwise they might never have made it out alive.

But perhaps he had already known. And bought up every other seat on that flight out of Harare just to trap her here. And now she was heading to Cape Town, just as he had ordered.

Casey's phone buzzed again.

She stared down and felt her heart twist.

It was Noah Hart's number.

Casey couldn't read it. She looked away from the phone, gazing across the shabby concourse. She thought about that pale face, that fawn hair plaited back tightly. The gleam of hope in the deep brown eyes.

What was the point in any of it?

Casey felt her eyes prickle, the sense of despair rising, choking.

Then she took a deep breath and opened the message. It was brief. To the point.

I thought you would want to know that Flora died this morning. I wish it could have been different. We kept her comfortable at the end. N.

And Casey stood in the sparse crowd of the airport and cried.

68

Delphine arrived with a sharp knock on the door. Casey had checked into a hotel in Camps Bay, the reception filled by tourists with burnt noses talking about cricket and Robben Island and District Six.

'Miranda called me.' Delphine walked briskly into the room. 'What the hell is going on, Casey?'

'I—'

'You've been crying, Casey.'

'A girl I knew … I don't want to talk about it.'

Delphine shook her head. 'There's an article on that bloody Papercut site, Casey. It says you had a meltdown somewhere abroad. That you deleted everything from your computer, hacked your colleague's email and resigned from the *Post*. It says you've gone completely batshit.'

The man had stood over her as she typed out the email to Dash. 'I would like to tender my resignation with immediate effect … '

Dash had called her several times since, but she had ignored him. Zac had called too, Casey pressing the red button again and again: end call, end call, end call.

'I know.'

'Who briefed Papercut?'

'I don't know … They have an email account to receive anonymous tips,' Casey muttered. 'Anyone could have told them. And it's half true, anyway.'

The most dangerous sort of truth.

'What? What's *happened*, Casey? Tell me.'

'Bailey wants the *Post* to write an article.'

'An article?' Delphine's voice was high-pitched. 'About what?'

'I—'

Delphine sat down on the bed. 'Casey, I'm worried. Tell me. What the hell is going on?'

'Elias Bailey wants us to write an article about an antibiotic,' Casey said robotically. 'A small piece about a brilliant new antibiotic that Adsero are working on at a special site in Zimbabwe.'

'I don't understand.' Delphine's face sagged with confusion. 'It doesn't make sense.'

'The article must appear in the business section of the *Post*,' Casey recited. 'It isn't to be a big piece, you understand. It must just be a brief interview with the Adsero chief executive.'

'But why?'

'In this article, there will be a passing reference to the fact that the lab in Zimbabwe has been relatively informal,' said Casey. 'Bailey's hobby, almost. But overall, it will be a positive piece.'

She spat out the last two words.

'And then what?'

'Nothing,' said Casey. 'That is the last story the *Post* will ever write about Adsero or Bailey.'

There was a long pause.

'But you can't.' The colour had faded from Delphine's face. She leapt to her feet, unable to stay sitting down. 'You can't do that, Casey. You know what Bailey has done.'

She strode to the window, staring out over the ocean.

'I know, Delphine,' Casey said to her back. 'But I don't know what else I can do. If I don't publish the article, he won't give me the Corax. And if he doesn't give me the Corax, Miranda will die. I can't let that happen. I *can't*. So it really is that straightforward.'

There's no one left for them to threaten. The self-pitying words of months ago popped into her mind again. There had been someone left, it turned out. She just hadn't realised.

Delphine spun around. 'But there must be something else we can do.'

'There isn't,' Casey said. 'All the way down here on the plane, I tried to come up with something else, and I can't think of a single way out of this. He's taken all my notes, wiped everything. Burned the documents. We can't take down Adsero based on memories and hearsay. We have no proof of anything.'

Delphine pressed her fists to her mouth, her eyes blazing. 'But he will get away with it. He will get away with everything. Those murders.' The word was a shout. 'He can't be allowed to get away with it, Casey.'

'I can't prove anything.' Casey spoke through her teeth, 'Without those documents, it's only circumstantial. We are to publish the article tomorrow, and then that's it. It'll be over. Miranda's going to talk to the business section now.'

Delphine moved towards the bed, her steps jerky. 'But we are so close.'

'I know.' Casey felt as if she were comforting Delphine. 'But it's Miranda, Delphine. *Miranda*.'

'And this article will say that Corax will be available soon?'

'No,' said Casey. 'That's the point. It will just say that Adsero are working on an antibiotic, not even specifying if it's saepio or Corax or something else. And that it will be available at some undefined point in the future. This article will run under our Cape Town stringer's name. The *Post*'s stringer, I mean,' she corrected herself.

'But why? Why does Elias Bailey want you to do this?'

'Because how many times have you read a puff piece in the business section about some antibiotic breakthrough?' asked Casey. 'It's quite boring, isn't it? Your eyes move on to the next thing. It doesn't tie them in.'

'Casey,' Delphine subsided onto the bed. 'I don't understand.'

'It's hiding the story in plain sight,' Casey said slowly. 'If the *Post* runs a piece saying Adsero is doing brilliant – albeit slightly unorthodox – research, it would be very hard to turn around three days later and say it's actually criminality on a grand scale. We'd need proper evidence for that sort of shift, and … ' Her voice dropped slightly, 'I've deleted all the evidence.'

'Never ask why,' Delphine's mouth twisted into a smile. 'As we always say. You can look at this story from one angle, or another.'

'It's where you point the spotlight,' said Casey. 'You know how it works, Delphine.'

'I do.' It was a sigh.

'It puts everything we can prove into the public domain,' said Casey. 'Exactly the way he wants it out there. And nothing else will ever see the light of day. Especially now that I've resigned.'

'And the business team will publish this piece tomorrow?'

'Miranda will tell them that Bailey is demanding it immediately, given my behaviour,' said Casey. 'Harassment, they're going to call it. *Harassment*.'

'Dash will take you back,' said Delphine. 'Miranda will explain, and you will explain. When this is all over.'

'Maybe,' said Casey. 'But that is why Bailey is making me wait four days for the Corax, isn't it? In four days' time, this will be history. The Papercut article saying I'm an obsessive, unreliable lunatic will have bounced all over the Internet like a virus. And that story … ' Casey almost smiled, 'has an element of truth to it too. My job depends on my word being reliable. They can't possibly publish an article based on just my memories after all this. The *Post* will publish a nice positive piece about Bailey and Adsero, and that will be the end of it. Bailey will get away with it, Delphine.'

Delphine jumped to her feet. 'He can't, Casey. He just can't.'

'But that's the thing. He can.'

'When are the *Post* going to do this interview?' Delphine asked. 'With Bailey.'

'I don't know. I suppose Miranda will talk to Isla as soon as possible.'

Isla Suchopar was the *Post*'s stringer in Cape Town. As budgets contracted, staffers had been axed all around the world. Instead, the *Post*'s foreign desk relied on a network of stringers. Freelancers available at the push of a button to write articles about murder and riots and hunger. 'No one bloody reads the stories at the back of the paper anyway,' Ross would shrug. 'Any muppet can write those.'

'I know Isla Suchopar,' Delphine nodded.

'I suppose I'll check it, to make sure she gets everything right. Then Miranda will send it to the business desk.'

'I could do the interview instead of Isla,' Delphine suggested. 'I'm a bit rusty, but it's not a tricky piece to write.'

'Bailey would google you,' said Casey. 'And see that you used to work with Miranda. We can't do anything to rock the boat right now.'

'Just say I'm Isla,' said Delphine. 'I'll go up there instead. I know Isla, and she's a gossip. If she got even a hint that there was something weird going on with this article, it would be halfway around Cape Town by teatime.'

'Isla wouldn't really have to know there was anything odd about it,' said Casey slowly. 'She'll just be commissioned to write 800 words about Bailey. But I suppose it doesn't make any difference if you do it.'

'Cool,' said Delphine. 'I'll pop home to get my stuff. Tell him I'll be there in two hours?'

'I will.'

Miranda rang later. 'Is everything OK?'

Casey was lying on her bed in the hotel, flicking lackadaisically through the television channels. She kept hearing Flora Ashcroft's laugh and seeing those little piles of blankets in small white cots: a tiny brown arm reaching up to the ceiling.

'Everything's fine,' Casey said listlessly. 'Delphine's just on her way to do the interview. She left her house in Constantia half an hour ago.'

'Constantia?' said Miranda. 'She lives in Camps Bay.'

'Sure,' said Casey, not listening. 'She said she'll be at Bailey's soon.' She glanced at her watch. 'So any minute now.'

'And are you all right?'

'As well as I can be. How are you feeling?'

'Fine,' said Miranda. 'Dash is getting a bit demented though. I've told him I'm off sick, but he won't believe me. He gave Hessa a right going over this morning too.'

'She didn't say anything?'

'No. Just hinted that you'd overstepped the mark with Bailey, and best not to ask any further questions.'

'He must be spitting tacks.'

'He is. The Papercut article hasn't helped. He wants to know where you are.'

'Don't tell him. I'm putting stuff on my own credit card, so it's none of his business.'

'I won't tell him,' Miranda sighed. 'Tell Delphine to file to me, and I'll put it through to the business desk. Probably best if we leave Dash out of this one. Nicky'll be pleased with a decent Adsero story. She won't ask any questions.'

'I hate it.'

'I know.'

'He's going to get away with it.'

'For now, yes. You don't land every story, Casey. Some of them get away.'

'But this one ... ' Casey felt the tears rise again. 'It's Ed, Miranda. How can I let Bailey get away?'

69

Casey couldn't stand the hotel room any more. She pulled on flip-flops, shorts, a flowery top that seemed absurd, and stepped out of the hotel room.

In the lift, she listened to bickering about Kirstenbosch and the Cape of Good Hope and how you'd expect a cooked breakfast in a place like this, really. And then she was across the lobby and out into the sunny courtyard, breathing in the scent of the pale pink roses.

A sudden movement on her left, and she flinched, turning with a jolt of realisation.

'Oh.' Casey came to a halt. 'You.'

'Yes,' he said sardonically. 'Me.'

'I thought you'd gone back to Mauritius.'

'Well, no, evidently.'

'You should. Go back to Mauritius, Zac. Or get on your yacht and hide somewhere in the ocean for a bit.'

She tried to sidestep him, but he moved too fast. Too tall and too strong, blocking her path.

'What happened in Zimbabwe, Casey?'

'Nothing happened.'

'Casey.'

'I don't want to talk about it.' She tried to feint past him again, but he cut her off. 'Stop it, Zac. Leave me alone.'

'I don't understand,' said Zac. 'The last time I spoke to you, you said you were off to Harare and you looked ready for anything. You were on the hunt, Casey. And now look at you.'

Casey recoiled from his stare. She wished, vaguely, that she had washed her hair, and then she shoved the thought away.

'We're not doing the story,' she said. 'I got it wrong and it's over. Now leave me alone, Zac.'

'Tell me what's happened, Casey.'

Casey thought of the bacteria racing around Miranda's bloodstream. Their numbers doubling, quadrupling. 'No, Zac. There's nothing to say.'

'I haven't heard from Garrick.' He changed tactics.

'Tough,' she said. 'I don't think you will. And I think he told Bailey everything anyway.'

'He probably did,' Zac shrugged. 'But he is his father, Casey.'

'I know. But I'm done. I'm not having anything else to do with Bailey.'

Casey pushed roughly past Zac, sensing dubious looks from the hotel receptionists. Zac caught her arm, spinning her back around again.

'Casey, I've seen this look in people before, remember? In Garrick, in Noah. In my own sodding mirror. What has Bailey done to you?'

'Nothing.' She yanked her arm away, 'Leave me alone, Zac.'

The bellboy took a step towards them, unsure whether to intervene or not. Casey remembered – just – that she didn't want to attract attention. She hesitated and turned towards Zac, forcing a smile on her face, and quickly trawling for an excuse.

'I'm just going to pop out and see Delphine.'

Zac smiled down at her, shifting his tone. 'Just round the corner? How lovely, darling. I'll come with you.'

'She lives in Constantia, my love.'

The bellboy looked relieved by the change in mood, strolling back towards the entrance.

'Camps Bay,' Zac trilled back. 'I popped over to her house while you were in Harare.'

'She lives in Constantia,' Casey said flatly, dropping the act.

'She doesn't.' Zac was serious now too. 'I did go to her house. While you were up at Njana, I bumped into her on the beach, and she invited me back for a braai. She's got a lovely place there.'

Casey stared up at him, trying to read his face. 'But … '

'What?'

Casey's mind was racing. She sat down on one of the little benches scattered around the courtyard, and pulled out her phone.

'Loelia.' Casey's voice was chatty. 'How are you? I'm not interrupting you, am I?'

There was a pause as Loelia adjusted to Casey's tone. 'Not at all, Casey. How are you?'

There wasn't much time for subtlety. 'This is a ridiculous question, Loelia. But Delphine told me I had to try her yoga class while I was in Cape Town, and I've gone and lost the details. You don't have them?'

'Of course.' Off the top of her head, Loelia recited the class times, the location, a chic Constantia yoga studio.

'Oh, it's in *Constantia*,' said Casey. 'I thought she went to a class in Camps Bay. That's where I am staying, you see.'

'Oh, sure,' said Loelia. 'That's a bit of a trek for a class, from Camps Bay to Constantia. I know some good studios that way too. I'll text you the details.'

'Great!' Casey said. 'Is that how you met Delphine originally? At your yoga class?'

'Yes, indeed.' Casey could hear Loelia pouring a glass of wine. 'Delphine joined the class just a few months back. We've become good friends. Great girl, don't you think?'

'Yes. Well, thanks for that,' Casey chirped. 'Speak soon.'

She hung up.

'What?' asked Zac. 'What is going on? Why the hell does it matter that Delphine decided to go to a yoga class in Constantia?'

Casey didn't respond, as another thought had struck her. She pulled up Twitter, searching for Flora Ashcroft. Flora had an account but hadn't used it much; there were long periods of empty silence. All those empty weeks when she was stuck in the Royal Brompton, Casey thought. She scrolled down and down through the feed, and finally she saw it.

'What the hell is going on?' Zac asked again.

'I don't know.' She stared across the courtyard. 'But Delphine made contact with Flora Ashcroft months ago. Look. They're chatting about having a coffee after a journalism lecture in this tweet. I bet it was Delphine who suggested to Ross that I speak to Flora. There are only about three people that man would call a friend, and he said it was a *friend* who gave him the tip about Flora.'

'OK. I don't know who Ross is, but OK.'

'Delphine must have hoped that if I went to that hospital, I would bump into Noah Hart.'

'What?'

'She must have realised,' Casey fitted the words together carefully, 'that if I went to the hospital, I might get a hint of the story from Noah. She may even have asked Flora to tip me off about Corax, for all I know.'

'That seems like a long shot.'

'Yes, but I don't know how many other breadcrumbs Delphine scattered. That could just have been the one tip I picked up on.'

Zac gave her an exasperated look. 'Maybe.'

'And she may have been feeding Flora snippets of information all along the way, that Flora passed on without even realising it probably. For all I know, it was Delphine who tracked down Bailey when he was talking at that wretched conference in Wrocław, for example. I could never work out how Flora had found out that he would be there. Flora was learning fast, but that was … That was Delphine. Delphine would just have told Flora they were helping us along, and they were, I suppose.'

'If you say so.'

'It was Delphine,' Casey was still thinking aloud, 'who told Miranda that Loelia had spoken to the *Argus* originally, and Delphine who told Miranda that they had ditched the story, too. And it was Delphine who told us that Bailey had been cheating on his wife. And that's why you and I headed down to Cape Town.'

'Why does that matter?'

'And it was Delphine who actually got me into Loelia's house.' Casey put her hand to her forehead. 'Loelia would never have spoken to me, left to her own devices. But Delphine had – quite coincidentally – joined Loelia's yoga class a few months ago although it is nowhere near where she lives, and they became pals very quickly.

Delphine said we were just round the corner from her home when I was walking along that road in Constantia, where she just happened to bump into me, and that was a straightforward lie.'

'Stop,' Zac interrupted her thoughts. 'What are you going on about?'

'It was Delphine,' Casey said slowly. 'All along. She was running this story, and we didn't even notice.'

'What?'

'Hansel and Gretel breadcrumbs,' said Casey. 'She was dropping them every step of the way.'

Zac was looking at her, something close to concern in his eyes. 'Casey, what are you going on about?'

'It was Delphine,' Casey repeated.

'OK,' said Zac. 'She wanted you to do this story. But why? Why go to all that trouble?'

'I don't know,' she said. 'I have absolutely no idea at all.'

70

'Stop,' said Miranda. 'You're not making any sense.'

'Delphine's gone to Elias Bailey's house,' Casey snapped. 'I don't know what she's doing, but she's at his house right now.'

Casey and Zac had raced back up to her hotel room. Zac was sitting on the window seat, listening as she talked to Miranda on speakerphone.

'OK,' said Miranda. 'But why does that matter?'

'What does Delphine want, Miranda? Is she working with Bailey?'

'Of course not,' Miranda said. 'Don't be ridiculous.'

'Why didn't she tell us?' demanded Casey. 'Why didn't she say she had a particular interest in Bailey?'

'I don't know.' There was a hesitation in Miranda's voice.

'She's working with Bailey,' Casey insisted.

When you stop and think about it, it looks different.

'Of course she isn't,' Miranda said. 'I've known Delphine Black for years, and she would never work with Bailey. She's … She's not that kind of person.'

Delphine Black.

There was something rattling in Casey's brain. An irritating feeling, like a label itching at the back of her neck. She pushed the sensation away, forced herself to think.

Delphine Black.

'I know sure she's lovely, Miranda.' Casey softened her tone. 'But she's been lying to us all the way through. And she's up at Bailey's house right now and we have no idea what she's—'

'Casey, calm down ... '

The feeling was back, prickling and itching and insisting. Casey pressed her hands against her forehead, pushing against her skull.

Then she looked up sharply.

'The Black Heart Fund,' muttered Casey.

'What?' Miranda asked. Zac gave Casey a baffled look.

'The Fitzgerald Brennan Trust.'

'Casey, I'm really worried about—'

'It's what he does,' said Casey slowly. 'It's what he does to atone.'

'What do you mean?'

'Bailey set up the Fitzgerald Brennan Trust after Ed and Professor Brennan died,' said Casey carefully. 'It funds scholarships. I think that's his thing. When he does something terrible, he sets up a foundation, as if to make amends. Offset the guilt somehow.'

'So what?'

'It's not the Black H-e-a-r-t Fund,' said Casey. 'We just assumed that's what it was called. It's the Black *H-a-r-t* Fund.'

Zac sat up abruptly. 'But ... '

'It was set up right after Abigail died,' explained Casey.

'Abigail?' questioned Miranda.

'Abigail Hart,' said Casey. 'She's the sister of Noah Hart. The Black Hart fund must have been set up two years ago, right after Abigail died. And it funds research in a rundown hospital in Harare.'

'Casey ... '

'That woman I spoke to in Taunton ... The Black *Heart* – H-e-a-r-t – Fund in Somerset gives books to local schools. It's got nothing to do with Harare at all. It's the Black Hart – H-a-r-t – Fund doing research in St Agnes.'

'Maybe, but ... '

'Who died a few years ago?' Casey asked, already knowing the answer. 'Who mattered to Delphine and died not long before Abigail Hart?'

There was a beat of silence.

'Delphine's husband died,' Miranda said slowly, unwillingly. 'Finlay Black died.'

'How did he die?'

'He was killed in a car crash,' Miranda said.

'*Another* car accident?'

'It was an accident, Casey.'

'I don't think it was.'

'It—'

'There are a lot of crashes on the roads in South Africa,' said Casey. 'But I don't think this one was an accident.'

'You don't know that.'

'No,' said Casey. 'I don't. But I think that Delphine does.'

71

Casey stood up.

'We have to get to Llandudno fast,' she said to Zac, and he nodded.

'I have a hire car. We can go straight away.'

'Wait,' said Miranda, voice echoing over the speaker.

'Bailey's expecting Isla Suchopar to arrive at his house,' said Casey. 'All set to write a nice little puff piece about him. But it's Delphine going up there. And we don't know what she wants.'

'She won't do anything.'

'How do you know that, Miranda? She's been manipulating us for weeks – months, even – to write a story about Bailey that finishes him off altogether. And I've just told her that her whole plan is going to come to nothing. That everything she's done was for nothing.'

'Yes, but—'

'Delphine is desperate for revenge,' Casey interrupted. 'She must believe that Bailey was involved in her husband's death, and she wants to destroy him.'

'She wouldn't—'

'How do you know? You don't, Miranda. You don't have a clue what that woman might do.'

'But Finlay Black was an architect,' Miranda protested. 'He had nothing to do with Bailey at all. Why on earth would Bailey have had him killed?'

'I don't know.' Casey clenched her fists.

'Maybe she just wants to confront him?' Miranda sounded desperate.

'Maybe she does,' said Casey. 'But neither of us believes that, do we?'

Zac's hire car raced along the coast road, beneath the disapproval of the Twelve Apostles.

'Faster,' muttered Casey. 'Hurry up.'

'I'm going as fast as I can.'

Casey was scrolling through the few brief articles about Elias Bailey for the hundredth time before she turned to Adsero's financial statements, frantic for any clue about Bailey's activities.

'There's nothing,' she shouted at last. 'There's nothing out there about anything.'

'Well, maybe there is nothing to find.'

'There must be … There has to be something that convinced Delphine … '

She had a photograph on her screen of a wrecked car, festooned in police tape. *Architect killed in horror smash.*

'Try Loelia,' Zac suggested. 'She knows more about Elias Bailey than anyone else. Try Loelia.'

Casey looked sideways at him. 'She'll think I'm insane if I call her again.'

Zac met her eye. 'You are insane.'

Her eyes on the ocean, Casey dialled the number, switching her voice to calm. 'Loelia, I'm so sorry to bother you yet again, but I am just putting together a last bit of research on Elias.'

'Yes, Casey?' Brisk.

'I'm just trying to piece together what he was up to three or four years ago. There doesn't seem to be much in the public domain.'

'Well, there wouldn't be, would there?'

'Why?' Casey hesitated.

'Casey, I really need to get on with my day … '

'Please, Loelia.'

'Well, I would have thought it was obvious, Casey. Just over three years ago, he was having his heart transplant.'

A chill. 'His heart transplant?'

344

'You and I talked about it the first time.' Loelia sounded irritable, 'Elias had a heart transplant right here in Groote Schuur. He had to be especially careful during Covid for that reason, too. Transplant patients had to—'

'A heart transplant … '

'Are you quite all right, Casey?'

But Casey was shutting down the phone, staring blankly through the windscreen.

'What is it?' Zac asked.

She couldn't speak, the words tumbling through her mind and making no sense at all.

'Casey?' Zac sounded impatient. 'What did Loelia say?'

'Finlay Black died at the same time as Bailey had a heart transplant,' Casey said. 'What if Bailey arranged that car accident too?'

72

As Zac drove, Casey rang Delphine again and again.

'*Hurry*, Zac.'

'I *am*, Casey.'

Hessa had sent Bailey's number to Casey again, but the phone rang out. The traffic was slowing on the coastal road, clotting like blood.

'Call Garrick,' she ordered.

'I've tried. He doesn't answer.'

'Try him again.'

Not taking his eyes off the road, Zac dialled again and again, and finally, the phone was answered.

'Stop calling me!' Garrick's voice was panicky, echoing out of the loudspeaker. 'Are you with that other journalist? I can't … I can't talk to another bloody journalist today!'

'What do you mean?' There was an urgency in Zac's voice. 'What other journalist?'

'Some woman turned up on my doorstep this morning.' Garrick sounded almost hysterical, 'I told her to bugger off too. I can't … '

'Who?' Casey mouthed.

'Which journalist?' asked Zac.

'She said she was called Jessica Miller,' Garrick grumbled. 'From the *Argus*.'

Jessica Miller, who ran a rival investigations team. Casey was texting Miranda as fast as she could. *Find out if Jessica Miller is in Cape Town right now.*

'What did you say to her?' Zac asked. 'To this Jessica person.'

'Nothing, of course.' Garrick sounded scornful. 'I called my father. He sent his bodyguards over right away.'

Casey pictured the bodyguards racing away from the house in Llandudno, rushing to Garrick's assistance.

And leaving the house unprotected.

'So you're talking to Bailey again?' said Zac.

'Yes.' Defiant.

A text back from Miranda. *I just rang the Argus switchboard. They put me straight through to Jessica. It def sounded like she was sitting at her desk.*

'Jessica Miller's nowhere near Cape Town,' Casey murmured to Zac. 'I reckon it was Delphine who knocked on Garrick's door, on her way out to Llandudno.'

'Where is your father right now?' Zac asked. 'I need to know, Garrick.'

'At the house in Llandudno?' Garrick guessed. 'I don't know. Didn't ask. Why?' An edge of panic. 'What's going on?'

'We think he's in danger, Garrick. You have to call him.'

'How? What?' Casey could feel Garrick scrambling to catch up. She stayed silent. 'What's going on, Zac?'

'Can you get hold of him, Garrick? It's important.'

'I can try ... I don't understand—'

'Do it. Right now.'

'Zac.' There was an edge of apology in Garrick's tone. 'He called me, and we spoke. And I know he's done terrible things ... But ... '

The weakness, the indecision, echoed in his voice.

'So you told him everything,' said Zac coldly.

A pause. 'He's my *father*.'

And abruptly, Casey knew how Bailey had pulled Garrick back into his circle.

'What did you tell him exactly?' Zac asked.

'He wanted to know about the girl at the Llandudno house,' Garrick went on sullenly. 'I told him that she was a journalist, an undercover one. I described her. And a few minutes later, he sent me a photograph of Carrie, with blonde hair now, up in Njana.'

There would have been security cameras at the ranch, thought Casey. She had been lucky, so lucky, to get off that reserve.

'What else did you tell him?' Zac asked again.

'He guessed about that politician Drummond being involved, too.' Garrick sounded pleading, 'I am sorry, Zac. I am so sorry about everything.'

'Call him, Garrick. At once. Your father may be in serious danger.'

The phone went dead without a goodbye.

Zac glanced sideways at Casey. 'Bailey turned him again.'

'Garrick is the sort of person,' Casey said slowly, 'who is persuaded by whoever is in front of him at the time. Insecure, indecisive. Inadequate,' she spat the words out. 'When Garrick helped me break into the Llandudno house, it was because we had fired him up with a sense of doing the right thing. But that meant it only took Bailey a few minutes to turn him again.'

'Garrick found out about the heart transplant, didn't he?' said Zac. 'That's why he left Adsero to set up Pergamex.'

'I think so. It fits in with the timeline.'

'Well, what the hell do you think Bailey offered him this time? After all that. Do you think he threatened Jeanie again? Or warned Garrick that he would be cut out of the will altogether.'

'Bailey might have threatened you,' said Casey thoughtfully. 'Adsero's mob might have worked out you weren't in Mauritius, and then Bailey just told Garrick he would hunt you down if he didn't start talking. I think that might have worked.'

Zac pulled a face. 'Doubt it.'

'It's possible.'

'You think Bailey offered him something else, don't you?'

'Well, it would have been easy, wouldn't it?' Casey said bleakly. 'And maybe Bailey finally worked it out. All he really needed to offer was love.'

At last, the traffic unfurled. They reached the turn-off for Bailey's house, and the hire car roared up the track, gunning around the switchbacks, racing through the rolling fynbos.

'Oh, god,' Casey cried. Far ahead, she could see a small figure wandering down the drive towards them. 'That's Delphine. What the hell has she done?'

Delphine looked almost dreamy. She seemed to be meandering along the track, gazing out at the ocean as she walked. She looked across as the car screeched to a halt, eyes hazy. 'Hello, Casey,' she said abstractedly. 'Hello, Zac.'

'Delphine!' Casey leapt from the car. 'What happened?'

Apart from her vague expression, Delphine looked normal, her clothes spotless.

'I'm very sorry ... ' Delphine's eyes reached Casey's face. 'About Ed. I'm very sorry he got involved ... '

'Ed,' Casey shuddered. 'Delphine, what have you ... '

'Elias Bailey killed my husband,' Delphine said simply. 'I had to do it.'

'Do what, Delphine? What did you do?'

'I didn't want it to be like this, Casey ... I wanted you to run the story. To finish him like that, all neatly. But you weren't going to do it.' Her eyes hardened. 'None of you had the guts.'

'What did Bailey do to Finlay, Delphine?'

'Elias Bailey killed Finlay.' It was almost a chant. 'He killed Finlay. He killed my beautiful husband.'

'How do you know? Finlay died in a car accident, Delphine. How can you be certain that Bailey had anything to do with it?'

Delphine was scraping her shoe against the rough gravel of the drive. Back and forth, she scored the gravel. Back and forth, back and forth.

'Delphine,' said Zac. 'Please tell us.'

'I didn't know at first,' Delphine said. 'Finlay went off to work one morning, just like he always did. It was a normal day, the sun shining. The boys and I were playing in the garden. Just a normal, ordinary day. And then I looked up and the police were there. In their uniforms, with their worried faces. They took me into the kitchen, and said there had been an accident. They said I needed to come right now. I could see the boys through the window, still playing. In the sandpit, building castles. I went out to them and I kissed them goodbye, and I said that everything was going to be OK. And then I left them. They were so young. The boys stayed with one of the officers but I could feel their eyes on me as I ran out the gate. They didn't quite believe me, but they trusted me all the same.

'The police rushed me to the hospital as fast as they could. I remember staring out of the car window at all these people going about their lives. People popping to the shops, picking up their kids, grabbing a coffee. I touched the window and it felt as if there was this thick, cold layer between me and the world, and there always would be now.'

Behind Delphine, Casey could see Bailey's house, perched on the hillside. From here, it looked normal.

'I'm sorry,' she said.

'And then I was at the hospital,' Delphine swallowed. 'They took me to his bed, and there were all these tubes and needles and everything. But he was lying still. So still. As if he was dead already. And the doctor looked up as I walked into the room, and I could see … Later, they said there was no hope. They were so kind, the doctors, the nurses. As kind as anyone could be. But they showed me all these scans and graphs, and you could see there was nothing to be done. His brain was … His brain was gone. He was gone.'

'You don't come back,' Zac said gently. 'Not from something like that.'

'Exactly.' Delphine was nodding. It was too big a movement, knocking her off balance. 'When they said there was no hope at all, when they said it was time to switch off the machines, I decided to donate his organs. I signed everything over because I wanted one good thing to come out of it all … Because it was the right thing to do. And Finlay always did the right thing. He always did the good thing.'

'I'm so sorry,' said Casey again. 'It must have been awful to have lost him like that. But how does that connect to Bailey? Why does it have anything to do with him?'

Delphine's eyes focused on her. 'Finlay had done a medical trial, you know? Not long before he died. He had done a medical trial, right here in Cape Town.'

'How … ' Casey struggled with the change of topic.

'Finlay took part in a medical trial, because he fit the criteria, and he thought it was important to help out when you could.'

'I don't—'

'It was an Adsero trial,' said Delphine flatly.

'But—' For a split second, Casey was back in the office at the top of Bailey's house. Clozapine and schizophrenia in Slovakia. Rheumatoid arthritis in Belgium. And a heart drug in Cape Town, just under four years ago.

'Adsero took down every detail about Finlay for that trial,' Delphine recited. 'Not just his blood type, but every single fact about his life. They did DNA tests, blood tests, scans of his heart. They even knew that he liked to go jogging.' She stopped, looking up at the sky. 'Adsero knew he had the perfect heart.'

'But that doesn't mean … '

'Of course, I never thought about it at the time,' said Delphine. 'But afterwards, you get a letter. It's what they do, you know? The medical authorities write you a letter, to make you feel better about donating the organs of your … So my letter arrived. And it was sweet. A 27-year-old man received one of your husband's kidneys, thank you. A 42-year-old woman received his corneas, thank you. A 55-year-old man received your husband's heart, thank you.'

'But … '

'And the donor recipients sometimes send letters too. You saved my life, I can never thank you enough. Heart-warming stuff.'

'You couldn't know it was Bailey though. That's not enough information.'

'And then one day I read an article,' Delphine spat. 'An article in my own bloody newspaper. That man talking about the miracle of his own fucking transplant. A transplant that happened right here in Cape Town, at the exact time, right down the corridor, from where my husband died. My husband's heart went to a 55-year-old man, just the same age as Bailey. A 55-year-old man who never wrote to his donor's family, oh no.'

'You still can't—'

'Bailey knew,' said Delphine. 'He knew he was getting to the top of the list, and that if someone died with the right blood type, he would get the heart. But Bailey had been waiting for years. I spoke to Loelia about it. Bailey knew he was going to die on the list, waiting for that heart.'

'You still don't know—'

'I *know*.' Delphine's eyes were crazed. 'I just couldn't prove it. Like you could never prove he killed Ed. So I looked into it. I did all the reporting. I went up to the crash site. His car smashed into one of the canyons, but it didn't make sense that he crashed where he did. The police thought that another car must have been involved, but they could never track it down. And someone called the police, too. Without leaving their name or number. They thought it must have been the other driver, out of a sense of guilt. But it meant that the ambulance got to him fast. Fast enough that his organs ... '

'But—'

'Then I spoke to Adsero about that trial, asking if I could write about the next one for the *Argus*. And I got some cheerful PR girl on the phone saying it was funny I asked, but that trial was the only trial Adsero had ever done in Cape Town. They usually did them in Europe, and so, sorry about that, I couldn't write about the next one. And it went on and on. I know what he did, Casey. I know it.'

'You don't ... '

'I knew you wouldn't believe me if I came to you. You'd think it was the mad ramblings of some over-the-hill hack. Some has-been. I knew that you and Miranda, you needed to work it out for yourselves.'

'Delphine—'

'I wanted you to destroy him, Casey,' Delphine snarled. 'You and Miranda, I *needed* you to do it.'

'Why?'

'I have children.' A wild gesture. 'I couldn't spend my life in jail ... So I ... But then you said you couldn't do the story. Wouldn't do the story. And I ... '

The sentences dissolved to chaos.

'What did you do to Bailey?' Zac's voice was icy. 'Where is he?'

Delphine turned, looking back up towards the huge house.

'He's up there.' She pointed, and smiled sweetly at Zac.

'Come on.' Zac grabbed Casey's arm. 'Get in the car.'

Casey let Zac shove her into the passenger seat, and then the car was roaring up the drive again, leaving Delphine by the side of the road, her eyes staring at nothing.

73

The gates were open and the guardhouse was empty. There was no sign of any bodyguards.

The front door was ajar, which looked ominous: a broken tooth in a gleaming facade.

Zac drove slowly into the courtyard, coming to a stop beside the smirking cupid. Delphine's black Range Rover sat silently in one corner, and Casey imagined the big gates opening with a purr, the housekeeper coming to the door. *Yes, of course, he's expecting you.*

'Why didn't she take the car?' whispered Zac.

'Maybe she's not running away.' Casey shook her head. 'Maybe she knows she's going to be caught. Come on.'

She climbed out of the car and hurried towards the polished white steps. As she pushed at the door, it swung open silently. The house was still, empty, an echo in the air. Casey moved forward, her feet quiet on the marble floor.

'Elias Bailey?' she called. 'It's Casey Benedict.'

Silence. She took a couple more steps. Now she could see straight through the house, out to the shimmering blue of the swimming pool. The bullet holes would already have been fixed, she knew. There would be nothing to show for that terrifying day.

Zac was behind her, staring up at a hammered gold chandelier and a gallery that ran around the triple height lobby.

'What a place,' he murmured.

'Elias?' Casey called again. 'Is everything all right?'

She edged across the hall to look out at the swimming pool, past the large white sofas and the never-used fireplace, piled high with pointless silver pine cones. The house was still, the only movement from the tiny motes of dust that caught the sunlight as it poured in through the huge windows.

Now Casey could see the staircase that led up to Bailey's office from the gallery. She shuddered at the thought of that room, with the grey files, the stolid wooden desk. She knew that invisible hands would have repaired the French doors, too, replacing the green lamp and mopping up the blood. Wiping away the terror, as if it had never been, swirling it all down the sluice. If only it were that easy. If only …

A tiny noise behind them, and Casey swung back towards the double doors that led to the kitchen. Mabel stood there, eyes wide. As Casey walked towards her, the housekeeper shrank away, almost cowering. She was shaking, Casey saw, bright smears of blood on her crisp white dress.

'Mabel!' Casey came closer, hands wide. 'We won't hurt you. Please don't be scared. Do you remember me? I came here with Garrick, Mr Bailey's son … '

The housekeeper shook her head, making a gesture as if to push Casey away.

'We want to help you,' Zac tried. 'We—'

But the housekeeper was ducking through another door that looked as if it led to a pantry.

'Do you know what happened, Mabel?' Casey pleaded, but the housekeeper had disappeared, the door closing with a bang.

Casey turned away. 'Come on.'

Wide corridors led towards the wings of the house. Casey forced herself down the one on the left. She nudged the first set of double doors, flinching as they swung open. But it was only a sitting room, the huge windows opening towards the pool. The room was immaculate – with large sofas, beautiful art, white curtains drifting in the breeze – and empty.

The next set of double doors along the corridor was closed. Casey took a deep breath and pushed down on the door handle.

Bluebeard's wife, climbing.

But this room was deserted too. Only a dining table that might sit a couple of dozen invisible guests.

Another deep breath, and into the next room. This was empty also, and she had the impression of pushing through the stagnant air of an abandoned fairy-tale palace.

'Mr Bailey,' Casey called out again. 'I am very concerned for your safety.'

Silence.

'Is there anyone here?' Zac appeared behind her. 'There's nobody in the other wing.'

'Let's try upstairs.'

They crept across the hall, towards the spiral staircase. Casey looked up at the stairs that led to the office. She imagined the bodyguards, alerted by Garrick, racing back across Cape Town, back towards this echoing home.

'Up there?' Zac followed her eyes.

'Maybe.' Casey raised her voice again, pulling out her phone as she spoke. 'Mr Bailey, I am calling the police. I am concerned about your safety ...'

There was a movement in the corner of her eye, so she was turning when the air exploded. Gunfire: blasting the room apart. Casey dived behind one of the white sofas as the room seemed to convulse. Bullet holes appeared in the wall above her head, sending chips of marble flying across the huge space, smashing into the gold chandelier so that it jumped and jangled, and spun around and around. Casey jammed her hands over her ears, folding herself into the smallest possible shape as the sofa thudded and jerked as bullets hit it, the stuffing erupting into the air.

The gunshots stopped, the sudden silence almost as shocking. Casey's ears rang and hurt. She lay completely still.

Time ticked past. Slowly, Casey uncurled herself and tried to look around. She was in a small space between the sofa and the wall. She rolled on to her stomach, waiting for the next eruption.

Nothing.

Zac, she thought. Where is Zac?

Very carefully, she inched forward, trying to look around the corner of the sofa. Fighting every instinct that screamed: stay *still*, stay *hidden*. She could hear muffled movements from the gallery above, and imagined Bailey pacing around, peering over, waiting for any motion down in the hall.

'Zac.' The quietest whisper. Nothing moved in the lobby or in the gallery above. She tried again. '*Zac*.'

The smallest groan.

Casey edged forward again, and now she could see him, lying on the cold marble floor. There was blood, she could see with a jag of horror, a pool of crimson trickling from his blue shirt. He was lying still, and she couldn't tell whether he was dead or dying or pretending to be dead.

'I'm here, Zac,' she whispered.

He didn't move. Nothing to indicate that he could hear her at all.

She had to get to him, couldn't leave him out there alone, his life ebbing away. She reached for her phone, patting her pockets, and realised it was gone. She had been holding it as the world exploded, she remembered. It was somewhere out in the room.

From above, there was silence.

She had to try.

Casey slid forward. Any minute, she would be out beyond the safety of the sofa, any minute she would …

The gun roared, and Casey jerked back behind the sofa.

She lay on the marble floor, tears hot in her eyes. Enough. She pushed herself up on her elbows with a burn of rage.

'What do you want, Bailey?' Casey shouted. 'This is over. You must be able to see that. You're not going to get away with this, not any more. Let me help Zac.'

'Shut up,' he shouted. 'Shut up, you stupid fucking idiot!'

Casey lay on the floor. 'Why? Why am I such an idiot, Mr Bailey?'

'Why couldn't you just leave things alone?' As Bailey spoke, Casey could hear a breathlessness in his voice. A creeping exhaustion.

'Mr Bailey,' Casey tried to sound soothing, 'I want to talk to you. I want to help you, if I possibly can.'

'Help me? You sent Delphine Black up here.' Bailey's laugh ended in a choke. 'You sent that bloody woman up here to kill me.'

'I didn't know … What did she do to you?'

'She shot me, didn't she? The bloody bitch shot me.' The words turned into a groan.

'If you promise not to shoot me, I will come up there. I'll see if I can help.'

There was a long silence.

Casey tensed, feeling her body healthy and intact for maybe the last time, and then she took a breath and stood up.

There was no movement from above, no blast from the gun. Zac lay ten feet away from her, stretched out on the floor. As Casey looked at him, his eyes opened for a second, gleaming at her. He was breathing, shallow, fast gasps. Alive for now, Casey thought. But he doesn't have long. *Hurry*.

She grabbed her phone from the floor, automatically switching it to record, and moved towards the staircase, its elegant lines sweeping up towards the first floor.

Casey forced herself up the stairs, with slow, unwilling steps, waiting for the roar of the gun.

But Bailey was slumped halfway along the landing. He was barely able to turn his head, propped up against the wall, blood oozing from his chest. She could see streaks of scarlet on the carpet. He must have scrabbled his way along the corridor. The gun lay a few inches from his hand.

Casey took three long strides along the passageway, and kicked the gun away. She fell to her knees beside Bailey. 'What happened? Where does it hurt?'

He looked up at her with oddly calm eyes. 'There's no point,' he said. 'You can't do anything now.'

'I might be able to—'

'No.' His voice was resigned. 'That woman knew what she was bloody doing.'

'But there might be … ' Casey looked at him despairingly. 'Why? Why did you do it all?'

He made a weak gesture. 'Don't you see? I had to … '

The words ebbed as Casey showed him her phone. 'I'm calling the police … Paramedics. They'll help.'

'No,' he said. 'There's no point.'

She ignored him, dialling the emergency number.

They responded in clipped, cool tones. Ambulance, yes. Police, yes. Right away, ma'am.

She turned back to Bailey.

He was dying, she could see that now.

'They'll be too late,' he said, almost pleased.

'Let me help you.'

'No. Don't you touch me.'

'But why?' The words burst out of Casey. 'Why did you do it?'

He stared up at her for a long time. Then he almost nodded, his tongue passing over dry lips.

'I did it because we don't need Corax—'

'But we do,' Casey interrupted, unable to let him carry on. 'There are people out there dying right now who would live if they could use Corax. One girl, she had cystic fibrosis … '

'No.' Casey was surprised by the strength in Bailey's voice. Somehow, he was pushing himself upright, leaving a smear of blood on the floor. 'You're not listening. We don't need Corax *yet*.'

'What do you mean?' Casey stared down at him in disgust.

'I was protecting it,' he hissed. 'I was keeping it safe.'

'But we need it right now.'

'No,' he said. 'We don't. We still have antibiotics we can use for now. But one day – not that long away – we will need Corax.'

'What?' Casey shook her head. 'That doesn't … '

'One day, there will be millions and millions of people dying.' Professor Jalali's words echoed in Casey's head as Bailey spoke. 'Antibiotic resistance will make coronavirus or Aids or cancer look like a walk in the park. And that is when the world will need Corax. Not now.'

'I don't understand.'

'You do. You just don't want to. From the very minute that some-one takes the first dose of Corax, bacteria will start trying to find a way round it. It will take a few years, a few decades maybe, because Corax is the best antibiotic ... But the bacteria will find a way in the end. If I kept it back, it would buy more time in the future.'

'That doesn't ... '

'Why do you think I kept the information at my house and not in the office?' Bailey gritted his teeth, agony in his eyes. 'If the Adsero board knew about it, they would get it out there at once. Get the prof-its surging in. I'd planned to tell them I was working on something after today's interview, but not ... '

'But—'

'Think of a child on Christmas Day.' Bailey sounded weaker. 'If he has thirteen presents already, he'll barely notice the fourteenth. But if you hold it back ... '

'All those people,' Casey murmured. 'You killed all those people.'

'It was to save the lives of millions,' said Bailey. 'Millions of people will live because five or six died now.'

'But ... you had Ed killed.'

'I had to scare you off.'

'And you killed Finlay Black,' Casey said furiously. 'You took his heart.'

'Who could I trust?' murmured Bailey. 'Who could I trust to keep Corax hidden? Corax is my lifetime's work. My gift to the world. It was my duty to stay alive for as long as possible.'

There was a fanatical glow in his eyes now.

'You did a whole trial,' said Casey. 'How could you?'

'I knew everything about Finlay Black.' Bailey's mouth twisted. 'Except for what his wife did for a living. I should have checked that.'

'It's how you've always worked, isn't it?' said Casey. 'Hold back this drug. Hold back that medicine. It's worth people dying so that you can carry on with your research. Keep the prices high, because the *research* is so crucial ... '

'The end justifies the means?' Bailey looked up at her. 'I think you understand that.'

The runaway train hurtling down the hill ...

'Flora Ashcroft couldn't wait,' said Casey. 'She died waiting for that drug. And the babies in St Agnes. Those tiny babies ... '

But Bailey's breath was slower now, his eyes glazing over. 'Tell ... '

The words were lost. Casey leaned nearer. 'What? What do you want me to say?'

Close to, Bailey smelled of blood: metallic and animal all at once. In the far distance, Casey thought she could hear the howl of the ambulance.

In time for Zac, she thought. Just in time. But not for Bailey.

'Tell Garrick,' Bailey whispered. 'There's a file ... upstairs ... For him.'

'You'll be able to tell him yourself.'

'And tell Loelia ... ' Bailey smiled, his eyes moving past Casey. 'Tell Loelia that I always loved her. That I was stupid, but I loved her always.'

'Hang on, Elias. Stay with me.' Now she remembered with a surge of adrenalin. 'The Corax, Elias. I need it. I need it for Miranda.'

Bailey had turned his head away. 'She wasn't given anything,' he said. 'I just wanted you to ... '

Relief, a wave breaking.

'You bastard.'

Something like a smile. 'I would never have given you a dose of Corax anyway.' His eyes were closing. 'I would never have let it out of my sight.'

'So Miranda is safe?'

'You'll write your story now,' he murmured. 'About me. In all its grim details.'

'Yes. Yes, I will.'

'Make sure you get that prat Drummond in,' he said bitterly.

'No,' said Casey, because it didn't matter any more, 'I won't. We promised that we wouldn't.'

A gleam of teeth. 'I recorded that bloody conversation in Wrocław too,' he gasped, getting the words out one at a time. 'I always record

361

meetings with sodding politicians. My secretary has the tape, and she'll know what to do with it. That bastard.'

And Casey laughed out loud, the sound strange in the echoing house.

Bailey's eyes were on the hammered gold of the chandelier. It glittered in the sunlight, sending a thousand diamond glints dancing around the room.

'So beautiful,' said Bailey.

'Yes.'

His eyes were closing now. 'I don't think Garrick believed me,' Bailey murmured, 'when I told him I ... '

The sirens were outside the house now. Casey heard a vehicle screech to a halt.

'Stay with me, Elias. You're not going to die.'

'I am.' For a moment, he smiled. 'Oh, I am. That woman ... That woman was aiming for her husband's heart.'

74

Blue flashes seemed to fill the house. The sirens howled through the front door until it seemed as if the very house was screaming.

Zac managed to smile at Casey as she sprinted down the stairs towards him, throwing herself to the ground next to him.

'Zac? Zac, are you all right?'

'Not really.' A cautious grin. 'But I'm not going to die either.'

'Yes, do try not to.'

She quickly told him what Bailey had said as paramedics flooded the room.

'I suppose it's what they have to believe,' Zac murmured. 'That it's their right to control these drugs ... '

His voice faded away.

Thou shalt not kill ...

Unless.

'He was quite used to choosing,' said Casey, 'who lives and who dies.'

Zac was gazing towards the sea. The curtains were whispering in the breeze.

'Is he dead?' he asked.

'Yes,' Casey said. 'He's dead.'

Zac's eyes shifted to her face. 'You love the hunt,' he murmured, 'but you hate the kill.'

'Maybe.'

'You'll write the truth now?' It took a lot of his concentration to look straight at her, she noticed.

'Something like that.' She took his hand, managed to smile. 'A part of it, anyway.'

'I think I'll go back to being a doctor.' The corners of his mouth lifted. 'A bit more chilled out than this.'

'You'll be great,' she said. 'You'll be brilliant.'

'Yeah, yeah.'

And a moment later, the paramedics scooped him up and rushed him away.

As the ambulance cornered away around the smiling cupid, Garrick appeared in the doorway. Out of breath, eyes wild. Behind him, the bodyguards hovered, as if already sensing they were no longer needed.

'Where is he?'

Casey's eyes went to the small group up in the gallery. Even as Garrick glanced up, Casey could see the defeated body language of the paramedics. One was pulling off his mask, turning away.

'No!' Garrick screamed. 'No.'

He ran up the stairs, racing around the gallery until he was held back by two policemen. 'We're sorry, sir.' The compassion was polite. 'You can't go that way. Not this minute.'

Casey thought about Delphine Black, wandering down the drive. The police storming up alongside her, wrestling her into handcuffs, forcing her to the ground.

She walked up the stairs behind Garrick. 'Come this way, Garrick.'

He looked around, bewildered by her appearance. 'You … ' His mind seemed stuck on the word. 'You … '

He was unable to take her in, mouth slack with confusion. Before the policeman had time to react, she led him up the second stair-case, to the office at the top of the house. Tears were running down Garrick's face, and his shoulders shook.

'My name is Casey,' she said. 'I work for the London *Post*.'

'My father … '

'I'm sorry, Garrick. I really am.'

'We'll never … Not now,' Garrick managed. 'We'll never … '

They stood in the room, the bright sunlight in squares on the floor. Garrick stared at the rows of grey files, stunned.

'He was my father,' Garrick said quietly. 'He called me last night. But I wasn't sure … I didn't know if he … ' He paused, the realisation choking him. 'I never told him that I loved him.'

There is forever, Casey thought. And suddenly there is nothing.

She carried on pacing around the room, then stopped and crouched down, pulling a file from the shelf.

'What's that?' Garrick was irritable. 'I'm … '

'*Fili mi.*' Casey read the back of the file. 'My son. He labelled it for you, like the file you found before. Open it.'

'I don't understand.' Garrick opened the file and leafed through the pages. He looked up sharply. 'It's about Corax.'

'Yes.'

Garrick sat down on the sofa, clutching the file to his chest. 'I don't understand.'

'Bailey wanted you to have it,' said Casey. 'He told me, just before he died. You'll have to decide what happens to Corax, Garrick. You're the one he entrusted with it.'

'But I don't understand.' He was still hugging the file close. 'How can I … '

'I don't know.'

Garrick stared into the distance. From downstairs, Casey could hear official voices making brisk decisions.

'What would you do?' There was a pleading note in Garrick's voice. 'What the hell should I do?'

'It's Pandora's Box,' said Casey.

'What?'

'Out flew disease and misery and evil,' said Casey. 'Despair and misery.'

'Yes.'

'And all that was left was hope,' Casey said. 'The only thing left was hope.'

'I don't understand.'

'Me neither.'

'So what should I do?'

'I don't know,' said Casey, and she almost laughed aloud.

And then she thought of Flora, waiting and waiting and dying, and her smile was gone.

Garrick turned towards her, still holding the file. 'I told him, you know?' he said. 'I told him you were investigating him.'

'Yes,' she said. 'It doesn't matter now.'

'Saepio will be an important drug,' said Garrick. 'He did a lot of good. In the middle of all the bad.'

'I know.'

'And Corax ... '

'Yes.'

The big French doors leading out to the balcony were unlocked. Casey pulled them open.

She gripped the chrome railings as the wind roared. The sea pounded against the huge granite boulders, endless and beautiful. Far above her head, a seagull screamed in the wind.

Another police car was creeping up the drive towards the house. She would have to leave soon, the legal procedures unfolding relentlessly.

And, in parallel, there would be a blast of stories. Headlines and outrage and big, angry photographs. Lawyers, arguing over every word. PRs, with their pert messages: *just so we're clear*. Adsero, cornered, raging back.

She would transform the hunt and the fear and the chaos into neat little words: black and white and mostly right.

This is the truth or this is our truth and this is what you should know.

Half the truth, lost forever.

But for a moment, it was as if Ed was there.

Ed, laughing. Ed, smiling down at her. Ed, waiting to say I love you.

Casey's eyes filled with tears, and for a moment she let them spill over. The sunlight glittered on the sea, so joyous, and it was as if the ocean was dancing.

He was gone.

She rubbed away the tears with her wrists. Moving slowly, she sat down on a bench and typed out a message.

It's all over, Miranda. It's all over, and you're safe, and I'm coming home.

AUTHOR'S NOTE

Zentetra, saepio and Adsero are fictional, as are Corax and Pergamex.

Drug dumping, including the consignment of antibiotics, was a serious issue for many years. After the flooding in Mozambique in 2000, 2 million ampoules of gentamicin with a shelf-life of four months were sent to the refugee camps. It is believed that most of this donation was destroyed.

ACKNOWLEDGEMENTS

'Why did you decide to focus on antibiotic resistance?'

'Because it's going to kill you.'

It was yet another jolly conversation in a random pub in London, this time with Ronan Doyle, a leading specialist in infectious disease.

We were out celebrating my brilliant friend Felicity Fitzgerald gaining her second (second!) PhD, and over the course of the evening I ended up in a long discussion about antibiotic resistance with Ronan, who is now based at the London School of Hygiene and Tropical Medicine.

The rest of the conversation was much jollier, but Ronan's bleak sentence stayed with me. I gradually became fascinated with the whole issue of antibiotic resistance – and eventually that interest turned into *The Hunt and The Kill*. Naturally, I stole Ronan's line for Noah Hart.

As part of my research, I ended up visiting Great Ormond Street, St George's Hospital in Tooting – where I was lucky enough to meet the brilliant Professor Mike Sharland – and the Public Health England site in Colindale, so I'd like to thank those organisations for allowing me access. I also visited a friend at the Royal Brompton Hospital, who was incredibly generous in explaining life with cystic fibrosis.

The painting described in early pages of *The Hunt and The Kill – Island Collaborations* – is a real painting by an artist called Kate Hughes, whose fascinating work was displayed in the Royal Brompton at the time of my visit.

I was lucky enough to see the work of Neotree – neotree.org – in action during a visit to Harare. Neotree is focused on harnessing technology to reduce newborn deaths in low-income countries, with a group of brilliant doctors and scientists working in extremely complex environments.

Life has changed in a hundred different ways since I wrote *To The Lions*, the first book in this series. The Pearce family – I can't name them all, this book is quite long enough already – have been especially wonderful, particularly Andy Pearce, Emma Faraday, Eleanor and Jessie, and Oscar and Evie Beamish (I know that is a confusing list of names given they're all coming under the 'Pearce family' category, but there we go). I feel that if I can survive Storm Francis in a tent, I can survive most things the Pearces throw at me.

A huge thank you to my lovely new Devon friends, especially Alex and Bertie Readhead, Nishanthi Silva and James Goodhand, Tess and Rory Hardick, Charlie Llewellyn and so many others.

Thank you in particular to James for reading this book before publication despite his very busy work at the RD&E – and flagging up some of the more egregious errors. Thank you, Flic, for reading it too. Both of these eminent doctors would like to make it clear that the remaining mistakes are very definitely all mine.

I wrote most of *The Hunt and The Kill* in early 2020, as the world changed with the most extraordinary speed. I knew that this book was due to be published in the summer of 2021, and eventually – with the help of my wonderful editor at Bloomsbury, Alison Hennessey – we had to try and guess where the world would 'be' by 2021. As I write these acknowledgements at the beginning of 2021, it is starting to look as if I was over-optimistic. Still. I am glad I approached the pandemic with optimism. It kept me going.

The usual thanks to the usual suspects. Sarah Mahmud, Jasmine Miller, Laura Millar, Cressida Pollock, Laura Roberts, Alex Marrache: you all continue to be fab. Collette Lyons and Paul Vlitos, now better known as Ellery Lloyd: it's been an utter joy watching *People Like Her* triumph. Claire Newell and Robert Winnett: thanks for being great. Alice Ross: thank you for general uplifting. Hooray too for Team VHS and the Author Support Group – Francesca Hornak and Kate Kingsley. Thank you to Vanessa and Harty for being the most fabulous fun in Mauritius. Justine Moxham and Toby Darbyshire, you've continued to entertain me and fill my life with pink plastic horror. As I write this list, it seems absolutely bizarre that I haven't even seen most of you since the pandemic began, although in Toby's case, that's definitely an improvement.

Huge thank yous to Alison, Sara Helen Binney, Lilidh Kendrick, Ella Harold, Amy Donegan and Philippa Cotton at Bloomsbury. You've all been fantastic, especially given the chaos the last year has inflicted on us all. Thank you to Andrew Gordon and Georgina Ruffhead at David Higham Associates for all your help.

But the biggest thanks – once again – go to my family, most especially Jonny and our gorgeous little Izzie. I'm so glad we're on this adventure together.

A NOTE ON THE TYPE

The text of this book is set in Minion, a digital typeface designed by Robert Slimbach in 1990 for Adobe Systems. The name comes from the traditional naming system for type sizes, in which minion is between nonpareil and brevier. It is inspired by late Renaissance-era type.